DANCE TO THE DEVIL'S TUNE

Lady Law and The Gunslinger
Series

Book Two

Adrienne deWolfe

Book design by eBook Prep
www.ebookprep.com

Cover design by The Killion Group Inc.
www.thekilliongroupinc.com

November, 2016
ISBN: 978-1-61417-888-0

ePublishing Works!
www.epublishingworks.com

"Looking for someone, mister?"

Sadie's voice was harsh when she surprised him, prowling through the dark hotel room.

Caught red-handed, Cass halted. "They call her the Devil's Daughter."

A moment passed. Then a light bloomed at her elbow. She lounged in an armchair, her chestnut mane spilling to her waist, lacy rosettes cascading from her breasts. The skimpy threads left little to his imagination. But what captivated Cass in that moment—what had *always* captivated Cass about Sadie—was the sensual fire burning in those hungry, tiger eyes.

"I got word you wanted me," he said.

"Lies."

He hiked an eyebrow.

"But since you made the trip," she added huskily, her trigger finger never wavering on her .32, "take off your clothes…"

LETTER TO THE READER:

Thank you for reading my *Lady Law & The Gunslinger* series. Now I have a special invitation for you! I would love to take you "behind the scenes" so you can enjoy the books even more. You'll get to watch how the series evolves, from brainstorming a new villain's name to inventing sneaky spy gadgets. Ask questions about the writing process; share ideas for new scenes; and win some fun prizes too.

If you'd like to join my book family, please visit this link: http://wildtexasnights.com/join-my-romance-club/.

Happy Reading!
Adrienne deWolfe
Austin, Texas, USA

CHAPTER 1

Pinwheels of light spun in the young woman's mind, blanking her memory, stealing her will.

One hour ago, she'd had a name. A conscience. A keen intellect and the heartfelt desire to save the world. But all that had changed the moment the clock chimed the midnight hour, and the music box with the enamel peacock began to play.

Now she was staring blankly at her reflection. The mirror hung in the master bedroom of the silver-mining tycoon she'd come to rob. If she'd still possessed the power to reason, she might have thought she looked a mess with her black curls spilling in a riot from her sealskin toque. She might have dusted powder across her chill-reddened nose or re-touched her lips with her favorite, strawberry balm. Certainly, she would have bemoaned the bloody smears on her indigo evening gown.

But her appearance no longer concerned her. Not since she'd found the attractively wrapped gift box, and the darling little novelty had mesmerized her with its tune.

Tripping the hidden latch behind the mirror, she swung the hinged, 24-karat frame away from the wall. Gaslight flickered over a numbered dial, protruding from the exposed safe. She tore off a leather glove and placed her ear against the cold steel. Listening for clicks, she turned the knob.

As a Pinkerton, she was more experienced at picking locks than cracking safes. Even so, she'd never set out to steal anything in her life—not until the vault finally swung open, and she stood staring at her prize. Nestled between several stacks of silver bullion, a heart-shaped ruby winked with a blood-red luster.

Ignoring neighboring emeralds, sapphires, and pearls, she snatched the walnut-sized gem she'd been induced to steal from Lt. Governor Horace Tabor, while he attended the theater with his family. In her haste to grab her rabbit-fur muff and close the vault's door, she forgot her glove.

Descending the circular staircase, she swept past the dead butler and two equally dead dogs before slipping through the kitchen door into the gardens. Touched by a surreal light, bare branches glimmered with frost in the crisp, Colorado night. The moon was beginning to set.

A spark of urgency quickened her feet. The carriage would be waiting.

He would be waiting.

Snowflakes tumbled across her hair and landed on her lashes. She never blinked. The pointy heels of her calfskin boots beat a steady tattoo as she marched across the cobblestones, looking neither left nor right. Puffs of steam curled above the dutiful horses in the street. Beyond them, a velvety, brassier-warmed blackness beckoned.

When she climbed through the open door of the carriage, he rapped the roof with his walking stick. The conveyance lurched forward. Ice crackled beneath its wheels. The sounds jarred her senses, but he murmured her name, caressing the word with a warm, buttery baritone.

All her awareness focused on him.

"Did you procure the Heart of Fire?"

She nodded, surrendering her plunder.

"Splendid. And the dossier?"

She raised her skirt to reveal ruffled bloomers and a large, plain envelope strapped above her knee. Without the slightest hesitation, she handed him three weeks worth of evidence she'd been compiling to indict him for coercion, burglary, and murder. No other copies existed.

"That's a good girl."

He settled into the shadows, his gloved hand resting atop the brass handle of his cane. He looked like he'd just come from the opera, with his silk top hat, Inverness cape, and polished black pumps. He smelled of lemongrass soap, Cleopatra Federal cigars, and cognac. The scents stirred something deep inside her, the memory of his taste. His touch. The insidiously sweet way his fingers had dipped between her thighs, working their dark magic.

She blinked.

"We're almost there," he soothed.

He called himself Maestro, partly because musical novelties intrigued him, partly because he specialized in various forms of mind control. Since she'd stepped inside the cab, he hadn't taken his eyes from hers. He knew about the .32 concealed inside her muff; he knew if she found a path through the fog inside her brain, she wouldn't have hesitated to put a bullet through his black heart.

But he was confident in his power over her. He'd told her, once, that hoydens with popguns amused him, and he considered them his favorite sport. He'd also told her to kill anyone who might get in her way at Tabor's mansion.

And she had.

The carriage rolled onto 19th Street and stopped. At this late hour, the road was deserted. However, she barely noticed the world beyond the isinglass windows. She was entranced by the pocket watch he'd tugged from his vest. When he pressed the stem, the timepiece started playing a sweet melody from her childhood. Her lips curved softly as she listened.

He handed the novelty to her.

"Run along now." He pushed open the carriage door. "You know what to do."

Obediently, she stepped down to the wooden planks beneath the carriage. Freshly fallen snow crunched under her boots. Rushing river water glittered in the moonlight, not far below. The South Platte was close to flood stage.

The bite of winter air burned her lungs. She blinked again. But the mechanical melody was insistent:

> *"London bridges falling down,*
> *Falling down, falling down..."*

When she jumped into the river, the carriage rolled away.

Ten Days Later

Sometimes Lady Pinkertons tackled the most bizarre cases.

But no assignment could be more bizarre than this one, reflected veteran agent, Sadie Michelson. She was posing as a grieving, Italian *contessa* so she could get bilked by an American flim-flam artist at a traveling spook show.

Definitely a case for my memoirs, she thought, hoping an attempt at humor would distract her from the stench of copal incense and unwashed bodies, shouting *Amen* beneath the red-and-white circus tent.

Yes, she was freezing her bustle off in the middle of Denver's Jewell Park, where Brother Enoch Fowler and his more zealous camp followers had been parking their wagons since August. According to rumor, environmental complications, ranging from wildfires on the plains, to an avalanche in Raton Pass, had prevented Fowler's retreat to a warmer climate.

But Fowler wasn't one to question Divine Providence. The preacher happily continued his stage shows, humbugging the superstitious suckers of Mile High City—especially the *nouveau riche*. In fact, one of his assistants was leading the prayer service now, so Fowler could shear some wealthy lamb inside his private lair. Judging by the rest of the brassier-toting sheep beneath the Big Top—and the army of females in Puritan costumes, ladling out hot cider—nobody minded the chill.

Except Sadie.

She grimaced. Careful not to discharge the pistol strapped to her wrist, she flexed stiff fingers so she could fish a timepiece from her hand muff's lining.

Hallelujah. Show time.

Suspecting she looked like a lemon popsicle—because that's how she felt—she shook out the topaz velvet of her skirt and widened the gap between the lapels of her sable coat. The whole reason behind her *contessa* disguise was to bait a mysterious jewel thief, named Maestro, with the obscenely large emerald nesting between her breasts.

According to a preliminary report filed by Agent Araminta "Minx" Merripen, Maestro was relatively new to Denver and had received *carte blanche* entry into the richest homes. Minx had named Fowler her chief suspect. Three days later, her body had been found floating in the Platte. That's why Sadie believed Fowler was connected to Minx's death.

Eager to come face-to-face with her quarry, Sadie abandoned her rustic bench at the rear of the camp meeting. Adopting a regal mien, she skirted late arrivals, including a couple of arguing Italians, with a bawling infant, and a Mexican, who was leaning against a tent pole. The *caballero* appeared to be snoozing under his sombrero, the way his hat rested on the tip of his nose.

But Sadie quickly forgot the immigrants when she noticed the commotion at the registration table. She figured the sight of an Italian noblewoman, in an ankle-length fur, had flustered the two females with the plain muslin bonnets and conservative, gray gowns. Careful to hide her amusement, she watched the younger of these Puritan Throwbacks whisper in the ear of her bespectacled companion.

The older woman fled like a pack of hounds was at her heels.

Sadie halted and sized up the adolescent, whose badge proclaimed her to be *Sister Rebekah*. Not a single strand of hair could be seen beneath the waif's snow-white bonnet. She was pale and mousy-looking with unusually intense, dark eyes. An enormous wooden cross hung from a leather cord around her neck. That cord stretched nearly to her navel.

"Buona sera," Sadie greeted in her best Italian accent. *'Finally,'* she thought, *'those grueling language lessons with my childhood opera coach are paying off.'* "I am the *Contessa di Montaldeo*. I am scheduled to meet with Brother Enoch—"

"You're late."

Sadie hiked an eyebrow. Was it her imagination, or was Rebekah glaring at her as if she were the devil's own handmaiden?

"Mi scusi," Sadie said politely, "but the clock on your table says—"

"The clock's wrong. Sister Abigail gave your appointment to someone else."

A muscle ticked in Sadie's jaw. Sister Abigail was the near-sighted woman, whom Rebekah had sent scurrying into the crowd. Sadie had no way to verify the waif's claim.

"Very well," Sadie bit out, "schedule me for the next available appointment."

"We're filled."

"Tomorrow, then."

Rebekah hiked her chin and shook her head, two sure signs she was lying.

"Next week?" Sadie persisted to confirm her suspicion.

"Come if you like, but we won't be here."

"And why is that?"

"Too much snow."

Sadie struggled with her notoriously short temper. Rebekah's lie wasn't the only reason why Sadie's patience was stretched thin. The *Rocky Mountain News* had sabotaged her plan to gain credibility among Denver's privileged class. Despite the effusive assurances of the editor, her elaborately concocted story about the *contessa's* adventures as a tourist had been relegated to a footnote in the morning edition. The editor had used the rest of the society column to praise the "lyrical virtuosity" of a Sicilian soprano, who'd stolen Sadie's thunder by debuting at Tabor's Grand Opera House last night.

Is it any wonder Rebekah doesn't know I'm supposed to be traveling with a fortune in jewels, any one of which would put the Heart of Fire to shame?

"*Signorina,*" Sadie said in reasonable tones, "surely we can come to an arrangement." Deliberately, she fingered her ostentatious gold and platinum collar, which weighed as much as the monstrosity was worth. She didn't enjoy lugging the necklace around Denver like an ox's yoke, but if diamonds and emeralds were to be the seeds of Maestro's destruction, then so be it. "I must be leaving for California soon," she improvised, "to inspect my dear, departed Luigi's vineyards. I have heard how Brother Enoch speaks to spirits, how he gives comfort to the living. It is a dreadful imposition, I am sure, but I was hoping he might make an exception for me. I must consult with my beloved *conte* and ask him how to invest—"

"Go away," Rebekah snapped. "I don't like you."

Sadie blinked. She was so stunned by this rebuff, she wondered if Rebekah had remembered her from some previous encounter.

But Sadie quickly assured herself their acquaintance was impossible. In her pre-Pinkerton days, she'd never performed her bawdy songs in a venue where children were allowed.

Besides, two nights ago, she'd altered her appearance, dyeing her hair a deep, dark chestnut to look more Italian. Even her lover, William "Cass" Cassidy, would have looked twice to recognize her now.

"I am grieved to hear that, *signorina,*" Sadie said dryly. "But the facts remain: the clock is not wrong, and I am not late. Now then. I am willing to overlook this unfortunate misunderstanding and tell Brother Enoch how helpful you've been to correct it. Or, if you prefer, I can distress him with the news that Sister Rebekah is an ill-mannered guttersnipe, who offends his paying customers."

Well, *that* stoked the fire in those burning, black eyes. Rebekah clutched her cross with two white-knuckled fists. "It would serve you right if I *did* take you to see Papa right now."

Papa? Sadie frowned. According to Fowler's Pinkerton dossier, he was supposed to be a bachelor: never married and no children.

"*Signorina* Fowler." Sadie locked stares with the brat. "I am not known for my patience. I demand that you point the way to—"

"*Grazie, carino,*" purred a female voice in dulcet Italian, somewhere to Sadie's rear. "How kind you are to ask. Of course, I shall autograph your opera program."

Sadie's heart nearly stalled. In the reflection of the clock face, she glimpsed a sloe-eyed, dark-haired beauty in a low-cut, scarlet gown, which was embroidered with tiny black treble clefs. The woman's companion, a gentleman wearing a cleric's collar, gallantly held aloft a tent flap for her convenience.

Holy crap! Fowler's entering the Big Top with Dolce LaRocca!

Sadie wasn't the only one who recognized the international singing sensation. A cry went up from the Italian immigrants with the bawling infant. Soon, their shout was sweeping like wildfire through the tent:

"It's Dolce!"

"I love you, Dolce!"

"Bless my baby, Dolce!"

The next thing Sadie knew, a swarm of euphoric admirers was rushing the entrance. They knelt, cap in hand, to kiss Dolce's hem or beg her blessing for sundry possessions, ranging from medicine bottles and crutches, to knitting needles and Bowie knives.

The soprano responded graciously to this public adoration. She blew kisses; she clasped hands; she patted toddlers' heads. When Sadie spied Sister Abigail, squinting happily in Dolce's wake, she deduced the reason for the scheduling mix-up: Sister Abigail couldn't see three feet in front of her nose. No doubt the woman had assumed, from Dolce's accent, that the soprano was the *contessa*.

Great. I can't approach Fowler now; Dolce will expose me as a fraud!

Tossing a dagger's glance at Rebekah—who was smirking in the most annoying way—Sadie ducked her head, turned up her coat collar, and hurried past the opera enthusiasts. In her haste to escape with her cover intact, she didn't notice how the Mexican roused himself to follow.

Twilight was rapidly stretching its tentacles over the Rockies. Sadie ducked behind a tower of cider kegs, located a discreet distance from the tent flaps. She didn't know where Fowler fleeced his lambs, but she reasoned his quarters couldn't be far.

Glad to spy no other stragglers, arriving late for the meeting, Sadie studied the grounds. About 20 yards from the Big Top, the makeshift boardwalk abruptly ended. Countless impressions in the ground told how hooves, wheels, and boots had trampled the grass that once carpeted the area. Now, only a few bedraggled islands of green rose amidst the frosted mud ruts. To the north, horses huddled for warmth before rough-hewn hitching posts. To the south, crisscrossing foot trails led to a road, which in turn disappeared into a stand of spruces.

Eureka. Sadie hiked her skirts. *Hopefully, Dolce will keep Fowler distracted long enough for me to search his wagon.*

Thunder rumbled. Brisk gusts of wind knocked tree limbs together, causing icicles to snap. Sadie shivered. A Texican by birth, she'd spent the last five months on assignment in her native state, sweating bullets in a drought. When headquarters had sent the urgent wire about Minx, Sadie had hopped the first train to Denver. She hadn't anticipated the need to adjust to a 50-degree drop in temperature overnight. Nor had she thought to stop at some emporium along the way to purchase a decent pair of boots. She'd been too busy ditching her favorite nuisance: a silver-tongued gunslinger, better known as "Eros in Spurs" in polite society.

And as Lucifire in my bed.

Her lips curved at the memory.

William "Cass" Cassidy was as hot as the devil's pitchfork with a temper to match. The snoop had learned how headquarters wanted her to investigate the disappearance of a fellow Lady Pinkerton—or Pinkie, as female agents were affectionately called. Cass wasn't the least bit convinced that women should wear badges, especially in a city where the chief of police was even more corrupt than its mayor. He'd insisted on tagging along for her protection.

Sadie had been equally insistent that Cass butt out of her Pinkerton affairs. He might be a newly minted Ranger in Texas, but in Colorado, he was still wanted for three counts of stage coach robbery.

Unfortunately, Cass had been determined to give her boss a piece of his mind. To prevent him from smashing Allan Pinkerton's face—or worse—Sadie had let the tawny-haired heartthrob tucker himself out, pleasuring her with whipping cream and drizzled honey. Shortly before dawn, while Cass had been recuperating from his erotic feast, she'd snapped manacles on his wrists and dumped his three lock picks—yes, *three* lock picks!—out the train's window.

Thus, while her lover had snoozed, blissfully unaware that he'd need a hacksaw to cut himself from his berth, she'd fled to Fort Worth's stage depot and had finally arrived for her debriefing in Allan Pinkerton's secret railroad car.

With any luck, Cass is still speeding his way toward sunny Laredo.

Sadie smirked at the thought.

But as she entered the grove of spruces, her amusement ebbed. Here, the bristling tree sentinels blotted most of the light from the sky. The deeper she roamed, the denser the shadows grew. When she finally entered a clearing big enough for a circle of wagons, her relief was short-lived. Judging by the wheel ruts, the abandoned wood piles, and the ashes scattered across the snow, Fowler's troop had camped here and moved on.

Damn. Where'd they go?

Teeth chattering, she hugged her muff to her chest and trudged a few yards further, wincing when her ankles wobbled on their spiky heels. She didn't know what bothered her more, the pits in the road or the unnatural silence of the conifer forest.

Suddenly, a twig snapped behind her. She gasped and turned. With her Smith & Wesson cocked inside her muff, she raked tawny eyes over the hulking shadows around her. Above the hammering of her heart, her straining ears could hear nothing but the soughing of the wind.

Then a white-tailed deer stepped onto the path.

Her breath loosed in a shaky rush.

'What were you expecting?' she scolded herself. *'An ax-murdering ghost from the spook show?'*

She shoved her pistol back up her sleeve and yanked her foot from a hole. That's when she heard the ominous sound that every fashionable female dreads: the crack of a breaking heel.

Son of a—

She'd only just begun to curse when a fine, freezing drizzle pelted the top of her sable hat.

It's official. I'm in hell.

The deer fled, probably because she was hopping on one foot and swearing like a bawd in a low-rent crib. But as she tried—unsuccessfully—to snap her other heel, she heard the rattle of an approaching carriage.

Praise the Lord. He hasn't forsaken me yet.

The vehicle was coming fast. Through ice-encrusted trees, she glimpsed polished brass lanterns and a perfectly matched team of Morgans—sure signs of wealth. She didn't recognize the crest on the carriage doors, but she reasoned that hitching a ride with rich folk was better than limping a quarter mile back to the spook show on one heel.

As the carriage rounded the bend, she hobbled to the intersection and waved her arms like a windmill. The whip, whose hat dripped icicles, didn't look inclined to stop. And who could blame him? The way the rain was pelting down, she probably looked like she'd fished a drowned rat from the river and plopped it on her head.

Fortunately, the hansom's occupants were more altruistic.

"Good heavens!" a young female exclaimed, rolling up the isinglass curtain. "Stop the carriage!"

The whip muttered, but he obliged. The vehicle bounced to a halt, spraying sludge all over Sadie.

She scowled, wiping a dollop of mud from her chin.

Luckily for you, pal, my study of Riggoletto *didn't supply me with the vocabulary to lambast coach drivers.*

The door swung wide, revealing an attractive, dark-haired couple, dressed in evening finery. The gentleman sized her up, his right hand tucked inside his hip pocket. No doubt he gripped a pistol, which meant he travelled smart. Lawless bands of road agents weren't above roughing up a woman, forcing her to play decoy for a robbery. If Sadie wanted on that coach, she would have to invent a sob story—and fast.

"Oh, *grazie, signore. Grazie!*" she gushed. "I am hopelessly lost in your wretched, American wilderness, and I think I was being chased by *il lupo.* A wolf!"

"A *wolf?!*" The dainty, blue-eyed female, who couldn't have been a day over 21, looked aghast. "You poor darling! You must be Lady Fiore, the *Contessa di Montaldeo!* I read in the *Rocky* how you came to Denver to attend Rothchild's art auction."

The gentleman tossed his companion a warning glance. "Madam," he addressed Sadie more warily, "you are quite safe now. I see nothing to indicate that you've been followed."

"And even if you were," his companion chimed in staunchly, "Dante is a crack shot. He'd turn that wolf into a pelt for sure!"

"My ward is understandably biased," Dante said in a smooth, cultured baritone that suggested Boston roots.

Repairing his lapse in chivalry, he stepped into the drizzle and swept a formal bow. When he straightened, Sadie found herself locking stares with one of the most alluringly sensual men she'd ever met. He sported a beaver top hat and a form-fitting Chesterfield overcoat, which accentuated his broad shoulders and lean waist. His eyes were dark and mesmerizing, and the cleft in his clean-shaven chin lent him an air of nobility. Sadie guessed him to be about 35 years old.

"Permit me to introduce my companion properly," Dante said. "This is Miss Wyntir Grayfell. And I am Dr. Dante Goddard, at your service."

Dante Goddard? The eminent psychiatrist?

Sadie's mood brightened at this stroke of good fortune. During her debriefing in Pinkerton's private railroad car, she'd learned how Minx had consulted with Dante, as well as a psychology professor, named Mendel Baines. At the time, Minx had been trying to determine if a wealthy dowager, named Lilybelle Welbourn, was as senile as her daughter-in-law claimed. More to the point, Minx had wanted to know if Lilybelle had been hoodwinked out of a fortune in heirloom jewelry by Enoch Fowler and his "spooks."

"*Grazie, Dottore* Goddard," Sadie said when he shrugged off his overcoat and wrapped it around her shoulders. The wool was heavy and toasty-warm. Dragging it closer, she enjoyed the civilized fragrances of him: applewood tobacco, lemon-spice cologne, and cedar hair tonic. "You and *Signorina* Greyfell are the answer to my prayers."

"We shall see you to your hotel," he assured her warmly. "Come."

But as Sadie stepped forward, her remaining heel skated

on ice. One moment, she was flailing for dear life; the next moment, she was clinging to Dante's neck and sliding down a chest like Colorado granite. When their stares locked, she glimpsed golden flecks, like kindling fires, in his dark eyes.

She sucked in her breath.

After working for 11 years as a professional seductress, Sadie had thought herself immune to masculine beauty. But with Dante's arm locked around her waist, and her muddy pumps dangling helplessly above his shoes, she couldn't quite bite back a nervous giggle. His lips curved in a lazy smile, leaving no doubt he was accustomed to making females giddy.

"Grazie, dottore." Sadie's cheeks flamed. She vowed to take an ax to her traitorous heel at the first opportunity.

"Please. Call me Dante. All my friends do."

I'll bet your patients do too. While they're naked on your couch.

"And you must call me Fiore," she said gamely, recovering her composure. *Might as well strike while the iron is hot.*

He helped her into the carriage, and she settled beside Wyntir, who fussed like a mother hen, shoving a brassier under her seat.

"Lady Fiore, I'm sorry you've had such a fright," Wyntir said, uncorking a silver flask and reaching for a demitasse cup. "Turkish coffee? To warm you up?"

Sadie wasn't a big fan of *café;* tequila was more to her liking. However, she was willing to make an exception, if only to thaw the blood in her fingertips.

Suddenly, from the corner of her eye, she spied a flash in the drizzle. Seeking the source of that light, she peered through the window and scanned the embankment. Through the ribbons of mist weaving through the spruces, she spotted the man in the vaquero hat. He was holstering his gun.

Damn! I knew I was being followed!

"Fiore?" Dante prompted as the coach lurched forward. "Is something wrong?"

For a moment, she struggled with guilt, worried that she'd endangered civilians. Then she reasoned that the Mexican would have already plugged her if he was willing to risk a murder warrant to snatch her emeralds. No, he was probably biding his time, waiting to see where she lodged so he could search her hotel room for plunder.

Based on that assessment, Sadie guessed the Mexican couldn't be Maestro. Denver's Prince of Thieves had no qualms about leaving corpses in his wake. By accepting this mission, she'd also had to accept that her emerald bait would attract opportunistic riffraff.

With as much dignity as she could muster, she pasted on a smile for Dante and tried to forget how her curls were hanging in disarray and her skirts were dripping with slush. *"Si, dottore.* All is well. You are my hero. And you, *signorina,* are my angel. I am so grateful for your willingness to drive me back to the Windsor Hotel."

Wyntir blushed as she passed the steaming demitasse cup. "Think nothing of it, Lady Fiore. Any good Christian would have done the same. You see, Dante?" Wyntir added with a touch of asperity. "There *was* a reason to take the high road today. Just like Brother Enoch said."

Distaste flickered over Dante's face. "An inspiring message, to be sure—if one could overlook the messenger."

Sadie hid her amusement. Clearly, Dante thought little of Enoch Fowler, and that was another reason to like Dante.

"Dear Lady Fiore, please don't take offense," Wyntir said, her blush deepening to a pretty rose. "You traveled a long way, and went through a terrible ordeal, to hear the voice of God today."

Sadie decided to let Wyntir believe her romanticized version of the truth. "You must call me Fiore, *carina.* We are all friends now, *si?"*

Wyntir nodded, looking pleased. "I shudder to think what might have happened to you, if Dante and I hadn't come along. Were you harmed by that odious wolf?"

Sadie pasted on a martyr-like smile. "I am quite well. But my sable, I fear, has seen better days."

"And your necklace," Wyntir commiserated. "Your servants will be digging out the mud between all those diamonds and emeralds for hours! Goodness," the younger woman added, leaning forward to take a closer look at Sadie's collar. "That stud is truly stunning. I daresay it could rival the Namdaran jewels—which, unfortunately, you'll never get to see. They were stolen recently from our museum."

Sadie was well aware of the theft. Her supervisor, Mace Ryker (better known as Agent Sledgehammer,) was working that case.

"This trifle?" Sadie said in bored tones. She fingered the cushion-shaped emerald, which was roughly the size of a robin's egg. "My little bauble is hardly comparable to the Heart of Fire. Now *that* gem is worthy of your high praise. A maharajah's wedding gift to his true love? Ah, *amare!* But I read in the *Rocky* how the necklace was stolen from *Signore* Tabor's mansion. *Che peccato*—what a shame."

Wyntir nodded sadly. "A tragic affair. Horace is beside himself. His butler was like a second father to him."

"You know the lieutenant governor?" Sadie asked in some surprise.

"Oh, yes. He and Papa used to play billiards at the Gentleman's Sporting Club before…before…"

Wyntir's bottom lip trembled, and her eyes grew bright with tears.

Dante reached across the coach and gave her hand a squeeze. "You must forgive my ward," he said, offering Wyntir his handkerchief. "Mourning is especially difficult for a young woman who faces the holidays without family."

Sadie fidgeted. Nobody knew that truth better than she did.

"Fortunately," Dante continued kindly, "Wyntir has a great many friends to support her since Edmund's death.

Why, all the First Families of Denver have RSVP'd for her 21st birthday party. The Moffats, Byers, Crokes, Welbourns—"

Sadie's interest increased exponentially. *The Welbourns?*

Wyntir's face brightened suddenly, as if a light bulb had switched on in her brain. "Dante, I've had the most wonderful idea! Fiore should come to my party! Since she's new in town, I could introduce her to all the important people, whom a *contessa* should know."

Sadie felt the warmth of Dante's approving gaze upon her face.

"I'm certain Denver's First Families would welcome you with open arms, Fiore," he said.

"Oh, *do* say yes!" Wyntir begged, giving an exuberant little bounce. "I'll send an invitation, of course, but the festivities will be held the Saturday before Thanksgiving."

Sadie was secretly thrilled that Wyntir had provided the social entrée to bait Maestro. "A birthday party would be a charming diversion," she purred.

For the rest of that journey, Wyntir couldn't stop blathering about her party. Every now and then, Dante would chime in with a droll observation about the guest list or a gentle reproach about the extravagance.

Sadie fixed a smile on her face and listened with half an ear. She kept glancing out the window and wondering if the Mexican was tailing the coach. The last time she'd had the nagging suspicion she'd been followed, a container of Greek fire had crashed through her window at Galveston's Satin Siren Casino and Saloon. She'd barely escaped with her life, no thanks to Mace, who'd been posing as her pimp at the time.

At long last, the carriage rolled under the Windsor Hotel's *porte-cochère.* Sadie returned Dante's Chesterfield, and he handed her his calling card. She accepted it graciously, lingering in the hostelry's doorway to wave good-bye. The ploy allowed her to scan the courtyard for suspicious-looking characters.

To her relief, she spied no vaquero hats.

Then again, a man could remove his hat, and Larimer Street wasn't the hotel's only entrance.

Doing her best to ignore the disdainful sniffs and disapproving stares of the Windsor's illustrious guests, Sadie hurried across the lobby in her bedraggled sable. The hotel had been financed, in part, by Horace Tabor and modeled after the famous British castle, which was probably why one of the turrets flew the Union Jack. The hotel also happened to be one of Denver's fanciest, with mirrors made of crushed diamonds; a suspended dance floor (so couples felt like they were waltzing on air,) a shopping hall full of boutiques; one elevator; two grand staircases; and three restaurants, boasting legendary chefs from Europe.

Sadie's stomach rumbled at the thought. *Too bad no maitre d will admit me while I look like a refugee from a mud hole!*

At long last, the elevator bell dinged to announce her arrival at the fifth and final floor. She glanced warily down the hall toward her penthouse suite, which had served as Tabor's love lair until March. That's when he'd ignored the fact that he was still married to his wife of 26 years and had wed his mistress.

Men are such dogs.

Pressing a coin into the elevator operator's palm, Sadie dismissed the car and dashed for her door.

Thank God. The wax seal's still intact.

She bolted the lock behind her.

The rise of a full moon cast twisted, claw-like shadows across the rose-patterned wallpaper and the towering, black-walnut furnishings. She figured the spooky silhouettes had contributed to her renewed sense of unease. The flame in the lamp by her bed flickered at its lowest setting, just as she'd left it.

Sighing, she shrugged off her coat and tossed Dante's calling card on the chiffonier. She'd made good progress for one day, meeting the psychiatrist and earning an invitation to mingle socially with Denver's First Families.

But the day wasn't over yet. She still had to attend Mendel Baines's lecture on hypnotism at eight o'clock. That meant she'd have to ring for water so she could scrub off her mud in Tabor's legendary, gold-leaf tub.

She turned for the bathroom. She hadn't taken three steps toward her goal, however, before the menacing click of a revolver froze her in her tracks.

"Buenas noches, señorita."

Sadie sucked in her breath. An alpine breeze riffled the curtains.

The Mexican had sneaked in through her window!

CHAPTER 2

S adie's heart crawled to her throat as a shadow emerged from the gold-silk dressing screen. An amber moon silhouetted a wide-brimmed vaquero hat, slanting across the intruder's brow. A plain gray poncho blanketed his torso like a tent. With the majority of light concentrated behind him, discerning his hair color, facial features, and breadth was impossible. His only identifiable characteristic was his scent: cedarwood soap, saddle leather, and damiana, a popular Mexican herb for cigarettes.

"I have looked forward to our meeting for a long time," the gunman gloated, his accent thicker than Mexican custard.

"So sorry to keep you waiting, *muchacho*," she rallied huskily, struggling to keep the quaver from her voice. "To what do I owe this surprise? A certain, comely necklace?"

His chuckle was throaty, reminding her of rawhide and sin.

"You Pinkertons think you know so much," he taunted in his gruff baritone. "But where are my manners, eh? You have had a trying day. You wish to change your gown and doubtless to bathe." A flash of white in that shadow-steeped face signaled a predatory grin. "Do not let me stop you, *querida.*"

Sadie's fingers twitched with the temptation to trigger the Smith & Wesson strapped to her wrist.

"Hands spread," he barked, as if reading her mind.

Her heart skipped. Even if she could draw her pistol, she couldn't fire fast enough to beat the bullet trained on her chest.

"I am told you are a dangerous woman," he mocked. "That you hide naughty toys in tender places. Let us start with the .32, *por favor.* Slowly. Very slowly. Unstrap the sleeve holster and kick it under the bed."

Who told him about my Smith & Wesson?

She mustered a seductive smile. "Come now. Don't tell me a big, bad *bandito* like you is afraid of a little popgun."

"Discard the .32," he snapped. "It gives my trigger finger the itch."

With a sinking heart, she watched her holster skate under the quilt.

"Next, you will remove the stiletto from your collar sheath."

Perspiration slid down her temple. Apparently, he knew the standard-issue weapons for Pinkies. But how? Had Maestro sent him to murder Minx?

Stalling for time, Sadie arched her spine, letting pearl buttons strain across her ample bosom. "I'm flattered you find me so fearsome, *señor.* It is rare to meet a man who admits his…impotence."

"Your clever tongue will dig your grave," he growled. "I am not the fool you think I am. Discard the knife. Now."

Reluctantly, she tossed the stiletto near the chiffonier.

"Next, remove the laudanum ring. And the hairpin dagger. Oh, and don't forget the cameo. I do not wish to be blinded by ink while teaching you the lesson you so richly deserve."

Bastard. Sadie's hands shook as she obeyed. He knew the Pinkie arsenal, all right. But what he didn't know was that she had an outlaw lover. Cass had taught her a few survival tricks over the years, not the least of which was how to rig a false sole in her boot. She'd concealed an extra knife there.

"Bueno," her bushwhacker said as her cameo joined the growing pile of weapons by the chiffonier. "Next, your corset."

"What about my corset?" she fired back.

"It hides dangers too, *no?"*

"Only if you're afraid of freckles, *mi amor."*

Again, that husky laugh. It was a rumble of pure wickedness. "To fill out so much whalebone takes more than freckles, I think."

"Such a suspicious *señor.* Come see for yourself."

"I prefer the view from here." He gestured, and his gun glinted with menace. "Remove your clothes."

Nervously, she moistened her lips, envisioning the blissful moment when she could get her hands on his balls. "I'll show you my treasures, if you show me yours."

"Does your man know you issue such invitations to *banditos?"*

She bit back a retort. Cass hadn't earned his nickname, Rebel Rutter, because he was known for his fidelity. Nevertheless, she battled a frisson of guilt. She might have been kinder to him in Fort Worth. She might have left a hacksaw within his reach...

She hiked her chin. Now wasn't the time to second guess her decisions. Doubt would get her killed.

"Variety is the spice of life," she rallied provocatively. "And I so adore spice."

He *tsked.* "Such a mouth. It should be gagged."

"Or kissed." She tilted her head, slowly, deliberately, licking her lips. "Mmm. I like exotic flavors. What does Mexico taste like, I wonder?"

"Muy caliente. Like chili, not Boston baked beans."

Her eyes narrowed. Was that a reference to Dante?

"I'm much hotter than a chili pepper," she bragged in sultry tones.

"I think all your fire's in your hair," he taunted.

"Try me."

"A tempting proposition, *querida.* But highly suspicious

while you are swaddled in satin. Prove your sincerity, and you may find me forgiving."

Forgiving?

She steeled herself against a scowl. Who *was* this Mexican? The kinsman of some *Tejano,* whom she'd arrested in Texas? "You're a long way from home, *amigo.* Why have you really come here?" she demanded.

"You have not guessed?" His grin turned lopsided as he reached beneath his poncho. "I have come to return the favor of these."

A pair of fur-lined handcuffs dropped at her feet.

She blinked.

Suddenly, understanding flooded her mind.

"Cass! You stinking weasel!"

He laughed, dodging the manacles she hurled at his head. "You sure took your time sniffing out my clues, *detective,"* he taunted, reverting to his native, Texas drawl.

Turning up the gas lamp, she glared at her lover. She couldn't remember the last time she'd seen Cass wearing any color except black—sinfully tight black. The reprobate had clearly gone out of his way to mislead her. He'd traded his sandalwood soap and clove cigarettes for cedarwood soap and damiana smokes. He'd ditched his fancy silver spurs and elaborately tooled Justin boots. He'd stuffed his blond, shoulder-length mane beneath a battered felt hat instead of his beloved Stetson. He'd even shrouded his lean, muscle-packed thighs in baggy trousers. But the drab shade of his poncho made the sapphire flames of his eyes burn that much brighter.

She found herself longing to trail her fingers along the tawny stubble of a week's growth of beard.

His lips quirked, as if he'd guessed her thoughts. In return, he studied her henna-darkened curls and pearl-studded bodice. The bold caress of her lover's gaze made her breaths catch.

"Does Allan Pinkerton have something against red hair?" he demanded.

"Only in Italian women."

"Since when did you become Italian?"

"About the same time you became Mexican, blondie."

He hiked a sun-gilded eyebrow. "Was that a slur against my parentage?"

"When's the last time you ever saw a tow-headed Mexican?"

"A new wardrobe, a new accent, and my disguise fooled *you,* Lady Pinkerton."

"Nonsense."

"*'Cass, you stinking weasel!'*" he taunted in a parody of feminine outrage.

She scowled. "You're a lousy mimic."

He chuckled, folding his arms across his chest. "You know what your trouble is?"

"You."

"Remind me to spank you later," he countered dryly. "No, *your* trouble is, you think you can wrap any two-legged male around your little finger. That's a flaw in your armor, Madam Pinkie. And someday, some bastard without a conscience is going to come along and use that flaw against you."

She snorted. Cass had been a Texas Ranger for two weeks. *Two weeks!* Yet the peacock had the audacity to tell her, a seasoned detective of four years, how to run her case?

"Oh, I get it," she said. "You traveled all the way to Denver, risking a domicile with bars, to teach me a lesson."

"Damned straight, princess. You're in over your head, and you're too stubborn to admit it."

"The term's *contessa,* wise guy. And if anyone's in danger, it's you. You don't even have a decent growth of beard yet. Set foot in any sporting house, and you'll be recognized. And that's just for starters. Do I have to remind you I'm working for Sledgehammer?"

"Who?"

"At the Satin Siren, you knew him by his alias, Karl Dietrich."

Cass snickered. "Agent Sledgehammer."

Sadie rolled her eyes. "Honest to God. It's like talking to a doorknob."

"I think it's time I got me a code name for undercover work," Cass drawled in lilting tones. "How about Agent Ramsbottom?"

She shot him a withering glare.

"Trouser Snake? Squirt Weasel? No?"

"Are you finished?"

He smirked. "Aw, *contessas* are no fun."

She blew out an exasperated breath. "Cass, I can't let myself get distracted. I have an investigation to conduct."

He shrugged. "So turn the case over to Sledgehammer, and come home to Texas."

"And do what? Sit in a rocking chair while you're dodging bullets with your Ranger badge?"

The amusement ebbed from his features. "You have friends in Texas. Rex and Wilma—"

"Minx was my friend too."

Actually, that wasn't quite true. Sadie had only met the 22-year-old Missourian once, at a secret Pinkie graduation, but Cass didn't need to know that. Minx had been a bored young debutante, fresh out of finishing school, when she'd decided to run away from Daddy's choice of husbands to become a Pinkie. Other than belonging to the small, female fraternity of field agents, Sadie and Minx shared little in common.

But that fact was moot, as far as Sadie was concerned. Minx had been a Pinkerton. And Pinkertons—especially Lady Pinkertons—took care of their own.

"I thought you wanted to help Wilma train Pinkies," Cass reminded her.

"What kind of role model would I be if I refused an assignment because my lover was worried I might stub my toe?"

"That's *not* what I'm worried about," he said grimly.

"Have a little faith in me, Cass. Pinkerton does. *Rex* does."

"For your information, Rex gave me orders to come after you!"

Sadie fumed at this revelation. Rexford Sterne was her mentor and ally, but the Ranger commander had a way of turning overprotective, like an Alpha wolf, whenever he got uncomfortable with the risk in her Pinkerton missions. Considering how Rex was 20 years her senior—and thoroughly infatuated with the Pinkie Chief, Wilma LeBeau—Sadie attributed his concern to a deeply ingrained southern chivalry.

"Neither you nor Rex has authority over me," she reminded Cass brusquely. "I'm a Pinkerton. I work undercover. Get used to it."

Cass jerked his head toward Dante's calling card. "Are you working under *his* covers?"

Sadie sighed. She should have guessed Dante was the real bone of contention in this debate. Cass and Dante were like night and day. The dapper Bostonian had probably been born on Beacon Hill, with the proverbial silver spoon in his mouth, and educated at the finest universities.

Cass, on the other hand, had grown up in a leaky sharecropper's cottage. He'd learned his life's lessons in saloons, brothels, and jails, graduating with a con man's knack for trickery and the well-deserved nickname, Coyote Cass.

Cass hated the privileged class.

Hoping to diffuse the bomb that Dante represented, Sadie modulated her tone with indifference. "Dr. Goddard is a psychiatrist. An expert witness in my case."

"Beans is an expert, all right. I saw how he put his hands on you."

"Would you have preferred me to sprawl in a ditch?"

"After I saw how much you liked being caught?"

"Oh for heaven's sake. Don't tell me the Rebel Rutter's jealous of a stuffed shirt."

Cass scowled, his gaze dropping to the ostentatious emerald between her breasts. "I don't like you posing as bait."

"You made that perfectly clear on the train, darling. And that's why I sent you to Laredo—in case you're wondering."

A muscle ticked in his jaw.

She blew him a kiss and started undressing. Cass could be a pain in the butt when his dander was up. She didn't have time for one of their explosive arguments or the fiery make-up sex that usually resulted. She needed to ring for bath water if she wanted to stay on schedule.

Earlier that morning, she'd learned that Minx had purchased a ticket for Mendel Baines's lecture, *Hypnotism and the Conditioned Response.* Sadie was hoping the psychology professor could shed light on Minx's case. About six weeks ago, the Pinkie had been hired by Sheridan Welbourn, who'd insisted that Lilybelle, her "old bat of a mother-in-law," had been tricked by the voice of a dead Indian into donating $200,000 worth of heirloom jewelry to Preacher Fowler.

Now Allan Pinkerton wanted to know why his female operative's custom-made, mohair-lined glove had been recovered from Tabor's mansion on the night the butler had been murdered and the Heart of Fire had been stolen. Male field agents, especially Mace, had speculated that Minx's "delicate mental balance" had been upset by field work, and she'd jumped off the 19th Street Bridge in a fit of remorse. To Sadie's disgust, her male colleagues had cited Minx as a tragic example of why the agency should end its "ill-advised experiment" with female operatives.

Sadie felt honor-bound to prove them wrong.

Padding across the hotel's plush carpet, she was arrested by her reflection in the floor mirror. Mud still dripped from her bedraggled curls. Splotches of dirt were caked on her chin. She groaned with embarrassment. *No wonder the hotel guests were sneering at me. I look like I wrestled a pig!*

Cass stepped behind her, placing his hands on her shoulders. Against the starched white muslin of her chemise, his long, sun-baked fingers were warm enough, dark enough, to pass for bronze. His grip was strong and possessive, but tender, too. He held her the way a seasoned trapper might hold a cougar cub he'd decided to rescue—or tame.

The notion caused alarm bells to toll in her head. Challenging his gaze in the mirror, she was surprised to spy a fleeting melancholy in his stare. That unexpected glimpse of sadness sent shockwaves to her soul. Cass never let the world see his pain. He was too accomplished as a trickster.

"What's wrong?" she murmured.

"You still have your clothes on."

He flashed his Coyote grin, but it couldn't fool her. Not this time.

"You're still angry about the handcuffs?"

A heartbeat passed. Maybe two. He seemed to be choosing his words—another novel phenomenon.

"I was. At first," he confessed.

"So what changed your mind?"

He reached for a stray, chestnut curl, rubbing it between his thumb and forefinger. "The notion that you cared. Even if you have a screwed up, harebrained way of showing it."

"Are you trying to piss me off?"

"Naw."

Her lips twitched. "Well...then I'm sorry. But you wouldn't listen to reason."

"Now there's the pot calling the kettle black."

"On second thought," she said dryly, "I'm not sorry."

His dimples peeked. "Hellcat."

"Horny toad."

"'Course, if the situation was reversed," he drawled gamely, "I would have made double sure you didn't escape *my* train berth."

"How so?"

"Trade secret." He wiggled his eyebrows.

She snatched off his hat, admiring the curtain of pale, golden hair that spilled to his shoulders. "In that case, I have ways of making men talk, Rutter."

He chuckled, snatching the hat back and sailing it onto the nearest bedpost. "Do your worst, Devil's Daughter."

He cupped her cheek, brushing his thumb across her lips in a whisper-soft caress. An expression of such profound tenderness washed over his sun-chiseled features that it stole her breath away. A starry radiance poured from his sapphire gaze. She blinked, half in awe, half in yearning.

But Sadie was quick to chide the treacherous dreamer, who lurked inside her. Cass knew how to flatter women. More than that, he knew how to steal the most guarded of hearts. He'd tomcatted his way across the West, setting brothel records in Dodge City, Cheyenne, Deadwood, and other male-dominated towns. She had no illusions about Cass. When it came to lovers, she was one in a harem of hundreds.

And that's why he must never, ever know I've fallen for him.

"I've missed you, Sadie," he murmured.

His inky fringe of lashes drooped. She recognized the primal calling in her lover's stare. In spite of her better sense, she thrilled to the heat of his virility. Cass could have any woman he wanted, married or widowed, virgin or whore. All he had to do was flash those dazzling dimples, or murmur sweet nothings with that throbbing, Texas drawl, and any female who possessed a pulse would be a goner. Sadie didn't understand why he was lavishing all his Coyote charm on an old flame with a muddy face, but she was just vain enough—and pleased enough—to ignore the passing suspicion.

She rose on tiptoe. He nuzzled her mouth wider. His kiss was the softest sweetness, like rose petals made of spun sugar. She licked his bottom lip, enjoying the flavor of honey laced with lemon and menthol. *So this is the taste of damiana?* It was heady. Aphrodisiac. She licked again, and her senses began to spin. To soar. She forgot the mud. She forgot the lecture she was supposed to attend. She clasped him tighter.

In the next instant, her knees buckled, and she oozed to the carpet.

Cass braced himself, catching her as she crumpled. He'd been counting his heartbeats. He'd been waiting for the opiate to kick in so Sadie would lose sense of time and space.

"Like I said," he murmured huskily, peeling a sheer strip of putty from his bottom lip. "Some bastard without a conscience."

Tossing the putty to the carpet, he swept up the woman he loved and carried her to the bed. He paused only long enough to fling aside a corner of the quilt. Then he was arranging Sadie's length on the mattress and smoothing her chemise around her ankles. She smiled softly, oblivious to his betrayal.

At least for the moment.

Hardening his heart, Cass reached behind her neck and slipped the hooks that latched her collar. A river of diamonds, emeralds, and gold-platinum spilled into his palm. He shoved the bait into the bag of loot swinging from his belt, beneath his poncho. The necklace clinked faintly against the peacock music box he'd discovered while poking through the false bottoms of her traveling trunks. Allan Pinkerton had gone to great lengths to accumulate the precious gems for Sadie's *contessa* disguise, gems that were supposed to lure the murderous jewel thief, Maestro, to her side. Cass figured the emeralds would fetch an especially handsome price from his criminal contacts in the Underground.

"Whether you like it or not," he chided her softly, tucking the quilt around her voluptuous curves, "a female tin-star has limitations. I would rather have you learn that from me than a Pinkie Killer."

He inhaled deeply, filling his lungs with the musky scent of woman, patchouli, and lavender-scented linen. He couldn't resist brushing a silken strand of chestnut from her breasts. Luscious, alabaster mounds rose high above the lace-covered whalebone of her corset. Wistfully, he watched the dance of darling, rose-gold freckles each time she took a breath.

His throat worked.

He forced himself to look away.

Retrieving his hat, he turned down the lamp and slipped out the door.

Shades of night spilled into the muted glow of the hall's crystal chandeliers. Hunkered down in a puddle of sawdust, a flinty-eyed, tow-headed youth sat whittling by the door. A portly raccoon, wearing a rawhide collar, snoozed by the boy's knee.

"Is it done?" Collie demanded, never missing a stroke with his knife.

Cass nodded curtly, tugging the door closed.

The coon snorted awake. Spying nothing out of the ordinary, Vandy flopped over, waved his paws in the air, and promptly fell back to sleep.

"Some watch dog," Cass muttered.

"Don't go busting your spleen on Vandy. Pinkerton's the one you're pissed at for putting your woman at risk."

"I got plenty of spleen to go around," Cass growled, envisioning the moment when he got his hands on Minx's killer. *So help me God, Sadie will not suffer the same fate.*

Four months ago, when the Satin Siren Casino had burned to the ground, and Cass had thought he'd lost her forever, he'd blamed himself for not finding some way to save her. Now he couldn't bear the thought of reliving that hell. He had to make Sadie see sense, to stop her from dodging bullets. Then he could finally concentrate on his own job: making Texas a safe place for little kiddies to play.

Maybe even our little kiddies.

"I'll take these rocks to the fence," Cass said, patting the pouch of gems under his poncho. "Don't let Sadie out of your sight."

"I ain't the push-over you are, Snake Bait."

Cass glared at his seventeen-year-old sidekick.

"Aw, lighten up," Collie said sheepishly. "You're Coyote Cass. Maestro's no match for you. You'll bait him. You'll trap him. He'll hang, and we'll all go home in plenty of time for Thanksgiving."

Cass nodded grimly. Turning on his heel, he stepped over Vandy and headed for the elevator. He hoped Collie was right.

Because Thanksgiving or no, Cass wasn't sure Sadie would ever forgive him.

CHAPTER 3

Cass pushed open the door of Porfirio Deinos's bakery. A yeasty warmth, scented with cinnamon and cloves, triggered an appreciative growl in his belly. Above the cheerful greeting of the bell, he could hear the muffled clanking of pans behind a blue and white curtain, resembling the Greek flag.

Just about everything else in the café was purple, owing to Porfi's fondness for his first name. Lavender linens filled the pastry baskets; violet tiles formed geometric patterns on the floor; grapes were the focal piece of the still-life covering the ceiling.

"Erre es korrakas!" the baker bellowed from his kitchen.

Cass hiked an eyebrow. Porfi had fenced his loot for five years, so Cass had learned the translation of certain pet phrases. "Go to the crows" was a scurrilous insult in Greek.

As if on cue, the kitchen's curtain whipped sideways, and an auburn-haired tenderfoot stomped past the counter. He looked like he'd done battle with a flour sack. Raccoon-eyes squinted from the only part of his face that wasn't white—no doubt thanks to the soiled spectacles peeking from his coat pocket. He kept cursing and bumping into tables as he zig-zagged across the café, a soiled pocket watch swinging from his fist. Flour flakes flurried in his wake.

A moment later, Porfi huffed into view, brandishing a rolling pin and bellowing at the top of his lungs, "A pox on your willy! May you never have sons! May your daughters be hag-faced!"

Cass cleared his throat, politely stepping aside so Flour Man could flip the bird and slam out the door.

"Trouble, Porfi?"

"Cass!" A cherubic grin of welcome stretched the Greek's pudgy cheeks. "Why would you think that?"

Draped in a purple apron and the traditional, baggy trousers of "the Motherland," Porfi was a mountain of a man—if you imagined the mountain had toppled sideways. Despite his girth and temperament, the blustery Greek was well-liked, even respected among the Italian, German, and Irish immigrants who dominated the Highlands. He never had less than three sloe-eyed beauties competing for his affection. At 68-years-old, Porfi's libido would have put a younger man's to shame. Cass knew this for a fact. He'd first met Porfi in the brothel owned by Denver's infamous, pistol-packing madam, Mattie Silks.

"That gent sure lit out of here in a hurry," Cass drawled, strolling to the counter and sniffing cooling racks of crispy, golden honey puffs. Porfi called the treats *loukounades* and described them as a doughnut, "minus the American waste of a hole."

"Bah. Good riddance. " Porfi sneered. "A professor should not have custard for brains. *Vlacas!*" He hurled this insult at the door's frosty window panes. Then he grinned, a sickle-shaped slash of white in his charcoal beard. "Amusing, no? The goat calls himself Baines. As in, 'bane-up-my-ass.'"

"Uh…the term is pain-in-my-ass, Porfi."

The rascal winked. "Think about it."

Cass chuckled.

"Help yourself to some *loukounades,* boyo. Or whatever you like. Then lock the door and pull the shade. I'll meet you out back."

Minutes later, Cass's mouth was watering as he entered Porfi's cluttered office. He couldn't wait to dig into the booty he'd heaped on his plate: *ergolavi* (almond cookies,) *baklava* (pistachio layer cake,) and *kataifi* (chopped walnuts wrapped in dough and glazed with lemon syrup.) To a poor kid, who'd stolen rags from scarecrows to stay warm, an invitation to help himself in a bakery was a dream come true.

Porfi shot an amused glance at Cass's cache and banged a platter of fish, olives, and feta cheese onto his desk. Next, he uncorked an anise-flavored liquor, called ouzo. Cass grinned. Ouzo usually led to dancing, dish-smashing, and jolly shrieks of *"Opa!"*

"Ya mas!" Porfi toasted solemnly. "May your days be merry, your women be willing, and your pockets be plentiful with pretties for me."

"Ya mas," Cass repeated affectionately. "And may your enterprises flourish in the Land of the Free."

They tossed back their shots.

Porfi grunted, settling his bulk across two chairs. As he spooned fish onto his plate, he groused about his flour-faced customer. Apparently, this Mendel Baines had been traveling from university to university, lecturing about hypnotism. Baines was trying to convince some academic board to fund a research project. He claimed he could hide a series of commands in a friendly conversation, and thereby induce a subject to do whatever he wanted, without raising the subject's suspicions.

Porfi snorted. "If the *malaka* was any good at his own research, he'd have rich folks hypnotized and forking over fortunes. Instead, he comes skulking around here, selling trifles to pay for gambling debts."

"Is that why you slugged him with a flour sack?"

Porfi widened roguish, blue eyes. "What, you think I waste perfectly good flour, pelting goats?"

"Baines sure didn't walk in your door looking like a ghost."

The Greek chuckled, pouring another round of ouzo. "He said Soapy Smith would give him a better price for his musical timepiece. The nerve! *Vlacas!*" Porfi spit on the floor for good measure. "I told him to kiss Soapy's *kolos* and never darken my door again."

"If you liked the pocket watch so much, why didn't you give him a fair offer?"

Porfi shot Cass a withering glare. "Shut up and drink."

Cass grinned. No one knew a fence's game better than he did. He'd been hocking marbles, slingshots, and tin soldiers since the age of six. As the years passed, he'd graduated to robbing stages and rustling steers.

The great irony, of course, was that he'd finally achieved his lifelong dream, the right to wear a Ranger badge, only to stuff the star inside his pocket five days later. Ranger jurisdiction was limited to Texas, and the special commission he needed to arrest Colorado felons had yet to be approved by the U.S. Marshal's Office.

But Cass couldn't sit around waiting for the bureaucrats if he wanted to protect Sadie from Minx's killer—or more aptly, from Pinkerton's harebrained scheme to use a woman as bait. Cass needed to weasel his way back into the good graces of Denver's crime bosses. And fast.

"So." Porfi lit a cigar and tossed Cass his matchsafe. "Another good meal with a good friend has come to an end."

Cass lit his self-rolled quirley, while Porfi swept dirty dishes to the side, using a massive forearm with purple porpoise tattoos.

"What pretties have you brought for Porfi to buy?"

Cass reached beneath his poncho and removed one of several, carefully organized pouches from his belt. When he tossed it into the space Porfi had cleaned, the Greek pasted on a bland expression and began pawing through the contents.

"Eh." Porfi shrugged at a charming broach mosaic, depicting a caged parrot inlaid with tourmaline, garnet, and citrine. *"Humph."* He pushed aside a butterfly-pendant

with silver, gold, and copper wings. He shook his head over a black opal bracelet that glittered with rainbows. When he found Cass's personal favorite—a diamond-and-topaz ring that flashed with the fire of Sadie's eyes—Porfi snorted.

"Something wrong?" Cass asked dryly. He knew the topaz, alone, was worth five grand.

"I invite you to my table," the Greek said in wounded tones. "I call you my friend. And yet, you bring me trifles?"

Cass did a masterful job of keeping a straight face.

"Well...there *is* this."

He produced the music box. Inside, he'd hidden a triple strand of pearls with an enormous, cushion-shaped sapphire. He'd "borrowed" the necklace from his friend, Mattie Silks, whose fancy man had stolen it from parts unknown. Mattie would hit the roof if she ever guessed Cass had relieved her of her favorite hot pearls—for her own good, of course.

Porfi cocked his head. He was studying the cloisonné peacock on the music box's black lid. Cass happened to know Porfi's favorite mistress had been begging him to procure such a novelty—which could be ordered from the Sears and Roebucks catalog for $1.98. But Porfi had his pride. He never paid retail.

"And what is this?" the fence inquired archly.

"A jewelry box. It plays a tune. I think it's the Greek National Anthem."

Porfi's eyes lit up. He flipped open the lid, and the tinny strains of a popular waltz, *Farewell My Darling,* reverberated through the cluttered, fish-scented quarters.

"Bah." Porfi slammed down the lid. "You think I traffic in girl's toys?"

"Look again."

"Eh?"

Cass gestured with his smoking quirley. "Under the false bottom."

Warily, Porfi dug his pudgy fingers inside the box. When he found the hidden latch and freed the necklace, Cass imagined he could hear the beads of an abacus clicking in the old scoundrel's head. If Porfi recognized Mattie's pearls, he didn't say. He never questioned where merchandise was procured. He'd explained to Cass, once, that curiosity was bad for business.

"The sapphire *is* something," the fence conceded grudgingly.

"Keep it," Cass said magnanimously. "Keep all of it. Consider these trinkets tokens of my esteem—in appreciation for all the favors you do me."

Porfi hiked a bushy eyebrow. "What favors?"

And now, the real game begins.

"I want you to spread the word on the street." Cass adopted a cheeky tone. "Denver has a new prince of thieves."

"You mean Maestro?"

Cass blinked, playing dumb. "Who?"

"The upstart from nowhere, who hit Tabor's place."

Cass frowned, tapping ash into an empty olive jar. "So what you're saying is, I have competition."

Amusement flickered over Porfi's craggy features. "You steal penny candy, boyo. Maestro steals the Heart of Fire."

Cass pretended to consider this disparity. "Is that why they call him Maestro? 'Cause he goes after loot no other thief has the balls to snatch?"

Porfi shrugged. "I call him Goat Stink. 'Cause whatever he steals, he doesn't trade with me. Or to any other local fence, as far as I can tell."

"Now that doesn't sound right."

Porfi agreed with a sneer. "He targets the grandest pieces—the Mother Lode of all rocks—and disdains the easy pickings. He is credited with stealing the Namdaran Emeralds two nights ago from the Museum of Antiquities, but he ignored the jewel-encrusted tankard in the same display case!"

"Maybe he's a teetotaler."

"Maybe's he's a *vlacas* with the brains of a sheep!"

Cass was careful to hide his amusement. Porfi wasn't the only criminal in Denver's underworld who carried a grudge against Maestro. Soapy Smith, the King of Con, resented him because the jewel thief left a trail of blood. Porfi and Soapy were both gentleman rogues at heart and adamantly against murder. They were also adamantly against interlopers, who muscled in on their turf.

"Maestro may be working for a collector," Cass said.

"Stingy bastards. That's what collectors are." Tossing back another shot, Porfi hurled the glass at the brick wall behind him. "May their balls rot off!"

Cass watched glass trickle from the stain on the bricks. The colorful mess was at least two feet wider than it had been five years ago. Porfi threw a lot of crockery at that wall. Cass suspected the Greek preferred smashing dishes to cleaning them.

"Seems like Maestro needs to learn his lesson, all right." Cass blew a leisurely stream of smoke. "What do you think he'll snatch next? I'm not afraid to run a little horse race. Tell you what: I'll beat Maestro to the loot and bring it to you."

Porfi grunted. Translation: he was interested.

"Well, there's this *contessa,* newly arrived in town," the Greek hedged.

"I've already won that round, pard."

At long last, Cass pulled out the booty he'd stolen from Sadie—or rather, the Pinkertons. Gold collars, platinum bracelets, ruby broaches, and emerald pendants tumbled from his pouch. At the sight of so many one-of-a-kind showpieces, never before seen by local fences, the pulse quickened in Porfi's throat.

"All this from one female?" he said in dubious tones.

"Yep."

"Her old man, he must be worth something."

"That's why I'm calling dibs on his widow," Cass said. "*Comprendé?* Tell your associates the Devil has come, and Maestro's reign is over."

Porfi uncorked the ouzo and reached toward a stack of clean shot glasses on his liquor cabinet. Cass suspected the fence was stalling for time, weighing the pros and cons of siding against an emerging power, like Maestro.

"So what's your beef with this *kolos?*" Porfi demanded, pouring another round.

"The truth?"

The Greek inclined his head.

"He killed a mark. A *girl* mark."

Porfi frowned, setting the bottle between them. "A lover?"

"Does it matter? Maestro kills women, Porfi. That means he's capable of any depravity."

Porfi's jaw hardened. He fingered Sadie's emerald collar. On the street, it was worth at least 20 grand.

"So you stole this candy to protect the high-stepper?"

"That's right. She's off limits even to Soapy."

Porfi blinked. "You told *Soapy* not to touch your candy dish?"

"Damned straight."

The fence threw back his head and loosed a hearty laugh. "I like you more and more, boyo."

Leaning across the desk, Porfi drilled Cass with a cagey, alpha-wolf stare. "But if you really wish to make chins wag in the street, you must strike fast. You must beat Maestro to Mephistopheles' jewels."

"Whose jewels?"

"Mephistopheles. " At Cass's blank expression, Porfi added wryly, "The demon who serves the devil in *Faust.* In the opera, the ingénue is sung by Dolce LaRocca, a celebrated Italian soprano. Her American tour arrived in Denver last week. In Act Three, the demon gives a box of jewels to Dolce's character. The Prop Master must have outdone himself, because Dolce was smitten by the paste baubles. Tabor got the bright idea to commission Tiffany's, in New York, to make a copy from real rocks. Last night, he presented Dolce with the necklace to commemorate her debut at his opera house. It's worth $50 grand, at least."

A rascally grin stole across Cass's face. He didn't know the first thing about opera, except that Sadie liked it, and she'd dreamed of singing someday on a stage as grand as Tabor's.

Porfi's scheme was ripe with possibilities.

"I'll make you a deal, Porfi. You keep my dish's candy safe—" he waved a hand at the Pinkerton jewelry—"and I'll make Maestro sorry he didn't pay you the homage you deserve."

A barn-sized grin split Porfi's face. "Deal."

They drank to their new partnership. Cass hurled his glass; Porfi followed suit. Shards tinkled to the unswept pile beneath the bricks. Fueled by ouzo and way too much sugar, Cass was ready to take on Maestro, Soapy, and the whole damned secret, Pinkerton army.

Outside the office, a broad-shouldered man with a hawk-like nose stood in the November night. Sheltered from blustery winds by the alley, he was smoking a Cleopatra Federal cigar and watching man-sized shadows stomp dishes behind the bakery's window shade. Between muffled shouts of laughter, the voyeur could hear lusty cries of, *"Opa!"*

His lips carved out a small, vicious smile.

Dance, Lucifire. Dance like a dead man at the end of a rope. Because that's exactly how your thieving days will end.

Tossing aside his burned-out smoke, the man turned on his heel and walked into the bitter blast of autumn, his Inverness cape fluttering behind him like dark, sinister wings.

CHAPTER 4

R *aw, primal fury.*

That's what Sadie felt when she woke at dawn to learn Cass had betrayed her. She cursed his name in every language she knew. She hurled bars of soap and tins of throat lozenges at the door, imagining the target was his head. She even considered kicking out the window glass he'd sneaked through, until she realized she'd have to bathe in sub-zero temperatures in the suite's ridiculous, gold-leaf tub.

Panting from exertion, she halted in front of the mirror and glared at the traitorous tears, streaking her cheeks. *Poor little idiot,* she scolded herself. *Did you really think a dyed-in-the-wool womanizer could care for you? That a lifelong outlaw could resist the temptation of the Pinkerton jewels?*

With a shaking hand, she touched the slender gold chain gleaming against her throat. Two weeks ago, Cass had loved her so completely, she'd been unable to speak a coherent word. In the aftermath, he'd draped this chain around her throat to hold her lost button-pendant, the only remaining memento of her father, Roarke Michelson. With the ice fortress melting around her heart, Sadie had been so overcome with love, she'd feared she might blurt the truth by singing a reprise from her song:

"Always yours I shall be,
Born for you...Destiny."

A tiny sound, like a wounded animal's, tore from her throat. Unable to bear the memories, she ripped the pendant from her neck, pocketed the button, and hurled the chain out the window. Her muddy, tear-streaked reflection curled its lip at her.

Love is a weakness, and romance is for fools. You got exactly what you deserved, Sarah Jane Michelson.

Flushed with shame, she couldn't bring herself to ring for bath water. Instead, she suffered the chill of the drinking water in her pitcher as she performed her morning ablutions. By the time the clock on her mantle was chiming the breakfast hour, she had repaired her makeup and twisted her hair into a puffy updo that trailed a sausage curl over her right shoulder.

For her gown, she'd chosen a coffee-brown walking dress with ivory stripes—not her best colors, even if they did make her watery, brandy-colored eyes look as bright as moons. She reminded herself she hadn't come to Denver to seduce a mark; she was supposed to be playacting a widow. Besides, the less attention she attracted from randy men, the better she could concentrate on her mission.

Just as she was gathering her gloves to leave the room, she heard a suspicious scuffling in the hall. Warily, she approached the door, her fingers itching to trigger the .32 strapped to her forearm.

To her surprise, she found her boss, Mason "Mace" Ryker, squatting to inspect the raccoon prints in the sawdust that was sprinkled over her threshold. Hastily, she glanced up and down the hall. Spying no other sign of Collie or Vandy, she released her breath.

Damn. She had enough troubles. She didn't need to worry about some smart-mouthed kid and his masked moocher getting arrested by a bloodhound like Mace.

"What are you doing here?" she demanded.

Still squatting, the senior agent tipped back his bowler.

He had hair the color of dirty straw, a jaw like a dimpled hatchet, and oversized fists that didn't need brass knuckles to crack bones. She'd seen Mace flatten larger men with a one-two-punch and never break a sweat. And yet, despite all his years of boxing, his nose remained unbroken—a feat which secretly impressed her.

"When you didn't attend last night's lecture," he answered in his gravelly, Chicago accent, "I thought you were dead."

"Sorry to disappoint you."

Amusement registered on his features. The pugnacious detective's pine-green gaze trailed up her skirt, passed her empire waistline, lingered for a moment on the demure lace that fluttered over her ample breasts, and finally focused on her eyes. Nothing had the power to irritate her more than an ogling from Mace Ryker. She'd heard rumors that the 33-year-old bachelor attended church between Pinkerton cases—probably to pray for darker beer and bustier women. God knew, Mace wasn't any saint, although he did his fair share of judging sinners. Mostly her.

"Someone got up on the wrong side of bed," he cajoled. "Late night?"

"I fail to see how that's any concern of yours."

"An aristocratic temperament suits you."

"So delighted you approve. What do you want?"

"Let's start with an invitation to come inside."

Biting her cheek to swallow annoyance—he *was* her boss, after all—she obliged, sweeping her arm toward the room.

Rising to his five-foot, ten-inches of muscle-packed brawn, Mace stepped past her, crunching throat lozenges underfoot. His eyebrow rose as he spied the broken tins and dented soap bars littering her rug.

A slow heat rolled up her neck. "What did you expect? You dropped in unannounced. I didn't have time to tidy up."

He didn't look convinced, but he must have had other things on his mind, because he didn't comment. Reaching beneath his Inverness cape, he withdrew a folded *Rocky Mountain News*. "Care to explain this?"

With a theatrical flourish, he let the bottom half of the newspaper drop to reveal the front page headline:

Contessa's Emeralds Snatched:
Denver Has a New Prince of Thieves!

Choking back an oath, Sadie grabbed the *Rocky's* morning edition from Mace's hand. The article read:

"Shortly before the dinner hour last night, an anonymous source reported that the Contessa di Montaldeo *was burglarized by the most dastardly of villains.*

"Calling himself the Daredevil, the thief scaled the five-story Windsor Hotel to climb through the Contessa's *window. This brazen reprobate escaped with the* Contessa's *entire travel-collection of heirloom jewelry, a heist estimated at more than $300,000 dollars.*

"Daredevil's demonstration of braggadocio has led police to compare him with Maestro, the mysterious night prowler who pinched the Heart of Fire from the mansion of Lt. Governor Horace Tabor just 11 short days ago…"

Sadie was seeing red before she finished the sentence. *I'm going to* kill *Cass!*

"Well?" Mace demanded.

"Well what?" she fired back.

"Judging by your lack of ornamentation—" his impertinent stare dropped once more to her breasts "—the story's true."

"Your job is to hunt for the Namdaran jewels, not chase sensational rumors in a newspaper."

"Spoken like a dame with something to hide."

"Don't be absurd."

"So you can produce the emeralds?"

Sadie's mind raced. As much as she wanted to punch a

hole through Cass's spleen, she didn't want Mace to break every bone in her ex-lover's body. Nor did she want Cass locked in a Colorado penitentiary for the next 20 years—even if he did deserve it. She had a conscience, after all.

"Everything's under control, Mace. I told Cass to leak that story to the newspaper. I didn't expect the article to be printed so soon, that's all. Don't worry. It's all part of my plan."

"Your plan?"

She hiked her chin. "What, you think I let Cass drug me with kisses and steal those emeralds? You insult my intelligence."

Mace looked skeptical, which fanned her ire.

"If you spent less time questioning my integrity," she snapped, "and more time hunting for evidence, we might know why Minx is dead!"

"Your integrity isn't in question," he said dryly. "Just your common sense where Cassidy is concerned."

"So you came here to insult me, is that it?"

Bold green eyes locked with hers. She knew he was trying to strip away her pretenses, to find the truth beneath her lies. Mace wasn't just a sledgehammer with his fists; he could shatter a man's will under interrogation.

But Sadie had 28 years of hard knocks to strengthen her resolve. She'd be damned if she let another arrogant, high-handed male make her question her competency as a detective. Like a mountain defying Armageddon, she stood her ground.

Finally, to her immense satisfaction, Mace grunted and dropped his eyes.

"Since you failed to show up at the lecture hall last night," he said, thumbing through a small, leather-bound notebook, "I took the liberty of doing your job. And while I was searching the desk in Baines's office, I found a journal with a record of his hypnotism experiments. At least one of the subjects will be familiar to you: Wyntir Greyfell. After her father's suicide, Wyntir began to suffer bouts of anxiety."

Sadie was surprised by this revelation. "Why would Wyntir want to consult Baines, when her guardian is a psychiatrist?"

"Maybe Baines's lap is more comfortable."

"Honestly. Must you reduce everything to its lowest common denominator?"

"The dame met Baines for six weeks in an office with a couch." Mace shrugged and spread his hands. "You do the math."

Sadie rolled her eyes.

"In Baines's desk, I also found several boxing stubs," Mace continued, "a betting form for a horse race, and the name of a bookie. Looks like our good professor runs with a rough crowd—Cortese Thomson among them. In fact, Cort was skulking around the lecture hall last night, looking suspicious."

"Who *doesn't* look suspicious to you, Mace?"

"So you and Cort are old friends?"

Sadie gritted her teeth. She didn't know what irritated her more, that Mace assumed she dropped her drawers for every scumbag in Creation, or that Mace was probably envisioning her butt-naked right now with Mattie Silks' Fancy Man.

"If I knew Cort *that* way," Sadie said tartly, "Mattie would have blown off my head already. She's fond of pistol-duels with rivals. But Cort *does* know me in the sense that he used to visit the Long Branch Saloon and watch my stage show."

Sadie frowned as realization dawned. *Damn. If I'd gone to the lecture hall last night, Cort would have recognized me. Cass saved me from getting my cover blown!*

"So it's a good thing you went to bed early," Mace deadpanned, as if guessing her thoughts.

She shot him a withering look.

"And while you were getting your beauty rest," Mace added, flipping two more pages in his notebook, "the museum curator was found hanging from an oak tree in front of his office window."

"What?"

"Looks like a suicide. Renfield left a note. He claimed he could no longer live with himself for bringing international shame upon the citizens of Denver. Apparently, he never got over the museum break-in. That pain-in-the-ass had the police turning this city upside down for the Namdaran Emeralds, when they should have been looking for Minx," Mace added grimly.

Sadie shared his upset. But she was confused by his report. Malcolm Renfield was renowned as a fussbudget, who did everything by the book. He'd served long, glowing tenures as a museum curator in prestigious institutions, located in St. Louis, Philadelphia, and Boston, despite the fact that at least two of his administrations had suffered break-ins before. In each instance, Renfield had turned into an avenging angel, using his own money to hire the Pinkertons. Sadie's colleagues had apprehended the thieves within days and recovered the relics. So why would Renfield give up hope on the Namdaran Emeralds?

She asked Mace these questions.

"Beats me. Ask your psychiatrist friend." He slid his notebook into the inner pocket of his frockcoat. "The police shook down all the fences, but they're not talking, of course. The police also crawled all over the exhibits, the curator's office, and Renfield's home. If there was any hope of finding those emeralds, the boys in blue probably bungled it. Curious, though."

"What's curious?"

Mace shrugged. "Two pocket watches were discovered on Renfield's corpse. One attached to his vest. One dangling from the buckle of his shoe. He must have dropped the watch when he jumped out the window. When the night watchman found him, the timepiece was playing that old hanging dirge, *Tom Dooley.*"

Sadie shivered. She knew the lyrics well. Occasionally, at Dodge City's Long Branch Saloon, a lonely cowboy had asked her to sing about the ill-fated lover, who'd murdered his mistress and was sentenced to hang from a white oak tree. Renfield must have been one creepy guy.

"So you're poking your nose into my Maestro investigation because you think he masterminded the Namdaran theft?"

"Now you're catching on," Mace said dryly. "Where did Cassidy go when he left here last night?"

She tensed at the question. "You think *Cass* is Maestro?"

"I think you have a hard time giving straight answers about your outlaw lover."

"*Ranger* lover," she snapped. "And I expect Cass went to the newspaper office."

"It doesn't bother you that Mattie and Cassidy are old friends?"

"Every man in this town is an old friend of Mattie's. I'd question a gent's manhood if he wasn't."

"Lucky Cass," Mace taunted. "Seems like he's got the longest leash in town. Poor Cort has to worry about getting his head blown off if he so much as winks at a skirt."

"Mattie would never plug Cort. He owes her too much money."

Mace smirked. "Ah, the course of true love never did run smooth."

A muscle ticked in Sadie's jaw. She didn't doubt for a moment he was referring to her and Cass.

Mace started rummaging in his frockcoat again. He withdrew a slender, velvet box.

"What's that?" she demanded.

"Open it and find out."

She reached for the black box the same way she might have reached for the wrong end of a Pinkerton parasol—the kind that fired a dart from its tip.

But when she cracked open the box, she was surprised to find innocent-looking, perfectly matched strings of iridescent beads. Nestled amidst the pearls was a brilliant, topaz teardrop that flashed with the fire of the sun. The pendant was the size of a silver dollar!

"What are these beads?" she demanded suspiciously. "Laudanum pellets? Smoke bombs?"

"Pearls," Mace answered dryly. "I figured a *contessa* wouldn't waste any time spending her dead husband's fortune to replace stolen jewels."

"Uh…right." She wanted to kick herself. "Did you expense these?"

"Gotta keep Agent Scarlet Diva safely undercover." Mace winked. "By the way. The next time you see Cassidy, tell him to keep his mitts off that necklace. Otherwise, Lucifire's gonna have a damned hard time drawing his guns—with ten broken fingers."

Sadie shot Mace a dagger's glare, but he was too busy turning for the door to see it.

Alone once more, she re-opened the box. Ignoring the voice in her head—the one that scoffed at her for being a pushover for pretty rocks—she eagerly lifted the necklace from the velvet. The pearls were heavier than she'd expected, good quality, with perfect luster. She'd never owned real pearls, much less a genuine Imperial topaz. Over the last 28 years, she could count on one hand the number of times a man had gifted her with jewelry. The vast majority of baubles she'd worn had been fakes, accessories for a dancing costume. Whenever she'd been lucky enough to wear real rocks, they'd been part of a Pinkerton disguise and therefore, subject to return.

A small smile curved her lips as she clasped the necklace behind her neck. Wistfully, she fingered the beads, glowing with a soft luminosity in the morning light. Pearls went with everything. This triple strand set off to perfection the creamy column of her throat, while the topaz matched her eyes. Her boss had a good memory for color. But then, he should. He was a detective. Mace had been trained to recall details.

Like the puffy red skin around my eyes?

She muttered an oath, leaning closer to the mirror to rub out the smudged kohl beneath her lashes.

That's when she realized that Mace hadn't answered her question about the business expense.

CHAPTER 5

L ater that morning, Sadie sailed past Cass in the hotel lobby and furtively flipped him the bird. That's when she received a welcome surprise. The freezing rain had driven Enoch Fowler's tent circus out of Jewell Park. Now his spook show was performing at the Windsor.

No wonder Cass was loitering near the assembly room!

The hotel was being mobbed by camp followers, thanks to an advertisement in the *Rocky* and the industriousness of a street-urchin army, which Fowler had paid to hawk flyers.

No one was happier about the new location than Sadie, who'd dreaded the idea of returning to the Big Top to freeze her bustle off. Now all she had to do was bide her time—and give Cass the cold shoulder, of course. She hoped the reprobate got frostbite from her glares.

She found a seat near the center of the packed house. Forcing herself to concentrate on her mission, she decided she was ready for any nonsense Fowler might dish out. After all, she'd learned to tolerate the idiosyncrasies of the Pinkie Chief, Wilma LeBeaux, who happened to be a Cajun Mambo. Wilma burned herbs and sewed poppets to ward off evil spirits. She also required Sadie to wear a *gris-gris* around her neck whenever she entered Wilma's house. Sadie didn't believe what Wilma believed, but she humored the Cajun because she loved her like a mother.

At precisely 10 a.m., Fowler took the stage amidst enthusiastic applause. He was an energetic, middle-aged man, with a commanding voice and captivating smile. Standing six-feet tall, with a gleaming ebony mane that shimmered with blue highlights, he led a prayer of thanks to the Lord—and also to his sponsors, which included some hair tonic company. Sadie wasn't surprised to see the vast majority of his audience was female.

Next, Fowler announced that he wasn't the show's headliner. With great fanfare, he introduced Rebekah, whom he praised as "a young protégé with an ancient wisdom." The adolescent adopted a mouse-like demeanor as she perched on a stool at the center of the stage.

"Relax, dear child," Fowler boomed in his resonant show-boater's voice. "Relax and allow the spirit of our Lord to speak through you."

Fowler began to swing a pocket watch before Rebekah's wide, unblinking eyes. Within moments, her face started to change. Her brow furrowed. Her jaw hardened. Her scowl made her look older and more masculine. Suddenly, a voice like thunder boomed from her lips: *"I am Emmanuel."*

Everyone jumped in their seats. Ladies in the front row began to sob.

Sadie rolled her eyes. *Here we go.*

Rebekah proved to be a masterful performer. She could answer any question posed about the Bible. In fact, she could quote the text backwards, starting at random pages. She could translate passages fluently in Hebrew, Arabic, and Greek. Whenever people accused her of spouting gibberish, she would turn her burning, black eyes on the skeptics and reveal their personal secrets, a feat which left them red-faced and sputtering.

Sadie wondered how much Fowler had paid these shills to sit in his audience.

By the end of the show, supposedly intelligent adults were prostrating themselves at Rebekah's feet. Ladies tore off diamond rings, pearl necklaces, and silver broaches. Gentlemen dumped out the contents of their wallets. As Sadie watched Denver's *nouveau riche* succumb to religious frenzy, she could completely understand how the doddering elder, Lilybelle Welbourn, might have pledged her family jewels to Fowler.

Sadie did some rapid calculations in her head. Fowler's troupe performed two times a day, seven days a week. Even if he'd arranged the usual 60/40 split with the house, she estimated a sell-out crowd would earn him $2,000 per performance—and that was just from the door receipts. Judging by the number of True Believers, who were now mobbing the reservation table for private appointments, Fowler could easily rake in another $1,000 today from the people who were clamoring to see Emmanuel—or rather, Rebekah.

Sadie's jaw hardened. The time had come to put this child-peddling huckster behind bars.

Plotting to search Fowler's hotel room, Sadie left her seat and jostled her way to the lobby. To her annoyance, she spied Cass with a smoking cigarette, waiting for her beside the elevator. Sheathed in his trademark black, he'd propped his athletic leanness against the wall and tucked a heel beneath his buttocks. This casual pose let his duster gape, as if to testify he'd shed his double-holstered rig, per the city ordinance. Nevertheless, Sadie had no doubt he was armed—and in places where most lawmen wouldn't think of searching.

Her feet faltered.

Her ex-lover stood as still as a lamppost amidst bobbing bowlers and jaunty beaver hats. Nevertheless, he got noticed. Frequently. Even when he wasn't trying, Cass exuded a feral magnetism. Appreciative ladies blushed and giggled in his presence; scowling beaux hustled their sheep-eyed sweethearts past his wolfish grin.

Sadie glared at the traitor.

Cass was looking at her—or maybe at Mace's topaz—with flame-blue eyes that shot sparks up her spine. Cass had always been able to melt the iciest virginal resolve. But after last night's stunt with the opium-coated putty, she'd be damned if she succumbed to his roguish charms!

She was just envisioning the pleasure of grinding her heel into his foot, when she noticed Mace. Her boss lurked among Fowler's camp followers, who had nothing better to do between shows than park their rears and clutter up the hotel's two staircases. Like a great hulking spider, the detective sat amidst the chattering sycophants. He was watching every move Cass made.

Sadie groaned. She didn't dare take the elevator now. If Cass challenged her about the topaz—and he would—all hell would break loose. Mace's suspicions about her missing emeralds would be confirmed.

Sadie turned toward the staircase, only to spy another obstacle: Collie and his ever-present…

Wait a minute. Where's Vandy?

Alarm bells tolled in her head. Collie's coon stirred up more trouble than a coyote in a hen house. She quailed to imagine the little fiend in her hotel room, gnawing on her lip paint or crapping on her pillow. She shot the boy a dark, foreboding glare, the kind Wilma drilled into chatty recruits.

But Collie wasn't a Pinkie recruit. He was a 17-year-old hillbilly, who regarded moonshine like mother's milk. He got his jollies by picking door locks and eavesdropping under windows.

As if guessing her thoughts, the boy smirked and tipped his hat.

"Lady Fiore!"

Sadie nearly jumped out of her skin to hear this panicked, female voice call her alias.

"Oh, thank heaven I found you!"

Cautiously, Sadie peered around a luggage cart, piled six-feet high with traveling trunks. Wyntir was navigating her way past a 10-foot sterling statue of Horace Tabor. Huffing and puffing, the young heiress clutched her blue-velvet hem just shy of the scandalous height of her ankles.

"Oh mio dio!" Sadie responded in her best diva voice. "Slow down, *signorina!* What is all the fuss?"

Wyntir dutifully reined in, but she looked on the verge of hyperventilation. "Please don't think poorly of me," she begged. "Dante so rarely leaves the manor house in the mornings. I took the opportunity to sneak into town. I never expected him to come *here!* I know it's a dreadful imposition, but please, oh please, tell him we've spent the morning together—shopping!"

Sadie hiked an eyebrow. *Trouble in paradise?*

Now she could see the handsome physician shaking rain from his overcoat. Apparently, he'd just entered the hotel through the Larimer Street door.

Sadie cast Wyntir a sidelong glance. "You attended the prayer meeting behind Dante's back?"

Wyntir blushed to the roots of her raven-black hair. "I know it sounds terribly childish, but I wanted to meet with Rebekah. Dante won't let me have friends who talk to ghosts!"

"You, uh, have *other* friends, who talk to ghosts?"

"Well…yes," Wyntir admitted. "Papa and I used to host meetings of the Spiritual Telegraph at Greyfell Manor. It was our way of being close to Mama. But after Papa's death, Dante forbade me to host séances at the house." Wyntir's eyes filled with tears. "How else am I supposed to speak to my parents? I don't have the Seer's Gift!"

Sadie fidgeted. Although she didn't share Wyntir's belief in ghosts, she did share the pain of being suddenly and cruelly orphaned. "To have such a protective guardian must feel confining," Sadie murmured in consolation.

"Oh no, you mustn't think that," Wyntir protested, looking chagrined. "Dante's the best thing that ever happened to me. He took me under his wing when I had no one else to turn to. He helped me through the most dreadful of times—times when I thought I might never be happy again. I love him! I couldn't live without him!"

Sadie steeled her features against a show of cynicism. Granted, there were things in the world she couldn't live without. But not one on her list was a man.

"Carina," she said gently, "have you told Dante how important your faith is to you?"

"Of course, but..." Wyntir bit her lip, twisting her handkerchief in her hands. "He doesn't believe in spirits. He doesn't even believe in *God,"* she whispered hoarsely, as if she feared she would be struck by lightning. "I pray for him every night before I sleep, and every morning when I rise. What else can I do? I couldn't bear it if he left me!"

With new eyes, Sadie watched the psychiatrist. Dante had stopped at the hatcheck counter to surrender his bowler. As he bent his head to sign a receipt, light from the lamp at his elbow shot rich threads of chestnut through his hair. He was one of those rare gentlemen, who disdained wax to avoid "hat head," probably because his hair was so thick, it defied compression. Sadie found herself admiring the incongruously playful curl, spilling across his high brow.

Suddenly, she felt compelled to raise her sights toward the elevator. Cass was tapping ash into a silver spittoon, conveniently located near his boots. He was frowning at the way she'd ogled Dante.

Good, she thought uncharitably.

"Yoo-hoo!" a croaking female yodeled across the lobby. "Is that you, Dante, dear?"

Wyntir sucked in her breath, digging cherry-red, lacquered fingernails into Sadie's forearm. "Matters just got worse!"

"They did?"

"Infinitely worse," Wyntir assured her.

The heiress's gaze was riveted on a wizened, stoop-shouldered dowager in a dilapidated fox stole. As the elder shuffled toward the hatcheck counter, she dragged an enormous orange-and-yellow carpetbag across the tiles and slapped the hands of any bellhop foolish enough to reach for it.

"That's Mrs. Welbourn," Wyntir whispered. "She was sitting beside me during Rebekah's performance. Come on! We have to head her off!"

Lilybelle Welbourn? Sadie hid her delight. For three days, she'd been trying to figure out a way to meet the Welbourn family without revealing her Pinkerton affiliation.

But as Wyntir made the introductions, Sadie's delight turned to bemusement.

"Well, I'll be dinged!" Lilybelle cried.

Squinting through gold-rimmed spectacles, the dowager leaned toward Sadie for a closer look. Breaths bearing the distinctive trace of chamomile, mixed with whiskey, wafted across Sadie's face.

"You're a *Skinwalker!*"

"I'm a…er, what?" Sadie inquired politely, wrinkling her nose.

"Don't you dare deny it!" Lilybelle wagged a gnarled forefinger under Sadie's nose. "I know a Skinwalker when I see one! You have yellow eyes, just like you do in your coyote form!"

Wyntir cleared her throat. "Um…Mrs. Welbourn spent some time among the Navajo people."

"That I did." The dowager loosed a raspy chuckle. "Took two braves as my lovers—under the same full moon. Now *that* was something to howl about."

Wyntir's face flooded with color.

Sadie's lips twitched.

"Fiore agreed to attend my birthday party," Wyntir said hastily, attempting to change the subject and prevent social suicide all in one breath. "Isn't that splendid?"

Lilybelle snorted. "Splendid is *my* age. Throw a party when you're 91. Then you'll have something to celebrate." She began rummaging in her carpetbag. Lots of mysterious clanking ensued. "So, Lady Coyote," she said, finally retrieving a sugar-dusted tin. "Did you come to Denver for the opera? I hear your compatriot, Dolce LaRocca, holed up here, in Tabor's toothpick palace. Maybe you should warn her about the Daredevil."

"That *was* frightful news," Wyntir breathed, turning wide, worried eyes to Sadie. "Dante and I were horrified when we read the account this morning in the *Rocky*. Thank heavens you're safe! You must have been terrified. Not to mention outraged!"

"Coyotes don't get mad," Lilybelle said sagely. "They get even."

Lilybelle doesn't know the half of it, Sadie mused, watching Cass prowl within earshot. He settled in a cowhide chair outside the Cattleman's Saloon and ordered a boot buff. Sadie had no doubt he was eavesdropping.

Weasel.

"You gonna put a curse on his dillywhacker?"

Sadie jumped half a foot at Lilybelle's question.

"That's what *I'd* do to the Daredevil," the dowager confided over Wyntir's sputtered objections.

"Such novel ideas you Americans have," Sadie said drolly.

Lilybelle flashed a cherubic smile. "Jelly donut?" she offered, thrusting the tin at Sadie.

"I know *I'm* famished!" Wyntir said, her laughter growing strained as she watched Dante shake the hand of an acquaintance. She tried to drag Lilybelle out of sight, behind the luggage cart. "Perhaps we should make our reservations for lunch."

"Nonsense. I didn't smuggle jelly donuts into Tabor's drafty firetrap because I want chilblains. I brought them to lure Tahoma back from the Great Beyond!" Lilybelle planted a lusty kiss on her fox's snout. "Strawberry was his favorite," she confided, "when he was in his human form."

Sadie fixed a smile on her face and tried not to groan. So Tahoma is the reason why Minx consulted a psychiatrist in the Welbourn case?

"But darling, you've eaten three of Tahoma's donuts already," Wyntir cajoled, desperately trying to hide her face from Dante. "Surely that can't be healthy."

"Ha! Three donuts a day keep the doctor away. I'm as fit as a fiddle. You see any other 91-year-old woman, strutting her stuff around this hotel?

"Dang," Lilybelle muttered. The donut she'd been waving under Wyntir's nose had spouted a leak. Red goo gushed between her fingers, plopped on the younger woman's skirt, and splattered Lilybelle's shoes.

The dowager scowled. "*Dante*," she bellowed in a voice three times her size, "bring Wynnie your handkerchief. She messed on me!"

Wyntir looked like she wanted to crawl into a portmanteau when a bemused Dante turned in her direction. If the good doctor was disturbed by the sight of his ward in a sea of Fowler's sycophants, he hid his annoyance when he crossed the lobby.

"Is there a problem, ladies?" he greeted in his cultured, East Coast baritone.

"My dress is ruined!" Wyntir wailed.

"Yeah?" Lilybelle retorted. "Well, my greedy strumpet of a daughter-in-law is trying to lock me in an asylum!"

Unperturbed by these outbursts, Dante nodded to Sadie, passed Wyntir his handkerchief, and acknowledged Lilybelle's complaint with a gallant bow.

"I won't let that happen, dear lady."

The dowager raised adoring eyes to her hero. "Of course you won't! That's why Harridan—I mean, Sheridan— stiffed you for your fee and hired that buggerhead, Baines." Lilybelle cackled, elbowing Dante in the ribs. "You should have seen the look on Harridan's face when I told her I tossed my diamonds in the Platte. I'm tempted to do it for real this time, just to see if she'll jump in after them!"

Sadie steeled herself against a frown. Had Minx been hired to solve a theft that never occurred?

"You are fond of practical jokes, *signora?*" Sadie asked, careful to keep the accusation from her tone.

"All's fair in love and court. Ain't that right, Dante?"

Dante smiled. A rare power, like dawn breaking through a storm, radiated from that smile. Even Sadie was momentarily captivated—which surprised her. God knew, she'd seen plenty of charming smiles on handsome men. Cass's roguish dimples came painfully to mind.

"Put your mind at rest, my dear Mrs. Welbourn," Dante said. "Professor Baines may have a reputation, but it fails to do justice to the profession of Psychology. As an expert witness in a conservator hearing, Baines would lack credibility with a judge, just as his hypnotism research lacks credibility with the university's Board of Regents. You have nothing to worry about."

"That's what Tahoma said." Lilybelle flashed her impish grin. "Only he knows where my diamonds and rubies went. And I had Brother Enoch swear *him* to secrecy!"

Dante frowned.

Wyntir fidgeted.

"Perhaps Brother Enoch's spirits could tell me where *my* diamonds went," Sadie interceded, dabbing woefully at the corners of her eyes. "I do not think this Daredevil means to return them."

"My dear *contessa.*" Dante turned to her, looking concerned. "You have been through an unholy ordeal. You are alone, vulnerable in a strange country. In good conscience as a gentleman, and as a medical doctor, I cannot allow you to spend a single *lira* on false hopes, which is all Enoch Fowler can provide. I traveled into town to offer my condolences, but more importantly, to offer my support to help you recover from such a reprehensible violation."

Pleased by his consideration, Sadie sneaked a glance at Cass. He made a great show of yawning behind his hand. She wanted to punch out his lights.

"How kind you are, *dottore.* It has been so long since I have had a *trustworthy* gentleman on whom I can rely."

"Dante, I was just telling Fiore—while we were window shopping," Wyntir added hastily, "that you were as horrified as I was to read the news about Daredevil."

Lilybelle nodded. "That young whippersnapper should have his hide nailed to an outhouse wall. And if I were 10 years younger, I'd do it myself!"

Cass grinned.

Sadie struggled to hide her annoyance. "A man who would commit such a crime must be very stupid, *no?*" She made sure she spoke loudly enough for Cass to hear. "To pit himself against your fine, American policemen? To waste his best years in some disease-infested prison?"

"The criminal intellect is often misunderstood," Dante cautioned her gently. "He might have a rare, hidden genius. A contempt for the trivial life. Most likely, he is thrilled by danger."

Cass nodded smugly.

Sadie wanted to groan. *Good Lord, don't encourage him!*

"What woman would be safe from such a man?" Wyntir breathed. "Fiore, you simply cannot spend another night in this hotel! Come stay with me and Dante. We have Dobermans, servants, and a spiky, eight-foot fence to keep out vandals. We can even bar the windows if we have to! You'll be safe with us on East Colfax Avenue. Won't she, Dante?"

Dante's deeply compelling stare made Sadie's skin flush. "Wyntir has a point. You should not be without an escort. Denver hasn't left its frontier roots far behind. This town is still teeming with men of questionable moral character. Clearly, the hotel hasn't taken sufficient measures to protect its guests. But at Greyfell Manor, you'll be among friends. We have plenty of bedrooms."

At his mention of *bedrooms*, heat sizzled from Sadie's scalp to her toes. Her libidinous flush embarrassed her. Even if the gold flecks in Dante's eyes smoldered like tiny bonfires, and she liked the mountain-fresh way he smelled, he'd given her no legitimate reason to conclude he was proposing a tryst. Indeed, he'd demonstrated nothing but professional courtesy since they'd met.

Maybe that was the problem, she mused. The respect he'd shown her made his hospitality especially tempting. A wounded part of her yearned for platonic comfort after Cass had been such a louse. A stay on Colfax Avenue might unearth all kinds of useful intelligence about Minx's disappearance.

Unfortunately, detective work often required a Pinkie to paste on a beard and crawl through a window in the dead of night. How was she supposed to explain such behavior to a psychiatrist? And how was she supposed to sneak out of Greyfell Manor while Dobermans were prowling the premises?

Reluctantly, she declined Dante's offer.

"You are like an answered prayer, *carino.* But I would not wish to insult *Signore* Tabor after he has given me his personal assurance, he will see to my safety," she lied glibly. "It is a matter of diplomacy between our two countries. I am sure you understand."

Wyntir looked disappointed.

Cass looked amused.

Don't flatter yourself, Rutter.

Suddenly, Sadie noticed a suspicious rocking in the trunks behind Lilybelle's head. She glanced lower, seeking the source of the movement. A furry felon was squeezing beneath the cart.

Vandy!

Sadie shot a murderous glance at Collie, who'd slapped a hand over his mouth to smother snickers. If she knew anything about that raccoon—and unfortunately, she did—Vandy had been stalking Lilybelle's donuts for some time.

"Is something amiss?" Dante asked politely.

"Yeah, Lady Coyote," Lilybelle chimed in. "You got your face screwed up like an opossum sucking persimmons."

Sadie forced a smile at this assessment. "Forgive me." As nonchalantly as possible, she stepped between Vandy and the fruit preserves on the dowager's toe. "Dante, what time do you have? Perhaps we can still make a reservation for lunch."

But petticoats weren't much of a barrier against a willful raccoon. Dante had no sooner tugged out his timepiece, than Vandy charged between her legs. He exploded like a rocket from under her hemline, knocking her off balance. She stumbled, slamming into Dante's arm.

He dropped the watch.

The flash of tumbling gold caught Vandy's attention. Showing his true colors, the furry felon swerved, snatched the prize in mid-air, and fled for the 18th Street entrance. He left a trail of strawberry paw prints in his wake.

"What the—?" Dante turned florid as Vandy's tail vanished into the drizzle.

"Tahoma!" Lilybelle cried.

"Um…I think that was a raccoon," Wyntir advised gently.

"Well, of course it was a raccoon!" the dowager snapped. "I was summoning Tahoma to catch the thief!"

"Did I hear something about catching a thief?" drawled a lazy Texas baritone, one which sounded far too smug for Sadie's peace of mind.

She shot Cass a *"get lost"* glare, but he didn't take the hint. Instead, he halted congenially by her side, tipped his hat to Lilybelle, and lavished his most dazzling smile on Wyntir.

"Trouble, folks?"

Wyntir giggled like a giddy child. She actually fanned her cheeks with a glove.

But Dante wasn't half as impressed by Cass's charm. The Bostonian raked narrow eyes over the Texican's immaculately brushed hat, past his half-grown beard and shoulder-length hair, all the way down the modest wool of his duster, to his gleaming Mexican-style spurs. A fleeting disdain registered on Dante's features.

"It appears vermin got into the hotel," he said, leaving no doubt he was referring to Cass.

The gunslinger bristled.

But Cass hadn't been dubbed "Coyote" because his wit was dull.

"Then it's a good thing I'm a kind of *exterminator,* eh, Doc?"

Wyntir fluttered admiring lashes at Cass's sun-baked face. "Do you work for the lieutenant governor, sir?"

"The name's Cassidy, Miss. William Cassidy." He flashed roguish dimples. "And regrettably, no. I'm just passing through town. Although I must say, the more I see of your fine city, the more I'm tempted to stay. Denver has some of the fairest young ladies this side of the Mississippi."

He winked.

Wyntir turned a pretty shade of rose.

Sadie ground her teeth. She caught a glimpse of Mace, shaking his head at her. She prayed she could find some way to prove that Cass hadn't blown her cover—again. If Mace filed another report, citing her for negligence, she would get drummed out of the agency!

"That...that *beast* stole Dr. Goddard's timepiece," she cried in her best offended, Italian accent. "Be on your way, Exterminator, and fetch the timepiece back."

Cass turned his insufferable grin on her. "Aw, the little rascal was just having fun, ma'am. Raccoons are mischief-makers at heart. They don't do a body harm—unless you try to cross one."

She suspected he was referring to himself, not Vandy, and that his veiled threat was intended for Dante.

But the Bostonian didn't take the hint.

"When a nocturnal beast prowls during the day, it is typically rabid," Dante chided, implying that Cass didn't know squat about extermination.

Cass hiked an eyebrow at his detractor. "I reckon it's not common for a refined, Yankee gentleman to know so much about night-prowling. Have we met before, Doc? At Mattie's place?"

"Who's Mattie?" Wyntir asked with all the innocence of her 20 sheltered years.

"She's a whore, dear," Lilybelle supplied helpfully.

Wyntir's hand flew to her mouth.

A muscle ticked in Dante's jaw.

Sadie figured she'd better look shocked too, considering her alias. "Vulgar man, be gone! You are unfit for polite company!"

"Aw, don't be such a fuddy-duddy," Lilybelle said, fetching another donut from her tin. "Boys will be boys. You need to get out of the palace more often, Lady Coyote. William, dear," she cooed to Cass. "I need a strapping young man to carry my carpetbag. Would you tote it to the assembly room for the next show?"

"I'd consider it an honor, ma'am."

Lilybelle tossed a smirk at Sadie, as if to say, *'And that's how it's done, Toots.'*

Sadie wanted to smack her.

Meanwhile, Wyntir had digested the "whore" news. Her heart-shaped face was as pale as the pearls at her throat. "Dante," she whispered, "is it true what Mr. Cassidy said about…about *Mattie?"*

Dante smiled down at his impressionable young ward. The warmth in his gaze caused two spots of color to bloom in her cheeks. "You mustn't trouble yourself, my dear. Mr. Cassidy and I have never met."

"Sure, Doc. Whatever you say." Cass winked. "A man's got to have his secret pleasures, after all. Wouldn't want a sweet, young heiress to think less of you in the suitor department."

Dante's smoldering glare locked with Cass's. A primal challenge, as palpable as a lightning strike, sizzled between the two men. Even Wyntir must have been aware of the static. She rubbed her arms, as if warding off goosebumps.

Dante noticed. "Are you chilled, my dear?"

"I-I feel a draft."

"Some foolish doorman must have left his post," Sadie improvised hastily, "and let the raccoon sneak inside the hotel."

"Or perhaps," Dante countered, draping his coat around Wyntir's shoulders, "the creature was a pet. I noticed a leather collar."

So the psychiatrist notices details, does he?

"Dante, wasn't that your grandfather's pocket watch?" Wyntir gazed anxiously into her guardian's veiled eyes. "The one that plays the waltz? I know how much it means to you. Perhaps we should notify the desk clerk."

"And offer a reward," Cass suggested. "Lost items have a tendency to turn up when a bounty's offered."

Dante's lip curled faintly. "I daresay you know a lot about bounties, Mr. Cassidy."

"No more than most. But I do know a fraud when I see one, Doc."

Sadie held her breath.

But Dante surprised her. He didn't escalate the verbal brawl, as Cass would have done. Maybe he suspected the younger man was a gunfighter. Maybe he considered himself too well-bred to trade insults with a rabble-rouser.

In any event, he dismissed Cass with a thin smile. "Ladies," he said mildly, "I believe we were discussing lunch. Fiore, would you do Wyntir and me the honor of presiding at our table?"

"How kind you are, *dottore!* I would be delighted."

With old-world chivalry, Dante extended an elbow. Cass stiffened when she took it. If the psychiatrist had been acting on a hunch that she and Cass were acquainted, Cass had just proven him right. Sadie needed to cast doubt on that hunch to protect her cover.

Fortunately, the way she was feeling about Cass, snubbing him didn't require much effort.

"It is always a pleasure, *carino—*" her smile dripped honey for Dante "—to dine with an educated man of refined tastes."

Turning her shoulder with glacial dignity, she left her ex-lover choking on her dust.

Cass dragged a restraining breath into his lungs.

"You're a hot-blooded one," Lilybelle said, arching an eyebrow at his hips.

That's when he realized he was flexing his hands over the holsters he no longer wore.

Cass forced himself to smile at her observation. "Shucks, ma'am. I've been trying to reform."

But he couldn't take his eyes off his woman. Not when she was walking away on the arm of another man.

Lilybelle shook her head. "A high-stepper like that can't see past the nose she's waving in the air. But if you want *my* advice, sonny, get a haircut."

Cass loosed a long, winding breath. Jealousy was like a spike, jabbing at his spleen. He wanted to know who had given Sadie the Imperial topaz to replace his gold chain.

But what really bothered him was the notion that Maestro might think that fancy rock was worth killing for.

CHAPTER 6

———◆———

Beans had left a foul taste in Cass's mouth, a taste that could only be washed down with whiskey.

Lots of whiskey.

But the next morning, Cass learned he had bigger problems. His special, Deputy U.S. Marshal's commission had been denied.

Rexford Sterne, Adjutant-General of the Texas Rangers and a part-time Marshal himself, had signed the paperwork, so Cass didn't understand the problem. Neither did Sterne. According to the Ranger's latest telegram, some anonymous pain-in-the-ass had challenged the application because of Cass's criminal past.

Sterne had advised, "Sit tight, and let me deal with it."

Right. And let my woman get killed?

So Cass had spent the better part of the day laying his trap to smoke out Maestro. Riding to the Gentleman's Sporting Club, he got friendly with the stable boys, who confirmed his suspicion that a dappled-gray mustang with a fancy, silver-studded halter, was none other than Ghost Dancer. The champion runner belonged to Cass's old *compadre,* Boone Wylie. The freighting baron's reputation for feats of daring had made him a legend in La Plata County, where he'd spent four years hauling ore smelters through the treacherous, snaking passes of the San Juan Mountains. Ironically, his real fortune had come from a poker wager 18 months ago.

Now Boone lived the good life in Denver, apparently, because to become a member of the Sporting Club, a man had to possess money or pedigree. Cass possessed neither, but he did manage to talk his way inside, out of the cold, while some snot-nosed attendant searched for Boone and passed him Cass's hastily sketched calling card: a bull's eye sprouting a devil's horns and tail.

Eventually, as Cass cooled his heels in the entry hall, he heard a floorboard creak above him.

"Lord thunderin' Jaysus, it *is* you, Billy!"

Cass grinned up at the rangy muleskinner, who was leaning over the gallery railing. Boone cleaned up pretty well for a cussing, tobacco-spitting, 38-year-old rascal. His rusty-brown, shoulder-length curls had been sheared to his ears and heavily waxed to hold a center part. He'd traded his duster for a shooting jacket and his dungarees for gaiters, but he'd refused to part with his bullwhip, Cass noted in secret amusement.

"I hear that barren patch of rock you won with your diamond flush was hiding a vein of gold," Cass called. "You sure were born under a lucky star, Boone."

"Me? Hell, you have more lives than a tabby. Last time you and Lynx rode shotgun on the Silverton run, I found you dangling from a bullwhip over a 4,000-foot gorge. I still can't believe you caught that payroll before the buckboard fell over the mountain."

"To tell the truth, I was grabbing for your whiskey cask. And missed."

Boone hooted. "That tale gets taller with every tellin', don't it? C'mon upstairs, Billy. I got a bottle of Scotch that needs a friend."

Cass followed the transplanted Texican into a rustic, raftered lodge with a menagerie of animal trophies, ranging from elk to bear. On the western wall, a picture window looked over the wooded grounds, which featured a shooting range and race track. Against the eastern wall, a fancy sideboard was loaded with wild game, including elk steak and a pot of squirrel stew. The room was moderately populated with gents, who were eating a late lunch or reading the newspaper in antler-framed chairs.

"You caught me with a quarter hour to kill," Boone confided, waving Cass toward a seat beside a granite fireplace, which looked large enough to roast a bison. "I'm not scheduled for the barber till half-past two."

"So that's what happened to those braided whiskers you grew clear to your belt. Seems a shame you lost them."

Boone winked, pouring Cass a dram of single-malt. "Lost a beard, gained a wife. I hear Lynx got hitched, too. Never thought I'd see the day when you and he would finally part ways. Sera must be one helluva woman."

Cass smiled wistfully, recalling the spirited preacher's daughter, who'd saved his life. Then she'd risked the anger of her kin and the contempt of the small-minded folks in her Appalachian town to elope with a Cherokee halfbreed.

"You think I'd let Lynx marry some shrew?" Cass rallied.

Boone chuckled, sitting back in his chair. "So you approve."

Cass averted his eyes. "Sure." He tossed back his dram. In truth, he missed Lynx and Sera more than he missed his own kin.

Setting his shot glass on the table, Cass glanced out the window and noticed a familiar figure in a Chesterfield overcoat. Goddard was walking along the snow-shoveled path to the stables. Along the way, he exchanged words with a pudgy, huffing fellow in an Inverness cape.

Cass watched speculatively. "Who's that tenderfoot outside, talking with Goddard?"

Boone glanced toward the window and grunted. "Wortham Welbourn. Sole heir to the Welbourn banking fortune. His older brother, Sterling, died about 25 years ago of pneumonia. According to the fogeys, it was quite the scandal: Sterling's wife wasted little time re-marrying her husband's kid-brother—Wortham."

"You don't say?" Cass hid his amusement. He'd figured Boone could dish the dirt on Goddard's pal. Boone lived to gossip.

"Yep," Boone said eagerly, his eyes twinkling as he spun the old tale for fresh ears. "But the joke was on the gold-digging wife. Wortham's mother still holds the purse strings. At 91-years-old, Lilybelle shows no sign of kicking the bucket. Sheridan, her daughter-in-law, got tired of living on an allowance, so she's trying to convince Wortham to send his mother to the Funny Farm."

Apparently, Lilybelle wasn't exaggerating when she'd claimed 'Harridan' wanted her committed.

"And Goddard?" Cass jerked his thumb toward the window. "What do you know about him?"

Boone shrugged. "Not much. Edmund Greyfell introduced him for club membership about six weeks ago, before tragedy struck. Greyfell shot himself, poor bastard. Didn't leave a suicide note, but the police ruled out foul play. Goddard was appointed guardian of Greyfell's heir, until she reaches her majority."

"So if Wyntir doesn't marry him, Goddard's out the door without a dime."

"That's about the size of it," Boone said. "Why? You thinking of marrying Wyntir yourself?"

Cass grinned. "Oh…you know me."

"Better than you think, Rutter!"

They shared a laugh over another dram of Scotch.

"I hear the museum got fed up with the railroad wars," Cass said casually. "I heard they gave you the freighting contract for the Namdaran exhibit."

Boone's humor ebbed. "That haul has been nothing but a damned nightmare. I had to pay 20 armed men for babysitting a life-sized baby elephant, cast from solid gold, not to mention a Maharajah's jewel-encrusted sarcophagus and a treasure chest of relics from some temple. We freighted the Namdaran load all the way from Leadville. But since Renfield's death, the Museum Board has been sitting on my money. Maestro's escapades are costing me thousands. Insurance rates are going through the roof."

"You're not worried about Daredevil?"

"Who?"

Cass's ego deflated a notch when Boone blinked blankly at his question.

"I read in the *Rocky,*" Cass said, "that some fella named Daredevil broke into the Windsor two nights ago and robbed an Italian *contessa* of her jewels. The heist was valued at $300 grand. The next morning, Daredevil challenged Maestro in the advertisement section. He wrote, '*Now who's Denver's Prince of Thieves? Long live the Devil.*'"

Boone grunted, tugging a stogie from his pocket. "Daredevil sounds like a craphead."

Cass shot his friend a withering glare. "You've got the vision of a one-eyed mole. I thought you owned a stake in the *Rocky.*"

"Worst investment I ever made," Boone grumbled, rummaging through his pockets. "Aw, hell."

"What's the matter?"

"Lost my match safe. A damned nice one, too: 24-karat gold. It played my favorite tune, *She'll Be Comin' Round the Mountain.*"

Cass shook his head and struck one of his own matches with a thumb. "You never could keep anything that wasn't tied down."

"Except the admiration of women," Boone quipped, lowering his head to puff his cigar to life.

Cass chuckled, extinguishing the flame. "So about this Daredevil."

"What about him?" Boone drawled, blowing a stream of smoke.

"Seems like he could help you fix your troubles with the *Rocky.* A fella like Daredevil could sell more newspapers than the gold strike in Durango."

"Why do I sense a Coyote Con coming on?" Boone said dryly.

"'Cause you got more horse sense than the average muleskinner." Leaning across the table, Cass lowered his voice. "Say you leaked a story to some wet-behind-the-ears reporter. Say Daredevil paid you a visit and got away with stealing—oh, I don't know. Something that would make the Namdaran Emeralds look like penny candy. You got any diamonds?"

"Maybe," Boone hedged. "What for?"

"So I can pretend to steal them."

"Pretend to steal them?"

"That's right. Every time Daredevil pretends to steal jewels, the *Rocky* will get first crack at the story. You'll also get an exclusive advertisement for the Classifieds, taunting Maestro to steal something bigger. Folks'll be so eager to see Maestro one-up Daredevil, papers will fly off the newsstands. When Maestro finally does take the bait, the police will be waiting to arrest his ass, and your insurance rates will go down. See that? Everybody wins."

Boone gaped, his forgotten stogie smoking between his fingers. "Have you lost your cotton-picking *mind?!"*

Cass glanced furtively around the room. When he was satisfied no one was watching, he flashed the Ranger badge pinned to the lining of his duster.

Boone sucked in his breath. "Thunderation!" He sounded awed. "You finally did it."

Cass's nod was grim. "But here's the rub. My hands are tied. I can't stop Maestro north of the Red River until I get my Marshal's commission. The best I can do is go undercover and help the police smoke him out of hiding. Can I count on your help?"

A barn-sized grin split Boone's face. "Hell, yeah."

They shook hands, and Cass passed the muleskinner a folded paper, wrapped in a greenback. "Here's your classified."

"Keep your money, son. This ad's on me." Rising, Boone gathered his whip and hunter's cap for his barber's appointment. "By the way," he murmured in Cass's ear, "I got something better than diamonds. Belonged to my wife's Swedish grandmother."

"Meatballs?"

Boone laughed, clapping Cass's shoulder. "Just for that, smartass, you'll have to read the news in the morning edition, just like everybody else." He winked. "But I'm pretty sure you'll be
amazed when you see how clever ol' Daredevil really is."

The next morning, Sadie sat idly outside Enoch Fowler's "Spook Room," waiting for her quarry to appear in the hotel lobby. Her goal was to secure a private appointment so she could set her trap. More to the point, she wanted to avoid Rebekah, who kept sending her away with claims that Fowler's waiting list was longer than the Colorado River.

Sadie was growing weary of Rebekah.

That's why she'd entrenched herself in the waiting area an hour early. She was hoping to corner Fowler and "implore his indulgence for a grieving widow, who wished to make a charitable donation."

In the meantime, she had nothing better to do at 7 a.m. then watch bellhops push trolleys and maids mop the Windsor's black and white tiles. Eventually, a balding, auburn-haired gent in a tweed coat settled in the boot-buff chair. Ordinarily, Sadie wouldn't have looked twice at a middle-aged man with patches on his elbows, but she was bored.

Patches tugged a self-rolled quirley from his pocket, sniffed it with pleasure, and flipped open a matchsafe. Sunlight glanced off the golden lid a heartbeat before her ears pricked to the faint, mechanical strains of an old African spiritual. She recognized the melody of *She'll Be Coming 'Round the Mountain.*

Since the shoeshine boy had left his post to visit the privy, Patches settled more comfortably in his throne-sized chair to wait. Pocketing his matchsafe, he adjusted his wire-rimmed spectacles and reached for the *Rocky* in his lap. Even at a distance of 20 feet, Sadie couldn't fail to notice the six-inch headline. It screamed from the page:

Daredevil Strikes Again!
Prince of Thieves Steals Swedish Crown Jewels

Sadie was pretty sure her jaw hit the tiles.

Hastily flagging down a newsboy, she purchased her own salacious copy. When she unfolded the rag, she learned, to her horror, that freighting mogul, Boone Wylie, blamed Daredevil for the theft of his wife's Faberge parure. The matched set of gold, pearl, and aquamarine jewelry included a tiara, earbobs, brooch, necklace, ring, bracelets and belt clasp. The parure had been designed for the late King Karl XV's favorite mistress, Tova. Tova, in turn, had gifted the set to her granddaughter, Astrid "Dimples" Gustavson, a former dancing girl at Denver's Bust-a-Gut Saloon and Wylie's wife of 10 months.

As if this report wasn't sensational enough, the article then directed readers to visit the Classified Section for a "thrilling message," written by Daredevil to challenge Maestro.

Cass, in his audacity, had penned:

What's the matter Theater Prig? Lost your muse?
You're 0 for 2 and counting.
Let's see you beat today's headlines.
The devil dares you.

My God, Sadie thought, *is he insane?*

Visions of Mace with a smoking gun in one hand, and a noose in the other, swam before her eyes. She was so alarmed by Cass's reckless gambit, she didn't notice the approach of the broad-shouldered gentleman in the form-fitting, Chesterfield overcoat until his shadow fell across her newsprint.

"My dear Fiore, is something amiss?" Dante inquired, his brow furrowing as he scanned her face. "You look a tad peaked."

Sadie struggled to pull herself together. Fortunately, she had years of stage experience to call upon. She loosed a mirthless little laugh. She fluttered a helpless hand over the newsprint in her lap.

"Forgive me, *dottore*. But I cannot help but be saddened by this proof, in your American newspaper, that the *polizia* have not yet captured this dastardly Daredevil."

"Ah." Dante nodded, his handsome features grave with concern. "I, too, found the headline disturbing. Unfortunately, the lack of progress in the investigation does not surprise me. At least half the police in this town are numbered among the criminals."

Sadie gasped with an appropriate show of outrage. "But that is not acceptable! Why does the army not come and clean the blackguards out?"

"In America, a governor must opt for other, more democratic remedies, " Dante said dryly, "such as our notoriously understaffed, federal marshals."

Sadie sighed, shaking her head. "I do not think I shall ever understand your American politics."

"I must admit—" a dimple flirted with Dante's lips "— Denver politics isn't the most cheerful topic. But I believe I have news that will brighten your mood." Reaching into his breast pocket, he withdrew three theater tickets. "I procured proscenium box seats at Dolce LaRocca's sell-out performance Thursday night. Pray allow me to escort you."

Sadie had no need to feign delight. *Box seat tickets? To hear the world's most celebrated soprano sing Marguerite?* She was hard-pressed not to bounce on her seat.

That's when she noticed Collie, her ever-present shadow. He was scowling and shaking his head at her. She did her best to ignore him, even though the boy was eavesdropping only about ten feet away. His chocolate-brown Stetson loomed like a harbinger of doom over Fowler's easel, which had been erected, along with its welcome sign, beside the entrance to the Baby Doe Room. As for Collie's irrepressible raccoon, Vandy was hiding in the sterling planter between his boots. She could see the Masked Moocher's snout, poking past the purple cyclamens.

Pests.

Sadie turned her shoulder on the scowling hillbilly and his coon.

"*Grazie, dottore!*" She lavished her brightest smile on Dante. "I would be delighted to accept your kind invitation."

Looking pleased, Dante took her cue to perch on the settee. "Splendid! I'm sure I don't have to tell you what a national treasure *Dama* LaRocca is."

"Her singing, it is transcendent," Sadie agreed, although she'd never heard a European opera star and could hardly wait for the opportunity. "In *Italia,* we are as proud of *Dama* LaRocca as we are of risotto, Donatello's David, and the Colosseum."

Dante chuckled at her boast. Joining in his laughter, she rocked forward, and their foreheads nearly touched. She caught her breath, arrested by the dark fires kindling in those mesmerizing eyes. When she realized she was blushing, the heat in her cheeks both disturbed and confused her. She was the one who usually flustered suitors, not the other way around. What was it about Dante that made her as giddy as a school girl? His magnetic smile? His debonair charm? The alluring spice of his cologne?

She averted her gaze and noticed his well-manicured fingers, stroking the package he'd placed so decorously between their thighs. Wrapped in brown paper and tied with twine, the bundle was about the size of an illustrated novel, although it was several inches deeper.

"You must tell me," she rallied in conspiratorial tones. "What's in the package? Is it a birthday present for dear Wyntir?"

Amusement warmed Dante's midnight-colored eyes. "If it were, I'd plead the Fifth, since you and my ward are as thick as thieves. But no, I stopped by the tobacconist to purchase a humidor—"

"Leave her in peace, you bugger!"

Sadie blinked in surprise. When she turned her head, she'd expected to find Collie looming over her, playacting her champion. Instead, she discovered Patches, his fists clenched, his knuckles bloodless, and his face mottled with outrage.

She climbed hastily to her feet. "*Signore,* I do not believe we have met—"

"Baines. Mendel Baines," he snapped in a grating, Boston accent. "And trust me when I say, you don't want *anything* to do with this parasite."

Now Dante was on his feet. She glanced anxiously at Collie, who stood flexing his hand uncertainly above the Remington in his pocket.

However, Dante showed enormous self-restraint. He did nothing more than curl his lip at his detractor. "You stink of gin, Baines. Come, Fiore." He offered his elbow. "Permit me to escort you—"

"To wreck and to ruin!" Baines interrupted hotly. "Like every other damsel you distress." He turned to Sadie in a huff. "If I were you, madam, I'd run long and far from this libertine. Knocking you up will be the least of his sins."

"Professor Baines." Dark fires smoldered a warning in Dante's eyes. "Since you seem determined to embarrass yourself, I suggest we continue this conversation outside."

But Baines refused to back down before that burning, black glare. "You'd like that, wouldn't you, Goddard? You'd like all of Denver to think you were a paragon of virtue, with your fancy silk cravats and your fussy, high-brow manners. But Beacon Street knows better!"

"What Beacon Street knows," Dante retorted acidly, "is that you were booted out of Harvard's hallowed halls for moral depravity and unethical research."

"*Liar!*" Baines howled, swinging a fist.

Dante ducked.

As if on cue, the door to the Baby Doe Room swung open. Cass stepped into the lobby with a giggling, eyelash-batting Rebekah. For a moment, Sadie stewed, watching Eros in Spurs work his magic.

But the commotion Baines was making couldn't be ignored. Her misguided savior was shrilling curses and throwing wild punches. Goddard was fitter and faster, but he seemed more intent on blocking blows than landing them. Sadie wondered if good breeding or the Hippocratic Oath forbade Dante to strike an assailant, who wasn't in his right mind.

"What the hell?" she heard Cass mutter.

He thrust Rebekah toward the safety of the assembly room and waded into the fray. So did two brawny, yelling bellhops. Eventually, the boys tackled the professor, while Cass shoved Dante away from the writhing bodies on the floor.

Suddenly, the matchsafe bounced from Baines's pocket. Sliding across the tiles, it plinked its melody all the way to Rebekah's square-toed shoe. The child recoiled, as if bitten by a rattler.

A police whistle shrilled. The circle of gawking spectators parted for the uniformed flatfoot, but by this time, the professor had been subdued. He flailed on his stomach, pinned by the bellhops. His nose was bleeding, his eye was swelling, and he looked like he'd wrestled a cyclone, thanks to his stalwart captors.

Dante, on the other hand, didn't look much the worse for wear, unless one counted his off-center cravat and the sable curl that spilled so rakishly across his forehead.

"You're under arrest!" the policeman barked, slapping cuffs on Baines.

"You'll pay for this, Goddard!" the professor yelled. "You'll pay for everything, you smug son of a—"

The policeman backhanded his prisoner, and Baines slumped, his head lolling. Blood trickled from the corner of his mouth.

Sadie winced at this police brutality. She couldn't help but feel sorry for Baines. Even so, she'd seen worse, far worse, in cow towns across the west.

Rebekah, apparently, had not. Fowler's shell-shocked disciple quivered like a mouse, her cheeks as white as her starched bonnet. Sadie's maternal instincts stirred.

But when she would have stepped forward to comfort the child, Rebekah's spine stiffened. Her dark eyes flashed like electrified steel.

"Beware the devil's tune," she boomed at Sadie in a voice like crashing thunder, "or marked for death you will be, mourning a loss as terrible as your sister's!"

Sadie gaped.

Rebekah slammed the door and turned the key.

Sadie's outrage surged, a welcome distraction from her plague of chills. *Rebekah knows about Maisy? Damn you, Cass! You had no right to tell her!*

Nothing was more sacred to Sadie—*nothing*—than the memory of her precious, five-year-old twin. Maisy had fallen into the river and drowned, despite every desperate attempt Sadie had made to save her.

Wounded to her core, she leveled a blistering glare at the lover who'd violated her trust. To Cass's credit, he turned gray under his tan.

Dante moved toward her, straightening his cravat. Cass hastened to retrieve his fallen hat—and the matchsafe. He snapped the lid closed and slipped it into his pocket before halting before her in his slightly rumpled duster.

"Are you folks all right?"

The question was addressed to them both, but Cass's eyes were on her. Only her. Maybe because she was trying so hard not to cry.

Dante seemed to sense her upset. He offered her his arm. She clutched it with trembling fingers.

"My companion needs fresh air," he answered with impeccable chivalry. "Come, my dear. I apologize for the unfortunate disturbance. Allow me to make it up to you over breakfast."

Sadie gritted her teeth. She knew if she unhinged her jaw, terrible things—unforgiveable things—would spew from her mouth to hurt Cass. To make matters worse, Dante, along with every bellhop, chambermaid, and snot-nosed guest in the hotel, would peg her for a trollop. Her cover would be blown.

Fortunately, not even the pleasure of lambasting Cass for his betrayal could compete with her determination to find Minx's killer. She murmured her acceptance of Dante's breakfast invitation.

Then, pasting on a frozen smile, she turned on her heel and stalked away from her *very* ex-lover.

CHAPTER 7

Twelve Hours Later

Nursing a tequila bottle, Cass sat in the red-velveteen parlor of the Rockies' most infamous brothel. At 11 o'clock, Mattie Silks's house was doing such a booming business, the bouncer was turning away Johns. Even if Cass had wanted a rut, he would have had to wait his turn.

To entertain her restless guests, Mattie had changed the musical program. The voluptuous blonde took center stage under an opulent chandelier. As she swelled her breasts to sing, a diamond cross glittered from her cavernous décolletage. Ironically, she was belting out the refrain of a bawdy ditty that Sadie had written—and made famous—four years ago in Dodge:

> *"Purty Pansy Primrose, now that she's full grown,*
> *Will jump a randy tycoon like a dog jumps on a bone!"*

Cass grinned as the local gents hooted, waving their top hats and stomping their opera pumps in time to the fiddlers.

Of course, Sadie's refrain would have been different in Dodge. "Cowboy," "wolfer," or "gambler" would have been inserted in place of "tycoon." But Mile High City wasn't a frontier town anymore, so Mattie had taken liberties with the lyrics.

Yes, pleasing her guests was what Mattie did best. That's why she no longer had to rut in a tent. The former Kansas whore now owned a three-story house with a mansard roof and lead-paned mahogany door. Liveried wait staff, bearing sterling trays and crystal champagne flutes, passed Cass's table. On slower nights, beautiful girls in stunning gowns conversed about literature, politics, and stock prices. Lonely travelers from as far as France and Austria could feast on caviar and blue-winged teal in the first-floor restaurant.

Tonight, Cass was hoping to overhear some useful gossip, thanks to Boone's front-page farce. Cass couldn't have been more pleased with the freighting mogul's invention. The story had helped him recruit other mischief-minded allies, who'd been only too eager to make headlines of their own.

For instance, Mattie's arch rival, Jenny Rogers, had jumped at the opportunity to "rub the Mayor's nose in the muck." Apparently, he'd tossed her over for a rich virgin with a pristine pedigree. In revenge, Jenny had agreed to tell reporters that Daredevil had snatched her favorite "love token," a lavish gold table clock, which the mayor had swiped from his deceased in-laws' estate.

Cass had also succeeded in recruiting Silas Tate, a steel tycoon, to Team Daredevil. A couple of years ago (and with the help of Lynx,) Cass had rescued Silas's infant daughter from a Cheyenne raiding party. To return the favor, Silas had agreed to tell the press that Daredevil had run off with a priceless gold-and-ivory walking stick, once owned by King Louis XIV of France.

Now all Cass had to do was recruit Dolce to his team— and write clever taunts for the classifieds.

Of course, he recognized his advertising scheme had drawbacks. Success hinged on the crucial element that Maestro read Daredevil's taunts, got incensed, and tried to steal Mephistopheles's Jewels. But short of getting plugged for asking too many questions in the Underground, Cass didn't know how else to communicate with Maestro and lure him to take action.

Preferably, against me.

A blast of cold air buffeted the chandelier. Cass glanced toward the brothel's entry hall. He'd chosen a table with a view of the front door, mainly because he liked to know what kind of trouble might walk in.

However, he hadn't been expecting *this* kind of trouble.

A masked bandit with a striped tail streaked past Pug, the bouncer. As the raccoon galloped across the alabaster tiles, he trailed slushy paw prints all the way to Cass's chair.

"Hey!" Pug yelled. "Come back here!"

But Vandy's wicked little varmint brain was intent on making mischief. He took a flying leap. Cold, wet paws landed in Cass's lap.

Aw, hell.

A message was tied to the rollicking coon's collar. Cass grimaced, pushing a slurping tongue out of his face as he wrestled the scrap free. Unfolding the paper, he deciphered what proved to be an abysmally spelled message from Collie:

Sady snuk in weering opra duds and a beerd.

Cass scowled. He could see the crown of Collie's chocolate-brown Stetson, gathering a heap of snow flurries.

"Hey, Cort," Cass called to Mattie's Achilles Heel. She was so smitten by the gambler that whenever he rode his horse into her house and threatened to damage the dance floor, she gave him more spending money. "Tell Pug to let the kid inside, will ya? Collie doesn't want a rut. Just a drink."

Cort grinned. He was seated at the next table, writing an utterly worthless I.O.U. to some whiskered dude, who apparently wasn't acquainted with the gambler's reputation. As usual, Cort's coffee-colored eyes were glassy, but for some reason, womenfolk considered him handsome. He had wavy black hair, a pencil-thin mustache, and an athletic build. In fact, Cort used to be a footracer and a guerilla fighter in the war, but these days, his fondness for opium usually kept him drooling on his butt.

"Sure thing, Cass," Cort hollered above Mattie's singing, which earned him dagger-like glares from everyone else in the room. "But you know the rules. Coons cost double."

"Yeah, yeah." Cass flipped the smartass a $20 gold piece. "I'll expect to win that back before you pass out tonight."

"Dream on, grasshopper."

Cort waved to Pug, and Collie stepped inside.

After a detour to the hatcheck counter, Collie stomped into the parlor, sporting a five-day growth of beard. The kid was dressed in his usual denim trousers and buckskin coat, garments that had once belonged to the heavy-fisted moonshiner, who'd been his pa. No one would have guessed those hand-me-downs weren't custom-tailored. Over the last six months, Collie had sprouted like a weed, filling out the coat's shoulders and the once baggy rump of the trousers. Long hours in a saddle had packed muscle on his skinny thighs, and his wrists had lost their bony look, thanks to daily quickdraw drills.

"Three bucks for a bottle?" he groused, banging down his bourbon and swinging a leg over a chair. "That's highway robbery!"

"Nevermind that," Cass retorted, leaning across the table so he could whisper.

Cort and the whiskered dude were headed for the gaming room; the nearest John slumped in his cups. With the symphony booming and Mattie yodeling, Cass figured he was safe to talk business.

"Where's Sadie?"

Collie jerked his head toward his coon. The varmint had scrambled out of Cass's lap—leaving him with a soggy crotch—and was now belly-creeping into the hall.

Vandy was the sneakiest varmint Cass knew. He had an uncanny instinct about people, whom he considered food dispensaries. Somehow, Vandy had figured out that Pug was busy, turning away another John. The coon sniffed his way into the foyer. Whether he was tracking pumpkin pie or patchouli-scented Tiger was unclear, but he did dash under the linen drape of an accent table, topped with a vase of peacock feathers. The table was located outside Mattie's audience chamber.

"Looks like Sadie's waiting for Mattie," Collie whispered dryly, uncorking his Wild Turkey. "She used a letter from Wilma to get inside the brothel."

Cass groaned. He'd forgotten how Mattie owed Wilma a life debt. "You shouldn't have let Sadie come here!"

"You said *protect* her, not tie her to a chair. Besides. You ever try talking sense into a firecracker?"

Cass didn't commiserate, even if his woman's temper *was* only rivaled by her tongue. "Did she see Pancake tethered at the hitching post?"

"Oh, yeah." Collie had the audacity to smirk.

Damn. Cass wanted to box the brat's ears. "What's she want with Mattie?"

Collie took a swig of bourbon. "Cort bailed Baines out of jail this afternoon—with Mattie's money."

"So?"

"So Sadie added Baines to her suspect list after a telegram came back from Boston, verifying how he got expelled from Harvard for conduct unbecoming."

Cass hiked an eyebrow. The matchsafe from Baines's pocket had rightfully belonged to Boone. Earlier that afternoon, Cass had met with the freighting baron, and Boone had identified the inscription inside the lid. What hadn't been clear from their meeting was how Baines had acquired the novelty.

"Matchsafes—even nice ones—don't strike me as Maestro's target," Cass mused. "But Boone did tell me that a thief tried to crack his office safe about the same time his matchesafe went missing. The vault was holding a fancy music box, newly arrived for the Rothschild auction. Boone's secretary surprised the thief, and he fled."

Collie grunted noncommittally.

"Speaking of music," the kid said, "you'd best get yourself a pair of opera shoes."

"Why's that?"

"'Cause Beans is beating you at your own game."

"The hell he is."

"Beans invited Sadie to his private theater box," Collie challenged. "How're you gonna compete with that?"

Damn that Yankee prig.

Cass scowled. Sadie adored opera. In her mind, nothing could compare with proscenium-box seating for some highfaluting musicale. Before her dreams of performing had been cut short by her father's murder and her mother's suicide, Sadie had rehearsed daily with a music tutor in the hopes of headlining on a fancy stage.

Cass, on the other hand, couldn't make heads or tails of foreign shrieking—which was how he privately viewed opera. For Sadie's sake, he'd tried to sit through Wagner, once. She'd lured him to the theater with promises of big-busted women wearing chest armor and horned helmets, but he'd fallen asleep during the overture. Needless to say, Sadie had been furious. She'd frozen him out of her bed—like she usually did when she was pissed.

Making a face, Cass poured himself a shot of Jose Cuervo. "Better Beans than me," he told Collie.

"What's the matter with you? If you took Sadie to the opera, she'd forgive you, and we'd all get back to normal!"

"Too soon. She needs to spit and claw awhile longer."

"So you're letting Beans win?"

Cass tossed back his shot. At the moment, he didn't have a choice. Even if he'd wanted to take Sadie to the opera, all of Dolce's performances were sold out.

"What part of, *'Beans is taking her to the opera,'* don't you understand?" Cass retorted.

Collie shook his head. "Wailing and whining. That's all you did for three lousy months after you thought that woman had died in a brothel fire—"

"I did *not* wail."

"Well, you sure as hell whined! You were like a big noisy mosquito in a Stetson! For 96 days, you yapped, yakked, and jawed our ears off. That's right," Collie added loftily, "me and Vandy *counted.* So go make peace with your woman. We're sick and tired of your boo-hooing."

"Since when does Vandy get a vote?"

Collie wiped his sleeve across his mouth. "When's the last time I slugged you? It seems like you're due."

Cass's amusement was fleeting. "Sleeves aren't for wiping. How many times do I have to tell you that? No wonder you can't talk your way into a high-stakes poker game. Or a classy brothel."

"Shows how much you know. Vandy does my talking. He gets me free drinks and casino credits anytime I want."

"Vandy didn't get you free *anything* tonight. I had to pay your entry fee."

Collie smirked. "You think on that again, Snake Bait."

A slow heat rolled up Cass's neck. He didn't know whether to be annoyed or amused by Collie's humbug.

"I sent you to protect Sadie so she could teach you some *manners,* you crazy corn-cracker."

"Manners?" Collie scoffed. "That skirt curses like a muleskinner."

"Good. Then the two of you found something in common."

Collie rolled his eyes. "Yeah. You drive us both to drink." He belched like a foghorn.

"Tarnation, boy! Were you born in a barn?"

"Worse." Collie's dimples peeked.

"Quit bragging." *Honest to God, teaching that boy charm is like teaching an alley cat how to fetch.* "Has Sadie gotten an appointment with Fowler yet?"

"Are you kidding? Rebekah can sniff out patchouli from a mile away."

Cass frowned. Rebekah *was* a tad zealous about managing Fowler's appointment schedule. She'd told Cass the waiting list was as long as Father Time's beard. But then, Cass dressed like a cowboy, not a tycoon.

Rebekah probably thought he was too poor to fleece.

"Sadie's supposed to be rich," Cass said. "Rebekah's supposed to be raking in money for Fowler. What's the problem?"

"You mean, besides Rebekah being a few pecans short of a fruitcake?"

Cass shot him a withering glare. "I found her perfectly cordial."

"Sure you did. You're the Rebel Rutter. Your sweat don't stink! But Rebekah told *me,* if I lived in Arabee, I'd get my hands chopped off, my tongue ripped out, and my eyes gouged!"

Cass hiked an eyebrow. "That's a bit harsh."

"You're tellin' me!"

"Maybe you shouldn't always let Vandy do the talking," Cass said dryly.

"Vandy was a perfect gentleman!"

Cass let the irony of this assessment pass. "In my experience, a young woman doesn't make threats unless she has good reason. So what did you do to her?"

"Nuthin'! I was standing in the hallway, just as nice as can be. When she got off the elevator, I tipped my hat and said, 'Howdy.' She's off her freakin' nut, I'm telling you. She cursed Vandy with a plague of locusts!"

Cass smirked. "Somehow, that makes sense."

Collie flipped him off.

"So let me get this straight." Cass was trying to keep a straight face. "You were standing in the hall earilier this evening?"

"Yep." Collie nodded. "On the fourth floor. Keeping a lookout for Sadie."

"And while you were getting bullied by a 14-year-old *girl,"* Cass taunted, "what was Sadie doing?"

"Crawling out Fowler's window, I expect."

"What?!" Cass was pretty sure the blood drained to his toes.

"It's not like she never did it before," Collie said sheepishly. "Remember Galveston? And Lampasas?"

"Those windows were on the second story! Fowler's room's on the fourth! Sadie could have broken her fool neck!"

"What did you expect her to do? Exit through the hall door and flash her badge? If Vandy hadn't chased his ball under Rebekah's skirts, she would have caught Sadie rummaging through Fowler's drawers!"

Cass struggled with his outrage. As much as he would have liked to pommel Collie for his poor judgment, Sadie's adventure hadn't ended in catastrophe—this time. "Did she *find* anything, at least?"

"A chunk of quartz, a corncob pipe, a pewter goblet—"

"Anything to *incriminate* him?" Cass amended impatiently.

"How about peyote?"

"It's not illegal, if that's what you mean."

"Then she didn't find squat. But if you ask me, Rebekah's the one you should really be worried about."

"Rebekah's a child. And even if she wasn't, she's not Maestro. Look at how she dresses. She isn't interested in pretty rocks."

Collie shrugged. "That doesn't mean she's not dangerous. She found out about Sadie's sister, didn't she? That's not common knowledge."

Cass frowned. Collie did have a point. But the real problem wasn't Rebekah. The real problem was how Fowler would respond, if the child convinced him Sadie was a threat. "Tarnation, boy, that's why I told you to stick to Sadie like a tick on a hound! If anything happens to her—"

"Yeah, yeah. Quit your whining. *Sheesh.* She's better armed than I am, with all her detective gadgets. 'Sides. What can go wrong? She's just on the other side of this wall, ain't she?"

Not for long, Cass thought grimly.

But before he confronted Sadie, he had another matter to settle with Collie. "Hand over Beans's timepiece."

"Huh?"

"You heard me."

The kid stiffened. "Vandy stole that watch fair and square!"

"Vandy's not supposed to be stealing *anything,* deputy. Besides, I need an excuse to reconnoiter Greyfell Manor."

Collie hiked his chin. "What happened to all that Coyote Charm that's supposed to open doors for you?"

"Charm doesn't work on Dobermans."

"So you're going to wave that watch in the air, and put the hounds in a trance?"

"How 'bout I wave my fist in the air, and put *you* in a trance?"

Collie snorted. "I'd like to see you try it, Snake Bait."

"Do you want to be a lawman or not?" Cass snapped.

The boy scowled. Thanks to Sera's influence, Cass knew that Collie didn't want to end up like his old man: drunk, reviled, and lynched. The kid was sweet on Sera. She was quite possibly the only person in Collie's universe who had the power to lift him to higher moral ground. He wanted to be the kind of man some future Sera would deign to marry. But before the boy would admit to such a thing, he'd have to be doused with kerosene and lit.

"I liked it better when I was a thief," Collie grumbled, gulping another swig of bourbon.

"Now who's whining?"

"Fine. You want the watch so bad? You can have it for 40 bucks."

"Forty bucks?! It wasn't worth that much new!"

"That's your problem. And don't bring me any worthless greenbacks, either."

Cass gaped. "Wait a minute. You're serious?"

"Hell yeah. I want gold pieces."

"I don't have any gold pieces!"

"Then you'd better win me some," Collie retorted loftily. "It's the least you can do while I have to stay sober enough to protect your woman."

* * *

Alone in Mattie's audience chamber, Sadie paced the fancy carpet. She'd been unceremoniously abandoned 20 minutes earlier. Now she could hear some woman belting out her pirated ballad, *Pansy Primrose.* That wasn't a good sign, Sadie mused. It meant at least one of the musicians from Dodge City's Long Branch Saloon had migrated to Denver—and worse, that he'd be able to identify her if he saw her unusual eyes.

Sadie cursed her luck. She'd figured she could avoid Cass, simply because he was upstairs, whoring, but the musicians were another matter. She would have had to walk past the bandstand to get to any other room in the house—except this one. That's why she'd insisted on a private meeting with Denver's reigning madam.

Mattie's audience chamber was fit for a queen. Red-velvet and gold gilt adorned the furniture; tinkling chandeliers scattered rainbows across the ceiling; the Persian carpet practically sucked Sadie's feet into the pile. Near the heavy bombazine that draped the window, a small table had been cozily set for two. Decanters with golden liquid beckoned from the sideboard. Sadie was tempted, but she restrained herself. Four years ago, during her first assignment as a "man," she'd made a pact with herself never to drink in the field—at least, not real liquor. Guns and gadgets could fail. The only things standing between her and the Angel of Death were a clear mind and a swift kick.

She halted before the mirror over the sideboard. Raising her blue-tinted spectacles, she studied her reflection, critically inspecting the putty on her freckled nose and the graying muttonchop whiskers that swallowed the lower half of her face under her beaver top hat. She was hunting for signs of cracking or peeling. Even though Wilma's letter had carefully omitted all reference to gender, Sadie didn't really expect to fool Mattie with black worsted swallowtails and a satin-lined opera cape.

The clock on the mantel chimed 11:30 p.m. Sadie muttered an oath. Had that blockhead of a waiter forgotten to pass Wilma's letter to Mattie? Sadie had never expected to wait this long. She wondered if she should call her Pinkerton escort inside. Pryce was posing as the driver of her hansom cab, mostly to guard the horses. If Mattie delayed much longer, Sadie was going to find a man-shaped icicle in the alley!

But as she headed for the hallway to rescue her colleague, she was surprised by the sound of a sliding door. Prepared to trigger her .32, she turned.

A tawny-haired devil stepped out of the rich, cherry wood paneling beside the fireplace.

Sadie scowled. *"You!"*

Cass grinned. "What a smashing chapeau, old chap. Have we met?"

Hilarious. He knew damned well who she was. In fact, Collie had probably told him where to find her.

Sadie watched Cass hang his lantern over a hook in the passage before letting the panel slide closed. As usual, the reprobate was dressed in his mouth-watering black. She was quick to notice that all his buttons and buckles were properly latched, which made the pain of seeing him in a whorehouse slightly less acute.

"What are you doing here? No, wait," she amended acidly. "Never mind. I can guess."

Ignoring her blistering glare, he strolled closer. The smoking sapphire of his gaze trailed leisurely over her disguise. "Sandalwood soap, nice touch," he drawled. "Muttonchops? Not so much."

"I was expecting Mattie." She kept her tone clipped, as businesslike as possible.

"Mattie's singing your song."

That explains a lot. "Good," Sadie snapped. "While I'm here, she can pay me royalties."

His grin turned lopsided. "That might clue her you're not a man."

Sadie ground her teeth. Right now, she didn't feel like a man, thanks to Cass's sultry heat, lapping over her skin. She struggled to ignore her traitorous female parts. "What's the matter? Afraid you won't get the chance to betray me again?"

Undaunted by her taunt, he let his wicked gaze drop below her belt. "You can't seriously expect Mattie to think you're a John."

Annoyed by her libidinous flush, Sadie turned on her heel and stalked for the door.

"Aw, c'mon, Tiger." He caught up with her, preventing her escape. "You know you're not safe here. If you were, you wouldn't have worn a disguise."

"Get out of my way," she growled.

"I have a better idea. Why don't you let me do the snooping?"

"Because I'm not talking to you."

His dimples peeked, boyish and endearing. "You just did."

"Only because braining you with this walking stick would be illegal."

"Sounds like another good reason not to wear a badge," he quipped.

"So *sass* is your idea of helping me?"

He backed her into the door, all sizzle and sin with a dastardly dash of incorrigible thrown in. "It could be worse. I could tug off your whiskers. Or steal your codpiece."

She hiked her chin. "And that's supposed to make me trust you?"

"Aw, c'mon, Sadie. You know I'm on your side."

She sniffed. "You sure have a lousy way of showing it."

"Truce?" he murmured, his lips parting hypnotically above hers.

She had to fight her screaming, female instincts—the ones that wanted him to forget her beard, drop her drawers, and prove why he'd earned the nickname, Rebel Rutter.

"Hell, no," she rallied. "What do you take me for?"

"I'll take you forever, if you let me."

Pain lanced her heart. Sadie knew he hadn't meant the words the way they'd sounded—like a marriage proposal. He was Coyote Cass, after all. He'd always been good at word games.

She shoved his chest, forcing him back a step. "Go spin your lies for some dewy-eyed virgin. I'm done being your—"

Footsteps echoed in the hall. They were heading for the audience chamber. She sucked in her breath. Cass cocked his head.

"There you are, Baines, my good fellow!" Cort's slurred, Texas twang called in the hall. "Enjoying your reprieve from the slammer?"

Cass reached for his shoulder holster; Sadie grabbed his arm and gestured for him to keep quiet. She and Cort had buried the hatchet, so to speak, and she didn't need Cass turning all Wild West on him—at least, not until she figured out why Cort had bailed Baines out of jail.

Cort liked to think of himself as a true southern gentleman. In other words, he was too proud to work. The Texican owed money to most of Kansas. To elude his creditors, he'd abandoned his wife and infant daughter so he could live off Mattie's earnings—which, ironically, hadn't stopped the louse from cheating on her. Four years ago at the Long Branch, Cort had tried to hike Sadie's skirts without paying a fee.

"I must admit," Baines said drolly, "the entertainments at the jail are less amusing than the ones you have here. I owe you a debt of gratitude."

"Don't worry, Doc. I'll think of a way you can pay me back."

Baines chuckled. "Of course, dear fellow. So tell me. Are you having better luck at the blackjack table?"

"Ten straight wins," Cort crowed.

"So now you admit my research has merit," Baines said smugly.

"Damned straight! That crazy finger-tapping exercise really works!"

"The exercise is called a *trigger*," Baines said dryly, "and it's designed to elicit a conditioned response. In other words, every time you tap your knee, your memory improves. Just like every time a fellow smells a sizzling steak, he gets hungry. Conditioned response is a scientific fact. There's nothing crazy about it. Unless, of course, you take it to extremes."

"You mean, like tapping both knees?"

"No, like winning 10 black jack games in a row."

"Aw, I was just practicing," Cort said sheepishly.

"Precisely. You were practicing *cheating*. Might I suggest a little discretion? I can't cure a smashed skull."

"But you said you could make a body impervious to pain!"

Baines sighed with martyr-like patience. "Under certain conditions, a number of scientific methods, including hypnosis, can trigger any conditioned response, from blind obedience to memory loss. But even hypnosis can't revive a corpse."

"That's not the *worst* news I've heard all night," Cort said, laughing.

Sadie's scalp prickled.

"Of course, there are other ways to deal with pain," Baines countered slyly. "You're an enterprising fellow. I daresay you know a lot of people. People who can make a…er, headache go away."

"I hate headaches as much as the next man," Cort quipped.

"Then I came to the right place."

"Absolutely! How many kilos do you need?"

"Not opium." Baines lowered his voice. "I have another solution in mind for this *particular* headache."

Is Baines referring to Dante? Sadie exchanged an uneasy glance with Cass.

She'd learned that the quarrel between Baines and Dante had deep roots. It started in 1870, when both men were graduate students at Harvard. Apparently, when the university's Ethics Committee investigated allegations that Baines fudged research for his thesis, Dante was among the students who testified against him. Dante graduated with flying colors, but Baines was expelled. Barred from every school in New England, he finally finished his graduate work at a less prestigious college in Philadelphia.

Now, 13 years later, that Harvard scandal continued to dog Baines's heels—even in the forward-thinking West. In the University of Denver's formal refusal to fund Baine's hypnotism research, the Chair of the Psychology Department had alluded to Baines's "contempt for the sanctity of fact-based evidence."

"Do tell?" Cort said.

"Not here," Baines countered. "Somewhere private."

"You've got me intrigued, Doc." A back slap ensued. "Follow me."

Their footsteps were coming closer. Sadie panicked.

"My eyes!" she hissed at Cass. "Cort will recognize me!"

Cass bolted the door.

Now someone was futilely twisting the knob from the other side. "Looks like Mattie's got company," Cort said. "C'mon. We'll try the Blue Room."

"Where's that?" Sadie whispered as their footsteps receded.

"None of your beeswax," Cass whispered back. "You're leaving."

"The hell I am." She reached for the bolt.

He grabbed her wrist. "If the Johns on Mattie's waitlist figure out you're female—"

"Who's going to tell them?"

"Christ, Sadie—"

"I know my way around a whorehouse, Cass!"

The muffled tattoo of a woman's stiletto heels echoed in the secret passage. Sadie cursed under her breath. Mattie had lousy timing.

"Follow Baines!" she whispered, retracting the bolt and shoving Cass into the hall.

"But—"

"You wanted to snoop, so snoop! I'll stall Mattie."

Cass didn't look happy about this change of plan, but he relented. She barely had time to close the door behind him before the panel by the fireplace slid open again.

A Rubenesque blonde, in a black corset and scarlet lingerie, sauntered across the carpet in a cloud of lily-of-the-valley perfume. At 35 years old, Mattie was earthy and undeniably attractive. She had stunning cerulean eyes and full, pouty lips that didn't need paint to look kissable.

Belatedly, Sadie remembered that she was wearing a beard. She doffed her hat and doubled over in a bow.

Mattie hiked a finely plucked eyebrow. She glanced at the letter in her hand. Sadie knew its contents by heart:

The individual bearing this letter has earned my full trust. The matter is not only delicate, but urgent. I implore your indulgence and discretion. We seek your help. Consider me in your debt.

Respectfully,

Wilhelmine LeBeau

Tucking the paper into her bodice, Mattie sucked on her long black cigarette holder. She puffed out a string of smoke rings. Several lengthy seconds ticked past as she let Sadie stew.

Finally, Mattie demanded, "Is this a joke?"

Sadie was annoyed to feel her cheeks heat. She'd expected Mattie to peg her for a female, of course, but not the moment they locked stares!

"No joke, Madam Silks," she said with as much humility as her fiery nature would allow. "Thank you for agreeing to meet with me."

"Wilma must have come into money lately. A *great deal* of money, to be wasting my time with masquerades."

And so the game begins, Sadie thought grimly.

She laid a $100 gold certificate on the table. "I won't take much of your time—"

"For that paltry sum?" Mattie snorted. "You have exactly one minute."

Sadie bit back her retort to save time. Mattie's less-than-cordial welcome made her wonder just how close Wilma and Mattie really were. "Sisterly" seemed optimistic. Mattie must still be sore about Wilma getting a marriage proposal from Wild Bill Hickok. Of course, the notorious, curly-haired gunslinger had been three sheets to the wind at the time. And he'd retracted his proposal the next morning by riding hell-for-leather out of Dodge. But Wilma had gotten his prized ivory-handled Colt, while Mattie had gotten egg on her face.

"Can you tell me anything about this young woman?" Sadie asked, withdrawing a daguerreotype from her pocket.

Through her haze of smoke, Mattie glanced briefly at the image. "A runaway?"

"A friend."

"You don't lie well."

"Wilma's friend."

"Wilma should take better care of her business assets."

Sadie struggled with her notorious temper.

"My friend goes by the name of Minx," Sadie said, "although she may have used an alias. She disappeared in October. The sepia tones in the photo don't do her justice. She has blue eyes. Black hair. A bubbling laugh. She turns heads. Maybe the wrong head. We were hoping she paid her respects when she arrived in town."

"She didn't."

"Are you sure?"

Mattie yawned. "I believe your time is up."

"But Minx is dead!"

"My condolences."

"Wait!" Sadie ground her teeth. *"Murdered,* Mattie. Minx was murdered. I think she was coerced to do something against her will. Through…hypnosis."

Mattie hiked a skeptical eyebrow.

Even to Sadie's ears, the accusation sounded ludicrous. But during Pinkie training, she'd been warned against nefarious methods that enemies might use to coerce field agents. The Agency had expounded on the dire consequences of hallucinogens and torture. Her trainer had even mentioned the fledgling science of hypnotism, although he hadn't taken it seriously. He'd believed that a Pinkie would have to sit still and agree to be hypnotized. And what Pinkie would do that?

Nevertheless, as Sadie had eavesdropped on Baines and Cort, the seed of a suspicion had bloomed in her mind. Fowler wasn't the only shady character in Denver, who purported to be an expert on hypnotism. Baines had written his doctoral thesis on the subject, and he'd planted "trigger" commands in Cort, a player in the criminal underground.

What if Baines had programmed Cort to do something far more nefarious than count cards? And what if Baines had programmed Minx to jump off a bridge to silence an inconvenient witness?

"Have any of your girls disappeared?" Sadie asked. "Or suffered a sudden, inexplicable loss of memory?"

"My girls don't disappear," Mattie said. "They have good lives here."

That much was true: Mattie spent $6,000 on each of her girls to outfit them with an annual wardrobe. In Mattie's house, whores lived like queens.

"You're close to your girls," Sadie persisted. "You'd know if one was…say, acting oddly?"

Mattie looked bored. "Did I mention your time was up?"

Grimly, Sadie tossed $1,000 on the table.

"You've been holding out on me, dear."

"Enough games, Mattie. Help me help your girls."

"I wasn't aware they needed help."

"Then pull your head out of the sand! Some predator, lurking in this tenderloin, is turning people into his personal puppets. He's making them steal and murder at his command. He avoids all suspicion, while they go to the gallows in his stead. We need to figure out who this bastard is and how to stop him, because no one is safe. Not you. Not your girls. Not even Cort!"

At the mention of Cort, Mattie's eyes narrowed. Clearly, she knew Cort was a guinea pig for Baine's experiments.

"Your theory's a bit extreme, dear."

Sadie battled the rise of frustration. She couldn't blurt out the real nature of her suspicions—that Cort might be an unwitting pawn, who stole for Maestro. Only a Pinkerton would pose an allegation like that. She, on the other hand, was supposed to be an agent for Wilma's brothel.

"Men coerce young women all the time, Mattie. I don't need to tell you that. Whether Minx was drugged, hypnotized, or a combination of both, is moot. Surely you don't want your girls—your *investments*—to disappear the way Minx did! Wilma wanted you to be forewarned."

At the mention of Wilma, Mattie made a face and averted her gaze.

A few moments passed. Sadie kept her tongue firmly clamped between her teeth, lest she overplay her hand. She was privileged to know one of Mattie's closely guarded secrets. Back in Kansas, when no one else had cared that a feverish bawd lay babbling in the gutter, Wilma had used her Voodoo and herbs to nurse Mattie back to health. But business being business, Mattie and Wilma continued to operate rival houses. Of course, Wilma was in Texas now, too far to be a threat to Mattie's earnings.

Mattie must have drawn the same conclusion. She shrugged. "I might know something. I might not. Johns talk. The word is, a pretty young reporter from the *Leadville Democrat* was asking questions about a jewel thief. He calls himself Maestro because he has a perverse interest in musical novelties. Anyway, this reporter fit the description of your Minx," Mattie continued. "I never met her myself. And she never came around here. She wasn't *that* kind of working girl.

"A couple weeks back, before Halloween, the reporter was interviewing musicians around town and asking questions about Maestro. She wanted to know what instrument he played, if he performed in a band at a local saloon—that sort of thing. At some point, the reporter agreed to dine with a violinist from the opera company. However, she never showed up for their appointment. I know this, because the violinist spent the night here, drowning his sorrows and lamenting the fickleness of brunettes. He kept calling the reporter, 'that cheeky minx.'"

Sadie's heart tripped.

"The next morning," Mattie continued, "the *Rocky* reported that an unidentified woman had jumped off the 19th Street Bridge, leaving behind a cape. My girls were macabrely fascinated, speculating about what might make a woman throw away her life. The violinist suggested, 'A guilty conscience for jilting her dinner companion.' At the time, I thought he was making a bad joke at the expense of a stranger. But now that I think about it, he might have known her."

"Does this violinist have a name?" Sadie demanded darkly.

Mattie chuckled, rubbing out her cigarette. "If you're truly Wilma's protégé, you know better than to ask that question, dear. Curious, though. You're the second person in two weeks, who's come sniffing around here, looking for Minx."

Sadie tamped down her frisson of unease. "I suppose your house is the first place people would come to look for runaway girls. After Jenny's."

"Maybe." Mattie swept the gold certificates off the table and stuffed them in her bodice. "Or maybe your Minx was friends with a Pinkerton."

Sadie did her best to look shocked. "Some bastard sent the cops here? How could you tell?"

"Undercover dicks all have the same—" Mattie curled her lip "—smell."

Sadie swallowed an oath. She made a mental note to warn Mace that one of their agents was walking around with a blown cover. "So what did you tell this Pinkerton?"

"The same thing I'm going to tell you, dear. If Maestro did kill your Minx, it was because she poked her nose into his business affairs." Crystal blue eyes, as cold as midwinter, locked with Sadie's. "Don't make the same mistake."

CHAPTER 8

———◆———

Reining in his temper—and his worry—Cass reluctantly left Sadie in Mattie's audience chamber. He wasn't happy about leaving her unprotected, but he figured Sadie could handle a brothel madam. Besides, the sooner he got the evidence Sadie needed to close her case, the sooner he could get her home to Texas.

When he reached the restaurant, he could see the door to the private dining room. It was shut. To complicate matters, the restaurant was full of bored Johns, who had nothing better to do than watch his comings and goings while they waited for a rut. Cass cursed under his breath. He couldn't possibly put his ear to the Blue Room's door—unless, of course, he wanted dozens of witnesses to see him eavesdropping.

He waited another few minutes to see which waiter was carrying drinks inside the private room. But when he realized Cort had commandeered the brothel's one-eyed mute for the job, Cass admitted defeat. Mattie had hired Vachel specifically because he couldn't read, write, or carry tales.

Damn.

Well, whatever scheme Baines and Cort are hatching, I'm not going to learn about it tonight.

Since Cass's first priority was Sadie's safety, he headed back to the parlor to wait for her. He picked a strategic seat by the entrance, one that allowed him to observe Pug and the comings-and-goings in the foyer.

Lord. How long are those skirts going to yak?

Cass scowled at the irony. Here he was, Dodge City's Rebel Rutter, sitting in a corner of Denver's fanciest sporting house, shooing away half-naked women eager for his sex.

Why?

Because he was an idiot, that's why! Ever since a certain tawny-eyed Tiger had gotten under his skin, he'd been struck by a chronic case of cat-scratch fever. At least, that's what Collie called it.

Not that Collie knew anything about sex, Cass thought dryly. That crazy corn-cracker would rather suck bourbon than a tit. Even now, the kid was seated at Cass's original table, glaring at a mouth-watering brunette, with scarlet lip paint and hungry green cat's eyes, who'd dared to reach her immaculately lacquered fingernails toward his private parts. Usually Vandy sat in Collie's lap, guarding those hallowed balls, but tonight, Vandy was hunting Tiger. Cass could see the coon's tail, sticking out from the linen-covered table beside Mattie's audience chamber.

Another five minutes crawled by. Cass shifted impatiently in his chair. He was seriously tempted to pound his fist on the wall. What could Mattie possibly say that would make Sadie risk her cover in one of Denver's roughest neighborhoods? More to the point, what had two tempestuous bawds found so consarned interesting, that they'd holed up for 15 minutes without tearing out each other's hair?

Are they talking about me?

Cass quailed at the thought. He tried to imagine life with his eyes gouged out, because that was the least Mattie would do, if she guessed he'd stolen her pearls. Not to be outdone, Sadie would set fire to the strips of flesh Mattie had left intact if she ever learned his other secret.

Or rather, Sterne's.

Cass wasn't happy about the promise he'd made to his boss before leaving Texas. Sadie had a right to know the Ranger commander was her real father. But what was Cass supposed to do? Waltz into Sadie's hotel room and say, "Guess what, doll? Your Ma was an adulteress. She screwed around with Sterne when Roarke was out of town, and oopsie! Guess who came along nine months later?"

Even Wilma was keeping Sterne's secret. The Pinkie Chief didn't agree that Sadie would be happier, believing Roarke Michelson had sired her. But Wilma had given Sterne her word. And her word was golden.

Suddenly, Mattie's door swung open.

Vandy's tail disappeared beneath the table.

Damn, Cass thought. *That coon is sneaky.*

Sadie emerged in all her bearded glory. Thanks to the dark swirls of her cape, Cass couldn't see a purse swinging from her belt, but he suspected Mattie had relieved Sadie of every cent she'd brought—and then some. However, the ruffians on Holladay Street were likely to view Sadie's fancy clothes with more optimism.

Sensitive to her cover, Cass didn't hail her as she swept down the hall. Judging by her brisk bootfalls—and the smart tapping of her brass-handled cane on the alabaster tiles—he guessed she was headed for the alley exit. He heard the guttural farewell of Mattie's second bouncer and the squealing of the rear door. Cass decided to give Sadie a couple of minutes to reach her coach before he tailed her. He wanted to make sure she returned safely to the Windsor.

He waved to Collie. The boy nodded.

"C'mon, varmint," Cass called to Vandy as he reached for his Stetson and stepped into the foyer. "We're leaving."

As usual, the coon ignored him.

"Cockleburr!"

No response.

Confound it. What was that idiotic flower-command Collie used instead of heel?

"Snap dragon! Pussy willow!"

Beady black coon eyes winked at Cass before disappearing beneath the linen. He would have sworn Vandy was laughing at him.

"C'mere you rotten, good-for-nothing, wannabe hat!"

Prepared to spank the furry little craphead, Cass raised the linen. Vandy bolted out the other side and galloped merrily for the door.

A newcomer was arriving in a flurry of snow. Vandy ignored Pug's shout. Squeezing his 50 pounds between the John's legs, Vandy caused the elderly gent to stumble and drop his spectacles. Cass could hear the ominous *crunch* as Vandy streaked like a silver bullet into the cold autumn night.

Aw, hell.

Collie chose that precise moment to emerge from the parlor. Jamming his Stetson on his head, the boy cast suspicious eyes up and down the foyer. "Where's Vandy?"

Cass jerked a thumb over his shoulder. "You see that man on the threshold, cursing like a muleskinner and wishing he'd brought his shotgun?"

Collie glanced at the outraged John, who was picking bent frames from a pile of glass. "Vandy sneaked *outside?!*"

"Don't look at me that way," Cass grumbled, feeling unaccountably guilty. "He's a coon, for crying out loud. He *belongs* outside. 'Sides. You know he never lets you out of sniffing distance."

Collie's face purpled. "You were supposed to be watching him!"

"I was supposed to be watching *Sadie!* And you were supposed to be—"

Suddenly, a gunshot exploded on the alley side of the house. Cass's heart leaped to his throat.

Sadie!

Shoving the kid after his coon, Cass ran to protect his woman.

* * *

Sadie knew she was in trouble the moment the metal door squealed closed. It had no knob, and she smelled blood.

"Evenin', mister." The stench of saloon rolled off the unwashed mountain of flesh, who'd been hiding behind the door. "That your carriage?"

The hansom cab loomed in the splash of moonlight serving as the alley's entrance. Her Pinkerton escort was missing. She suspected the smell of blood was coming from Pryce's corpse.

"Hard to tell," she hedged. Mentally, she cursed her lack of foresight. She was right-handed. Her .32 was strapped under her sleeve, above the same fist that gripped her walking stick. She'd have to create some pretext for juggling the weapons if she wanted to use them both. "But you're welcome to the cab. I'll call another."

"Ain't that neighborly?" the Mountain jeered.

"More neighborly than your driver," menaced a second man, who stepped out from behind a refuse pile near the opposite wall. He was munching a dried strip of meat, called pemmican.

"My apologies, gentlemen," Sadie said as nonchalantly as her hammering heart would allow. "I'll speak with the blackguard immediately."

"Your driver ain't feeling so good," Mountain confided.

A third ruffian, lean and weasel-faced, chortled in the shadows to her right. "And you won't be feeling so good neither, if you don't hand over your purse."

"Sounds like a perfectly reasonable request, Friend." Sadie juggled her cane to her left hand. "Allow me to—"

Mountain's gun hammer clicked, freezing her right hand near her belt.

"We're gonna take a ride first, *Friend*," he taunted.

Sadie drew a shuddering breath. Any outlaw with half a brain knew that a John, leaving a brothel, would emerge with spare change. These thugs weren't after money. They were after blood.

Did Maestro send them?

A low, hungry growl reverberated through the alley.

"What's that?" Mountain squinted into the moonlight.

A humped-back form prowled closer. Sadie glimpsed whiskers and a ringed tail before her three-foot champion promptly vanished in the shadows.

Vandy!

"Hell. You see a dog, Harry?"

Pemmican Man craned his head over his shoulder. He made the mistake of dangling that dried meat from his fingers. Suddenly, 50 pounds of salivating coon were leaping for the treat.

Merciful God.

In that moment, all Sadie could think about was a dead coon, a grief-stricken boy, and the guilt that would haunt her for the rest of her days because Vandy was too damned trusting of people.

Swinging her cane with all her strength, she smashed Mountain's gun arm, triggered the .32 up her sleeve, and fired to disarm Pemmican, who was shrieking at a bewildered and snarling Vandy.

Meanwhile, Weasel, who'd been deciding whether to plug her or the coon, made up his mind. The slug pounded into her chest. She slammed into the bricks. Dazed and winded, she dropped her .32, fighting to shake off the pain of being saved by a bullet-proof vest. She knew her good fortune wouldn't last if Weasel fired a second shot at her head.

"Vandy!" she wheezed, as Pemmican booted the yiking coon and sent him somersaulting into the wall. *"Beggarticks!"* It was the command she'd once heard Collie yell to make Vandy hide.

Mountain and Weasel were both turning their guns on her. She muttered a prayer. Her walking stick only fired one bullet.

Suddenly, the door crashed open. Cass loomed on the threshold. Bullets starting flying from his .45.

Sadie took advantage of the distraction to duck behind the metal barricade. Ripping a button-bomb off her vest, she hurled it at Weasel's boots. Smoke billowed up around him. *Big mistake.* The door separated her from Cass. Now she was cornered with Weasel!

Eyes stinging from sulfur, ears ringing with the outlaws' shrieks, Sadie could scarcely think. All she could do was react. When she glimpsed the glint of steel, slicing through gray billows toward her throat, she lashed out with her cane. She heard an *oomph* and the clatter of Weasel's knife as it skittered across the cobblestones. Like a rabid dog, he lunged again. This time, he swung his fist. She managed to block his arm with her cane, but they grappled. He was too close; she couldn't raise the tip to fire.

"Hey!" His breath smelled like curdled beer and rank tobacco as he leered at her breasts. "You're a woman!"

"And you're a dumbass," she said, driving her knee between his legs.

He yiked and staggered backwards, doubling over.

A man's hand snaked through the dissipating smoke. Steely fingers closed over her forearm. She was prepared to smash her assailant's face until she realized Cass was trying to drag her around the door and shove her inside the brothel.

She also realized that Cass had turned his back on Mountain. The wounded outlaw was edging on his belly, reaching for his Colt. She fired the walking stick. Her bullet struck the .45 and sent it skating across the alley. For a moment, she had the satisfaction of watching Cass's eyes grow bigger than twin moons.

"Damn!" he muttered. "I need to get me one of those!"

Pemmican saw his chance. He rolled to his haunches and drew back his arm. Steel glinted in his fist. Cass moved so fast, Sadie's eyes couldn't follow. Fire spat from his revolver. A pinging sound accompanied sparks. For a fraction of time, a knife was illuminated in mid-air, changing its trajectory. Then came the tell-tale clatter on the cobblestones.

Cass had shot down the knife!

"You boys don't know when to quit," he growled, looming over the three fallen outlaws like the devil's own henchman.

"You ain't got but one bullet left!" Pemmican spat.

"And there's three of us," Mountain menaced.

"Count again," Cass said in lethal tones. A Smith and Wesson slid down his left forearm into his fist. "I've got five bullets. Who wants one?"

The outlaws quailed.

"That'd be murder!" Weasel whined, still clutching his balls.

"You see any tin-stars around here?" Cass retorted without a hint of irony. "Any lawman who gives a rat's ass if your brains get splattered all over the wall?"

An uneasy silence settled over the outlaws. Even Sadie knew the local law didn't come to Holladay Street—except on Payoff Day.

"You have five seconds to get your sorry asses out of this alley." Cass cocked his .38.

"You can't shoot us in the back!" Weasel cried.

"Four seconds," Cass growled.

The outlaws didn't waste another second. Limping, cursing, they scrambled for the street as fast as their wounds would allow.

Sadie drew a shuddering breath.

Cass holstered his guns.

Collie stepped out of the cab's shadow. He was carrying a shotgun. "The driver ain't dead, just knocked out. I bound his bloody arm the best I could."

Vandy ventured out of hiding. When he limped into Collie's arms, the boy shot Sadie a murderous glare. She wanted to yell at the kid, *"If you would stop following me, your precious coon wouldn't get hurt!"*

But Cass drew her fire first.

"What the hell's the matter with you?" he snapped. "You told your driver to wait in *this* neighborhood? Why didn't you just shout up the street, 'Come back in 20 minutes and rob me, boys!'"

"Piss off."

"Come again?"

"Not that it's any of your business," she bit out, "but Pryce was doing his job. He works for Sledgehammer."

"Well, *that* explains everything. 'Cause I never did meet a bigger, weasel-mouthed polecat—"

She hauled off and punched Cass in the gut.

He wheezed, doubling over. "So Sledgehammer gave you that topaz necklace, eh? Now it's all becoming clear."

"Interfere in my business again," she ground out, "and I'll do a helluvalot worse than give you a licking."

He straightened, grimacing. "I'm not opposed to a licking from you, sweetheart."

She flipped him off.

"Any time."

She made another fist.

"Go on." He spread his arms wide. "Get it out of your system."

"Oh, for God's sake," Collie grumbled. "Just kiss her."

"Shut up!" she snapped.

Vandy growled in defense of his boy.

"You too, Tubby!"

"Don't you be calling my coon names!"

"Now Tiger," Cass chided, as if he were speaking to a petulant child. "Don't be spitting and clawing at Vandy. He's a hero. He saved your life. And he's got the war wounds to prove it. The least you could do is let him gnaw your shoe while Collie drives you back to the hotel."

The furry little monster blinked big, shiny eyes at her as if to say, *"I love shoes!"*

Sadie was in dire danger of erupting, geyser-style. She didn't like being ambushed. She liked even less that Cass had been the one to save her. His 'I-told-you-so' was a bitter pill to swallow after he'd drugged and robbed her. The jackass deserved a whole lot worse than a bruise, and she would have dearly loved to walk to Larimer Street to spite him. The trouble was, she wasn't likely to survive the trek.

"Just so we're clear," she said in gravelly tones. "On no account does your fancy shooting exonerate you for your traitor's kiss."

"Aw, but you saved my life with that whiz-bang walking stick." He flashed endearing dimples. "That's gotta mean you still like me."

"What it means," she said acidly, "is that even ratfink scum-buckets don't deserve to get plugged in the back. Stay out of my affairs. Or God help you, the next time, you'll be answering to Sledgehammer."

Cass watched through narrowed eyes as Sadie snatched her .32 from the cobblestones and stalked toward the unconscious Pryce, whom Collie had propped against the wall. She knelt beside her comrade, checking his pulse and inspecting the makeshift bandage the boy had ripped from his shirttails.

"Pryce is fine. He's gonna live," Collie groused, shooing her into the cab. "But *you* aren't, if you keep strutting around Holladay Street, oozing sex under that beard."

"What?!"

"You heard me." He shoved Vandy into her arms. "Here. Make yourself useful. He likes belly rubs," Collie added, slamming the door and muffling her protest.

Cass's amusement was fleeting as the boy clambered onto the driver's seat and slapped the reins.

So Sledgehammer gave the order that nearly got Sadie killed?

Cass flexed his fists gunfighter-style as he watched his woman roll away in the cab.

Sounds like it's time for me and a certain Pinkerton to get acquainted.

CHAPTER 9

Cass figured any man who called himself Sledgehammer frequented prizefights.

Leaving Pryce in the excellent care of Mattie's physician, Cass cantered along 19th Street to the Highlands. Never mind that bare-knuckles boxing contests were illegal. Immigrants, especially Irish immigrants, considered fisticuffs the epitome of manly strength and courage. Dozens of Denver's police had risen from the ranks of Irish sluggers, so contests rarely got raided, especially in the Highlands, where promoters only received a wink and a nod. In truth, Cass expected to see many of Denver's off-duty constables at the Bust-a-Gut Saloon. He could hear the roar of bettors a block away.

The exhibition ring was located inside the saloon on an elevated stage overlooking the ice floes in the river. This arrangement allowed irate bettors to haul losing pugilists out the door and heave them into the Platte.

Silhouetted against the glare of lanterns, Porfi wasn't hard to spy above the booing, hissing crowd of all-male spectators. The boisterous Greek stood atop a chair, behind a makeshift counter that spanned two pickle barrels. Stacked before him were pork gyros, cheese pies, and lamb kebobs. He was swinging his apron over his head and bellowing, "Dunk the *vlacas!*" at the top of his lungs. Apparently, Porfi had bet on the beefy, red-haired palooka who'd just been KO'd by a well-muscled, Indian half-breed.

Cass smiled nostalgically, remembering his long-time *compadre,* Lynx. The Cherokee had rustled, smuggled, and hurrahed alongside him for 11 straight years until Sera had made an honest husband of him. Nowadays, Lynx worked as the sheriff of Blue Thunder, Kentucky, but during his outlaw career, he used to brawl like a wildcat.

Cass waved to catch Porfi's attention.

"Didn't I always tell you, 'Bet on the Injun?'" Cass yelled over the sea of bobbing bowlers and caps. "Lynx only lost me two wagers in 11 years!"

Porfi scowled at Cass's taunt and slapped his hand away from a basket of cheese pies. "Just for that, boyo, *pitakias* will cost you a buck."

"I'll give you two bucks to help me find a particular nobody."

"Favors cost five."

"So Dame Fortune knocked you on your *kolos* tonight, eh?"

"You want to owe me ten?" Porfi growled.

Cass grinned. "Only if you toss in a *pitakia*. With plenty of honey."

"You're a *malaka*. But you have a deal." Porfi reached for the honey pot. "So." He was drizzling amber-colored sweetness over the biggest cheese pie in the tray. "Have you attended the opera lately?"

"Soon," Cass said breezily.

"Must I be on my deathbed for this prize you promised?"

"Hope not."

Porfi shook his head in exasperation. "I shoulda put my bet on *him.*"

Cass snorted at this reference to Maestro. "You mean the fella who cuts you out of every deal?"

"At least he's a *working* man."

"Aw. You hurt my feelings."

"Good." Porfi thrust the pie, wrapped in wax paper, into Cass's hand. "If you wait much longer, you won't be the new prince of anything."

Cass sucked honey off his thumb. "Why? You hear something?"

"I hear a lot of things."

"Like what?"

"Like he set his sights on Italy."

Cass stiffened.

"A humidor that makes music," Porfi added.

Cass's shoulders relaxed. Porfi wasn't talking about Sadie. "You think he'll make an appearance at the Rothschild's auction?"

Porfi nodded. "Word is, he likes novelties. Jewelry boxes, pocket watches, wind-up toys—anything that plays a tune. Rothschild's will be auctioning a green cigar box that's worth a fortune to collectors."

Thoughtfully, Cass bit into his pie. He'd always thought the jewelry box with the enameled peacock was a bit too frou-frou for Sadie's tastes. Maybe she'd been keeping it as evidence.

He made a mental note to ask her.

Porfi changed the subject. "Who's this Nobody you're looking for?"

Cass shrugged. "I don't know his name. He's middle-aged. Probably German. He's got mallet-sized fists and a build like a brawler. I don't think he's been in the ring, though, since his nose is as straight as a razor. He's a few inches shorter than I am. Sandy hair. Green eyes. Talks like he's chewing on gravel. The cleft in his chin could roost a canary."

Porfi chuckled. "A German who roosts canaries on his face. Now that rings a bell."

"Does it?"

"Nope."

Cass shot him a withering glare. "Now who's the *malaka*?"

A flash of white in Porfi's beard betrayed a mischievous grin. "From my point of view, a grunt like that would be sucking suds, not stuffing his pie-hole with cheese." He jerked his head toward the staircase.

Cass followed Porfi's gaze and spied Sledgehammer, standing apart from the bettors with his shoulder propped against the railing. He was polishing off a brew.

"Much obliged," Cass said, flipping a coin.

"Don't you forget it," the Greek retorted, deftly snatching the half-eagle from the air.

As the intermission crowd descended like locusts on Porfi's counter, Cass took a circuitous route to Sledgehammer. He used this time to study the Pinkerton, noting how the older man seemed to blend into the stairwell's shadows. This feat surprised at least one red-faced bettor, who tipped his hat and stammered apologies for nearly colliding with the detective.

Sledgehammer wore his bowler low over his forehead and disdained the comfort of gloves, which let Cass notice, again, just how big the Pinkerton's knuckles were. Even if Sledgehammer wasn't a contender, he should have been. He had beefy arms and a barrel-sized chest that would have strained the buttons of his Chesterfield if the charcoal wool hadn't been tailored so well.

By the time Cass drew close enough to sneak up on the detective, Sledgehammer was tugging a stogie from his coat pocket.

Cass let the hiss of a striking match announce his arrival.

Sledgehammer didn't look surprised to see his rival materialize beside him, which annoyed Cass. In truth, a lot about the detective annoyed Cass, not the least of which was Sledgehammer's failure to protect the women under his command.

"Thought you'd want to know," Cass said acidly, cupping the flame so Sledgehammer could light his cigar. "Pryce survived his drive to Holladay Street. Barely."

Sledgehammer's expression never changed as he puffed, focusing on the tip of his smoke. "Is that name supposed to mean something to me?"

Cass reined in his temper. He didn't know what response he'd expected from the detective, but at the very least, Sledgehammer should have inquired after Sadie's well-being.

"Maybe you know this Pryce by another name. Like Lickspittle. Or Screw Up," Cass added, lighting a pre-rolled quirley for himself. "In any event, he got the tar beat out of him in Mattie's alley. Which served him right. He let the woman he was protecting fight off three bushwhackers with a button and a cane."

Sledgehammer exhaled a stream of smoke. "Sounds like a helluva woman."

"And you're a sorry bastard."

"Funny. She said the same thing about you. The morning after you robbed her."

Cass's eyes narrowed. Somehow, he couldn't picture Sadie confessing to the man who had the power to send her back to the whorehouse that she'd been duped by her outlaw lover.

"Your boss must pay screw-ups good wages," Cass countered, referring to the Galveston brothel that had burned to the ground last summer. "Otherwise, you wouldn't be able to afford an Imperial topaz for my woman."

Sledgehammer didn't bat an eye. "Is that why Daredevil was born?"

"Is that name supposed to mean something to me?" Cass fired back.

The ghost of a smile touched Sledgehammer's lips. "You mustn't read the newspaper much—contrary to the claims made by a certain dame."

"Who has time to read? I want to trap a coyote, not cogitate about it. Speaking of which, I don't appreciate your choice of bait in this hunt."

Sledgehammer raised his shoulders in an indolent shrug. "The *bait,* if you haven't noticed, keeps insisting on the role, much to my aggravation."

"What's that supposed to mean?"

"It means, if I had my way, she'd be safe and sound in Texas."

Cass digested this news. He wasn't sure he believed it. Sledgehammer had already lied to him once tonight.

But Cass knew the value of alliances, even the uneasy ones. Eleven years ago, when he'd stumbled across a Cherokee half-breed, who'd needed saving from the Ku Klux Klan, he'd forged a lifelong bond with that stranger. Lynx had eventually become his most trustworthy friend.

"Sounds like we have something in common," Cass said grudgingly.

"We're both bastards?"

"That makes two things in common."

Sledgehammer's lips twitched. "I saw you talking to the Greek."

"He bakes damned good pies."

"Uh-huh."

"You got a problem with pies?" Cass demanded.

"Only when they're baked with rocks."

Cass was careful to keep his Poker face. Porfi was rumored to bake loot into his confections so he could smuggle jewels out of his shop. "You're barking up the wrong tree if that's where you're looking for a certain silver magnate's missing rock."

"And you know this because…?"

"Me and Porfi go back a long way."

"And of course, Porfi never lies to his friends," Sledgehammer said dryly.

"Maybe if you had a few friends of your own, in the right places, you wouldn't be so quick to judge."

"And what places might those be?"

"Places that welcome coyotes, but not the fellas who hunt them."

Sledgehammer tapped ash. His eyes were fixed on Porfi; his expression remained as placid as a pond on a windless day. Still, Cass sensed the detective was considering the proposal.

"Seems like the right coyote could be useful," Sledgehammer conceded. "If he has a knack for digging. And the smarts not to get caught."

Cass snorted. He'd assumed Sledgehammer was familiar with his legend. Since going on the run at the tender age of 13, Cass had been brought to trial only once, and that was because he'd surrendered to clear his name. Last summer in Texas, the courts had exonerated him for killing Cousin Bobby's murderer in self-defense.

Dropping his smoke, Cass rubbed it out with his toe. "I'll be in touch, pard."

Mace continued to puff his cigar as he watched Sadie's outlaw lover stroll toward the exit with his usual, cocksure gait. Cassidy had arrived on a whiff of sandalwood. Now, thanks to the steady breeze blowing through the windows, the fragrance of lemongrass soap warned Mace another male was approaching.

"Damn," whispered the mousy-haired youth with the wire-rimmed spectacles. "Who was that?"

"Picture the same mug without the beard."

The junior agent sucked in his breath. "*Lucifire?*"

Mace frowned at the admiration in the youth's tone. He happened to know Sadie had written the *Ballad of Lucifire* long before Cassidy had set foot in East Texas for the first time in 11 years. Cassidy had adopted the name to fuel his legend. He fancied himself a "devil with a gun."

And sure, Cassidy was a showboating quickdraw; Mace would give him that. Cassidy was also a crass southern cracker, a notorious debaucher, and an unrepentant felon, whose thieving record stretched longer than Mace's arm.

"But the warrants say he wears a double-holstered rig," the junior agent protested. "And he always carries two guns!"

Mace's smile was mirthless. The young Pinkerton— better known as Ambrosius "Brodie" Darling—had spent all of three months in Denver. He'd left his home to save the world because, apparently, Bloomington, Indiana, didn't need saving.

"A man doesn't need a hip holster to carry a gun," Mace reminded his trainee.

"Right." Furrows creased Brodie's high, sensitive brow. "So what's the plan?"

"We'll wait. See what he turns up."

"Then he *is* on our side," the First-Year concluded eagerly.

Mace snorted.

Brodie's scrupulously shaved face turned crimson. "I just thought, maybe, since he offered to help us out, you'd want to retract your complaint," he whispered uneasily. "You know. About that *special commission.*"

"Hell no." Mace's lip curled as he tossed aside his stogie. Brodie had read too many penny dreadfuls, touting the courage, honor, and invincibility of Rangers. "This isn't Texas. And I'm not a fool, like Rexford Sterne."

Sadie lay muttering in her bed, plagued by a recurring dream with a frightening new twist.

"Sing the fairy song, Sadie!" Maisy called, blowing dandelion seeds on the wind.

Mama had told them to hike to the riverbank, a half-mile from their east Texas home. She'd given Maisy and Sadie strict orders not to return until their wicker basket was full of blackberries. At the rate they were going, that would be midnight. Maisy, the perennial dreamer, was hunting for daisies to fashion a circlet for her flame-red head, and Sadie was shoving a berry in her mouth for every two she picked.

She set down the basket in a shady patch of grasses, beneath a grand old cypress tree. Hiking her stained pinafore, she curtsied before her older twin and belted out a spring song. Maisy joined in the second verse, which was her favorite part:

> *"The fairies spread their sil'vry wings*
> *To shower love on earthly things,*
> *The dewy grass, the fragrant flowers*
> *Bloom with beauty from fey powers…"*

Laughing, Maisy twirled around, losing a blizzard of dandelion seeds. An errant gust of wind snatched the bonnet off her head. Giving chase, the innocent fluttered her arms like make-believe wings.

That's when Sadie noticed the stranger.

Ageless and timeless, with a pale face that somehow resisted the heat, the man stood on the riverbank, silhouetted against the sun. Despite the mid-day hour, he'd dressed in immaculate evening attire, from his gleaming silk top hat to his dove gray gloves and polished opera pumps. He wasn't overtly threatening as he leaned upon his walking stick, but Sadie sensed something about him wasn't right. For one thing, the wind didn't riffle his long swallowtails or slicked back hair. For another, his eyes were black. All black.

Laughing and leaping, Maisy was too busy pretending to be a fairy in flight to notice the silent sentinel with the creepy eyes. When her bonnet tumbled past his shoes, the stranger didn't lift a finger to fetch it. Nor did he call a warning about the rushing river, like other adults would have done.

"Let the bonnet go," Sadie called uneasily. "You can wear mine!"

"But Mama will be angry," Maisy said, swooping for the fluttering muslin.

That's when the unthinkable happened. Maisy slid in the mud and rolled down the bank. The sound of her splash was like an alpine blast to Sadie's soul.

Desperately, she hiked her skirts and ran after her sister. But the horrible, black-eyed man raised his palm. A cypress root snaked out of the ground, snagging Sadie's ankle. She struggled against the evil cypress tree as the relentless current swept Maisy further and further away in a bubbling froth of green dye. Sadie screamed and screamed Maisy's name until she grew too hoarse to squeak. But Maisy's precious, red head never surfaced again.

Sobbing, Sadie turned helplessly to the man, who could only have been the Angel of Death. In his arms, he held a freckled, curly-haired child—a child wearing a circlet of daisies and shining angel wings. Smiling her ethereal smile, Maisy blew Sadie a kiss with a dimpled hand.

"Maisy, don't leave me!"

"I'll always watch over you, sister."

Suddenly, the sky grew dark, and the wind began to keen. Maisy disappeared with the stranger. In their place appeared another muslin bonnet, burning black eyes, and an enormous, wooden cross.

"Beware the devil's tune," Rebekah intoned in a voice like crashing thunder. *"Or marked for death you will be..."*

Sadie gasped and jerked awake. Daylight was edging across her pillow. She sucked down great gulps of air, trying to sooth the erratic speeding of her heart. Her limbs were shaking. Her skin was clammy.

Thank God. It was only a dream.

Turning her head to check the clock, she came face to face with black eyes and a furry snout. She nearly shrieked.

"Son of a—"

Vandy whuffed affectionately and snuggled against her breasts.

Sadie scowled. The coon had been sleeping on his side, his head resting on her pillow. Tucked under his jaw was his right hind leg, which had been bandaged in what looked suspiciously like a piece of her other pillowcase.

"Who let you in?"

Vandy's tail flopped possessively over her bare arm. He yawned, revealing formidable fangs. The stench of carrion wafted over her face.

"Is that a flea on my quilt? So help me God, that had better not be a flea!"

Vandy licked her nose.

I'm going to kill that kid.

A jaunty rap rattled her door. "Room service!"

Sadie's eyes narrowed suspiciously. Throwing back the quilt, she rolled off the other side of the bed, grabbed her .32 from the nightstand, and snatched a black satin robe from the post.

"I didn't order room service!"

"Compliments of the fine gentleman," insisted that muffled, male voice from the hall.

Fine gentleman? Sadie's heart quickened. *Did he mean Dante?*

Hastily tying her belt, she padded on bare feet to the door. When she cracked it open, she spied a mahogany-skinned bellhop in blue hotel livery. He was accompanied by a linen-draped cart with a silver-domed serving dish. He looked legitimate. Slipping her pistol into a pocket, but keeping her thumb on the hammer, she pulled the door wider.

That's when she spied Lucifire, leaning against the wall in his trademark Stetson, black shirt and chaps.

"Mornin', Sunshine," he drawled.

The bellhop had already wheeled the cart's front wheels across the threshold; otherwise, she would have slammed the door in Cass's face.

"I'll take it from here," he told the kid with a wink.

The bellhop grinned and caught Cass's coin before retreating for the elevator.

Sadie seethed, and not just because her ex-lover had hoodwinked her again. At 6:45 a.m., after a restless night, her hair resembled an exploded mop, and the rings beneath her eyes made her look like Vandy's next-of-kin.

By comparison, Cass's wind-riffled ruggedness lent him a mouth-watering, outdoorsy appeal that made her private parts twitch. His eyes were as stunning as polished sapphires set in a face that the sun had baked to honey-colored amber. His grin was a slash of pure mischief in his closely cropped beard. She wanted to smack him for his disgusting cheerfulness.

"I should have told the bellhop you smuggled a *fleabag* into the penthouse," she grumbled.

He pushed the cart into the room. "Is that any way to talk about a hero?"

Vandy had been busily scratching his ear beneath the quilt. Now he popped his head out from his goose-down igloo and licked his chops.

"I brought all your breakfast favorites," Cass said.

"If you think a plate of gingerbread can excuse you for—"

"I wasn't talking to you," he interrupted loftily. He raised the platter's sterling dome to reveal a smelly, dead trout, an apple wedge smeared with peanut butter, a saucer heaped with pumpkin guts, and a pile of shelled pecans. At the center of the tray was a crystal bowl brimming with water. "A feast fit for a king!"

Vandy wriggled enthusiastically and barked.

Sadie wrinkled her nose. She wondered if it was too late to shout for the bellhop to remove the stinking travesty— and Cass along with it.

"All right," she bit out. "You've had your fun. Now get out."

"What, no chit-chat? No foreplay?"

"I have a gun. Don't make me use it."

He chuckled, lowering the platter to the carpet. Vandy hopped off the bed—favoring his leg—and promptly made a mess of things, tracking peanut butter and pumpkin guts across the pile.

"Aw. Look how tidy the little tyke is," Cass crooned without a hint of irony. "He's washing his paws."

"That's not all that needs washing," Sadie groused. "Collie had better clean this slop up. That kid has a lot of nerve, picking my lock in the middle of the night and stealing my pillowcase for a bandage."

"Now Sadie, the boy only has two shirts. And you have four pillowcases."

"That's not the point!"

"Yeah? Then what is the point, detective? That a beardless pup sneaked inside your bedroom while you were sleeping? And if he can do it, Maestro can?"

Humiliation burned its way up Sadie's neck. As loath as she was to admit it, Cass's argument was sound. A bad dream was no excuse for letting down her guard. However, she wasn't about to concede her failing. An army of inquisitors couldn't make her give Cass that pleasure!

"Oh, I get it," she said snidely. "I'm supposed to fear Maestro will murder me in my sleep. Well, your plan isn't working, Rutter. You've used up all your free sex tokens for my bed."

"Aw, don't be that way. We're on the same team now. I talked with your field boss."

"You did *what?!*"

"I convinced him how much he needs me. *Contessas* can't snoop around the Underground, after all."

Sadie quailed to think of Cass exposing himself to a bloodhound like Mace. There was a saying in the Agency. *'Don't piss off Mace Ryker. He's got a long memory and an even longer arm.'*

"My God, do you have a death wish? After you slandered him all over Galveston, word got back to Chicago. He was called to headquarters for a drubbing. Sledgehammer doesn't forgive—"

"You mean Mace?"

Sadie blinked, momentarily derailed from her tirade. *Dammit! Did I just blow Mace's cover?*

Cass smiled cherubically. "Rangers know how to investigate with telegrams too, sweets."

"Don't call me that!"

"Sorry, sugar."

Sadie's chest heaved. This was bad. This was *really* bad...

"If this mission goes south because of something Mace can pin on you—"

Cass snorted. "No tin-star has ever pinned anything on me."

"That's because you never tangled with *Pinkertons!* You have no idea what you're up against. God help you if you squeal, because if harm should come to Mace—"

"Whoa. Slow down. You think Mace is your *friend?* I got news for you, sweetheart. Mace sold you out. He tried to make me believe you fingered me as Daredevil. Then he went and admitted he wants you out of the agency."

Sadie ground her teeth. She didn't doubt the last part of Cass's story. Mace had never minced words in his reports about her "unsuitability" for field work. As proof that she couldn't keep a cover, he'd blamed her for the fire that had razed the Satin Siren, during their investigation of a corrupt Texas senator.

"If Mace had his way, all Pinkies would have their badges revoked," she said grimly. "He thinks women are liabilities in the field."

"And Minx proved him right."

"Don't you *dare* presume that! Especially about me!"

Cass raised his palms in conciliation. "All right, Tiger. Sheath your claws. Let's take a deep breath and start over. This conversation clearly got off on the wrong foot."

Stooping, he rummaged under the cart's linen drape. Clattering and clanging ensued. A few moments later, he finally emerged with another covered plate.

"Do you know how hard it is to find blueberries in this town?"

"It's snowing," she said uncharitably. "What did you expect?"

"Well, you can't have blueberry pie without blueberries. I think there's a law about that somewhere. Even in Colorado." With a grin, he swept off the plate's sterling dome. *"Tah-dah!"*

She looked suspiciously at a tin heaped at least six inches high with mounds of whipping cream. "I don't see any blueberries."

"That's 'cause you're looking in the wrong place." Thrusting a finger into the dessert, he shoveled cream into his mouth and wiggled his eyebrows suggestively. "To find the little rascals, you're gonna have to undress me."

If she hadn't been so hurt—and angry—she might have been amused by his game. Their long history of "whipping cream wars" had begun in Dodge, when she'd been suffering one of her perennial diets to fit into a slinky, fishtail stage costume. He'd brought her a lavish dessert; she'd thrown it at his head; and they'd spent the next half hour scraping goo off the wall and smearing it on each other's private parts.

She sighed at the memory. "You'd better leave."

"That doesn't sound better for anybody."

"Don't push your luck, smartass. I woke with a very itchy trigger finger."

He *tsked.* "Sounds like drastic methods of persuasion are required. Fortunately, I have just the thing."

He stooped again. More clanging and clanking echoed in the mysterious depths of the serving trolley. Finally, he emerged from the linen tent with a rectangular black box. Careful not to disturb the turquoise bow that partially obscured the lid, he set the present next to the pie.

She hiked her chin. "And what's *that* supposed to be? A guilt gift?"

He smiled pleasantly and ignored the bait. "A music box. To replace the one I borrowed."

Borrowed, my ass.

"Take it back." She folded her arms across her chest. "I don't want it."

"Then maybe you could send it to Minx's folks. The original box belonged to her, right?"

Sadie was secretly impressed by his deduction. By the time she'd arrived in Denver, Minx's personal belongings had been packed by Brodie, who'd catalogued every item in painstaking detail, right down to the missing glove that Tabor had eventually found in his wall safe. The only item Brodie hadn't been able to match against Minx's expense reports had been a black music box with a striking, enamel peacock. Mace had given the novelty to Sadie with the instructions, *"Find out where this came from."*

Her best guess had been the Sears & Roebuck catalogue. But Sadie knew better than to report such an obvious conclusion. Mace wanted her to dig into the box's significance, and he wouldn't settle for a hunch. Facts were the only things Mace cared about.

'So why would Minx buy herself a music box?' Sadie mused privately. While Pinkies were on assignment, they

were under orders not to introduce into their lodgings any item that might broadcast personal preferences, which could be used against them.

As if guessing her thoughts, Cass said, "A fence told me Maestro favors musical novelties. He's supposed to be interested in one of the Italian humidors that Rothschild's is auctioning."

Sadie's eyes narrowed in speculation. "Minx asked questions about Maestro around the opera house. She was fraternizing with a violinist. Maybe she was on to something."

"Well, *you* can't ask questions around the opera house. Not with those golden eyes and that fake Italian accent. Dolce LaRocca will expose you as a fraud."

"I'm perfectly aware of that," she snapped.

"Good thing I have a plan, huh?"

"You have a plan?"

"Yep." Cass was grinning from ear to ear.

"Do I want to hear this plan?"

"Probably not."

"Is *Daredevil* involved?"

"Like I said." Cass's wink was roguish. "You're better off not knowing. That way, you won't have to lie to that big-knuckled gorilla you work for."

She exhaled in exasperation. "Detective work isn't a game, Cass. Real people in this case have lost their property and their *lives*. Maestro needs to be stopped."

"That's what I aim to do. Stop Maestro."

"How?"

"You'll have to trust me."

"Trust you? After the stunt you pulled?"

"Okay. Bad choice of words. But—"

"Don't try to placate me!"

"Have it your way. Would you rather I hogtie you? Or kiss you into submission?"

She was seriously tempted to bean him with the pie lid. "If you try either of those tactics, Rutter, your new nickname will be Eunuch Bill."

He laughed.

"You think that's funny?"

"Look. I get it, Sadie. You're still pissed at me, but—"

"No, *buts!* What you did was cruel and childish. More than that, it was *unconscionable!* Dante Goddard would never treat a woman that way. Even Mace wouldn't treat a woman that way! And you know why? Because Dante and Mace are *gentlemen!* You're little better than a rutting hooligan!"

A dark stain crept up Cass's neck.

"In case you're forgetting," he retorted, "Doctor La-Di-Da didn't run into the alley to take a bullet for you last night. And neither did Agent Knuckle-Dragger. I was the one who had your back at Mattie's place."

"Oh. I'm sorry. Did my damsel-in-distress routine interrupt your *orgy?*"

"No," he bit out in gravelly tones, "I was looking for Minx's killer, the same as you."

"Do you really expect me to believe that? To believe anything you say? You betrayed me with a Judas Kiss!"

Her voice broke. To her utter mortification, a tear slipped past her lashes.

He swallowed hard.

"Sadie." He looked considerably paler now. "You have to understand. I've been crazy worried about you! No lawman worth his salt would expect a woman to act as bait in a murder investigation. Pinkerton put you in real danger! When you wouldn't listen to reason, I had to do something to make you see sense—"

"You succeeded," she interrupted bitterly. "You opened my eyes. Now get out."

She turned away. She couldn't bear to look at him. Against all her warnings, all her counseling, her heart had lowered its defenses. It had dared to trust him in a way it had never trusted a man before. For that immeasurable act of bravery, her heart had been crushed—not once. Not twice. But *three times*.

Cass had left her as an adolescent in Texas, and again, at the age of 21 in Kansas. Still, the pain she'd suffered those times had been possible to rationalize, mostly. He'd been running from the law. She'd been indentured to white slavers. He couldn't afford to buy her brothel contract, and if he had helped her escape, the greatest kindness the bounty hunters would have dealt him was a swift death.

But in Denver? When he'd planted that Judas Kiss? He'd jeopardized an aging whore's last hope of keeping a roof over her head. He never planned to marry her; they both knew that. Otherwise, he wouldn't have accepted a Ranger commission. Cass could offer her nothing but excuses and farewells. He didn't have any right to tell her how to earn a living!

"I can't forgive what you did, Cass."

A moment passed. An eternal, aching moment filled with a deafening silence.

"Ever?"

She didn't trust herself to answer. She heard the creak of leather chaps. She smelled the spice of clove tobacco and his favorite sandalwood soap. He stepped close behind her. The heat of his palm hovered over her shoulder, hesitating. Waiting for some sign of capitulation, perhaps? She squeezed her eyes closed. When his skin finally connected with hers, she winced.

"Please go," she whispered hoarsely.

Vandy whined. The sound was plaintive and worried as he pressed against her shins.

At long last, Cass obliged. Her bedroom door swung closed with a lonely, hollow click.

CHAPTER 10

S adie kept telling herself she'd be better off if she forgot she'd ever met Cass. But the scoundrel wasn't making it easy. The next day, she found an arrangement of chrysanthemums and a bottle of perfume outside her door. The following day, she found a sterling breakfast platter, heaped with gingerbread, blueberry muffins, and French lavender soap. The next evening, a rollicking raccoon scrambled through her window, his collar sporting a new gold chain to replace the one she'd tossed into the snow. Vandy was also carrying a love poem. The rhyme was a reprise of her *Ballad of Lucifire*. Cass had penned:

> *"Lucifire they call him,*
> *His heart is broke to bits*
> *Because the Devil's Siren,*
> *Continues to resist.*
> *The riches of his kingdom,*
> *Are nothing more than Hell,*
> *'Cause Sadie won't forgive him–*
> *Doesn't want him*
> *Doesn't need him;*
> *'Cause his Sadie cannot love him,*
> *He is ash inside a shell."*

Hardening her heart, she crumpled the poem and tossed it in the hearth. Vandy galloped merrily after the paper ball and retrieved it from the grate.

She scowled. "I'm not playing fetch!"

He dropped the poem at her feet and blinked expectantly at her.

She pointed sternly at the window. "Go home!"

The varmint flopped on his back, kicked his paws in the air, and tossed her a furry grin.

"I am *not* feeding you!"

Rolling on his belly, Vandy wriggled closer and licked the toe of her slipper.

She sighed. *I think I'm losing this battle.*

But Sadie forced herself to ignore her traitorous female impulses. Yes, she secretly missed Cass's teasing quips and playful seductions. But she couldn't let the yawning emptiness of her bed tempt her to call him to her arms. Her lover had put her mission at risk. Right now, finding Minx's killer had to take priority over erotic love-making with Cass.

So the next morning, Sadie dressed for battle. She boosted her breasts. She primped and perfumed. She donned a form-fitting gown that was only one shade darker than her stunning, golden tiger eyes. With Mace's topaz glittering from the deep recesses of her décolletage, her appearance was guaranteed to make men drool.

Today, by God, I'm going to meet Enoch Fowler.

But when the elevator doors rolled open in the lobby, Sadie was arrested by the sound of a haunting melody. She recognized the tune: it was a lover's lament. The ballad had been popular several years ago. In fact, she used to sing the song by request for lonely cowboys, who'd come to drown their sorrows at Dodge City's Long Branch Saloon:

> *"In moonlit dreams, I called thee mine,*
> *A silv'ry fey, who charmed my heart..."*

She strained her ears above the normal, lobby hubbub of rattling luggage carts, dinging counter bells, and murmuring voices. The mechanical plinking of the melody led her to the tobacco shop. Curious, she hid behind a life-sized, wooden Indian to peek inside the store. She spied Mendel Baines, his face unpleasantly bruised and swollen—probably from his tussle with the bellhops. Sighing soulfully, he stood over an ivory humidor. The cigar box was playing the music.

Sadie frowned. Why on earth had the hotel doorman let Baines back inside the building?

The answer to Sadie's question rustled forward, wearing a scarlet-silk walking dress and an exquisite parure of rubies and pearls.

"Do you like it?" Wyntir asked like an eager-to-please child. "Oh, please let me buy it for you, professor. It's the very least I can do after your brilliant suggestion to play Mama's music box so I could fall sleep. Not even Dante could cure my night terrors. That lullaby saved my life!"

Sadie's eyes narrowed speculatively. So Wyntir was still consulting with Baines behind Dante's back? And Baines was prescribing music-box therapy?

A sudden, unnerving possibility occurred to Sadie. Maybe Baines had given Minx the peacock jewelry box. Maybe he'd hypnotized her, and that innocuous-looking novelty had been the trigger!

Sadie shivered to think that music—something that brought her so much joy—could be perverted to serve a madman's scheme to kill. The music-box theory would certainly explain why Minx had stolen the Heart of Fire and jumped off the 19th Street bridge!

Baines, meanwhile, was blushing under his bruises. "I shall return your loan at the earliest opportunity, Miss Greyfell."

"Oh, no. You mustn't! The humidor is my gift."

An accusatory *eh-hem* sounded behind Sadie. Flushing with guilt, she turned and saw Rebekah, who'd sneaked up on her. The adolescent was wearing her Puritan stage costume and her usual, gargoyle's scowl.

Sadie tamped down irritation. *"Si?"* she demanded.

Rebekah snorted. "That's your problem. You *don't* see."

Insolent pup.

"But you are speaking of the spirits, yes? " Sadie rallied in woeful tones. "The angels who advise your papa? That is why I wish to consult with him. To communicate with my dear, departed Luigi."

Rebekah didn't look the least bit sympathetic. "Wyntir is my friend. I won't let you hurt her. Or Papa, either."

Sadie's brow furrowed. "But why on earth would you think—"

Raised voices were coming from the tobacco shop now. Distracted by the argument, Sadie peeked inside. Wyntir was biting her lip and wringing her hands. Baines was clenching his fists and turning florid. Before him stood a tall, broad-shouldered man in a black frockcoat and a white cleric's collar.

"I assure you, professor," Fowler was saying in his resonant, soothsayer's voice, "you *don't* want this humidor. And you mustn't let Miss Greyfell buy it for you."

"I don't recall asking for your advice!"

"You misunderstand, professor. The advice isn't from me. The *spirits* are urging you to remove all musical novelties from your residence."

"The spirits, huh?" Baines curled his lip. "No doubt the spirits also told you this humidor is one-of-a-kind, and you won't be able to buy another one like it in the city."

"That is not the point, my good fellow—"

"Listen here, you crackpot. What Miss Greyfell does with her money is none of your business." Baines snatched a brown-papered bundle, wrapped in twine, from the hands of the nervous tobacconist. "I suggest you and your demons return to the hellbroth that spawned you!"

Rebekah sucked in an outraged breath. Like an avenging angel, she swept into the tobacco shop.

"Mendel Baines, you are a wastrel, a dullard, and a swine!" she bellowed in her Emmanuel voice.

"Rebekah," Fowler chided mildly. "Come, daughter." He held out his hand. "Professor Baines has been quite clear. He does not wish to hear the word of God."

"You *both* should be locked in a padded cell," Baines flung back. "Forgive my outburst, Miss Greyfell, but I can't be responsible for my behavior if I hear another word about *God* from these two hucksters. Good day!" Baines stalked out of the store with the package under his arm.

Wyntir's face puckered. She looked on the verge of tears.

"There, there," Fowler soothed, patting her gloved hand. "You mustn't let that crass, uncivilized man disturb your peace. You were doing a charitable act, motivated by self- less kindness. The spirits know your heart is true."

A muscle ticked in Sadie's jaw. Like Baines, she couldn't tolerate much more of Fowler's pretentious posturing as a heavenly messenger. Deciding to rescue Wyntir from the charlatan's clutches, Sadie strolled through the door.

"Oh mio dio," she greeted lightly. "So much noise for such a small shop."

"Oh, Fiore," Wyntir sniffled, tugging a handkerchief from her reticule. "I am so glad you're here. The most awful thing has happened—"

"She knows," Rebekah said tartly. "She was eavesdropping outside the door, like a great, big *spider.*"

Sadie pasted on a strained smile. *Somebody's backside is in dire need of a paddle.*

"I could not help but overhear an angry gentleman shouting about a cigar box," Sadie agreed smoothly. "You must be Brother Enoch. Permit me to introduce myself. I am Fiore Torchia, the *Contessa di Montaldeo.* I am delighted to make your acquaintance, *signore.* For many days now, I have been trying to schedule a private consultation with you."

Fowler hiked an eyebrow at Rebekah. The adolescent had the good grace to blush.

"I *told* you about her," Rebekah whispered behind her hand. "The little red-haired angel, remember?"

"Ah yes." Fowler flashed his toothy smile. "Did you find what you were looking for on the fourth floor of the hotel, *contessa?*"

Sadie's heart skipped. *He knows I searched his room?* "I'm not sure I understand," she countered warily.

"No matter." His tone was as pleasant as a balmy summer day. "I trust things will become clearer soon. In the meantime, I suggest you consult with your lady friend from the bayou. I believe her insights will prove most valuable when she arrives."

Sadie's eyes narrowed. What did that mean? Was he referring to Wilma? Surely not! Wilma wasn't planning a trip to Denver.

Too spooked to protest, Sadie let Fowler sweep a bow and step past her with a gloating Rebekah.

"Um, Fiore?"

Sadie started. She'd forgotten about Wyntir.

"Would you care to join me for brunch? I hate to eat alone."

Grasping at the shreds of her composure, Sadie smiled. "What a lovely idea, *carina!* I accept your kind invitation."

And you can tell me everything you know about that shyster and his juvenile moll.

Brunch turned into shopping, and shopping led to the requisite stop inside Greyfell Manor for afternoon tea. Wyntir just *had* to have the *contessa's* opinion about her Thanksgiving decorations. The grieving heiress so desperately missed her father that she chirped for 45 minutes about Papa Greyfell's holiday traditions.

Despite her misgivings about the hour, Sadie found herself listening attentively. She ached to recall her own father, Roarke Michelson, whom she'd adored to the point of worship. Before he'd been lynched by the Ku Klux Klan, Daddy and she had developed holiday traditions, too: on Halloween, they would bob for apples; on Thanksgiving, they would break a wishbone; on

Christmas, they would leave a festive wreath on Maisy's grave.

Sadie blinked back tears.

Wyntir tugged a handkerchief from her cuff and sheepishly dabbed her eyes. "You must forgive me for rattling on, Fiore. It's just that you're such good company. And I've so desperately missed talking to a woman…"

Sadie forced a smile. "Not at all, *carina.* I am touched you would open your heart to me."

They sat knee-to-knee on an elegant, horsehair settee, the cooling tea and buttered cinnamon cakes forgotten on the sterling tray that the parlor maid had left on a low, cherry wood table. Dante, who was presumably unaware of her visit, was upstairs in his office, writing patient reports.

"I'm so grateful you're my friend, Fiore. No, *better* than my friend," the lonely young heiress gushed. "You're like the sister I never had! Can I tell you a secret?"

Sadie sighed inwardly and glanced at the mantel's clock. Wyntir's school-girl secrets weren't exactly the intelligence a Pinkerton hoped to wring out of an informant. Sadie was anticipating yet another dreamy recounting of Dante's virtues: How charming he was. How considerate he was. How he cared about lost puppies, stray kittens, and muddy urchins who picked pockets on the street. If one could believe everything Wyntir said, the psychiatrist should be canonized.

"The real reason I went into town today was to meet with Professor Baines," Wyntir confided. "I felt like I owed it to him, after that horrible drubbing he received in the society pages. I mean, Dante *was* partly to blame for the brawl. Thank heavens the reporter didn't mention him by name." Wyntir fidgeted, averting her eyes. "Anyway, I worry about Professor Baines. After the *Rocky* lambasted him as a common ruffian, how can he hope to drum up clients?"

"The *professore* did throw the first punch," Sadie reminded her gently.

Wyntir shook her head. "You don't understand. This whole mess *really* started when Dante made me cancel three months worth of hypnosis appointments. That's when Professor Baines started struggling financially. Can you blame him for resenting Dante?" Wyntir said unhappily. "The professor was kind to me after Papa's death and so…I try to help him out."

"You mean, you loan him money?"

"Oh, no. *Donations.* For his research. He really is quite brilliant. I would go back to him in a heartbeat. I always felt so much peace and contentment after our sessions. But Dante, of course, wouldn't hear of it." Wyntir sighed. "I honestly think Professor Baines could help you, too, Fiore. You've been so brave about the *conte's* death. But surely your heart is hurting. Professor Baines calls it denial."

"Does he indeed?" Sadie struggled with her flare of temper. Wyntir was too tender-hearted for her own good. No wonder Dante forbade her to associate with Baines! "Did the professor ask you to petition me?"

Wyntir looked troubled. "No. No, he didn't. But he did ask me to convey his sincerest apologies. After seeing you with Dante at the hotel, he seems to think you're in need of…counsel.

"Fiore, please don't be angry with me," Wyntir pleaded. "You're my friend. I want you to be happy. I know what it's like to lose someone you love. And Dante is the most wonderful man in the world: compassionate. Caring. Even heroic! I can understand why you might feel drawn to him…um…the way a woman might."

Sadie had no trouble guessing where this seed of suspicion had been planted. She wanted to punch out Baines's other eye.

"Carina, if this professor suggested I behaved improperly—"

"I know you would never want to hurt me. And Dante wouldn't either." Wyntir's eyes were bright with unshed tears. "The truth is, I'm a little jealous." Her laugh was short and hollow. "I mean, you're so clever and confident around men. I feel so dull and inexperienced compared with you. I've hardly traveled anywhere, and certainly not outside the country.

"Papa only approved of me having two gentlemen callers before Dante came along. And I've never even been kissed! I'll be turning 21 in four days, but I can't help but wonder if I'll ever be woman enough for Dante. I don't want him to think of me as a child anymore. Or worse, a helpless invalid!"

"Now why would Dante think that?" Sadie soothed.

Wyntir worried her bottom lip. Glancing nervously toward the parlor entrance, as if she thought someone might be eavesdropping, she lowered her voice. "Ever since Papa's death, I've been waking from dreams— *horrible* dreams!—about shadow figures doing terrible things. Sometimes, my arms are black-and-blue. Sometimes, my legs are bruised. Once, I even had scratches on my neck!"

Sadie's scalp prickled. In light of Wyntir's continued association with Baines, her admission wasn't good news.

"What does the *dottore* make of this?"

"He thinks I'm sleepwalking." Wyntir turned as red as her flawlessly lacquered nails. "He thinks I bump into furniture at night, or I trip and fall. He gave me a sedative, but I don't want to take it. Sedatives make my head fuzzy, and I can't concentrate after I wake up." She began twisting the handkerchief in her lap. "The trouble is, when I don't take the sedative, the nightmares come back. So Dante suggested he sleep with me. To give me comfort and keep me from leaving the bed. But we're not *married!"* Wyntir added in scandalized tones.

"Fiore, you're a woman of the world," the heiress whispered anxiously. "Do you think I'm being silly? I *do* love him. I couldn't live without him. But I want him to feel the same way! If I let him hold me through the night, do you think he might come to love me the way a husband loves a wife?"

Sadie squirmed before the hope in the innocent's sky-blue eyes. She couldn't help but recall the night when she'd lost her own maidenhead. After Pine Grove's townsfolk had learned how the Klan lynched Daddy for being a Yankee spy, she and Mama had become pariahs. Sadie had begged the new Yankee marshal for help, and he'd let them sleep in his hayloft.

Because of the way he looked at her, Mama had predicted he would climb the ladder one night. Mama had tried to explain what to expect from a lover. Sadie had been afraid, but Mama had ordered her to cooperate. They needed a man's protection, Mama had said; they had nowhere else to go. At 13 years old, Sadie had experienced her woman's courses only once before the lawman finally did come to her bedroll, reeking of whiskey and sweat. When he'd started pawing her thighs, she'd thought the pumping and grinding would never end.

A few days later, her "lover" had dumped her and Mama on a brothel doorstep.

Sadie drew a shuddering breath.

"Sleeping with a man will not make him love you," she told Wyntir in a voice made harsh with secret pain. "If you do not wish to take the sedative, then put a cot in your room and hire a lady's maid. Frankly, I'm surprised a gentleman of Dante's caliber didn't suggest the maid himself."

Wyntir winced.

But before the infatuated young heiress could rise to her guardian's defense, the Dobermans started barking in the hall.

The doorbell pealed.

Wyntir's brow furrowed. "Dante must have forgotten he scheduled a patient."

Sadie rose. "Then I should take my leave, *carina.*" *And get Mace to put a tail on you.*

"But I was hoping you'd stay for dinner!"

"Alas, I have an engagement in town."

Wyntir looked disappointed, but she accompanied Sadie to the foyer, where she intercepted the butler and sent him to fetch Sadie's driver.

Standing before a convenient hallway mirror, Sadie took extra time with her hat so she could spy on Dante's visitor. She glimpsed the reflection of a familiar black Stetson bobbing in the window. Wreathed in a cloud of frosty breaths, like an undeserved halo, Lucifire stood waiting on the porch.

Damn you, Cass. Are you following me again?

Wyntir called off the dogs and opened the door. "Mr. Cassidy, what a surprise!"

"Good afternoon, Miss Wyntir." His smoky drawl would have made the angels blush. "You look as pretty as a sunset in that red dress."

Fuming, Sadie hung back in the shadows, watching Cass flash his dimples. She recognized his Schoolboy's Smile, the one he donned to hide his Wolf from unwed innocents. He liked to use other, wickeder grins to charm the bloomers off more experienced prey. But for the moment, he was playacting the gentleman, which meant he was up to no good.

"Those are mighty fine watchdogs," he said, outwardly unperturbed by the show of fangs.

Then again, Sadie mused, *why should Cass worry about dogs?* He never dressed without an arsenal at his command. She had half a mind to warn Wyntir she was flirting with a felon, who was wanted for three counts of stage coach robbery!

"Thank you, Mr. Cassidy. Papa raised them from pups."

"They sure are fond of you." The throbbing caress in his drawl elicited suspicious rumbles from Wyntir's furry bodyguards. "What do you call them?"

The sheltered young heiress was hopelessly out of her league. She squirmed. She giggled. She patted a dog's head.

"This one's Maximus," she said, *shushing* her nearest protector, who sported a black collar. "And the one with the red collar is Brutus."

"So that's how you tell them apart. You must sleep like a baby, knowing they're guarding your bed."

A muscle ticked in Sadie's jaw. The reprobate had needed 20 seconds—*only 20 seconds!*—to work Wyntir's bedroom into the conversation.

But if Wyntir's maidenly sensibilities objected to this scandalous topic, she ignored them.

"Oh no, Mr. Cassidy! My Persian, Tallie, sleeps with me. If the dogs so much as drool on my quilt, Tallie claws their noses! The cat rules the upper story, but the dogs don't mind. They get the kitchen."

Cass chuckled. "I reckon your cook has to guard Doc's steaks with a cleaving knife."

"Maximus and Brutus do tend to get banished at mealtime," Wyntir admitted, blushing prettily. "But I promise, Mr. Cassidy, you're perfectly safe to come inside. Dante gets lots of visitors. Isn't that right?" she called to Sadie.

Sadie made a concerted effort to unclench her fists. Little did Wyntir know, she'd just volunteered enough intelligence to let Cass rob her house.

Drawing upon a nerve she'd honed while glaring down wolf-whistlers from a saloon stage, Sadie strolled into the slanting shafts of afternoon. Cass looked surprised when she rustled into view in her golden walking dress, shot with silver threads and loaded with ivory seed pearls. The gown had cost Alan Pinkerton an amount equal to six months of her salary.

Cass, who was an expert on ladies' clothing—or rather, an expert on *removing* ladies' clothing—grinned appreciatively. She was somewhat mollified to learn she still had the power to swell his crotch, even though he'd come to Greyfell Manor to seduce a younger, far richer beauty.

"Howdy, Lady *Contessa*," he greeted drolly. "You weren't hiding from me, were you?"

"I assure you, *signore*," she lied with practiced indifference, "the thought of you never crossed my mind."

"I reckon the doc must be keeping you busy. You look kinda tuckered out."

She pasted on a catty smile. "You have no idea."

Possessive, gunfighter's eyes raked her from hat to toe. Cass could see a dewdrop on a silver maple leaf at 50 paces. If she really had a love nip or kiss-bruised lips, no amount of face paint or powder could have disguised them.

"Sorry to hear you've been under the weather, ma'am. I was just about to tell Miss Wyntir, here, why I came to call on the doc."

"You suffer delusions of grandeur?"

Amusement flickered over the chiseled planes of his sun-gilded face. "Aw, shucks. I never knew a purtier lady with a jollier sense of humor. But to tell the truth, ma'am, I thought the doc might like his watch back."

Wyntir sucked in her breath. "You found it?"

"Sure did," Cass said, overdoing the braggadocio. He liked his enemies to think he was stupid. "I wrassled that rascally coon for it. Made myself a hat." He winked, hooking his thumbs over his belt buckle. "Tell the doc there's no hard feelings. I'll even cut my finder's fee in half."

"Oh. Um…I see." Wyntir pasted on a smile. "Won't you come in, Mr. Cassidy?"

"Thank you kindly." He hiked an eyebrow at Maximus, who'd begun growling again. "Maybe you should take the dogs to the kitchen, ma'am. They look hungry."

"Yes. Yes, of course. Please make yourself at home. The parlor's that way," she added with a wave of her hand. "Dante! Mr. Cassidy is here! He found your pocket watch."

Sadie shot her ex-lover a withering glare as his brawny shoulders filled the doorway. The long, golden rays of daylight flared around him, limning his shadow-steeped figure in flames.

Somehow, the image was appropriate.

"What the hell are you doing here?" she whispered.

He flashed unrepentant dimples. "Doing a little reconnaissance. Earning a little poker money. If I play my cards right, I'll score dinner too."

"You mean *dessert,*" she accused.

"Well, since you mentioned it—" he reached playfully for a sausage curl, spilling across her bodice "—I do have a hankering for chestnuts."

She slapped his hand away. "Louse."

"Jealous?"

"Not in the least. I'll leave the spitting and clawing to Tallie."

"I'm not worried. Pussies like me."

She was sorely tempted to punch out his lights, but she was distracted by the creaking of an overhead timber. Dante appeared on the landing, tall and regal in his impeccably tailored broadcloth. A moment passed as his dark eyes rested on her. Then he sized up his visitor.

"Mr. Cassidy." Something akin to martyrdom twisted Dante's handsome features. He began to descend. "We meet again."

"Today's your lucky day, Doc."

"Indeed." Dante paused at the foot of the stairs and lavished a heart-tripping smile on her. *"Contessa."* He raised her glove to his lips. "Always a pleasure. You are staying for dinner, of course."

Sadie felt, rather than saw, Cass stiffen. As much as she would have liked to encourage Dante's flirtation and watch Cass stew, the risk to her cover was too great—especially with Cass's unleashed mouth on the premises.

"You are most kind, *dottore.* Perhaps another time. I have an engagement in town."

"Disappointing. But you will allow me the opportunity to catch up at the opera next Thursday."

"I shall count the hours, *carino,"* she purred, mostly to piss off Cass. She just wished she could be confident that Wyntir's love for Dante would make the younger woman immune to Cass's Coyote Charm.

With a cool nod to her lover—*ex-lover,* Sadie reminded herself harshly—she gathered her skirts and marched down the steps to her rented cab.

As the coach bounced over the frozen ruts in the road, she gazed out the western window and pondered the next step in her mission. Her day with Wyntir had given her a great deal to think about.

At first, Sadie had been eager to pump the younger woman for information about Fowler. But Wyntir was better acquainted with Rebekah, who, apparently, had been the preacher's ward for six months. According to Wyntir, Fowler had adopted the catatonic Rebekah from an asylum because "her lost and grieving spirit had come to him in a dream, begging for help."

Honestly, how could Wyntir believe such rubbish?

Sadie supposed she could get Brodie to make a few discreet inquiries, via telegraph, to uncover the truth. But even if Fowler *had* adopted Rebekah after her parents died in a fire, his motivation had surely been to make a fortune from her mental instability. Sadie refused to believe Fowler was "a messenger of angels," as Wyntir professed him to be. To Sadie's way of thinking, Fowler was a wolf, and Wyntir was hopelessly gullible.

Despite her private misgivings about Fowler, however, Sadie was beginning to think Baines was the more likely Maestro suspect—especially after she'd seen him drooling over that musical humidor.

But the biggest strike against Baines was Wyntir's confession that she'd been donating money to his research. Knowing what Sadie now knew about the professor's shady past, she deduced that he'd hypnotized Wyntir to be his cash cow, and worse, that he'd induced her to do other things against her will, as evidenced by the bruises she couldn't explain.

Now all Sadie had to do was prove Baines had been responsible for Minx's death. Unfortunately, that task was going to be easier said than done. But Sadie had been fortunate in one respect. She'd tracked down the lead given to her by Mattie Silks. Disguising herself as an elderly "worried aunt," Sadie had snooped around Tabor's Grand Opera House, learning that the First Violinist had, indeed, been smitten by the Leadville reporter, "Claudia Dunlap." When he'd described this Claudia's appearance, he'd described Minx—right down to the tiny gap between her front teeth.

"Naw, I didn't give your niece a music box," the violinist said sheepishly. "To tell the truth, ma'am, I think she was sweet on some other guy. She never mentioned him by name, but she was always busy in the evenings. I figured he made her a better offer the night she didn't show up for our dinner appointment. Sorry I couldn't be more helpful, but your niece seemed chummy with that high-society miss, Wyntir Greyfell. Maybe you should pay her a call."

Strangely enough, Wyntir had no recollection of Minx. When the undercover Pinkie had called at Greyfell Manor to consult with Dante, surely Wyntir would have been curious about her. The two women were similarly aged. Wyntir was heart-breakingly lonely. Minx would have had no trouble earning Wyntir's trust. And yet, Wyntir had blinked blankly at Sadie when she'd described Claudia Dunlap.

Did Baines hypnotize Wyntir to forget Minx?

A nasty bump in the road jolted Sadie from her musings. She grabbed the leather strap above her head to keep from bouncing off the seat.

The day star was dipping behind the mountains, setting the sky aflame with streaks of tangerine and gold. She shivered, glad for the warmth of the brazier. She still wasn't used to the rapid drop in temperature when night enveloped the plains. She was looking forward to a stiff drink before she had to report to Mace.

Suddenly, her ears pricked to the sound of pounding hooves. A horse was gaining on the cab. She heard the driver call out. Masculine laughter followed. Warily, she let her .32 slide into her palm even as a puff of steam fogged her window. Moments later, the nose of a laboring buckskin bobbed into view, followed by a familiar, black Stetson and a cocksure grin.

Cass waved at her.

She flipped him off.

He blew her a kiss.

She yanked the shade over the window and holstered her gun.

In the next instant, the door banged open, Cass vaulted inside, and Pancake veered away from the cab.

"Are you insane?!" she shouted as he slammed the door. "You could have been killed!"

The scoundrel's eyes were bright with mischief. They gleamed like the Ranger star he'd pinned to his vest.

"Naw." He was crouching on the bucking floorboards, riding them as effortlessly as he'd ridden his gelding. "Me and Pancake chase down runaway coaches all the time."

She groaned. "Remind me to put that epitaph on your tombstone. Right under the code name, 'Screw Up.'"

"I like the screwing part."

"You would."

"'Sides. Your naughty middle finger invited me inside."

"*No* part of me invited you inside."

"*Challenge accepted!*" he cried like P.T. Barnum's ringmaster. He plunked his derriere on her seat.

"Why don't you go back to Mattie's," she said testily, "and stop harassing decent, sophisticated gentlemen in their homes?"

Cass snorted. "Decent my ass. Beans made Wyntir write the bank draft for my $200 finder's fee."

"*Two-hundred dollars!* That pocket watch was barely worth $20!"

"You can't put a price on sentimental value."

Sadie shot him a withering glare. "No wonder Dante gave you a bank draft. He was hoping some teller would recognize you on a Wanted Poster."

"It takes a crook to know a crook."

"As far as I can see, Dante's only crime has been his kindness to me!"

A muscle ticked in Cass's jaw.

He sidled closer. "Making up is fun, huh?"

"Go away."

"You'd miss me."

"Are you kidding? I can't seem to get rid of you."

"That's 'cause you and I go together," he crooned. "Like sarsaparilla and fizz."

"More like dynamite and a fuse."

"I don't mind." His grin turned wolfish. "I like when your eyes get all fiery with silvery sparks."

Irritably, she pushed his prowling paw off her thigh. "You must be confusing me with some other woman."

"Never."

She retreated as far as the cab's narrow confines would allow. "For your information, my eyes don't have silvery sparks."

"Sure they do. Like a zillion miniature stars, all orbiting the sun. They get glittery, like diamonds, when your volcano heats up."

She felt the tingling flush of lust as he stalked her across the red-leather cushions. He smelled like wind and leather, mountain and sandalwood. The fact that he was right, and she was starting to cream, only made her more irritated, mostly at herself.

"Think right highly of yourself, do you?"

"I *am* the Rebel Rutter," he said shamelessly. "Which reminds me. Why don't you pull down that shade while you're over there?"

"Hell no."

"How come?"

"'Cause you want me to."

"Then I don't want you to hike your skirts. Or sit in my lap. Or ride me like a demon tornado till you rain fire on my thighs."

"You think I'm an idiot?"

"Naw. I think you're hotter than the devil's pitchfork."

"Which is why you're bird-dogging a 20-year-old heiress?"

His dimples peeked. "See that? You *are* jealous."

"Dream on," she said loftily.

"I do. Every night. Of you, in all your freckled glory."

"Apparently, you used your best lies in your poems."

When he reached for her curl, she tried a Judo move to numb his wrist. He deftly snared her hand, rubbing her fingers over his beard, pressing wet kisses into her palm.

"You want to start picking your teeth off the floor?" she growled.

He chuckled, biting the mound below her thumb.

"Ow!"

"Sissy."

"That does it, Cassidy."

She took a swing at his nose, but he blocked her jab, seizing her forearm. Her struggles made her toque hat tip, plunking to her nose. She cursed, wasting precious seconds to shake off the hat. He took full advantage of her blindness, stretching her wrists above her. An ominous jingle sounded over her head.

"Cass! Don't you dare!"

She aimed a kick at his crotch, but the force of her blow was dampened by the wad of muslin, lace, and seed pearls sheathing her legs. He pinned her hips with his greater weight. The next thing she knew, furry bracelets snapped around her wrists. She was bound to the leather strap.

"You didn't think I forgot the train, did you, detective?"

She sputtered every expletive she could think of. He gave her a naughty wink, sliding the handcuffs' key into his vest pocket—ironically, the one where he'd pinned his Ranger badge. Then he drew the shade of the eastern window. Midnight-blue shadows slid across his devious grin.

"Comfy?" he asked, removing his Stetson.

"Paybacks are a bitch," she menaced.

"They sure are."

He made short work of the buttons on her bodice and the hooks on her corset. His fingertips were callused but warm as they dipped boldly beneath the lacy cotton of her chemise. Her traitorous nipples hardened, all too eager to jut into his palm.

His breaths tickled her ear. "What do you dream of, *Contessa?*"

"Nooses." She hated how her skin shivered in a mixture of anticipation and delight as he massaged her thighs. "With your name on them."

"Liar. I bet you dream of great big, Italian pepperonis."

"Then you'll lose every cent."

He chuckled. The velvet depths of his eyes glowed red, mirroring the coals in the brassier. Lucifire lurked in that wicked gaze, and her temperature raised another notch. She licked her lips.

"You want to know a secret?" he whispered, flicking his tongue inside her ear.

She tried to jerk her head away, but he tangled a fist in her hair.

"Let me guess." She sounded much too breathy for a woman who was supposed to deplore the man who'd betrayed her. "You kiss that Ranger badge every night before you fall sleep."

"Nope."

"You kneel before it and chant prayers?"

"When have you ever known me to kneel for anything?"

A knife twisted in her chest as she thought of the marriage proposal he would never give. "A little humility wouldn't hurt you. Especially when it comes to guns."

"Fess up. You *like* my gun."

With his free hand, he pushed her skirts all the way up her thighs. She gasped as the chill of the Colorado twilight rushed past the slit in her bloomers.

"I don't think we're talking about the same thing," she rallied desperately, her exposed places throbbing with renewed sensitivity.

He nuzzled the corner of her mouth. "We were talking about my gun. And how you downright worship it."

"Like I said. You suffer from delusions—"

She bit back a tiny mew of pleasure as his forefinger snaked past the petals of her femininity.

"You're so wet," he said, supremely smug.

She writhed, and he tipped her hips, wedging her thighs wider for his love play. Her struggles were futile. To make matters worse, they started to resemble an age-old rhythm.

"You like that, huh?"

"I hate you!"

"Not *all* of you hates me."

"Yeah? Well, just because you think you can make me come—"

"Who said anything about coming?" he taunted silkily.

He tormented her with catlike finesse, stoking her volcano, fanning her need until she fairly dripped with lava. She was panting. He was grinning. And all the while, she teetered on the edge of the bouncing seat, her wrists twisting futilely to break her bonds, her thighs shaking in their obstinate pride not to wrap his waist as her anchor.

"Why must you be so ornery?" he whispered.

It was a rhetorical question, because his tongue began fencing with hers. She sucked him deep into her mouth, and he growled. She heard the chinking of metal from somewhere near his waist. Erotic images tantalized her as only his dancing, darting fingers could. She imagined the glint of moonlight on his uncinched buckle; the tawny man hairs springing through the buttonholes of his fly; the swollen phallus jutting so proudly toward its slick and steamy goal. Her nostrils flared to the delicious scent of sex—*his* sex—for even though she would rather swallow her tongue than admit it, she had never wanted another man. Not since their ill-fated love affair four years ago in Dodge.

He rubbed and teased. Half in, half out. The perfect angle, the ideal speed. Thrust after maddening thrust, he kept her dripping, quivering, and aching for more. Her nerves were licked by fire. Her senses threatened to splinter. She stretched, but he broke the rhythm, defying her best attempts to control the game. Never in her life had she wanted a man to ride her harder and faster!

"Was that a whimper?" he taunted huskily.

"Never," she panted.

"Never's a long time, kitten." He climbed behind her, hooking her thighs wider with his calves. "You won't last another five minutes," he teased, his breaths tickling her ear.

She squirmed, but he had the strength of a man who'd busted broncos and hogtied steers. His steely hands gripped her hips, holding them prisoner, hoisting them just high enough so his slick, swollen head could rub her into a renewed frenzy. Her breaths whistled past her teeth. She squeezed her eyes closed to stop the stars from spinning.

"I know what's best for you," he growled. "And someday, you're going to admit it. Even if I have to hogtie you, row you to a prison island, and lock you in a goddamned dungeon to keep you safe!"

Shivers galloped down her spine. Cass rarely turned Dom on her. He knew better: she would spit and claw and bite his ears off—not to mention what she would do to his private parts. She refused to let a John control her. The bedroom was her realm.

But echoes of pleasure from love-games past reverberated through her smoldering core. He'd fanned her fever to a volcanic pitch. Surely if he kept her smoking, she would explode!

"You wouldn't dare," she wheezed, desperately dredging up a shred of defiance.

"Then you don't know me as well as you think," he retorted. "Bend over."

"Go to hell."

"I did. From August to October."

"What are you talking—"

"Bend," he commanded again.

She trembled.

Her traitorous spine yielded.

He rewarded her with deep, plunging strokes that soon had her writhing, moaning, and hating herself for wanting more.

She was all tiger now, all instinct, lust and need. Above her ripping breaths and the primitive sounds that tore from her throat, she barely heard the deep rumble of his confession.

"When you died, I died. I thought I'd failed you. *You.* My woman. Do you know what that was like, day in and day out for three months? *Torture!* It was goddamned torture, Sadie."

Finally, the blissful release came. Only "blissful" was too tame a word to describe the experience. Rapture pounded through her. Ecstasy shattered her mortal restraints. Like a shooting star, she blazed across the cosmos, burning bright enough to rival any sun.

From far away, she heard his vow:

"You will *never* put me through that hell again."

She lost touch with time. One moment, he was wrapped around her, his heart hammering her spine. The next moment, he was crouching before the limp dishrag her body had become. She blinked, trying to see past the rainbows glazing her eyes. A long, wet trail glimmered on his cheek. Her disembodied mind tried to make sense of the sight. Was that a tear? *Cass's* tear?

Surely not.

She was spiraling back to earth now, slamming into the fractured feelings and jumbled sensations that her flesh had become. She groaned. Parts that had burned with pleasure only moments ago now shivered with chill and ached with fatigue.

He was tugging down her skirts. "After we find Minx's killer, I'm taking you home to Sterne."

"Sterne?" she rasped. Her tongue felt like sandpaper against the roof of her mouth. "My God. You still think I'm sleeping with him?"

He winced, averting his eyes. "Sterne is as worried about you as I am."

"Get over it! I can handle myself in the field."

"So you've said. And yet, here you are. Handcuffed inside a cab."

"You set me up! Unlock these manacles. Unlock them *now!"*

"Your Pinkerton days are numbered."

"You have no right," she choked, futilely twisting her wrists. "Crawl back into the slime hole you came from. My life was better—a *helluvalot* better—before you darkened my doorstep! I had friends. *Sophisticated* lovers, damn you!"

He gripped her chin with powerful fingers. He forced her gaze to collide with his. She grew worried, then, that she'd gone too far. The dark intent in that relentless, gunfighter's stare chased goosebumps down her spine.

"Just so we're clear," he said flatly. "If Goddard touches you the way I touched you tonight, I'll kill him."

She quailed. Never had she heard more conviction in Cass's voice.

He unlocked her left arm—the one without the pistol strapped to her forearm—and pressed the key into her hand. Then he kicked open the door and whistled. Pancake magically appeared. The cab hadn't been moving fast; perhaps the gelding had been trotting after the vehicle. In any event, the well-trained cowpony drew abreast of the coach. Cass jumped into the saddle.

Her last glimpse of him, before the door slammed, was of his duster, fluttering like the wings of a fallen angel against the rising moon.

CHAPTER 11

One Week Later

Dolce LaRocca was scheduled to perform before a sell-out crowd of 1,550 Denverites at the Tabor Grand Opera House.

Cass was scheduled to steal her Tiffany reproduction of Mephistopheles's Jewels.

Well, sort of.

Yesterday, he'd secretly conferred with the diva, revealing his scheme to protect her assets. He'd explained how she was in danger from Maestro. He'd insisted that her best protection was to leak to the press some cock-n-bull story about how Daredevil had robbed her of Mephistopheles's Jewels. After Cass turned on the charm and flashed his Texas Ranger badge, Dolce was only too delighted to cooperate. Because she was a foreigner traveling through America, she had no idea his jurisdiction ended north of the Red River.

So kiss my grits, you stinkin' Pinkertons.

In truth, Cass was surprised Mace hadn't approached Dolce with an offer of protection. But then, Mace struck Cass as more of a *Can-Can* enthusiast. And who could blame him? The only reason Cass was attending *Faust* tonight was because he was honor-bound to keep Dolce safe from "dastardly jewel thieves and rapacious theater ruffians," which was how the diva liked to describe them. Dolce was blessed with a vivid imagination.

Cass scanned the lobby crowd for suspicious characters. Just beyond the frost-encrusted windows, his gaze lighted on a carriage that bore the Greyfell coat of arms. Wyntir's driver was jockeying through the chaos of private hacks and neighing horses to secure a parking spot by the curb.

The coach's door swung open. Dressed in all his gentlemanly frou-frou, Goddard stepped into the flurry of great, puffy snowflakes, the red-satin lining of his opera cape swirling around his legs. He waved off a valet and offered a hand to Wyntir, who looked especially scrumptious in midnight-blue silk.

Cass's eyes narrowed when he next glimpsed the twinkle of a tiara inside the coach's dim interior. A moment later, a buxom, chestnut-haired beauty extended her white glove into the glow of street lamps.

Sadie.

Cass drew a restraining breath. Beneath her ivory, feather-trimmed opera cape, she was dressed in slinky black damask, whose ruches winked with extra shimmer, thanks to a coiling pattern of jet seed pearls. When she clasped Goddard's hand, she smiled lusciously into the prig's clean-shaven mug.

All right, prig *may not be entirely accurate,* Cass conceded as he recalled his run-in with the dapper Bostonian three days earlier.

At the time, Cass had been hunting for Boone at the Gentleman's Sporting Club—or more precisely, at its shooting range.

Cass didn't know who'd been more surprised by his chance encounter with the psychiatrist, him or Goddard. Frankly, Cass would never have pictured a fussy, book-learned snob, blasting holes through a bull's eye. But then, Goddard would never have pictured a Texas "exterminator" possessing the pedigree for such a hoity-toity club. The fact that Goddard had pegged him for White Trash made Cass hate him even more.

"You're pretty handy with that popgun," Cass had jeered as Goddard pumped a new round of bullets into his Smith & Wesson. "Practicing to shoot some patients, Doc?"

Goddard's smile was wry. "You do *read*, don't you, Mr. Cassidy? The *Rocky* has been reporting almost daily on the dueling jewel thieves, who've been pillaging mansions along Colfax Avenue and Pennsylvania Street. It's just a matter of time before they strike Greyfell Manor. A man has to be prepared to defend his home."

"You mean Miss Wyntir's home," Cass retorted. "Greyfell Manor belongs to her."

"Not until Saturday. When my ward reaches her majority."

Turning a chilly shoulder, Goddard leveled his revolver at a fresh target. Cass watched the Yankee drill five additional rounds through the bull's eye without blinking. Even so, Cass wasn't impressed. Any Texas toddler could shoot out a knot-hole at 40 paces. Try hitting a penny, flipping end-over-end in the wind. Now that took real skill.

"You sure do shoot straight," Cass said dryly. "I reckon you'll be able to bag yourself a thief, all right—as long as Maestro's the polite type, who stands still and doesn't shoot back."

A dark flush rolled up Goddard's neck. "No doubt you'd like to show me how a gun should be fired, Mr. Cassidy."

"Naw." Cass winked. "I don't have any quarrel with you."

"Just Maestro."

Cass locked stares with the psychiatrist. Despite the bourbon-smooth quality of Goddard's voice, something about his observation grated on Cass's nerves. It felt like a challenge.

"What makes you think I have a quarrel with Maestro?"

"You mentioned him by name."

Cass shrugged, hooking his thumbs over his belt and instantly regretting it. The habit was a dead giveaway to anyone who knew anything about gunfighters.

"I couldn't let you go on thinking I don't know how to read a newspaper," Cass quipped with practiced jocularity.

"No indeed." Goddard's lips twitched. "So tell me, Mr. Cassidy. Where did you and the *contessa* first meet?"

Cass stiffened. He hadn't been prepared for that line of questioning. "Who?"

"Who indeed." Goddard's smile was mocking.

"If you got something to say, Doc, spit it out."

Goddard shrugged. "You strike me as a realist, Mr. Cassidy. A man who knows his place in the world."

"And Italy's a long way from home, is that it?"

"Precisely."

Cass had to dig deep to keep his tone light—and his tongue firmly in check. "A man can dream."

"Then he wouldn't be a realist."

Cass kept smiling through his teeth. "Sounds like you got an uncommon interest in the pretty things Italy has to offer. Like the imported treasures at Rothschild's."

To Cass's disappointment, Goddard didn't rise to the bait. He merely holstered his gun and reached for his bowler.

"We live in such a small world," the psychiatrist said, "thanks to steam ships and railroads. I daresay if a man waits long enough, the very thing he desires can be transported straight to his hands."

Cass's eyes narrowed. He was trying to decide whether that last comment hid a double meaning when Goddard executed a perfunctory bow.

"A pleasant day to you, Mr. Cassidy."

Cass's jaw hardened at the memory. If Goddard really was Maestro, he was too adept at lying to tip his hand. At least, in casual conversation.

That's why Cass was chomping at the bit for Saturday night and Wyntir's birthday party. He wanted to break into Greyfell Manor and search the upper stories. He figured Wyntir's party would give him the perfect opportunity to sneak into the manor.

In the meantime, Cass watched darkly as his rival escorted Sadie and Wyntir through the crowded lobby and into the glittery hubbub of the auditorium.

Sadie didn't bother to look his way.

A knife twisted in Cass's heart. Trying to ignore it, he directed his thoughts back to his quarry.

Yesterday in the newspaper, the contest between Maestro and Daredevil had escalated to the next level. The *Rocky* had printed the following headline:

Maestro Strikes Back!
Master Thief Beats Daredevil to Ruby Parure Valued at
$150K

Flipping eagerly to the classifieds, Cass finally found the challenge he'd been waiting for:

"Dance, Devil. You're playing my tune.
In your case, it's a dirge."

Snorting, Cass promptly dashed off a counter-challenge so Boone could print it in the classifieds:

"Mess with Mephistopheles, *and you'll get burned.*
Keep your greedy mitts off my rocks, Opus Dopus."

After a taunt like that, Cass figured Maestro would have to save face and snatch Dolce's necklace. The thief was running out of time. Her show closed on Sunday.

Unfortunately, tonight was Thursday. That's why Cass wanted Dolce to leak the news of Daredevil's theft in the morning. In good conscience, Cass couldn't let Dolce serve as bait any longer than dawn.

Doing his best to fit in with the opera buffs, Cass tipped his hat to a prune-faced matron, who snubbed him with a haughty snap of her fan. Among the stately swallowtails and jewel-toned gowns of the lobby's milling crowd, his immaculately brushed Stetson and coarse wool duster made him stand out like a tumbleweed in a rose garden.

Not that I care.

Resorting to his usual defense—swagger—he strolled into the auditorium, where the stench of a thousand perfumes made his temples throb. A mincing, nose-waving usher demanded to see a ticket, so Cass demonstrated the clever mechanism attached to his forearm. When the .38 slid into his fist, the usher stammered an apology and fled, most likely to rustle up a posse of liveried Nancy Boys like himself.

Cass's amusement was fleeting.

If ever there was a fish out of water, he was it. Sadie's accusation, that he was little more than a "rutting hooligan," haunted him every time a common store clerk or bank teller harrumphed at his duds. The memory of Lilybelle's admonition, that he should get a haircut, made him wish he was guzzling rotgut at the Bust-a-Gut Saloon. Even Dolce had suggested—with the utmost politeness—that he get a shave before the performance.

But then, she had no idea that he was hiding his mug because he was wanted for three counts of stage coach robbery.

Women.

Cass sighed, wishing he was guarding Dolce's dressing room with Collie. Somehow, the tedium of door-watching seemed more pleasant than wading through the horde of wasps, who buzzed, tittered, and sneered at his rustic attire.

Craving a cigarette, he stuck a match in his mouth instead, and watched the gaslights flicker, signaling the orchestra. He'd chosen a hiding place close to the stage, behind a massive cherry wood column. However, with more than a thousand people in attendance, and the glittery, cut-glass chandelier growing dimmer in the dome, surveillance was proving more complicated than he'd anticipated.

He did manage to spy Enoch Fowler. Standing beside his ward, the preacher was chatting with one of his plumper, richer donors in the orchestra section. Rebekah's eyes were glued to the carpet. She looked the very model of docility.

Cass smirked to recall Collie's claim that the mousy woman-child had cursed him.

Lilybelle sat in the front row with Wortham Welbourn on her right. Cass suspected that the snooty, brunette beauty on Wortham's other side was the infamous Sheridan—or Harridan, as Lilybelle liked to call her. Mendel Baines sat beside Sheridan.

No wonder Lilybelle looks grumpier than a bullfrog in a dried up puddle.

Cass next spied Wyntir Greyfell. Dripping with sapphires, the young heiress stopped by the front row to chat with the Welbourn party. Cass watched her curtsey to Baines and whisper in Sheridan's ear.

Where's Wyntir's escort? Shouldn't she be on her way to her seat?

Cass scanned the gilded proscenium boxes, with their lace lambrequins, mohair cushions, and tapestry-covered ceilings. He finally spied the slicked-back, well-heeled Goddard, sitting comfortably between two chairs. One was vacant. The other held a chestnut-haired firecracker with a sparkling tiara.

A muscle ticked in Cass's jaw.

At that precise moment, the gaslights flickered again. Preacher Fowler bowed gallantly over his sycophant's hand and led Rebekah to their seats.

Wyntir waved good-bye to the Welbourns and hurried toward the proscenium stairs.

Lilybelle kissed the snout of her stole and settled the fox in the empty chair on her left.

Goddard reached into Sadie's lap to take her gloved hand.

As darkness swallowed that cozy theater box, Cass ground his teeth hard enough to crack one.

Collie grimaced as the first tenor aria reverberated through the opera house, making the roof in Dolce's dressing room quake.

"You'd think rich folk would have better taste in music," he groused to his faithful, ring-tailed companion. "I can't hear a single jaw harp through all that yodeling. And I can't hear any jugs, spoons, or washboards, neither. Can you?"

Hiding behind a silk dressing screen, Collie was using his whittling knife to peel the apple Vandy had swiped from a fruit basket on the vanity. The basket had been smuggled into the room by a pudgy Dolce-admirer, who'd been wearing a red soldier's costume. The thespian had arrived about five minutes after the diva had sailed out the door in a ruffled, white night gown—presumably for the stage.

But Collie couldn't be too sure about Dolce's destination, considering all the shenanigans that went on backstage at an opera house. Girl dancers with bare buttocks bounded around like jackrabbits; big-bellied men with heavily rouged cheeks ordered other men to lace them up in corsets; and some fussy soprano in britches kept complaining about the "lunkhead seamstress" who'd left a pin in her codpiece.

Those eyebrow-raisers were just for starters. While Collie and Vandy had been cooling their heels behind the screen, five intruders had barged into Dolce's dressing room. One had snatched a rose from a vase and fled; another had grabbed a gown from a costume rack; two more had carried out a padded bench with rolled arms; and the fifth had turned the wall clock forward eight minutes. Apparently, Dolce was notorious for dawdling during intermission.

As a life-long sinner with a talent for scrounging, Collie considered himself a good judge of thieves. That's why he didn't seriously believe any of these theater folk were Maestro. A master jewel thief wouldn't have wasted his time stealing roses, gowns, or furniture.

Collie glanced once more at the clock and sighed. Act II was still crawling by.

"Do you really think Maestro will take Cass's newspaper bait?"

Vandy whined eagerly in response, his dark eyes shining like chocolate stars as he watched Collie nip a slice of apple from his knife.

"Me neither," Collie confided. "Fact is, he'd have to be a halfwit to come to the opera house. All of Denver—including those lamebrains at the police station—are following the rivalry between Daredevil and Maestro in the classifieds."

Vandy rose on his hind legs and begged for fruit.

Collie hiked an eyebrow. "What's your problem?" he taunted. "Didn't I feed you last week?"

Dropping to all-fours, Vandy galloped in circles, snapping at his tail.

"Liar," Collie scoffed. "Don't you think I see those crumbs on your snout every time you crawl out of Sadie's window?"

Vandy flopped to his side, heaved a sigh, and grew still.

"Stop that! You are *not* starving to death, you big faker! 'Sides. You licked all the peanut butter outta my tobacco tin, remember?"

Vandy suddenly lost interest in the apple. Bounding to his paws, he pricked his ears and pointed his snout at the door.

Collie cocked his head. By coon standards, he was practically deaf, but by human standards, he was an expert eavesdropper with weasel ears—at least, that's how Cass described him. Sometimes, Collie worried that Cass had fired too many trick shots over his left shoulder.

In any event, Collie could hear better than Cass, which was why he soon detected a light step in the hall, accompanied by the rustle of skirts. Figuring a dancing girl was hurrying toward the stage, Collie popped another apple wedge into his mouth.

Vandy's ears swiveled.

The footsteps halted outside Dolce's door. But that didn't worry Collie. Half the theater troupe had passed through the diva's dressing room at some point tonight.

For a long moment, nothing happened in the hall. Collie licked his knife clean. He snapped it closed and tossed the last apple wedge to Vandy. But the coon ignored the treat.

Now *that* was worrisome.

His heart quickening, Collie wiped his sticky hands on his dungarees. Just as the roof shook with deep, pounding drum rolls, Dolce's door whispered open. Collie wrinkled his nose. He smelled a light, floral fragrance—lilac. The female on the other side of the screen couldn't possibly be Dolce. The diva liked woodsy scents.

The door clicked closed.

Now the intruder was creeping around the room. Judging by her attempts to search the wardrobe without turning up the gaslights, he felt certain she was up to no good.

So Maestro's a skirt?

It figures.

Women always seemed to be the villains in Collie's life. The orphanage had been run by one. The school had been run by one. And a couple of weeks ago in Texas, his boss's wife had tried to poison him.

Just another normal day in Collie Town.

He slipped the tether from his Colt and strained to catch a glimpse of Maestro's face. The thief was wearing a dark cape that shrouded her weight and build. Maestro's hair, which was neatly twisted and pinned to the back of her head, appeared brown in the flickering gaslight.

At last, he glimpsed her profile. She was wearing a golden mask that stretched from her hairline to the tip of her nose. He decided she must be a member of the theater troop. In preparation for Act II, at least a dozen dancers had hooked glittery masks behind their ears, thanks to the Props Master, who'd bellowed down the hall, *"Don't forget your masks for the Golden Calf number!"*

Uh-oh. Collie frowned. *Something ain't right about this skirt.*

Maestro had caught the hem of her cape in the wardrobe's door. Surely, she had to feel it tug in resistance, but she just kept walking. She didn't look back. As she approached the vanity, the garment slid from her shoulders.

When she shoved aside a vase of roses, she scratched her hand but didn't flinch.

When she shook open a box of face paint, powder exploded all over her shimmery silk dress. She didn't cough or curse. She didn't even gasp.

Collie hiked an eyebrow. What skirt doesn't wail about a ruined evening gown?

As if in answer, she turned toward the floor mirror. Too late, he noticed his reflection in the glass. Without batting an eye, she whipped a pistol from her pocket. Once, twice, three times, she fired. As waves of applause rocked the chamber, she unloaded the entire cylinder at his reflection.

Then, as calmly as any church lady, she turned her back on the glass fragments, tinkling off the frame, and started rummaging through Dolce's vanity.

The clock ticked off another few seconds of Collie's life.

Finally, he loosed his white-knuckled grip on his revolver. He'd come close—*damned* close—to peeing his pants.

Vandy tossed him a sideways look as if to say, *"That skirt's bonkers."*

Collie couldn't have agreed more. He was seriously considering telling Vandy to bite her.

Unfortunately, it occurred to him that Maestro might have another gun. Or a head full of poisonous snakes. Or a gaggle of blood-sucking harpies at her command.

As the applause thundered on, sweat trickled down his temple. He was trapped in a cluttered box of a room, in the empty cast hall, where no one could hear him scream. He didn't think it was fair that some stupid etiquette rule said he wasn't allowed to shoot Maestro, just because she was a woman. From where he was sitting, Maestro looked like his worst nightmare: a flesh-eating zombie with breasts.

In a fit of desperation, he tried an experiment. With the stealth of the wild creatures he'd befriended in the Kentucky backwoods, he eased Dolce's paste necklace from the shelf of masks, gloves, and fans at his elbow. Little did Maestro know that Dolce had four strings of fake beads. The Props Master was a fussy little fellow who prided himself on preparing for every catastrophe: smashing, melting, chipping, and loss.

Good thing he doesn't prepare for coon theft. Otherwise, me and Vandy might be maggot food right now.

Moving with the silence of a stalking panther, Collie stepped to the edge of the screen and hooked the necklace over Dolce's peach-chiffon dressing gown. Then he ducked into the shadows with Vandy to watch.

Sure enough, Zombie Queen eventually spied the glitter of fake, translucent gemstones in the low light. Triumphantly, she snatched the prize, shoved it down her bodice, and headed for the door. She didn't fetch her cape. She didn't look back.

Collie breathed a sigh of relief. Now all he and Vandy had to do was tail Maestro until she took off her mask.

But in Collie Town, nothing was ever simple. As Maestro scurried along the hall, voices floated down the stairwell. Apparently, Act II was over. Members of the troupe were clambering down the steps in their golden masks. Collie bit back an oath. Soon, the hall became an obstacle course of petticoats, tin pikes, helmets, and wooden shields.

Moments later, Dolce parted the sea of thespians amidst a rousing round of applause. Cass walked at her side, his arm linked with hers. The Props Master hurried after them like a well-trained hound. Since the diva was too busy batting her eyelashes at Cass to notice anyone else, the mincing little man tugged on her sleeve.

She ignored him.

He tugged again.

She scowled.

About three steps later, the exasperated diva finally turned and lifted a string of glittery, paste jewels from the Prop Master's box.

That's when all hell broke loose.

Maestro stopped dead in her tracks. She drew her pistol and aimed it at Dolce. Sopranos shrieked; baritones ducked behind their wooden shields. Cass thrust Dolce behind him and triggered the .38 up his sleeve.

Visions of nooses danced before Collie's eyes. Before his best friend could ruin his Ranger career by shooting a woman who was gripping an unloaded pistol, Collie grabbed Maestro from behind. Vandy tripped her up, sinking his teeth into her hem.

They needn't have gone to the trouble.

The minute Collie tore the pistol from Maestro's hand, she crumpled to the carpet like a sack of potatoes.

CHAPTER 12

◆

Before the end of intermission, Sadie heard the rumor: a heroic hillbilly and his raccoon had saved Dolce LaRocca from a thief.

The whole opera house was buzzing with the news. Before the curtain could rise on Act III, Mendel Baines and Wortham Welbourn had started hustling an indignant Lilybelle from the theater. As the dowager passed the proscenium boxes, she hollered up at Dante:

"I always said Harridan couldn't be trusted! Now that she's been stupid enough to prove me right, why should it wreck *my* evening? Tell these two knuckleheads I want to watch Mephistopheles ruin Faust in peace!"

Titters and gasps circulated through the audience.

"Poor Mrs. Welbourn," Wyntir breathed, her eyes as big as blue moons.

Dante patted his agitated ward's hand. "It appears Lilybelle needs a friend. Do not fret, my dear. I shall go to her. Fiore, pray forgive me. A doctor's work is never done. If this matter should escalate, do me the favor of escorting Wyntir to Greyfell Manor at the end of the show."

"Of course, *dottore.*"

He flashed his devastating smile, which made Wyntir sigh and Sadie's blood heat. Then he parted the curtains, vanishing into the shadows as completely as the phantom of another, more infamous opera house.

Wyntir wrung her handkerchief and slid onto Dante's vacant chair. "I was so hoping tonight would be different," she whispered, her eyes brimming with crocodile tears.

"Different, *carina?*"

"Dante never seems to have time for me anymore."

Sadie sighed. She wasn't surprised. Wyntir had turned him away from her bed. Either Dante was exercising gentlemanly restraint by avoiding his ward, or he was punishing Wyntir in a fit of hurt pride. In either event, Sadie suspected Dante had little trouble finding substitute bedmates.

Wyntir toyed with the ringless third finger of her left hand. "I wish I was more like you, Fiore," she blurted out. "You're so wise in the ways of men. And marriage…"

Wyntir let the plaintive word hang in the air. Sadie's heart went out to the younger woman, who'd been left all alone in the world without the guidance of a mother. The real question wasn't, 'Would Dante propose?' The real question was, 'Would he propose because Wyntir inherited a fortune on Saturday night?'

"You've been trained to think of Dante as a parent," Sadie said gently, squeezing Wyntir's hand. "A child expects to be the center of a parent's universe. But a wife understands she must share her husband with children, parents and siblings, colleagues and clients. When Dante is your husband, he will always have patients, who need him more than you do. Your love must be big enough to allow this. A doctor needs a wife with a selfless heart."

Wyntir nodded, her eyes brimming with gratitude. "Yes," she whispered, dashing a tear from her cheek. "Yes, you are right. Thank you, Fiore. Of course, Dante must put his patients first." She straightened her spine in her chair. "And I couldn't be prouder of him for dashing off to help Lilybelle. What do you suppose she meant about Sheridan, proving her stupidity?"

Thoughtfully, Sadie turned her attention back to the orchestra level, where the Welbourns were making a scene. Wortham gripped his mother's left arm; Mendel Baines gripped her right. Wearing masks of grim determination, the two men were dragging the protesting dowager through the lobby doors. Sheridan was nowhere in sight.

"I cannot begin to guess," Sadie said as the houselights dimmed. *And it's going to be an excruciatingly long evening before I learn the facts.*

Around 2 a.m., after leaving Wyntir in the protective custody of her Dobermans, Sadie returned to the hotel to find an encrypted message from Mace. It read:

> *"Cassidy botched the stakeout. Learn what you can*
> *about the Welbourns' relationship with Baines,*
> *and Sheridan's attempt on Dolce's life."*

Sadie was pretty sure her jaw hit the carpet. *Sheridan tried to kill Dolce?!*

The other gaps in Sadie's knowledge were filled in by the morning edition of the *Rocky*. The newspaper reported the entire, salacious incident on the front page, along with this malicious quote:

"What possible reason would Sheridan Welbourn have to steal a necklace?" said her attorney, Jason Abercrombie. "Mrs. Welbourn's heirloom jewelry collection, a gift from her husband upon their marriage, is valued at close to a million dollars. Mr. MacAffee, on the other hand, is a drifter from Kentucky with a lengthy history of theft charges. No doubt he stole Mrs. Welbourn's cape and planted it in Miss LaRocca's dressing room to divert suspicion from himself.

"If I were the district attorney, I would question how this boy is associated with Maestro or Daredevil. The two thieves have been flagrantly one-upping each other for weeks, not to mention publically plotting to steal Miss LaRocca's necklace in this very newspaper."

Sadie groaned and tossed aside the rag. After the debacle at the opera house, Maestro wouldn't have trouble linking Vandy and Collie to Cass. Nor would the police. The newspaper might have quoted Dolce, praising Collie and his "adorable raccoon" for saving her life from "that mad woman," but Sheridan's attorney would get the police to poke around. With Maestro out for his rival's blood, Cass could no longer take refuge from local tin-stars in the underground.

Sadie drew a shuddering breath.

It was time to bring that jewel-thieving bastard to his knees.

The bell tower in the Methodist Church was chiming 11 a.m. when Sadie sailed into Rothchild's Auction House in full *contessa* regalia. To attract her quarry, she'd chosen her most advantageous color, green, and she'd boosted her bosom a tad higher than social convention allowed. Her *piece de resistance* was Mace's obscenely large topaz, glittering like a supernova from her décolletage. If Maestro didn't come sniffing around her skirts before the auction's end, then he would have to be dead.

Or female, she amended, thinking of Sheridan.

Pasting on an appreciative expression, Sadie strolled through the exhibition hall, pretending to examine the auction items. The displays included a barn-wide tapestry, elaborately depicting the dust, sweat, and blood of a chariot race; a sundial, hammered from pure gold; and a dark green humidor, featuring ivy-wreathed satyrs, dancing with nymphs to the plinking, mechanical melody of an old Italian drinking song. She figured Maestro would be targeting that humidor.

However, the most popular items, by far, were the naked statues. Sadie was amused to note the vivid imaginations of Italian artists, particularly when depicting their ancient gods below the belt. She was surprised to see so many of Denver's fair sex, gawking at the physiques of Apollo, Jupiter, and Mars.

As if on cue, she heard a peal of laughter from an especially curvaceous blonde, who'd craned back her head to gaze at a sword-wielding Hercules. When the woman turned, her face was veiled by black net, but Sadie recognized the flashy, diamond cross on the blonde's chest. Hastily, Sadie ducked behind a case of Legionaire armor and buried her nose in her program as Mattie Silks and Cort Thomson strolled by.

Whew! That was close.

Around 11:15 a.m., Mace entered the building. As usual, he managed to appear beneath everyone's notice. How he accomplished this feat mystified Sadie, since he wasn't a small man. Or a shy man. He wasn't even a plain man, with those piercing green eyes and that hooked beak of a nose. When he combed his hair the right way, he could be downright attractive. Especially when his chin softened in a dimpled grin.

But this afternoon, Mace wasn't smiling. When he was on the job, he was as focused as a tournament chess player. If he engaged in chit chat, flirted, or sucked down suds, his behavior was calculated to get him one thing: information.

Sadie wasn't surprised to see her boss breeze past her without a glance. He'd slicked his hair flatter than a flapjack, so his nose was especially prominent beneath his high brow—not his best look. With his Inverness cape fluttering around him like wings, he reminded her of a hawk, fiercely silent, always circling, always hunting prey.

She shivered.

For today's stakeout, Mace was posing as the agent of a wealthy, absentee bidder. She heard him mimic a New York accent as he surrendered his outer wear at the hat check counter. Declining champagne, he moved through the hoity-toity art patrons with a casual gait. Nobody hailed him; but then, nobody was supposed to know who he was. Mace had the enviable ability to forgo elaborate disguises. He could stoop and stammer, limp and shuffle, and pass himself off as any number of characters, ranging from a hayseed to a foreign general. He possessed all the theatrical skills a Pinkerton needed to survive, but he rarely used them. His greatest concessions to today's alias were a drooping mustache and a well-trimmed beard. They made him look commonplace—of little consequence.

Thus, while Denver's elite snubbed him, Mace was left to do his detective work in peace. Sadie, on the other hand, had to deal with Lilybelle.

Clearly relishing the ripple of whispers generated by her arrival, Lilybelle blew kisses to her detractors, who were scandalized that she hadn't cloistered herself at home to share her family's shame. The scrappy dowager confided to Sadie, "I came to see what all the fuss was about. According to the *Rocky,* Vesuvius erupted to punish the citizens of Pompeii for carving dillywhackers out of marble.

"But then, anyone who writes for that rag is a half-wit," Lilybelle said tartly. "The reporter from the opera house painted Harridan as an absent-minded ditherer, who got lost on the way to the privy. Horse feathers! Everybody *knows* she's a greedy, grubbing witch. And get this: Harridan claims she can't remember a thing that happened last night." Lilybelle snorted. "Too bad the raccoon didn't bite her.

"Oh look." With an impish grin, she elbowed Sadie in the ribs. "There's Bacchus rutting with a goat."

After a quarter hour in Lilybelle's company, Sadie began to suspect she'd misjudged the dowager. Lilybelle wasn't senile; she was cannier than her fox. A mischief-maker at heart, Lilybelle liked to shock people for attention. More than that, she liked to watch the *nouveau riche* scratch and claw for her approval—which was the highest rung on Mile High City's social ladder.

"Come meet the Duchess. She's just ducky!" Lilybelle crowed whenever one of Denver's jewel-spangled matrons wandered by. "Fiore's got more money than I do. And *I've* got more money than God!"

Sadie fixed a smile on her face and gave up trying to explain to the gold diggers that she was a *contessa,* not a duchess, and she wasn't in line for any thrones.

But even Lilybelle didn't have much patience for brown-nosers. Eventually, the Queen Bee would command in disgruntled tones, "Get along now. Those statues aren't gonna buy themselves." Then she'd roll her eyes behind the retreating offender's back.

"I am curious, *signora,*" Sadie said as the 91-year-old spitfire latched onto her arm for another stroll around the exhibit cases. "Why haven't you shooed me off as well?"

"Your turn will come, Toots. Say, is that Dante?" Lilybelle's grin turned lopsided as she straightened her spectacles. "Hot damn! He's looking fine!"

Sadie hid her amusement. Even a professional seductress, like her, had trouble staying immune to Dante's charms. He was the kind of man she'd dreamed of in her school-girl days: sophisticated, chivalrous, and swoon-worthy handsome.

As usual, he looked like he'd stepped off a fashion plate in the *Saturday Evening Post.* Today, he'd opted to wear charcoal-gray pinstripes with dove gray gloves and spats. In truth, everything about Dante was a pleasure to look at: the sable curl that spilled over his intelligent brow; the golden flecks of fire in his intoxicating eyes; the adorable dimple in his scrupulously shaved chin. If his hair had been longer—and he'd been wearing a toga—he would have resembled the sculpture of Hercules.

Sadie wondered wickedly if Dante was Hercules's twin beneath the sword belt too.

"Yoo-hoo! Dante!" The irrepressible Lilybelle dragged a handkerchief from her reticule and fluttered it like a banner.

The handsome physician noticed her. He inclined his head. But when he noticed Sadie, the dark fires in his eyes kindled in the most flattering way. He began to make his way across the room.

Lilybelle winked at Sadie. "Looks like we roped ourselves a stud pony."

Sadie had a hard time keeping a straight face.

"Good morning, ladies." Dante's bow was flawless, like everything else about him.

"Buongiorno," Sadie purred.

"Where's Wyntir?" Lilybelle demanded.

"I left her at home to make last minute arrangements for her party. My ward's innocent, young mind shouldn't be exposed to erotic art."

Lilybelle snorted. "Your ward turns 21 tomorrow. That gal needs the kind of education that isn't found in books—unless you've got a *better* idea how to teach Wyntir to be a wife. And that reminds me." Lilybelle's sky-blue eyes twinkled with mischief. "I need to snap Harridan out of her mope." Opening the auction program, she shoved a page under Dante's nose. "I can't read this tiny print. Which one of these gods has the biggest willy?"

Dante reddened in the most endearing way. "My apologies, dear lady. I haven't previewed the statuary."

"Aw, c'mon. A red-blooded fella like you? Surely you sneaked a peek at Venus, doing the wild thing with Mars by the door!"

Sadie decided to help Dante save face. "Perhaps I can read the program for you, *signora,"* she said dryly.

"Eh?" Lilybelle hiked a bushy white eyebrow. "You read American?"

Too late, Sadie realized she'd risked her cover. "I practice whenever I can," she recovered gracefully, "but I do not promise perfection."

"Oh." Lilybelle seemed to lose all interest in her prank, possibly because Dante had recovered his composure. "Nevermind." She shoved her program inside her reticule. "I think I'll buy that green cigar box instead. The one Buggerhead Baines keeps drooling over. That'll be a sweet revenge."

Sadie glanced around the hall, with its cherub-painted ceiling, plush Brussels carpets, and armed, private security at every entrance. Finally, she spied Baines. With his hands clasped behind his back, he kept circling and re-circling a towering metal cage. The sign on the display read, *"Musical Humidor. Satyrs and Fauns. Verde Malachite. 18th C. Florence."*

Sadie's eyes narrowed speculatively.

"And what on earth will you do with a cigar box?" Dante chided Lilybelle.

Her craggy cheeks creased in a sparsely-toothed grin. "I'm gonna stuff it full of peyote. So I can smoke my pipe."

Dante frowned. "A hallucinogen?"

Lilybelle feigned innocence. "What's that?"

"You know very well. And contrary to Navajo rhetoric, I'm not convinced it cures rheumatism."

Lilybelle waved away his concern. "If it ain't killed me after 76 years, it ain't gonna. Say! Do you think Harridan stole a pinch from my peyote pouch? That would sure explain a few things. Especially about last night."

"Without Wortham's permission to examine his wife," Dante began in long-suffering tones, "I couldn't possibly diagnose—"

"Yeah, yeah." Lilybelle patted his arm. "You're a dear boy. But my son is a troll; his wife is a hag; and they're not gonna pay you diddly. I keep telling them, you're a real doctor, and Baines is a blithering idiot, but they won't listen to me. They won't listen to *anybody!* At dinnertime yesterday, Brother Enoch stopped by, and Harridan threatened to sic the dogs on him."

Sadie's ears pricked at this news. "The dogs, you say?" She was careful to keep the irony from her tone. "I should think the messenger of God would be a comfort to your family."

"That's because you don't know the greedy grubbers like God does. In any event, Enoch rode up the drive just as the soup got served. He claimed he had a message from Emmanuel, and he warned Harridan to stay away from the theater."

Dante raised his eyebrows. "Fowler *threatened* her?"

Lilybelle snorted. "Enoch? Hardly. But Harridan's superstitious. She doesn't believe in angels—just demons. Last night, after she went bonkers, she claimed Enoch put a curse on her." Lilybelle rolled her eyes. "And she thinks *I* belong in the loony bin."

As if on cue, the self-proclaimed Shepherd of Men's Souls entered the hall. Fowler was dressed in his usual, immaculate black, except for the starched white of his cleric's collar. Displaying the steely nerve of a confidence man, he stopped to exchange pleasantries with a security guard, who was stationed by a gold-and-lapis ring, bearing an intaglio of Julius Caesar. Then Fowler weaved through jewel-toned skirts and jet-black frockcoats until finally, he stepped into the auction room.

Speculatively, Sadie watched the handsome grifter disappear through black-velvet draperies. *How interesting that a man of the cloth would attend an auction that had been touted, far and wide, for its fornicating statuary.*

"Fiore?" Dante inquired politely.

Sadie started, her cheeks flooding with heat. Apparently, she'd lost track of his conversation with Lilybelle.

"Forgive me, *carino,*" she purred. "You were speaking of Gounod's libretto, *si?*"

He nodded, his forthright gaze delving into hers. "I was curious what you thought of last night's performance."

Sadie didn't need to pretend; she was delighted to discuss her greatest joy: music.

"The symphony was superb. The singing, *magnifico! Dama* LaRocca delivered a stellar performance as Marguerite. Her exquisite *Jewel Song* brought down the house!"

Dante inclined his head. "Wyntir said you appeared to be pleased."

"Why, of course, *carino.* Why would I not be?"

He shrugged. "I did not find Dolce's Marguerite as compelling as her Juliette, when I caught her performance in *Romeo and Juliette* in Edinburg. And her Lucia di Lammermoor was much more impressive in Florence. But then, Denver has an unsophisticated crowd. Perhaps Dolce thought she might slide by. *Che cosa ne pensi?*"

Sadie's heart skipped. *Uh-oh. Dante never mentioned that he speaks Italian! Or that he visited Florence!*

Her mind raced. Somehow, she had to diffuse this bomb. She wasn't entirely certain, but she guessed that he'd asked for her opinion.

"Ah, you are a music aficionado, *dottore,*" she teased in sultry tones. In her experience, if she could get a man to think with his pecker, he'd forgive everything else. "Your ear will not tolerate the slightest imperfection. But the voice, it is not like a piano or violin. It is a living instrument, susceptible to altitude and climate.

"And speaking of climate," she continued enthusiastically, steering the conversation far away from Europe, which she knew little about, "I hear California is sunny all year round. I am so looking forward to curling my toes through warm, golden sands after trudging through your Rocky Mountain snow. In fact, I purchased my train ticket to San Francisco just this morning!"

"Bah." Lilybelle wrinkled her nose. "If I wanted golden sands, I'd visit Jamaica."

Dante ignored her.

"You're leaving us?" His voice throbbed with a hint of disappointment. "But surely not before Thanksgiving. My ward would be heart-broken if you did not share our turkey feast."

"That *does* sound like a valid reason to prolong my stay," Sadie drawled, parting moist, cherry-red lips in invitation. "Tell me, *carino.* Can you think of another?"

To her secret amusement, his eyes dilated.

"You flatter me, *contessa.*"

"How charming that you think so, *dottore.*"

Lilybelle pouted. Apparently, she didn't like being ignored. "All right, Lady Coyote. Your time's up. Dante's coming with me to meet Adelaide Hartwell. Her husband's dead, and she's got a face like a hatchet. Trust me when I say, she needs a psychiatrist more than you do."

Dante looked bemused when Lilybelle linked her arm through his. "It seems I have little choice." He tossed an apologetic glance at Sadie.

"That's right," Lilybelle said. "Duty calls. Time to make money." She marched him off in the direction of the chariot tapestry.

Chuckling to watch the unlikely pair, Sadie turned her thoughts back to her mission—or more specifically, to Baines. He was still pacing around the humidor. She drew a fortifying breath as she considered that she was about to confront her most likely Maestro suspect.

Show time.

She set off on a meandering route to intercept her quarry. He seemed agitated, perhaps because he was attracting stares and sneers from the other art patrons. Sadie suspected the *Rocky's* report about his arrest was only partly to blame. Baines looked like hell—worse, in fact, than he had looked in the tobacco shop. He'd tried to conceal his freshly bruised face with a wide-brimmed hat, tan stage make-up, and a stiff white collar that was high enough to choke a horse. However, these valiant efforts weren't adequate to hide the proof of his brawling.

For all his education, Sadie thought snidely, *Baines is nothing more than a thug.*

Pasting on a smile, she halted on a collision course with the pacing professor. Since he was past the age of puberty—and breathing—she'd expected him to be arrested by the vision of patchouli-scented breasts and the obscenely large topaz nesting between them.

But Baines was wholly focused on that humidor. With his hands clasped behind his back, he kept muttering and circling the cage that protected the artifact. If she hadn't cleared her throat to announce herself, he would have bowled her into the exhibit.

Searching for a weakness in the fortifications, Baines?

"Eh?" Irritably, he adjusted his spectacles. When his eyes rose to hers, they were bloodshot and glassy.

Sadie suspected opium, since Baines fraternized with Cort.

"Buongiorno, professore. The verde marble, it is exquisite, *no?"*

A deep flush rolled up his neck. "Indeed." He turned his shoulder on her.

Sadie blinked at this unexpected snub. But she reasoned he was embarrassed by the memory of his brawl. Or maybe he was self-conscious about his swollen face and scratched throat.

Strange. Her eyebrows knitted as she gazed more closely at the skin above his collar. Those marks were blistered and raw, looking more like insect stings or rope burns than knuckle punches.

"Professore," she began in conciliatory tones, "I am saddened by the misunderstanding at the hotel. I am sure you were only—"

"Sticking my nose where it didn't belong?" he finished for her acidly. "Like you're doing now?"

Apparently, he noticed me staring.

"My apologies, *signore.* I did not mean to offend—"

"What do you care? Unless he sent you to spy on me."

Her smile stiffened. Ironically, he wasn't as paranoid as he sounded. "Who would wish to spy on you?"

"You know damned well."

His stare remained fixed on the humidor.

She frowned. *"Professore,* you are a proud man. And pride makes you hard-headed, it seems. *Signorina* Greyfell told me you have been seeking patrons for your research—"

"You don't give a rat's ass about my research."

Her heart quickened. She wondered if she'd inadvertently blown her cover; if Cort had recognized her on a crowded street and identified her to Baines.

As if drawn by magnetic force, her gaze rose above the humidor's cage and locked with Mace's. He was standing near the refreshment table, stirring a cup of coffee.

Damn! That's all I need: to botch this mission with my boss in plain sight. Mace won't hesitate to send me back to the whorehouse!

"Professore," Sadie tried again, figuring that a desperate *contessa* would swallow her pride and tamp down her

annoyance. "*Signorina* Greyfell confided your methods were most helpful. She said she sleeps like a *bambina,* now, because you cured her of night terrors after her papa's death."

Baines locked stares with her again. This time, confusion muddied his bloodshot glaze. "I cured her?"

"*Si.* She recommends you highly. She says the nightmares are gone, and the grief has nearly passed too. That is why I wish to consult with you—privately, of course—about my own complaint."

He swayed for a moment, as if he'd grown dizzy. Then he muttered something. The words were muffled behind the hand he scrubbed over his face. But Sadie could have sworn he'd said, *"I don't remember."*

"Professore?" A reluctant concern crept into her voice. "Are you well?"

He sucked down a shuddering breath. His eyes clouded with chagrin. But just when he seemed on the verge of apologizing, Cort exited the privy. Sniffling the white powder on his mustache, Cort slipped a snuff box inside his hip pocket.

"C'mon, Doc!" the addict bellowed across the room. "Let's get our seats. Mattie gave me a loan!"

Baines turned beet red. Harrumphing, he tucked his calling card into her palm. "Of course, *Contessa.* It will be our secret. Come by my office Monday afternoon. One o'clock. But a word of caution before we part. Forget the humidor. For your own good."

Is that a threat?

Sadie watched in speculation as Baines passed through the black velvet draperies that framed the entry to the bidding room. If the ill-mannered professor was Maestro, she would need more than his obsession with a music box to convict him.

What would Baines do, I wonder, if the contessa *pulled some strings to get his coveted humidor taken off the market?*

But before she could act on her idea, Dante rematerialized at her side with two champagne flutes and zero dowagers.

Sadie pasted on a smile, hoping to distract him from the card that she was furtively slipping into a secret pocket in her skirt. She didn't want Dante to know "the *contessa*" had set an appointment with his arch rival.

"You escaped," she greeted warmly, accepting a glass.

"The same might be said of you." Those exotic, gold-flecked eyes made her temperature rise as they assessed her for damage. "No ill effects from your run-in with Baines, I trust?"

"How kind you are to concern yourself with my welfare," she purred, sipping from her fizzing flute. "Rather like my own personal knight in shining armor."

His lips curved, and his lashes drooped, veiling the tantalizing heat of his gaze. "My pleasure." He offered his arm. "Come. The auction awaits, m'lady."

A sudden ripple of applause circled the room. Turning toward the main entrance, Sadie noticed the crowd was parting in waves. Apparently, the ovation was for Dolce LaRocca. She'd arrived with a well-heeled gentleman, who sported a beaver top hat and a fashionable, double-breasted frockcoat. The stunning, porcelain-skinned diva flashed her brilliant smile and acknowledged her fans as her bearded, dark-haired escort raked piercing, sapphire eyes over the crowd.

When those smoldering, blue eyes locked with Sadie's, her jaw dropped. She sucked in a strangled breath.

Dolce's escort was Cass in disguise!

CHAPTER 13

Cass's sunny mane had been cut and dyed the color of a starless night. His sleek, athletic build had been swathed in finely tailored broadcloth. Sadie was so stunned by this transformation, all she could do was gape.

Then Dolce reclaimed his attention. Cass turned his head and lavished heart-tripping dimples on her—dimples that would have made Venus swoon.

A sick feeling settled in Sadie's stomach.

Cass never went anywhere without his beloved Stetson and Justin boots. Yet he'd ditched every last stitch of cowboy clothing to please another woman—an elegant, *sophisticated* woman, whose enviable singing voice had garnered the stage success Sadie had been dreaming of since childhood.

On top of every other betrayal—the stolen emeralds, the Judas Kiss, the more talented diva—how could he escort a woman who speaks fluent Italian to the auction, knowing she could blow my cover?

Dimly, through the roaring in her brain, Sadie heard her champagne flute crash at her feet.

"Fiore."

She blinked, and Dante's handsome face began to take shape through the glaze of her tears.

Lilybelle hurried forward. She started snapping her fingers under Sadie's nose. "C'mon, Lady Coyote." The dowager's voice sounded like gravel, crunching under water. "Snap out of it."

Sadie staggered. The room was spinning, and her corset felt like a boa constrictor. "I-I can't breathe!"

"Damn," Lilybelle muttered. "I never carry smelling salts. Don't need 'em myself…"

"Step aside," Dante commanded, thrusting his champagne into her hand. "I'll handle this."

He hoisted Sadie effortlessly into his arms. In that moment, she didn't know what was worse, that he was carrying her through the gasping crowd like a sack of feathers; that Mace was present to witness her shameful attack of vapors; or that she was on the verge of a real swoon for the first time in her life.

Cass's heart ricocheted off his ribs. Sadie had grown as limp as lettuce. At first, he'd thought she was faking. Sadie had the constitution of a horse, so he'd figured a pretend swoon was her calculated ploy to remove herself from the building. That way, Dolce couldn't expose her rudimentary knowledge of Italian.

But as the seconds ticked by, Cass realized Sadie needed help. Even she couldn't fake turning whiter than new-fallen snow. However, when he would have charged to her rescue, Mace breezed past, whispering in dire tones, *"Do nothing, or risk everything."*

Now Cass was struggling to keep his fists in his pockets so he didn't smash something. And by something, he meant Goddard's face.

"Che peccato. What a shame," Dolce lamented, her coffee-colored eyes fixed speculatively on the Bostonian's retreating back. "I shall not get to meet this mysterious *contessa.* The one I never heard of."

Cass shot her a warning look. Although Dolce was 10 years his senior, the dark-haired siren had proven as willful as a two-year-old. He'd tried damned near everything to divert her from her scheme to win Lady Fiore as her patron. He'd even submitted to Dolce's tailor and barber.

True, he'd needed the make-over to go undercover at this high-security shindig. But Dolce's motherly fussing, combined with three hours of dyeing, clipping, and pin-pricking, had made for a teeth-grinder of a morning. In truth, Cass had suffered the degradation less to avoid tin-stars than to keep Dolce from pounding on Sadie's hotel door.

But even his agile mind wasn't able to distract Dolce forever. Exhausted of ideas, he'd finally relented and accompanied her to the auction for one reason, and one reason only: to stop her from blowing Sadie's cover.

Perhaps he should have been more worried about his own "cover."

During their carriage ride, Cass had never had so much trouble keeping on his trousers in his life. To his bemusement, he discovered that the married diva possessed a libido rivaled only by stud ponies and bulls. If he'd known Italian women were so lusty, he would have made Collie pose as Dolce's tin-star hero. The last thing he wanted to do was give Sadie another reason to hate him.

"Carino," Dolce purred, when he couldn't resist sneaking another peek after Goddard, "I am *here."* She snapped her fingers under his nose.

Steeling himself against annoyance, Cass turned his full attention on the scene-stealer. She had flawless olive skin, which made him wonder if she was part Gypsy and fond of hexing rivals, the way the chorus girls liked to whisper.

He pasted on a roguish smile. "That's why I'm the envy of every man in this room. You've left them breathless in your scarlet silk."

"How good of you to notice," she said slyly.

"That's me. Good to the bone."

Her gaze dropped suggestively below his belt. "I look forward to proof of your boast."

He cleared his throat. *Christ, am I blushing?*

"We've been over all that," he said sternly. "I'm sworn to protect you. I must remain alert at all times. That's why I'm forbidden to fraternize. The rule is for *your* safety."

"Your Ranger Code is deadly dull."

"Shh," he hissed, wanting to spank her. In a moment of desperation, he'd invented the 'Ranger Code'—or more precisely, the part about keeping his pecker in his pants. "I'm undercover, remember?"

She smirked.

Oh, she remembered, all right.

"Perhaps I shall hire another protector," she said with a pretty pout. "Perhaps I shall hire one of those Pinkertons, I've heard so much about. Then you'd be free to take the night off. And you could show me more of Texas," she added wickedly.

"How 'bout I show you downtown Denver? And while we're sight-seeing, you could report to the *Rocky* your necklace was stolen—as we agreed."

She was too crafty to be dissuaded so easily.

"But *carino,* you read the newspaper. After that madwoman broke into my dressing room last night, I cannot cry wolf so soon. No one would believe me."

"You underestimate your performance abilities," he said dryly.

"Perhaps you are right." She fluttered long, feathery lashes. "But there *is* the other problem."

"What problem?"

"You are a Texas Ranger and my bodyguard," she said silkily. "If I say Daredevil succeeded so soon after Maestro failed, you would earn the reputation of…how you say? A nincompoop."

Cass wasn't fooled by this magnanimous consideration. The hellcat was stonewalling him. "For your safety, *signora,* I would gladly suffer the consequences."

Annoyance flickered in those hungry eyes. "Such admirable restraint you Texicans have."

Score one for the nincompoop.

But Cass's sense of triumph was short-lived. He'd lost sight of Goddard. He didn't give a rat's ass if the Bostonian was a doctor. He didn't trust him. Not with Sadie.

Did Goddard carry her out to his coach?

This notion sparked Cass's memories of his wild, twilight ride with Sadie. He tried to blank from his mind erotic visions of his woman, with her corset unhooked and her lush breasts bared—to Goddard's mouth. In desperation, Cass searched the room for something to inspire a new topic of conversation with Dolce.

Damn. Why does every sculpture in this gallery show bared bosoms or rock-hard peckers?

He spied a sign that read, Musical Humidor. Satyrs and Fauns. Verde Malachite. 18th C. Florence.

"Um, there's a nice music box over there," he told Dolce. "It's etched with goats."

"You mean satyrs."

Whatever. "Let's look."

She dragged her heels. "For mechanical movements, I prefer Swiss craftsmanship."

"Isn't that kinda like saying, for Texas chili, I prefer Michigan pinto beans?"

Amusement flickered over her exotic features. "Shall I purchase the humidor for you?"

Now he really was blushing. Just because he'd let her swaddle him in broadcloth didn't mean he'd become her pet! He was preparing to tell her so, when his attention was diverted by a commotion at the hall's entrance.

Porfi was waddling into the room in his Sunday best. The barn-sized baker sported gold frou-frou everywhere he could: the hoop in his right ear, the stick pin on his coat lapel, the rings on his fingers and thumbs. Flanking him like romping kittens were three adoring females. Not one of them was over the age of 25.

"Who's the Greek?" Dolce demanded, her speculative eyes following the blustery, granddaddy of a fence as he made a beeline for Aisle 12 and that musical humidor.

"What makes you think he's Greek?"

"He has the accent. And the libido."

Before Cass could respond, a bell chimed, signaling the start of the auction. An attendant arrived to carry the humidor into the bidding room. Porfi followed.

"Let's watch," Cass said, dragging Dolce after the attendant. After all, Porfi had said that Maestro was interested in a green musical humidor.

"Carino, one does not attend an art auction to watch," Dolce said loftily. "One attends to wrest treasures from rivals. That is the fun of the game."

Only if you're richer than Midas, Cass thought, parting the curtains and observing the assembly of high rollers, seated in their furs and silks. Most were idly fanning themselves with bidding paddles.

"How much do you suppose the humidor is worth?" he whispered, pulling Dolce into a plush gray seat beside him.

"A pittance." She sniffed. "The true valuables are scheduled later on the program."

Then why did Professor Baines start salivating like a hound when the humidor was carried to the front of the room?

The attendant played the humidor's plinking melody for the crowd. Dolce covered her ears and compared the sound to a braying donkey.

Baines sat straight up in his chair.

Porfi waved his paddle to open the bid. Fowler upped the ante by $100.

Within minutes, that "pittance" of a cigar box reached $8,000. The fretting Baines fell out of the contest early. Fowler quit $2,000 later.

After a quick, heated consultation with Baines, Cort jumped in, waging a valiant battle against Porfi. But at $11,800, Mattie compressed her lips in a grim line and shook her head. Apparently, Cort's allowance had its limits.

Just as the auctioneer was preparing to pound his gavel and bellow, "Sold for $12,000 to the bearded gentleman in the first row," Dolce flashed a cheeky smile and raised her paddle.

Porfi turned in his seats—his bulk covered two—and tossed a dagger's glare at his newest bidding rival.

"I told you, I don't want the cigar box," Cass whispered urgently.

"Sì, carino," she soothed, "but I don't like him."

"I didn't think you knew him."

"I don't have to. He's Greek." She smirked, raising her paddle again. "Besides, someone has to flush out this madman, who kills with music."

Cass muttered an oath, envisioning Dolce's neck snapped and the humidor—along with Mephistopheles's Jewels—gripped triumphantly in Maestro's black-gloved fist.

Cass snatched Dolce's paddle before she could tempt fate further.

Porfi won the bid at $16,000.

Dolce pouted. "Have I mentioned you're no fun?"

Cass sighed, removing her prowling fingers from his thigh. He imagined two more days of hell, enduring the diva's shimmies, wiggles, and groping before her show finally closed.

If Sadie doesn't kill me, Dolce Duty will.

CHAPTER 14

Nine Hours Later

Dressed in a billowing robe of lacy, black silk, Sadie paced the Windsor's penthouse, wringing her hands and anxiously checking the clock.

Only 9 p.m.? Damn! Where's Cass? What's keeping him?

Tears glazed her vision. After the debacle at the auction house, she just knew he would show up at her door. The question was, would he show up as a lawman or a murderer?

Her stomach roiling, she recalled his threat, how he'd promised to kill Dante if the Yankee tried to woo her. The aftermath of her swoon was still foggy in her mind, but she did remember waking under a tree, in Dante's arms, with the November sun flaring around his head like a golden nimbus. Surrounded by frosted grasses, she'd clung to his neck, shivering against his warmth, fighting off the twin demons of humiliation and grief as she realized she'd keeled over like felled timber in front of Mace and half of Denver.

And it was all Cass's fault!

"I-I don't know what came over me," she gasped, her teeth chattering, mostly from shock. "I never get the vapors!"

"Relax," Dante crooned. "I'm a doctor. Just breathe. You're safe."

And ironically, she did feel safe, even though he was tugging open her corset hooks in a public yard; even though the brass buttons of his frockcoat pressed like chilled coins into her flesh. She felt confused. Aroused. *Vulnerable.*

Blinking helplessly into the dark fires of his mesmerizing eyes, she let him massage the base of her skull. She let him murmur softly in her ear—so softly, she heard the comforting tone, not the words. A deep shudder moved through her body when his lips grazed her neck. She sank further under his spell.

He smelled like wool and winter, but where he straddled her thighs, he felt hot and primal. His breaths whispered over her lips—spicy. Intoxicating. He was so close, so tantalizingly close. When his lashes drifted lower, her mouth watered for the taste of him.

Suddenly, his kneading fingers tightened under her skull. She gasped. Colors exploded in her brain—colors, lights, and sounds. In that moment, her brain went numb. She could only form a single, coherent thought: *Is he going to kiss me?*

His lips edged closer. Hovered. Parted. Those dark, smoldering eyes promised all kinds of sin as he continued to squeeze and release. Squeeze and release. The shifting pressures at the base of her skull were so soothing...

Suddenly, a chocolate-brown Stetson blotted the sun from the sky. A lanky, tow-headed youth loomed over Dante with a murderous frown.

"You sure you're a doctor?" Collie growled, the butt of his .45 peeking from the fringe of his buckskin coat. "'Cause I don't see any healing going on. Just a lot of groping."

Groaning at the memory, Sadie pressed clammy palms to her cheeks. Halting before the floor-length mirror, she stared, aghast, at her guilt-ridden reflection. She'd been angry; she'd been hurt. She'd let Dante's lips touch her throat. Collie was sure to tell Cass. And if Cass blew off Dante's head, she would never forgive herself.

Dammit, Cass, get back here! I need to know you didn't turn vigilante again.

As if on cue, a knock rattled the door. She nearly jumped out of her skin. Sucking down a ragged breath, she pinched her cheeks so she wouldn't look like death-warmed-over. Then she hurried to the door and threw it open.

"Mace!"

Silhouetted in the hall's flickering lamplight, her boss looked refreshingly dapper in his trademark black bowler and Inverness cape.

She scowled at the notion. "Come back later. I'm not dressed."

He blocked the closing door with his boot. "Got company?"

"Got manners?" she wanted to fire back. "No. Tonight I'm entertaining intruders, apparently. What do you want?"

His impertinent eyes traveled from the ebony rosettes she clutched so protectively to her throat all the way down to her bare, freckled toes. "You've been crying."

"Allergies."

"Is that the cock-n-bull story you fed Goddard when you swooned?"

"Pretended to swoon."

"Uh-huh." He pushed his way into the room. "You might want to work on that accent, *Contessa.* It's slipping."

She ground her teeth as the door swung closed behind him. "Cass isn't here."

"I can see that."

"Good," she snapped. "Now that you've confirmed the obvious, you can leave."

He turned to face her, those pine-needle green eyes too sharp and discerning for her peace of mind.

"First, I want to make sure you're all right."

She stiffened. Mace was concerned about her? *Genuinely* concerned? This slope was slippery. She didn't know how to respond.

"Of course, I'm all right. Never better. What's that package under your arm?"

"Don't know. I found it on your doorstep."

Sadie was relieved to learn he hadn't snooped through the contents—yet. "Where's the card?"

"It didn't have one."

Yeah, right. That piece of evidence was probably tucked in Mace's pocket. Hadn't he admitted to Cass he wanted her off the case?

Irritably, she tossed the box onto the mattress. It clanked with a metallic sound. Although its plain, brown wrapping didn't have an inscription, she had a pretty good idea who'd left it in the hall. Cass had been showering her doorstep with flowers, love poems, and naughty love toys for a week.

Mace hiked a bushy eyebrow. "Aren't you going to open it?"

She folded her arms across her chest. *And let my boss see my outlaw lover's ingenious, fur-lined manacles? Do I look like an idiot?*

"It's probably from Cass."

"A guilt gift, huh?"

She shot Mace a withering glare. "Don't you have any *criminals* to harass?"

"Sure. You want me to arrest Cassidy?"

"Hell, no. If anyone's going to arrest him, it'll be me."

"Then here's a tip. You can't arrest a fugitive after you've blown out his brains."

"I'll keep that in mind," she said darkly.

Mace grinned, flashing boyish dimples that made him look far less annoying than usual. "Stay sweet."

With a wink, he pinched the brim of his bowler and turned for the hall. She frowned when the door swung closed after him. She couldn't remember the last time Mace had tipped his hat to her.

Her limbs trembling from fraying nerves, she crossed to the marble vanity and poured herself a shot of fortitude. Considering the week she'd had, her tequila bottle was growing alarmingly low. Slamming the glass back on the table, she wiped her mouth and finally faced her gift. A niggling doubt had begun to gnaw the back of her mind.

I've been in this room since sunset. Surely Cass saw the light under my door. Why didn't he knock?

Warily, she crossed to the bed.

When Cass got his dander up, he was usually a beat-down-the-door kind of Neanderthal. He didn't hesitate to pick locks, either. So the good news was, Collie mustn't have told him about Dante's kiss. Yet.

Maybe Collie intercepted Cass and sent him to cool off.

Torn between hope and dread, she finally reached for the package. She told herself no amount of poetry or frou-frou could excuse Cass's treachery at the auction house. He'd risked her cover. He'd made her faint in front of Mace. All she wanted to do now was stop Cass from killing Dante and getting himself hanged.

Grimly, she tore off the wrapping. She found herself holding a black, enamel music box with a peacock mosaic on the lid.

Suddenly, Rebekah's warning knelled in her mind:

"Beware the devil's tune!"

Sadie's blood ran cold.

"Collie!" she shrieked, dropping the ominous little gift to the carpet and racing for the door. *"Collie!"*

A moment passed. Finally, the boy poked his shaggy head into the hall. He'd picked the lock of the maid's closet so he could hide from Mace. "You wanna wake snakes?" he hissed.

"Who left that package by my door?" she demanded as Vandy raced across the hall, trampling her slippers to wriggle his way into the room.

"What package?"

She waved the boy inside and pointed a shaking forefinger at the cheerful little box of death, which Vandy was now snuffling for food. She knew the box couldn't be the one from Minx's hotel room. Minx's box had been scratched beside the winding mechanism.

Collie shrugged. "Beats me. Why?" he added suspiciously. "What's wrong with it?"

Sadie swallowed. *Everything.*

"Find Cass. I need him."

Collie's lip curled. "Wouldn't you rather be rubbing navels with Beans?"

She bit her tongue, forcing herself to remember that 17-year-old males believed the only reason for a man to associate with a woman was sex. "I don't have time to argue."

"Why? You gonna faint again?"

"I *told* you, I was faking!"

He snorted.

She grabbed a fistful of his collar and shook hard. "So help me God, boy, I'll skin you alive if you keep sassing me!"

She had the satisfaction of watching shock flare in those streetwise, pewter eyes.

"What put a bee in *your* bonnet, woman?"

"Maestro! He was the one who sent the music box!"

Satisfied that Collie was keeping watch over Sadie, Cass had only one obstacle standing in the way of his greater mission to apprehend Maestro: Dolce.

Fortunately, Italian divas weren't much different from American wedding-bell chasers. Cass had lots of experience eluding the clutches of would-be brides. So after Dolce took her final bow, and her last bewhiskered admirer got shooed from her dressing room, Cass sneaked out of the opera house, intent on tracking Mendel Baines and learning what plot he and Cort were hatching that involved musical humidors.

Cass made sure that Dolce was too busy changing into her street clothes to notice him leaving. He also made sure he left her well-protected. Even so, he figured the diva would pitch a fit when she realized he'd left her under the surveillance of four stalwart stagehands.

Then again, Dolce certainly has the stamina for a four-man orgy...

Some bell in a distant church was tolling 10:30 p.m. when Cass trotted Pancake past a faded signpost that read, *Highlands.* Mounds of snow covered the boardwalk, but the main road had been sufficiently trampled to make travel easy. He urged the gelding around a whiskey bottle, gleaming in a puddle of moonlight. But Pancake, clown that he was, defied command. He slowed and stretched his long neck to sniff the frozen dribbles of amber.

"Seriously? You want *tornado juice?*" Cass scoffed. "That coon has been a rotten influence on you."

Pancake snorted, prancing a few steps.

"Don't get high-and-mighty with me. You and I both know you're little better than a belly on hooves."

Pancake promptly hiked his tail and let one rip.

Yes, if mooching ever became a sport, Vandy would have serious competition in Pancake. The cowpony would happily follow an apple to the ends of the earth. Cass should know. That's how he'd rustled the big, lovable oaf in the first place.

Now Cass was saddled with Pancake until he found a well-intentioned buyer. The quarter horse might not be the kind of mount that enhanced a tin-star's reputation, but Cass didn't want Pancake turned into dog food. He liked ol' Batter Head.

Besides, it wasn't Pancake's fault he was a natural-born goofball. Goofballs had their place in the world. That place, unfortunately, wasn't under a Texas Ranger. Cass needed a steed that could race locomotives, swim raging rivers, and buck audacious rustlers to the moon. He was hunting for a four-legged partner who could grow his legend, the way Steel had grown Rexford Sterne's.

Cass spurred Pancake down a side street to buffer the wind. "Now don't take it personal," he said, falling into an old cowboy habit: talking to his horse. "But when we get home to Texas, I'm gonna find you a nice, new owner. Probably in Oatmeal. Sounds like your kind of town, right?"

Pancake tossed his head.

"Well, of *course* that's a real town! In Burnet County. *Sheesh.* Calling me a liar. You'd best mind your P's & Q's, or I'm gonna sell you to some wolfer in Lick Skillet..."

About ten minutes later, Cass found the ramshackle building he'd been looking for. It was partially obscured by a pair of clotheslines, bearing a type of poor men's longjohns: grain sacks with neatly whip-stitched arm and leg holes.

Pancake eagerly sniffed the food sacks. Cass rolled his eyes.

"Dream on, Hay Burner. You'll find more oats in Oatmeal."

Dismounting, he slapped the gelding's rump, and Pancake found a nice, cozy spot between the clotheslines, where the canvas protected him from the wind—and hid him from horse thieves.

Cass raised his eyebrows. *Dang. I should've thought of that.*

"Don't eat the underwear, you hear? It'll give you gas."

Smirking at his joke, Cass turned toward the wooden, two-story general store, which looked about as sturdy as a building made of matchsticks. The structure was leaning into the wind. Its sign—which hung from its left chain and banged above the door—was painted in some language Cass couldn't understand. Tenants lived on the second story. Baines was supposed to be one of them.

The professor should have stayed in jail. He would have slept warmer there.

A light burned behind a tattered curtain. Cass checked the address. Sure enough, the room was Baines's rental.

Suddenly, a second story door squealed open. Tinny strains of music spilled into the night. Baines appeared, silhouetted against the clutter of newspapers and books. Despite the brisk wind, he wasn't wearing a hat, overcoat, or gloves; indeed, he didn't seem to mind the biting cold.

He descended the outside stairs. Clutched under his arm was an ivory humidor. It proved to be the music's source.

Cass found himself recalling the lyrics of the once-popular lament:

> *"In moonlit dreams, I called thee mine,*
> *A silv'ry fey, who charmed my heart..."*

Goosebumps tiptoed down Cass's spine.

"Hey, Baines!"

If the professor heard him, he didn't react. Cass watched in bemusement as the man plowed through calf-high snow drifts to reach the street. Glassy-eyed and expressionless, Baines didn't seem aware of his surroundings; in fact, his unblinking gaze was fixed on some distant point on the horizon.

Cass popped two fingers into his mouth and whistled. Pancake's head jerked up, but the professor remained oblivious.

Cass jogged after his quarry and waved his arms in the professor's face.

"Hey, Chuckles! I'm talking to you!"

Baines didn't flinch. He simply pushed past Cass's shoulder and continued his measured gait along the trampled snow in the street.

Now Cass was getting the heebie-jeebies. Baines was acting a lot like Sheridan had acted at the opera. Deciding to follow—mostly to protect the professor from thugs—Cass swung back into the saddle. The Highlands wasn't the type of neighborhood you wanted to roam after dark, unless you had a death wish or you were accustomed to dealing with devils.

Which says a lot about me, I suppose.

But as Cass scanned the dilapidated porches, with their icicle drips and boarded windows, he decided he'd seen worse. Hell, he'd lived in worse. As a sharecropper's son, he'd spent more nights than he cared to recall, huddled before the smoky old potbelly stove, while the wind keened through the chinks in the walls and frost crystallized on his backside.

Pancake's ears swiveled west.

Yep, someone's tailing us, all right. Cass glimpsed a man-shaped wraith, flitting between buildings. Snow crunched. Porch planks groaned. Cass drew a .45. But all he could see through his steaming breaths was the tip of a flapping shadow as it vanished behind the undertaker's shack.

Cass wasn't spooked by this observation, just wary. An outlaw couldn't be too careful. That's why he never went anywhere, including the privy, without the fire power to blast an escape route from hell. Tonight, he carried three double-action revolvers, a Bowie knife, and a stiletto. His saddle boot held a Winchester rifle and a Whitney shotgun, and his torso was wrapped in the kind of bullet-proof vest that had saved Sadie in Mattie's alley.

Besides, Cass didn't believe in ghosts. He'd chalked up the wing-like flapping of that fleet-footed shadow to a cape. Some flesh-and-blood human was tailing him. Cass hoped the spy was Maestro. That way, he could beat the bastard senseless, slap him in cuffs, and leave an anonymous present on the police chief's doorstep.

In the meantime, Baines plodded on, oblivious to his pursuers, the ruts he stumbled through, and the wind that pelted him in the face.

So this is what a trance does to a body, eh? No wonder Collie nearly peed his pants when Sheridan cornered him in the dressing room.

A few blocks later, Baines ducked into Porfi's alley. Now Cass was sure Baines was up to no good. The bakery's windows were dark. The sign on the front door read, "Open 6 a.m.," in great, block letters.

The waltz was fading out of hearing. Cass spurred Pancake faster—and not a moment too soon. Gunshots exploded in the night. Lights flared in several neighboring buildings.

Cass cursed. Galloping around the corner, he arrived in time to see Porfi's kitchen door sag from its hinges. He heard a reverberating crash, a female shriek, and blood-curdling Greek.

"You will *never* get your hands on my humidor, goat-stink!"

Cass threw himself from the saddle and sprinted after Baines. An upstairs window was cracked open. Silhouetted against the partially drawn shade, Cass could see three sets of pert young breasts and a human wall with a beard. Porfi and his women were throwing on clothes, which meant they would soon be charging into the kitchen, where more crashing, splintering, and gunfire could be heard. Cass worried he'd have a massacre on his hands.

But Porfi proved cannier than Cass had imagined. The Greek had smeared grease on the stoop. Cass learned this the hard way, when he went skating for dear life through the moonlit chaos of a booby-trapped kitchen. Flour billows filled the air. Forks twanged from the wooden doorjamb. Baines lay flailing in a heap of pots, pans, and broken crockery. A broken trip-wire wrapped his ankle.

The scene might have been comical, except for one hair-raising fact. Amidst all the racket, Baines didn't yell. He didn't curse. His face looked like it was carved from white marble as he kept firing wild shots at the copper kettles swinging overhead.

"Stand down, Baines!" Cass shouted when the professor's sixth and final bullet shattered the window over the sink.

But the warning did no good. In his trance state, Baines felt neither fear nor pain. He was heaving off wooden shelves as easily as he might have hurled feather pillows. When Cass tried to disarm him, Baines swung a fist. They wrestled, but the grease tripped them up, and they crashed into a heap of burlap sacks. Sugar flooded Cass's nose and mouth. Choking, he kicked blindly, but Baines weighed more and rolled on top. His eyes burning like demon fire, Baines grabbed a sack and tried to smother him.

"Thought you could steal from an honest baker?" Porfi was meanwhile bellowing from the top of the stairs. "Welcome to my kitchen, *malakas!* Here a thief gets eaten alive!"

Amber ooze rolled down Baines's forehead and into his eyes. Porfi's mistresses were yelling and leaning over the railing, dumping syrup and hurling eggs. Taking advantage of Baines's momentary blindness, Cass heaved the professor into a stack of cooling racks.

"My *loukoumades!*" Porfi cried as the honey puffs went flying.

Cass glimpsed the outraged baker through a flurry of flour, his striped mobcap askew on his nappy head, his tent-sized nightshirt falling off one tattooed shoulder. He was pumping a shotgun in his beefy hands.

"Porfi, wait!" Cass gasped. "Baines is under a spell! He doesn't know what he's doing!"

"I'll tell you what he's doing!" Porfi howled. "He's going to hell!"

That's when Cass heard the menacing click. Somehow, Baines had stolen a .45 from his belt.

Porfi's women shrieked.

Cass reached for his other Colt.

But Baines surprised him. Instead of mowing down the females who'd doused him with goo, he raised the revolver to his temple.

"Don't do it!" Cass yelled.

Baines never batted an eye. He pulled the trigger and jerked backwards through the explosion of light and powder.

"Sonuvabitch," Cass choked.

The aftermath was sickening. Blood and brains oozed down Porfi's oven door. Cass averted his eyes. The three girls clutched each other, rocking on the stairs and bawling like lambs. Even Porfi was momentarily stunned. When he finally collected himself to bark an order, his mistresses fled hand-in-hand to his living quarters.

The grim-faced Greek turned lethal eyes on Cass. Despite his crooked nightcap, the flour flaking from his beard, and the sheer cotton nightshirt that strained across the massive rolls of his belly, Porfi didn't look clownish. Not when he held that scattergun with the expertise of an infantryman.

"In my country," the Greek growled, "we do not suffer thieves to keep their hands."

Cass gaped at this threat. Then he remembered he'd gotten his hair cut and dyed.

"Whoa, Porfi. Take it easy. It's Cass."

Those glacier-blue eyes narrowed. Porfi braced the butt of his Whitney against his massive shoulder. "You think an old man is a fool, eh?"

"I see only one fool in your kitchen," interceded a gruff, Chicago baritone near the shattered window. "I think we can all agree, it's not you, Porfi. Stand down. Cassidy made a visit to the barber, that's all."

Mace stood illuminated by a splash of moonlight, his broad shoulders draped by an Inverness cape. Suspicion dawned as Cass watched the detective holster his Remington and Porfi lower his Whitney.

"You turned informant for the *Pinkertons?"* Cass accused, glaring daggers at the Greek.

A sheepish smile curved Porfi's lips. "Sorry, boyo."

"No sorrier than I am," Cass snapped, stung by betrayal. Struggling with his anger, he locked stares with Mace. "You want to tell me why the hell you've been tailing me?"

"Not you. Baines. He's been talking for days—mostly at Mattie's poker table—about raising the money for that Italian humidor. He vowed to have it, so Porfi did me the favor of making sure he lost the bid. With Baines's underground connections and his desperation for cash, I figured he'd lead us to Maestro. But you let him steal your Colt and blow out his brains."

"So it's *my* fault you don't have a pot to piss in?" Cass was livid. "Serves you right, *partner.* Maybe next time, you'll let me in on the particulars!"

"The way you let me in on your Daredevil scheme?" Mace countered acidly.

A muscle ticked in Cass's jaw. He wanted nothing more than to smash Mace's perfect nose. But what would be the point? If he didn't cooperate with the Pinkertons, he wouldn't get Sadie back.

"The way I see it," Cass jeered, "Daredevil's your ace in the hole."

Mace's lip curled. "You overestimate your usefulness."

"And you're a dick."

Cass stalked past a bemused Porfi. Wading through rivulets of sugar, he retrieved his fallen Stetson and Colt.

"Now if you *vlacas* will excuse me, I'm going to finish the job I started. With or without your help."

Much to Cass's annoyance, he left Porfi's bakery looking like a licorice lollipop. He couldn't very well search for Cort at Mattie's house while he was coated with sugar. So Cass made a quick detour to the Albany Hotel, where he traded his duster and Stetson for his detestable opera attire.

Fifteen minutes later, Cass was climbing the stairs to the brothel, when he spied Collie cantering down Holladay Street. The kid was recognizable beneath the waning moon, partly because of his ever-present scowl, and partly because he had a raccoon stuffed in the knapsack on his back.

Cass intercepted Collie in the gutter. "Now what?" he greeted.

"Take a guess," the boy said acidly and dismounted. "I've looked here for you twice already. And I looked in every other public brothel in this town, plus a few that *aren't* so public."

"You're welcome," Cass said dryly. "Learn anything?"

"Not the way you mean," Collie snapped. "Your woman damned near scrambled my brains!"

"Pissed her off again, did you?"

"*I* didn't do nuthin'."

"Vandy, then."

"What the hell kind of female doesn't like furry little animals?"

Cass hiked an eyebrow. Vandy, who was gleefully chomping hardtack in Collie's ear, dropped biscuit crumbs down the boy's collar.

I'll consider that a rhetorical question.

"Fight your own battles, kid. I don't have the time," Cass said, turning toward the brothel again.

But before he could take another step, Collie blurted out: "Sadie sent for you."

Cass frowned. Considering their estrangement, that message should have come as good news. But when Cass faced Collie again, the boy avoided his eyes.

"Is she sick?" Cass demanded.

"Not anymore."

"What then?"

"She got a present."

"From Goddard?"

"Don't know. The card got lost before she opened it."

"So you told her it was from me?" Cass smirked. "That was quick thinking."

Collie fidgeted. "The package was waiting by her door when she got back from the auction. She didn't see it until Ryker showed up."

"So?"

"So…inside the wrapping was a music box. She thinks it came from Maestro."

Cass went cold. A long, uneasy silence stretched between them.

"And now she thinks her cover's blown," Cass guessed grimly.

Collie dragged him away from the light of Mattie's picture window. "I told her that box could have been left for lots of reasons," the boy whispered in conspiratorial tones. "She might have a secret admirer. But even if Maestro did leave his calling card, that doesn't mean he knows the truth. He might still think she's filthy rich. He might be after the jewels he thinks she has in Italy."

"But she can't take that chance," Cass pointed out.

"At least Ryker doesn't suspect," Collie said darkly. "He thinks the box is from you. Apparently, Sadie wants to keep it that way. So if I were you, I'd get my ass back to the penthouse before she changes her mind again."

"Again?" Cass repeated dubiously.

Collie grimaced.

"What aren't you telling me, boy?"

Collie threw up his hands in exasperation. "How should *I* know what goes on in that crazy skirt's mind? She's your woman! And if you want to keep her, you'd better stop whoring with Mattie and Dolce!"

"I'm not whoring with—" Cass bit off his protest. As far as he was concerned, Sadie had no right to tell him where to take his pecker while she was freezing him out of her bed. "Hey! Where are you going?"

"Anywhere," Collie flung over his shoulder. "S'long as it's got bourbon, and neither of you are there."

"Now that's hurtful. We think of Vandy as family."

"Shut up." Collie heaved himself into his saddle. "Me and Vandy are done being in the middle. The next time you need a babysitter, tell her daddy to do it. He wants to see you double pronto."

"Wait a minute. *Sterne's* in town? Why didn't you say so?"

"I just did! And considering where you're headed, it's a good thing I found you before he did!"

Cass winced. The kid had a point.

"Where's Sterne staying?"

"Grand Central Hotel. Look for Mr. and Mrs. Robinson. Wilma tagged along." Collie spurred Rhubarb. "By the way. That's *another* one you owe me, Snake Bait!"

"Put it on my tab," Cass hollered after him.

Collie flipped him the bird, and Rhubarb broke into a canter.

No light poured from the crack under Sadie's penthouse door. Cass frowned. He'd expected her to be waiting up for him.

Then he heard some distant bell chiming the hour.

Damn. Midnight! He hadn't planned on spending so much time at the Grand Central Hotel.

Sterne had wanted a full report, mostly about Sadie's progress with her mission. Needless to say, Cass had kept his mouth shut about the more interesting anecdotes: how Sadie had handcuffed him to his train berth; how he'd stolen the Pinkerton emeralds; how he'd given Sadie a carriage ride she'd never forget. He'd also thought it prudent not to mention how he'd mislead Dolce into believing his Ranger badge gave him authority in Colorado. He'd figured Sterne would have a conniption fit, since the Ranger commander did everything by the book.

Yes, Sterne was a pain in the ass, but he'd won the war with the Marshal's Office. He'd arrived in Denver, toting the holiest-of-holies: a Special Deputy U.S. Marshal's badge. He'd even sworn Cass in. Now that Cass had his commission, he didn't have to worry about getting thrown in jail for his old stage coach robberies. Better yet, he could blow off Maestro's head, nice and legal-like, if the bastard threatened another woman.

Sadie should sleep easier, knowing that.

Tugging a widdy from his hatband, Cass picked the penthouse lock in three seconds flat. *Collie would be proud,* he thought wryly, slipping inside the room.

Hastily closing the door on the hall light, he allowed his eyes to adjust to the shades of pitch. A single moonbeam pierced the slit in the curtain, illuminating the long lump in the bed.

Sadie's sleeping, all right.

Not wanting to wake her, Cass tiptoed toward the headboard. When a body had been thieving as long as he had, it learned how to move in silence.

Or so he'd thought.

But the click of a revolving cylinder quickly cast doubt on his effectiveness as a sneak.

"Looking for someone, mister?" Sadie's voice was harsh. And slightly slurred.

His lips twitched. He could smell the tequila in the room.

"They call her the Devil's Daughter."

A moment passed. Then a light bloomed at Sadie's elbow. She was lounging in a striped, pewter armchair, her chestnut mane spilling to her waist, lacy rosettes cascading from her breasts. The skimpy threads between each flower left little to his imagination, especially when she drew breath.

But as enticing as that quivering vista of patchouli-scented freckles was, what captivated Cass in that moment—what had *always* captivated Cass about Sadie— was the sensual fire burning in those hungry, tiger eyes.

"I got word you wanted me," he said.

"Lies."

He hiked an eyebrow.

"But since you made the trip," she said huskily, her trigger finger never wavering on her .32, "take off your clothes."

Cass's amusement was fleeting. Nothing would please him more than watching Sadie watch him strip. And lick her lips.

But tonight she was angry and hurt. He glimpsed a smudge of kohl beneath her lashes, a sure sign she'd been crying. He remembered how she'd arranged the covers to look like she was sleeping and how she'd challenged him when he'd crept toward her bed. Those ploys hadn't been part of a seduction game, he realized now. She'd been scared that Maestro would enter her room.

But Sadie, being Sadie, would never admit her fear. If Maestro did get the best of her some dark and lonely night, she would roast his manly parts in hell.

Imagining Sadie's vengeance made Cass love her even more.

He decided she needed a diversion. An excuse so she could let him make her feel safe. Tossing his top hat on the chaise, he leaned an indolent shoulder against the bedpost and crossed his arms over his vest.

She looked displeased by his challenge. "Is that the best you can do?"

"Tell you what," he taunted. "You come over here, and I'll show you what I can do."

Those feral, feline eyes narrowed. "Prisoners don't get bargaining rights."

"So shoot me."

He strolled into the line of fire. He kept walking, enjoying the flash of warning in her glare. When he planted his hands on her armchair, he leaned close to the muzzle of that expertly held pistol.

"You gonna play nice?" he demanded.

"Never."

Striking faster than a viper, he knocked the gun from her hand and dragged her into his arms.

"I was hoping you'd say that," he growled, slanting his mouth across hers.

Sadie sank against all those rugged, roughrider muscles, hating her weakness for wanting him, but needing the consolation. He was leather and rawhide, sandalwood and steel, something strong and familiar to cling to while the world was spinning out of control.

Nevermind that he was the reason for most of the chaos. That he'd lied. That he'd betrayed her. That he was sleeping with God knew how many other women. When she'd called, he'd left those other lovers to come to her bed. And that was saying something, wasn't it?

Besides, it was just sex, she reminded the traitorous Dreamer who lived inside her heart. Wild, primal, orgiastic sex. No one did it better than Cass, when the demon was in his blood. If she clung to that thought, she wouldn't have to remember how she'd hoped—so desperately hoped, in the secret, walled off chambers of her heart—that he would become more than a passing affair.

"This changes nothing," she growled, mostly so her brain could hear the vow, because her hands seemed to have a will of their own. They were yanking off his vest and tugging his shirt tails from his trousers.

He chuckled, arching her over his forearm, sucking her nipple deep into the tantalizing pressures of his mouth. Her eyelids fluttered closed. *Damn.* He knew what she liked. It was aggravating.

It was wonderful.

He kicked off his opera pumps and swept her up in his arms, carrying her past the lump in the bed. "Shh," he teased, laying her down and smoothing her riotous curls over a pillow. "Don't want to wake your other lover. Or did you put a bullet in his head, because he failed to please?"

"I was thinking more about putting a bullet in your head."

"Just like old times."

"Don't flatter yourself. I used to like you then."

"So you admit it."

She glared up into his sapphire eyes, laughing so wickedly in the moonlight. "Doesn't your mouth have anything better to do than gab?"

His smirk was incorrigibly male. "Well now. Rewards are reserved for obedient prisoners."

She scraped vengeful nails down the rock-ribbed planes of his abdomen. "If you keep making me wait—" she grabbed a fistful of his swollen fly "—you'll lose something *very* precious to you, Rutter."

His inky lashes fanned lower, veiling the hunger in those flame-blue eyes. "Nothing could be worse than losing you, Sadie."

She swallowed hard when he threw her that bone. *That's the trouble with tequila. It makes liars sound sincere.*

She pushed her tongue into his mouth. He gripped her butt cheek, tipping her hips with a strong, possessive hand. Lightning crackled down her nerves as he rubbed her throbbing mound. The fever didn't take long to build. She tugged impatiently at the brass buttons of his fly; he wrestled off her negligee, pushing wads of lace out of his way.

Soon there was nothing between them but sizzle and heat. Legs tangled, tongues fencing, they writhed in an age-old rhythm. Her breaths ripped when he lengthened his thrusts, plunging in, sliding out. Desperately, she arched for more. He drove deeper, but not deep enough. Her breaths splintered when he left her wet and wild, quivering on the brink, cursing him and all his ancestors.

He grinned. "Say it."

"You're a pig-headed louse!" she panted, locking her thighs around his flanks, trying to drag his princely shaft back for another ride.

"You know what I want to hear."

"That your stamina was better in Dodge?"

He chuckled, his callused thumb rubbing with fiendish gentleness over her sensitized nub. "Try again."

She whimpered.

He squeezed.

She nearly came. *Nearly.*

"Damn you!"

"Nope. That's not it either."

"Why do you hate me?"

"I don't hate you," he crooned.

"You have a lousy way of showing it."

He relented, filling her aching emptiness with his shaft once more. "I need your forgiveness, Sadie."

Her bottom lip quivered. Tearing her eyes from his, she blinked back a traitorous glaze. "I'm not ready," she whispered hoarsely.

"When?"

"I…I don't know."

"You can't stay angry forever," he whispered.

His voice sounded so sad.

She dared to look at him then. She found herself drowning in his eyes, in those ocean-deep pools of endless, aching blue.

"Can't it be enough that I want you?" she demanded helplessly. "Still?"

He didn't look happy, but at least he was moving again. Tenderly. Soulfully.

"I'd give you the world, if I could, Sadie. Why won't you believe that?"

She didn't know how to answer.

Fortunately, he didn't give her the chance. His mouth covered hers, and she sighed into him, shoving logic into a distant corner of her mind. She wanted pleasure. She *needed* pleasure, the kind that Cass gave so masterfully. She didn't want to apologize for it, not even to her heart.

The room was spinning now, crackling with intensity. Cass was both catalyst and anchor; she clung to him for dear life. In the final moments, before the stars exploded and the moon skyrocketed out of orbit, nothing in heaven or hell could have separated them. They were a primal power. A force of nature. He gasped her name. She cried out his. All the savage beauty of life—the grief and the hurt, the love and the bliss—roared through their bodies in a tumult of feeling.

She rolled to her side. In the aftermath, he was quiet for once. No quips. No jests. She considered it a blessing.

Curling into a ball, she was too exhausted to protest when he wrapped his arm around her waist and settled in for the night. Many minutes passed. She found herself staring at the embers in the hearth. In spite of every hurt, every disappointment, she couldn't escape the truth:

She still loved him. She would always love him.

But as his breaths evened out and his fingers grew slack in her hand, she was forced to realize a painful truth:

She was too cowardly to tell him.

CHAPTER 15

The sun jabbed an impertinent finger into Sadie's eyes. Grimacing, she rolled to her back, flinging a forearm over her face and doing her best to ignore the tequila hammers pounding in her skull.

But her reprieve was momentary. A rattling sound reached her ears, followed by an insidious, mechanical clicking.

What the—?

Blinking blearily, she squinted in exasperation through the patchwork of shadows and morning. Cass was fully clothed and standing by the vanity. Apparently, he'd been shaking Maestro's music box to inspect it. Now his nimble fingers were winding the key.

Holy crap!

Sadie flew out of bed. Heedless of her hangover—and the blast of November that chilled her naked flesh—she bolted across the carpet to snatch the booby trap from her unsuspecting lover's hands.

"Good God, don't play it!" she gasped. "You don't know what it can do!"

He raised jet-black eyebrows. Honestly, she didn't know if she would ever get used to him being brunette, especially since he'd dyed his hair to please some other woman.

"Okay. I'm listening. Shoot."

She blew out her breath. Her head really did hurt, and the flood of memories—Cass with Dolce, the humiliation of fainting, Collie's watchdog posturing—wasn't making her any less cranky. Setting the music box safely on the vanity, she reached irritably for her robe. Her teeth were chattering with cold.

"First off, this is Pinkerton business—"

"Not that again."

"You said you were listening," she snapped. "That means the pie-hole stays shut."

His lips twitched. "My apologies, *Contessa.*" He bowed in the grave manner of a certain, Yankee psychiatrist. "Pray continue."

He was mocking her, the louse!

"Don't get me started," she growled. "You're on thin ice. Don't think I forgot how you strutted into Rothchild's yesterday, on the arm of the one woman in town who could blow my cover."

He rolled his eyes. "Give me some credit, Sadie. I was trying to keep Dolce away from you."

"By bringing her to the *auction?*"

"She's been trying to meet Lady Fiore all week. The only reason she hasn't hit you up to be her patron, is because I've been keeping her busy."

"I'll bet you have," she said tartly. She ignored his withering glare. "In any event, I think I finally figured out what happened to Minx. Why she robbed Tabor's mansion and jumped off the bridge."

She told Cass her suspicion about Minx's peacock music box. She described the "lullaby therapy" that Baines had prescribed for Wyntir. Sadie then revealed how the young heiress had complained of blacking out, and that she'd waked with inexplicable scratches and bruises.

"An unethical hypnotist might use a combination of methods," Sadie speculated, pacing in her agitation, "including drugs, to make a subject perform unconscionable acts. I think Maestro is commanding his puppets to steal and kill. Renfield, Minx, and Sheridan were all unwitting accomplices."

Halting in mid-stride, she drew a shuddering breath and faced Cass. She'd expected him to burst out laughing, to tell her she had an over-active imagination, to demand proof of her wild accusations.

Instead, he was frowning.

"Well, that certainly explains a few things," he said grimly.

"Y-you believe me?"

His jaw hardened. "Yes. I do."

Her breath released in a giddy rush of relief. She was tempted to throw her arms around his neck. Never had she loved him more than in that moment.

"Thank you," she said humbly. "That means everything to me, Cass. *Everything.*"

Those sun-crinkled eyes narrowed. She sensed something was bothering him.

"Mace would never have believed me," she hastened to explain. "He thinks women have fluff for brains. He places no stock in intuition, instinct, or hunches. Without solid proof to back my accusations, he would have laughed in my face.

"But I'm pretty sure where to *look* for proof," Sadie continued eagerly. "All we have to do is find some shred of evidence that will stick in court. Then we can prove Mendel Baines has been hypnotizing people to—"

"Baines is dead," Cass said flatly.

Sadie wheezed. With three small words, Cass had just obliterated her best Maestro theory—a theory she'd spent long, arduous hours building against the brawling, debt-ridden, morally bankrupt professor.

"When? *How?!*"

"He shot himself in the head. Around 11 o'clock last night," Cass added grimly. "I tried to stop him. But he was in a trance, probably triggered by the humidor under his arm. It was playing music."

Goosebumps prickled Sadie's scalp. She didn't know which was scarier, that she still didn't know who Maestro was, or that the bastard was leaving musical novelties at her door—and at other doors too, apparently! Baines had fallen prey to the sinister mastermind.

Struggling to form an alternative theory, she grasped at the first idea that presented itself. "Fowler was Minx's original suspect in the Welbourn case. It's no secret he uses hypnosis. He knows all the players: Lilybelle, Sheridan, Wyntir, Minx—"

Cass grunted.

"What?" she demanded warily.

"Fowler's not the only one who knows all the players."

"What's your point?"

"Right before the opera, Wyntir was hugging Sheridan and whispering in her ear."

Sadie frowned. "That hardly qualifies as hypnosis."

"But it could qualify as a trigger. Wyntir wasn't at the auction. She could have left that music box at your door."

Sadie didn't like where these accusations were leading. "Rebekah wasn't at the auction either. *She* could have left the music box at my door."

Cass didn't look convinced.

"Just because you dislike Dante," Sadie flared, "doesn't mean he's Maestro!"

"And just because you *do* like him, doesn't mean he's not."

She threw up her hands in exasperation. "Dammit, Cass, I *knew* you'd think the worst when Collie told you! He's 17, for God's sake. All 17-year-old boys have sex on the brain!"

Cass grew uncommonly still. A slow, dark flush rolled up his neck. "And just what was Collie supposed to tell me?"

Sadie's heart lurched. *Uh-oh. The kid kept his mouth shut about Dante? Dear God, I'm such an idiot.*

In retrospect, Sadie didn't flatter herself that Collie had kept quiet to do her any favors. He'd been trying to keep Cass from a guaranteed trip to the gallows.

Clenching her fists at her sides, she drew a shuddering breath and tried desperately to ignore her hangover. She had to get her story straight. What she said in the next few breaths could save lives—including Cass's.

"Dante was trying to help me when I fainted," she said firmly. "He carried me outside and loosened my corset. He's a *doctor,* Cass."

Cass frowned. His coyote instincts told him something wasn't right. Despite what Sadie believed, Collie was skirt-shy. Although the boy didn't know much about sex, he did know the ways of doctors. He'd spent nearly a year under Doc Jones's roof, fetching water, bandages, and splints whenever Sera wasn't around to help her older brother. If Collie saw something inappropriate pass between a doctor and a female patient, he would recognize it.

"So let me get this straight," Cass said slowly, his keen, sniper eyes watching every nuance of emotion that flickered over Sadie's face. "You fainted."

"Which was your fault!" she fired back. "You damned near gave me a heart-attack when you entered Rothschild's with your hair dyed and that bowler on your head. That woman had *no right* to sink her claws into you and swaddle you in swallowtails for her amusement!"

Cass recognized Sadie's temper tantrum for what it was: a diversion. She was hiding something. He ignored the outburst.

"And after you fainted, Goddard unbuttoned your corset."

"So I could breathe," she reminded him testily.

"Then what did he do?"

"Nothing! He massaged my neck. He whispered a few comforts in my ear. All perfectly normal doctor behavior."

"Did he kiss you?"

"Of course not."

"Did you want him to?"

Color flooded her face. Her jaw opened and closed.

Finally, she blustered, "I was dazed. I was reviving from a *faint,* for heaven's sake."

"Did you want him to kiss you?" he demanded again in gravelly tones.

Her eyes glistened, growing bright with unshed tears.

"I..." She swallowed hard. "I didn't think it would matter," she confessed tremulously. "You were with *her,* you'd changed to please *her,* and I needed his comfort!"

A cold, bitter wind blew into Cass's heart.

He'd known it. He'd sensed it. From that first moment in Jewell Park, when he'd spied Sadie with her arms around Goddard's neck; when he'd seen the Yankee smiling like a hungry wolf and Sadie batting her eyelashes at him, Cass had known his woman was falling for that smooth-talking, college-educated, over-dressed *prick!*

"Cass, please," she begged. "Don't do anything rash."

He shook her hand off his sleeve. Turning on his heel, he crossed to the vanity, picked up the music box, and smashed it against the marble counter.

"Cass, stop! *Stop!* That's Pinkerton evidence!"

"I'm done apologizing for protecting you," he snarled, pocketing the battered, musical cylinder. "Until you wise up, or Maestro's behind bars, I'm putting you on notice. Stay out of my murder investigation."

"I don't take orders from Rangers!"

"You'll take orders from me," he snapped, fishing a star from his coat pocket and stabbing it into his lapel.

Sadie quailed. That wasn't his Ranger star. The lettering on the five-sided cutout clearly read, *Special Deputy U.S. Marshal.*

She fumed as realization set in. *Rex is in town. Dammit, why didn't he tell me he was coming?*

Cass stalked for the door. He wrenched it open and paused on the threshold. "By the way," he flung over his shoulder, "nothing would please me more than to lock some high-and-mighty Lady Pinkerton in jail."

"You wouldn't dare!"

"Try me, sweetheart."

Cursing like a muleskinner, Sadie grabbed one of his guilt gifts—a perfume bottle—and hurled it after his tyrannical head. The missile smashed against the slamming door, creating a kaleidoscopic spray of honeysuckle and glass. But the gesture was an impotent one.

Cass was already gone.

After his row with Sadie, Cass was too angry to wait for the Windsor's elevator. Pocketing his Marshal badge, he stomped down five flights of stairs and slammed through the lobby door—and the lobby door slammed into the pimple-faced bellhop, who'd been helping Wyntir with her shopping.

An explosion of milliner's boxes flew from the youth's arms. Ladies' gloves and stockings rained down on the black-and-white tiles. Cass choked back an oath. He'd inadvertently trampled the pristinely white egret feathers of a hat.

"Oh, no! My birthday chapeau!"

Standing like a blue-satin lighthouse in a frothy sea of frou-frou, Wyntir looked torn between embarrassment and despair as the sputtering, red-faced bell hop desperately shoved her unmentionables into tissue-lined boxes.

Sheepishly, Cass stooped to retrieve the hat, but the confounded feathers had snapped off in three places. He was just about to stammer an apology when Wyntir got her dander up.

"Good golly, mister, where's the fire?"

Mister?

Cass's Coyote instincts went on alert. The petite beauty was glaring daggers at him. In fact, she was looking him straight in the eye without a single, blessed hint of recognition. Apparently, his top hat and dye job were more effective disguises than he'd thought.

The Coyote in him smelled opportunity.

Steeling himself against a smirk, Cass bowed in imitation of her snooty butthead of a guardian. "A thousand apologies, *senorita,*" he drawled in his best *caballero's* accent. Sadie wasn't the only one who could put on airs and pretend to be royalty. "I am—how you say—*inconsolable* to cause a lady such distress. *Por favor.* You must tell me how to repair my honor. I am *Don Reynaldo Dominar, Marqués de Oro Gran Polla y La Libido Asombroso.* At your service," he added with an impossibly straight face.

The rough translation of this lampoon was, *"I am the Ruling Dom with the golden pecker and the amazing libido—at your service."* Sexual propositions always sounded so much more refined in Spanish.

Wyntir's brows knitted. "You…um…are a Spanish nobleman?"

Funny how women only hear the royal part.

Cass clicked his heels and bowed his head. *"Sí.* Don Dominar. But you must call me Dom."

"Oh. Um, I see."

"I beg your forgiveness, *senorita.* A gentleman knows not to burst through doors. I have no excuse for my manners, other than the angels."

"The angels, *señor?"*

Cass pressed a hand to his heart. "Cupid lent wings to my feet so I might gaze upon your lovely face before you departed."

Wyntir giggled.

"Did you say it was your birthday, *señorita?"*

"Well, not officially. But at midnight—"

"Bueno! I shall buy you presents!"

Wyntir turned rosebud-pink. "I'm sure that's not necessary—"

"I insist! To replace what I have soiled is my responsibility as a man of honor!"

Cass didn't know how he was going to pay for roughly $200 worth of female frippery, but he decided to cross that bridge later. The important thing was to get Wyntir to trust him. And to spill her guts about Goddard.

Within two hours, Wyntir was doing just that. She snuggled under the brazier-warmed blankets of a garland-draped sleigh, driven by a toothless geezer and his gelded paint. The horse sported an antler headdress. Cass had arranged this silliness because Wyntir had shyly confided to Don Dom (as she now affectionately called him,) that she'd always wanted to ride in a reindeer-drawn sleigh. Her guardian wouldn't hear of such nonsense, because she owned two sensibly roofed coaches to ward off snow.

"And croup," she'd confided with a giggle.

Now she blew steam off the whiskey-infused toddy that the enterprising geezer had warmed in an Arbuckle's can between his boots.

"This coffee is yummy. It makes the snow sparkle. With rainbows!"

Yes, Wyntir was three sheets to the wind and slumming in the Highlands, although she didn't seem to mind. Nor did she seem to mind the whooping ragamuffins throwing snowballs, fencing with icicles, and sliding down hills in cardboard cartons. In fact, Wyntir had been eager to join the fun. About ten minutes earlier, she'd climbed down from the coach to help a quintet of red-headed urchins fashion a "Mother Snow Lady," whose "hair" looked particularly fetching with the feathers from Wyntir's damaged chapeau.

For a hoity-toity heiress, Wyntir is all right.

"Your guardian," Cass drawled, "he is—how you say—a bit stuffy, *no?*"

"Oh, he's *very* stuffy," Wyntir confided, much to Cass's amusement. "A proper Bostonian. Harvard-educated and all that. I did spy a hole in the bottom of his shoe once. Dante was mortified, but I didn't mind. Papa was always giving promising young businessmen a chance."

So Goddard was a penniless nobody until Greyfell took an interest in him?

Wyntir sighed. "Dear Papa. He had a heart of gold—he really did—even though he was so grouchy. His mood swings were due to a plague of headaches. A mining shaft collapsed a few years back, and he got struck by falling timbers. He was afraid that old neck injury would get him addicted to morphine. Unfortunately, opiates were the only solutions the doctors had to offer—at least, until Dante came along."

"Did Dante hypnotize your Papa?"

"Oh no. In fact, he got angry when I participated in one of Professor Baines's hypnotism experiments. After Papa's death, I kept waking up crying. By day, I started hyperventilating. Professor Baines said I was having anxiety attacks. The hypnotism seemed to help, but Dante said it was dangerous." She shrugged. "So I sought the advice of Preacher Fowler."

Cass hiked an eyebrow. "The man who talks to ghosts?"

Wyntir's cheeks turned rosebud-pink. "You don't have to make it sound so creepy! Preacher Fowler talks to perfectly nice ghosts, like my Mama and Papa. And angels, too.

"But Dante said Preacher Fowler was preying on my innocence," Wyntir continued, looking troubled. "He said I was delicate and impressionable. As my guardian and physician, he insisted on treating my anxiety himself.

"Now Dante won't even let me invite Rebekah to my birthday party! He said she should be returned to the asylum. Isn't that just dreadful? Rebekah is doing so well under Preacher Fowler's care! Sometimes, I think Dante's afraid of her."

Cass found this confidence intriguing. "A grown man? Afraid of a child? Why is that, *querida?*"

Wyntir's heart-shaped face took on the look of a crusading mother. "Because Rebekah sees things. *Really* sees things. Even though she never visited Greyfell Manor when Preacher Fowler came to call, she told me that my favorite diamond necklace could be found in the oddest place: a hollowed out book in Papa's library. I didn't even know the pendant was missing! But when I searched for the volume, there was my necklace, exactly as Rebekah had described it! Papa was furious when I showed him the vandalized volume. He fired the butler and two maids over it."

A muscle ticked in Cass's jaw. No one had to convince *him* that Second Sight was real. Before becoming Lynx's wife, Sera's visions had proved her future husband was innocent of a murder charge. "Was Dante living at Greyfell Manor when your pendant went missing?"

Wyntir blinked impossibly big, ocean-blue eyes at him. "Goodness. That's an odd question."

"Humor me," Cass said grimly.

Wyntir's eyebrows knitted. She began to rub her forehead. After a few moments, she seemed to give up.

"Strange." She loosed a strained little laugh. "I haven't thought of that incident for so long. And now, I honestly can't remember."

CHAPTER 16

The trouble with pitching perfume, Sadie fumed, was that the mess had to be cleaned up. Adding to her annoyance was her realization that she'd wasted 30 minutes scrubbing the door and the wallpaper, and the room still reeked like a bordello. At that point, she was in no mood for the trials of corsets and garters.

So she stabbed her legs into trousers, pasted on a beard, and hooked blue-tinted spectacles over her ears. Finally, she set off for the lobby. Her intention was to find Rex's signature in the ledger. After she figured out his room number, she planned to give the traitor a piece of her mind.

But as she exited the stairwell, she was intercepted by Collie, in what might have passed for a disguise. He'd stuffed his bleached hair under a slouch hat and draped a ratty duster over his buckskin coat. Sadie hiked an eyebrow, wondering if he'd stolen his battered duds.

"We got trouble," he greeted gruffly.

She sighed in exasperation. Vandy was nowhere in sight.

"What did the coon do this time?"

"Vandy ain't the problem."

He jerked his head toward the Windsor's registration counter. Two bellhops had replaced the usual clerk. Although they raced frantically around their post, neither of them seemed to be as effective as the man they'd replaced. A disgruntled crowd was clamoring for the valuables they'd stored inside the safe. A pair of steely-eyed constables prevented them from storming the business office.

"I'm being watched," Collie whispered, slapping a rolled newspaper into her hand. "Don't believe what you read. Keep your window open. I'll send Vandy with updates."

Fifteen seconds after he'd hailed her, the boy was stalking off, looking older and graver than his 17 years.

Uneasily, Sadie ducked behind the tobacconist's wooden Indian to read the headlines:

Can No One Stop the Daredevil?
Audacious Felon Nets $500K from Windsor's Safe

Sadie's stomach clenched. Dear God. *Someone set up Cass!*

By the time she tracked Rex to the Grand Central Hotel, the clock in the Methodist Church tower was chiming half-past eleven. Sadie despaired of catching the Ranger commander asleep in his bed. However, the hotel register had been signed, *"Mr. and Mrs. Robinson,"* in Rex's bold, slanting scribble. That could only mean one thing: he was traveling with Wilma. And Wilma was a night owl who rarely rose before noon.

Sadie banged hopefully on the lovers' hotel door.

"C'mon," she muttered, checking her pocket watch for at least the tenth time. With any luck, neither Rex nor Wilma had seen the *Rocky* yet.

But luck failed her. Mace threw open the door.

"Oh good," he greeted dryly. "You saved me the trouble of hunting you down."

Alarm bells tolled in her head.

"Well?" He hiked an eyebrow. "Are you going to join us or turn tail and run?"

Donkey butt.

Warily, Sadie shoved past her boss's broad shoulder. She spied Rex standing by the drawn shutters of the window. The handsome, pewter-haired Ranger commander was dressed in his Sunday best, sporting a black vest and matching string necktie, although he'd refused to trade his beloved Justin boots for "city shoes."

Wilma was also stylishly attired. The sheen of her navy satin day dress coaxed midnight-blue shimmers from the dark curls piled so elegantly on top of her head. She perched demurely in an armchair by the writing desk, a sheet of paper in her gloved hand, an envelope in her lap.

"Where's Cass?" Sadie demanded.

"That's what we want to know," Mace countered.

The Ranger shot the Pinkerton a glacial glare. "Has anyone told you you're an ass, Ryker?"

"Daily." Although Mace was 17 years younger than Rex, he wasn't intimidated by the Ranger's Alpha Wolf growl. "That's why I run the tightest ship in the agency. Let's get down to business.

"Sit," he told Sadie, sweeping his hand toward the only other chair in the room: a spindle-backed affair with an embroidered seat cushion that still bore the impression of his rump.

Sadie obeyed, but only because she didn't want to rumple the quilt. It had been tucked tightly enough around the bed to bounce a quarter. She suspected Rex's handiwork.

"Where were you between 11 p.m. and midnight?" Mace demanded.

Sadie eyed him resentfully. "Why?"

"Answer the question."

"Am I on trial here?"

"You'll be an accessory to a crime if you don't cooperate," he said flatly.

She darted a furtive glance at Wilma. The Pinkie Chief didn't look happy. In fact, she was glaring daggers at Mace. Sadie breathed a little easier, knowing Wilma was on her side.

"I was in my hotel room."

"Can anyone verify your statement?"

"Cass was with me."

"When did he arrive?"

"I didn't check the clock," she snapped.

His cool green stare was uncompromising. "You can do better than that, detective."

She wanted to kick him. "Church bells were tolling," she conceded. "It must have been midnight."

"Interesting." Mace scribbled something in his notebook.

"What's interesting?"

He ignored the question. "Describe how Cassidy was dressed."

Sadie was rapidly losing what little patience she'd walked in with. "Tuxedo and top hat."

"What was he carrying?"

"How the hell should I know? My lamp was doused." *God only knows what would happen to Cass if I confess he entered my room with a lock pick!* "Before I answer another question, I demand to know why I'm being treated like a suspected felon!"

Mace wasn't in the least bit daunted. "You want to be treated like a Pinkerton? Prove you deserve it. What do you know about the theft of Dolce LaRocca's necklace?"

"I know what I read in the *Rocky*."

"Which is?"

A muscle ticked in Sadie's jaw. "Sometime last night, the Windsor's vault was robbed. The heist was estimated at half a million dollars. The perpetrator escaped with small valuables, mostly jewelry."

"You mean *Cassidy* escaped," Mace challenged.

"Like I said, Cass was with me."

Mace flipped a page in his notebook. "According to Rex, Cassidy left the Grand Central Hotel around 11:15 p.m. The attendant at the Windsor's livery claims Cassidy stabled his horse around 11:40 p.m. If he arrived at your room at midnight, that leaves 20 minutes unaccounted for. Twenty minutes is plenty of time to crack a safe."

"Or smoke a cigarette," Sadie fired back. "Or bribe a stableboy."

"All right. I'll bite. What's your theory?"

"Cass was set up—or rather, Daredevil was. It's no secret that Daredevil and Maestro have been one-upping each other in the *Rocky*. Maestro's not the type to suffer a rival. In fact, he likes to eliminate human complications. My guess is, the hotel clerk was working for him. The clerk cleaned out the vault, gave the jewels to Maestro, then obeyed Maestro's orders to hang himself."

"Zut alors," Wilma muttered, blanching. "But why would the clerk do such a thing?"

"Maestro uses some combination of hypnosis and drugs to elicit mindless obedience. Then he gets rid of witnesses. That's why Baines shot himself, and Renfield hanged himself."

Mace hiked an eyebrow. "You have proof of this?"

"I'm working on it."

Mace grunted. "That's what I figured." He ignored her blistering glare. "Your theory doesn't account for Sheridan Welbourn. She's still alive."

"For now," Sadie said grimly. "And that doesn't mean I'm wrong about Renfield and Baines. But what I really don't understand is why the *Rocky* would print that cockamamie story about Daredevil."

"You mean, because the most recent anonymous tip didn't come from Boone Wylie?" Mace's smile was mirthless. "Yes, I interrogated the muleskinner this morning. Wylie claims Cassidy hasn't communicated with him. By the time Wylie learned about the Windsor story and tried to quash it, 200 papers had hit the streets. Dolce read one and went through the roof. She marched into our office around 9 a.m., demanding that we recover her Tiffany necklace."

So Dolce *sicced the Pinkertons on Cass?* Sadie bit back an oath.

"Brodie took her statement," Mace continued dispassionately. "She described how Cassidy impersonated a law officer to gain her trust. She said he persuaded her to put Mephistopheles's Jewels in the hotel vault. He urged her to wear one of a half dozen fakes for her protection. Then he surrounded her with guards and sneaked out of the opera house around 10 p.m. She claims he stole her jewels and rode out of town."

Sadie's chest heaved to learn how Cass's Maestro trap had backfired. She didn't doubt that Cass had jilted an international singing celebrity, since discarding women was the Rebel Rutter's way. *But he didn't ditch Dolce to steal her necklace. He ditched her because I sent for him!*

"As for the hotel clerk, Mr. Jonathan Stewart," Mace said, heedless of Sadie's growing upset, "he left no suicide note. No wife. No family. He slept in a room behind the Windsor's office and devoted himself to the hotel's guests. Everyone I spoke to said he was an exemplary employee. Tabor was grooming him for manager. Suicide makes no sense, but I agree with Sadie. Murder might. I want Cassidy for questioning."

Sadie's jaw dropped to hear Mace use her theory to incriminate Cass. "That's ridiculous! Cass wouldn't kill an unarmed man! He's a U.S. Marshal now."

"I don't give a rat's ass if he's president of the United States. He's a suspect." Mace drilled her with a no-nonsense glare. "Where is he?"

"How should I know?"

"You sleep with him."

"What the hell does *that* have to do with anything? Your entire case against Cass is built on an anonymous tip—which any halfwit can see came from Maestro—and the vindictive rant of a jilted lover. A woman like Dolce would be *desperate* to remain the darling of the press. If her American tour got cancelled, she'd have to pay back her thousand-dollar-a-performance price tag!"

"Maybe," Mace said grimly. "And if you're right, Cassidy has nothing to lose by turning himself in. Just like you have nothing to lose by telling the truth."

"I *am* telling the truth!"

"Cassidy is my responsibility," Rex interceded. "I'll find him."

Air whistled past Sadie's teeth. "Y-you don't believe he's innocent either, Rex?"

Something primitive and volatile flickered in the Ranger's slate-gray eyes. Was the emotion worry for her? Fury with Cass? Sadie couldn't say. All she knew was that Rex turned his face away. He strapped on his holster and reached for his Stetson. "When I have him, I'll bring him to the office."

"What office?" Sadie demanded.

"Colorado District. U.S. Marshal."

Mace nodded, tucking his notebook into his breast pocket. "The Pinkertons will want routine updates. I'll send a messenger to the office. One you can trust. You'll know him by the code word, *Slammer.*" He threw on his cape.

But before Mace followed Rex out the door, he paused on the threshold. He locked stares with Sadie. Something human flickered inside those hard, gemstone eyes. Regret, maybe? A reluctant sympathy? She wasn't certain.

In the next moment, he was all business. All *Pinkerton.*

"If that hillbilly kid comes sniffing around for information, keep your mouth shut," he said gruffly. "And don't make matters worse by getting in the way. Or else, you'll leave me no choice."

"No choice but what?" she fired back.

"To put you under house arrest."

She gaped.

The door slammed behind him.

This is bad. This is really, really bad...

Sadie was shaking. There was a roaring in her brain, a burning in her eyes. She bit her lip, tasting blood, vowing she'd bite it off before she cried.

"Come, *chere,*" Wilma crooned, reaching for a porcelain tea pot. "Let us have refreshment."

"How can you possibly think of tea at a time like this?!"

Wilma extracted a dainty silver flask from a pocket in her skirts. "Because it goes so well with bourbon."

Sadie blew out her breath. Wilma considered hospitality next to godliness. *All in good time, and all in its proper order.* That was Wilma's motto, unless, of course, she was staring down the barrel of your gun. At that point, you had better kill her—and fast—because Mambos could make life one big, endless torment while they had enough breath to curse you with. According to Wilma, *"There are worse fates than hell."*

Impatiently, Sadie waved away the cup the octoroon offered. If Sadie was going to drink bourbon—and she still might before the morning was over—it wouldn't be diluted with tea.

"Cass didn't do it, Wilma. He might be a loose cannon and a philandering jackass, but he didn't steal Dolce's jewels. And he certainly didn't put a noose around that clerk's neck!"

Wilma inclined her head in her gracious, southern manner. Whether she believed in Cass's innocence was unclear. Wilma knew him as well as Sadie did: every heroic impulse, every unexorcised demon. In fact, it was Wilma who had given birth to his Rebel Rutter legend back in Dodge, in a moment of whimsy, after his youthful stamina had accomplished what no other man had ever been able to do: win her wager to earn free ruts in her brothel.

"I am sure this matter will be resolved soon," the Cajun soothed in her husky, buttered-toast voice. "In the meantime, we have our own case to solve, *n'est-ce pas?"*

Setting down her cup, Wilma reached for the spectacles that hung from a delicate, gold chain around her neck. That chain was one of her few concessions to Father Time. A madam's most cherished secret was her age, and Wilma guarded hers more fiercely than most—with charms, incantations, and herbs.

"I received a letter from Minx."

Sadie struggled to concentrate. "But how—?"

"Her older brother, Geoffrey, brought it to my attention. Apparently, this is the last family letter she wrote."

Every hair on her scalp prickling, Sadie dragged her chair closer. She recognized Minx's handwriting. The letter was dated Oct. 15, which also happened to be the day the young Pinkie had sent her last telegram to headquarters, proving she was alive.

Sadie's eyes narrowed. "When did you get this?"

"Two days ago. Apparently, Geoffrey was away on business when the letter arrived at his home. He traveled to San Francisco immediately after Minx's funeral. He didn't know about the letter until he returned to his estate last week."

Grimly, Sadie took the page from Wilma's hands and scanned it. Much of Minx's reminiscences had to do with social gatherings, as might be expected. To protect her secret mission, she'd told her brother she'd traveled to Denver to visit an old school friend—"Wynnie" Greyfell.

Sadie caught her breath at this revelation. In all their conversations, Wyntir had claimed not to remember a woman of Minx's description!

Uneasily, Sadie read further:

"So sad, the news about Wynnie's father. The poor darling is devastated. She fired her papa's lawyer. Can you believe it? Benjamin Hoyt was like a second father to her! He served Edmund Greyfell for 26 years! Apparently, Hoyt counseled Wynnie to assign the bulk of her cash inheritance to a trust fund..."

Goosebumps scuttled over Sadie's scalp.

"What else did Geoffrey know about Wynnie—or rather, Wyntir?" she demanded.

Wilma was pouring more tea. "You know this woman?"

"I developed a relationship with her."

Sadie explained how Wyntir's blackouts led her to consult with Baines behind Dante's back.

"Interesting." Wilma lowered the teapot. "You are fond of this Dante."

Embarrassment burned its way up Sadie's neck. "No more than any other man."

Wilma didn't look convinced.

Sadie shot her friend a withering look. "You were telling me what Geoffrey knew about Minx."

Wilma nodded. "He calls her Minta. In a fit of rebellion, Araminta dubbed herself Minx when she left home to become a Pinkerton."

Somehow, the name change didn't surprise Sadie, given what she already knew about the adventure-seeking debutante.

"It is my understanding," Wilma continued, "that Geoffrey is unacquainted with his sister's friends. He is nearly 20 years Minx's senior. But Geoffrey did say, that on graduation day, Minx gave her friends a hand-made journal as a special memento. She was quite proud of it; she sent Geoffrey one too. Apparently, she pressed the pages from a special pulp mixture made, in part, from her trademark mint leaf. If this Wyntir is a friend of Minx's, she couldn't fail to remember such a gift."

"Not necessarily," Sadie said grimly. "Wyntir's memory may have been altered. She submitted to hypnosis on numerous occasions at the hands of our chief suspect."

Quickly, Sadie told Wilma everything she knew about trance states. How Maestro's puppets appeared to be triggered by music. How Fowler and Baines had argued over the musical humidor. And how Sheridan Welbourn had been in a trance when she tried to rob—and then kill—Dolce LaRocca at the opera.

"From the beginning, Minx suspected Fowler was Maestro. Somehow, he stayed one step ahead of us at every turn. He even knew you were coming to Denver!"

Wilma hiked a coal-black eyebrow. "Impossible. My decision was made at the last minute."

"I'm telling you, Wilma, he *knew*. Last week, he said straight to my face, 'Consult with your lady friend from the bayou. Her insights will prove most valuable when she arrives.' I think we have a mole in the agency!"

Wilma's expression remained placid. But few things flustered Wilma. Sadie had seen the older woman face a knife-wielding ruffian and teach him respect with her whip. Wilma's reputation as a dominatrix and a Mambo was usually sufficient to keep predators in line—which was fortunate. Only a handful of men knew she was a Pinkie Chief.

"Very well," Wilma said. "I shall take your concerns under advisement. What's next?"

"Wyntir's birthday party is tonight. I'll question her about Minx."

"And Fowler?"

Sadie glanced at the mantel clock. "It's 12:15," she mused, doing some rapid calculations in her head. "Fowler should be hosting one of his spook shows. If you could confirm—"

A polite knock on the door interrupted her.

She tensed, her eyes locking with Wilma's.

"Company?" Sadie whispered.

"No one's supposed to know Rex and I are here except Collie."

Wilma started to rise, but Sadie waved her back to her seat. After all, Wilma wasn't the one dressed as a man with a shoulder holster hiding under her coat.

Unbuttoning her duster, Sadie drew her .32 and crossed to the door. But when she spied the visitor, waiting so patiently in the hall, her jaw hit the carpet.

"Oh, hello, *Contessa.*" As if encountering a bearded woman with a cocked pistol was an everyday occurrence, Enoch Fowler doffed his bowler and flashed his congenial smile. "I hope I'm not too late. I came to see the Marshal. To turn myself in."

CHAPTER 17

"Hands up!" Sadie barked, waving Fowler into the room.

Wilma hiked an eyebrow. "And who is this?"

"Permit me to introduce myself, madam. My name is—"

"Shut up," Sadie snapped, yanking him around. Her heart was crashing against her ribs. There was no telling what insidious weapon Fowler had hidden under his coat: Guns. Dynamite. Lethal drugs.

"Hands on the wall. Legs spread." She forced his skull forward, so his forehead butted against the rose-patterned paper. "Frisk him, Mrs. Robinson," she said, careful to maintain Wilma's cover.

"I assure you, ladies—" Fowler's chin was tucked in his collar, so his voice sounded muffled "—I am quite harmless—"

"Did I say you could talk?" Sadie growled, her gun hammer clicking by his ear.

He sighed.

"He's not armed," Wilma concluded after patting down his clothes.

"Check for bombs. It would be just like Maestro to send someone here to blow us up."

"Nothing's ticking," Wilma advised, wrestling his shirt tails from his waistband.

Sadie was relieved to see no wires or timing devices strapped to his torso. "All right, cuff him."

Peeking over his shoulder, Fowler gawked as Wilma hiked her skirts to produce a pair of manacles—the all steel, all Pinkerton kind.

"Goodness. What a clever place to hide—"

"Shut up!" Sadie smacked the back of her prisoner's head. *So help me God, if he gets a hard on, I'll bust more than his chops.* "Sit." She shoved him into the spindle-backed chair.

At last she felt safe enough to step back and take her thumb off the gun hammer.

Wilma hiked a questioning eyebrow.

"Enoch Fowler," Sadie supplied finally. "Or more likely, Maestro."

"May I speak now?" he asked.

"When spoken to," Sadie fired back. She glowered at the disheveled preacher, whose expression was far too complacent for her peace of mind. "If I had my way, you sack of turds, I'd be handing you to a female lynching mob, not an all-male jury."

"I'm sure I would feel the same way, if—"

"Don't try to placate me!"

Wilma cleared her throat. "Mr. Fowler—"

"Reverend," he corrected her politely.

"Very well. Reverend Fowler, did I hear you correctly? You came here to turn yourself in?"

"Yes, madam. To save us all a bit of time. Someone is going to arrest me anyway."

Sadie sneered at this gall. "You got that right."

Wilma hiked an eyebrow. "And why would someone want to arrest you, Reverend?"

"Let's just say I have enemies. People who don't like to hear the truth."

"Because you blackmail them with it?"

Indignant, Fowler stiffened in his chair. "Madam, whatever you may think of my sources, I assure you, I am nothing more than their channel. I told as much to your young colleague before her death. Now I understand that individuals within your organization—" he tossed Sadie a pointed look "—are trying to implicate me in that tragedy. The only way to prove my innocence is to help you catch the real culprit. That's why I'm here."

"So you've been listening at keyholes," Sadie bit out.

An unmistakable challenge gleamed in Fowler's intensely blue stare. It locked with hers. "Your ragdoll is buried with your twin. At the time, it was your most treasured possession."

Sadie's breath whistled past her teeth. For a moment, she was so astounded, all she could do was gape. How the hell could Fowler know something so private about her childhood? She'd never told that story to Cass or Wilma. She hadn't even told it to Mama!

In fact, Mama had forbidden her to go near the casket. Mama had blamed her for Maisy's death. Sadie had been forced to sneak Dolly inside the pinewood box so Maisy wouldn't be scared to go to heaven alone.

Wilma was frowning. She waved Sadie to a circumspect silence. "Tell me, Reverend. What exactly do you think our line of work is?"

"Most recently? Undercover investigations."

Sadie and Wilma exchanged uneasy looks.

"And you believe this because—?"

"My dear madam, I do not wish to offend. Only to help. Oh, good," he continued with unmistakable relief. "There's the marshal now. I wasn't too late, after all."

As if on cue, Rex's spurs jingled in the hall and his key scraped in the lock.

"Blast. I grabbed the wrong—" His explanation trailed off as the door swung open.

"Badge," Fowler finished for him. "Yes, good sir, you left your marshal badge in your duster. Left breast pocket."

Rex gaped to see Sadie drawing a bead on a handcuffed man. "Who the hell is this?"

"Reverend Enoch Fowler," Wilma said dryly. "Apparently, he talks to spirits."

Rex hiked a bushy gray eyebrow. "Talking to spirits is a crime now?"

"It's a little more complicated than that," Sadie snapped. "Fowler's the chief subject in Maestro's crime spree, including the murder of Minx Merripen."

"I thought Minx jumped off a bridge."

"Her murder *will* be difficult to prove," Fowler said sadly.

Sadie was sorely tempted to hit him again—and a lot lower this time.

Meanwhile, Wilma was rummaging in the left breast pocket of Rex's duster.

"For God's sake," Sadie told her, "you can't seriously believe—"

The Mambo's expression grew grim. She withdrew her hand to display the marshal badge.

Goosebumps tiptoed down Sadie's spine. "Lucky guess," she insisted stubbornly. "He probably saw Rex take off the star and slip it into his pocket. Or maybe one of his followers did. God knows, hundreds of them are polluting this town."

Fowler shot her a reproachful look. "My dear young woman, a little faith wouldn't hurt you. Surely, you don't think you survived that brothel fire simply because of your lock-picking skill. Meg and Maisy watch over you."

This dig incensed Sadie. "Just Mama and Maisy?" she sputtered, desperate to poke a hole in his eerily invasive insights. "Not the ghost of my father?"

"Your father isn't dead."

"Liar!"

Rex blanched. Lunging between her and Fowler, he plucked the gun from her fist.

"That's enough," he growled. "Unless you have some evidence to charge him, you can't cuff this man and hold him against his will."

Sadie hiked her chin. "He turned himself in."

"Is that a fact?" Rex drilled Fowler with his steely lawman's glare. "You have a confession to make, *padre?*"

"Yes, marshal. I confess I speak to spirits. They have information that can help you solve Maestro's crimes."

"And these spirits are just piping up now, are they? Convinced you to be a Good Samaritan, did they?"

"What would you have me say, sir? You're the law, and you don't believe me, even though I just *proved* I know the unknowable. Such is my fate among lawmen. Nevertheless, I do try to help in my way.

"When I foresaw Maestro's coming, I urged Lilybelle Welbourn to hide her jewels and hide them well. I cautioned Malcom Renfield not to work alone in the museum after dark. I warned Mendel Baines to rid his home of musical novelties—" he hiked a challenging brow at Sadie "—as you'll no doubt recall, since you were eavesdropping. However, he called me a crackpot.

"I don't have to tell any of you what happened when Professor Baines ignored the spirits' advice," Fowler continued with an unpleasant hint of righteousness. "Now I fear for Wyntir Greyfell. She is young. She is impressionable. And she will inherit a fortune at midnight."

Sadie wasn't sure what to believe. Fowler was the consummate showman. He could be lying through his teeth.

Her troubled gaze flicked to Wilma. The Mambo was staring at the window, as if she could see past its latched, wooden shutter. She'd grown unusually quiet. Sadie fidgeted, wondering if her outburst had offended Wilma. In all their years of friendship, Sadie had schooled herself to discretion, outwardly tolerating Wilma's arcane practices: the tattoos of writhing snakes on her hands; the pouch of protective herbs around her neck; the little straw poppets dressed like friends—and enemies. But secretly, Sadie was spooked by Wilma's Voodoo.

"Tell me, Reverend." The Mambo was winding the cord of her *gris-gris* around and around her forefinger in the most disturbing way. "Are your financial affairs in order?"

Fowler stiffened.

Wilma's dark, compelling stare finally fastened on the preacher. "You are a gifted clairvoyant, *m'sieu*. Of this, I have no doubt. Your visions warned you about the Federal agents combing the Windsor for you, even as we speak. The Denver police cannot prevent your arrest for tax evasion. But a U.S. Marshal? Perhaps he can."

A dark flush rolled up Fowler's neck. But he didn't deny the accusation. "Madam, I cannot pay the penalty. They will throw me in prison and lock Rebekah in an asylum. I can't let that happen to her. If your spirits are good and true, then they've shown you her fate. The child will not survive another institution."

Rex shot Wilma an exasperated look. Sadie knew him well enough to understand his frustration. Rex didn't have the freedom to interpret the law. All he could do was enforce it.

"A plea bargain might be possible," he conceded in grudging tones. "But you can't go to court spouting mumbo-jumbo, *padre*. Hard evidence. That's what a judge wants. And the district attorney will want Maestro's conviction."

"I am prepared to do whatever I must. For Rebekah," Fowler added staunchly.

"You have taken the first step, Reverend," Wilma soothed. "Now you must trust the process."

Tears filled his eyes. "Please, madam. Watch over my ward. Without me, she has only the spirits to protect her. And sometimes, spirits aren't enough."

"My friends will rally around her," Wilma assured him. "The child will be well guarded. You have my word."

"Thank you," Fowler whispered hoarsely.

As Rex caught the preacher's arm and helped him from the chair, Sadie struggled with a surge of guilt.

Maybe I really did misjudge Fowler. Maybe he really does care about Rebekah.

Then again, murderers weren't immune to love. Crimes of passion produced corpses all the time. Fowler could be playing them all for fools.

As if sensing her skepticism, Fowler glanced over his shoulder. Their eyes met.

"Eat nothing," he urged suddenly. *"Drink nothing at the party unless it is poured by your own hand. He will be watching."*

"Who?" Rex demanded, yanking Fowler's arm so hard, the preacher nearly stumbled to his knees.

"She knows," Fowler gasped.

"You think that's the kind of talk that'll make you friends in court?" Rex growled, shoving his prisoner out the door.

Sadie shivered, avoiding the speculation in Wilma's all-too-knowing eyes.

Sadie did indeed know whom Fowler had meant.

But she didn't want to believe it.

"Psst!"

Cass hiked an eyebrow at the snow-dusted bush, hissing so urgently at him beside the porch of the Bust-a-Gut Saloon.

"You talking to me, Four Eyes?"

The young Pinkerton blew out his breath. "I'm supposed to be *disguised,"* Brodie grumbled.

Cass hid his amusement. Little did the intrepid, junior detective realize, he might as well have been waving a red flag above his stakeout. Little puffs of steam were rising above the dark, green leaves of the boxwood's foliage.

Strolling through the slush, Cass propped his derriere on the railing beside the bush. *Yes, Mace Ryker isn't the only one who can recruit allies from the other side.*

Night was creeping over the mountains, and the temperature was rapidly dropping as Cass fished in his duster pocket for his tobacco. Leaning his shoulders into the corner of the building, away from the wind gusting across the river, he lit a quirley, mostly for an excuse to sit and talk to a bush.

"Sterne's still hunting for me, I reckon."

"Oh, no, sir!" Brodie protested. "Not anymore. I threw him off your trail. I told Ryker you were spotted out by Union Station."

"So Sterne and Ryker both think I fled by train? Much obliged."

Brodie grew pink with pleasure. "I want Maestro caught as much as you do, sir. Did you win the $200?"

Cass shoved a jingling leather pouch through the branches. Brodie sucked in his breath.

"Jeepers! That's $500!"

Cass smiled to himself. Brodie might be four years older than Collie, but he possessed the street smarts of a toddler.

"Wait a minute," the junior agent said suspiciously. "Is this a bribe?"

"Can you be bribed, son?"

"Absolutely not, sir!"

"And Pinkertons, Rangers, and Marshals are all on the same side, right?"

"Yes, sir!"

"Then it can't be a bribe, now can it?" Cass blew out a lazy stream of smoke. "So tomorrow, I want you to dress as Don Dom's valet and take 200 of those dollars to Miss Wyntir. The rest will buy you a horse and tack."

"But I already have a horse."

"No. You have *Dumpling*."

Brodie's sigh was wistful. He clutched his plump new money bag a wee bit tighter. "Giving Dumpling a new name sure would be a lot cheaper."

"A nag's a nag, son. Changing her name won't turn her into a runner—or even a walker. 'Sides. If working magic was that easy, I'd have re-Christianed Pancake. Named him something useful, like Bountiful Springs of Whiskey."

Brodie's muffled cough sounded suspiciously like a snicker. "I suppose Dumpling isn't much of a deputy's horse. Or even a valet's, I *reckon,*" he added, testing the unfamiliar Westernism on his Hoosier tongue.

"Son, a crippled monkey wouldn't ride her."

This time, Brodie's strangled laughter came out as a snort.

"Shh!" he whispered fiercely, pocketing his bribe. "You want folks to wonder why this bush wasn't here 20 minutes ago?"

Cass suspected that question was rhetorical because Brodie launched into the rest of his report.

"Marshal Sterne took Fowler into custody. Mostly for protection, I think. The rumor is, Fowler has some dirt on Maestro, and he's using it to plea down tax fraud. Since Maestro might retaliate, Miss Wilma sent Collie to protect Rebekah. Collie wasn't too happy about it."

Cass's lips twitched. "I don't suppose he was. And Sadie?"

"Ryker's with her."

A muscle ticked in Cass's jaw. Brodie fidgeted while Cass sucked on his smoke.

"Can I ask a personal question, sir?"

"Shoot."

"Why don't you become a Pinkerton?"

Cass shrugged, tapping ash. "'Cause I'm a showboater, I reckon. Undercover work is for fellas who like to keep to the shadows, where they can't be seen."

Brodie digested this news. "But you've worked undercover before. Besides, Pinkertons can get married. Mr. Allan has a wife."

"You think a lawman can't survive without a wife?"

"No, sir! It's just that…well, I see how you look at her."

"Her, who?"

Brodie snorted.

"Dolce? Mattie?"

"Miss Sadie would claw out your eyes," Brodie protested, aghast.

"You think?"

"And fry your balls!"

Cass grinned. "She does have a fiery nature."

"Like a supernova."

"Sounds like *you* want to marry our shooting star."

"Me? Heck, I wouldn't know the first thing about keeping a woman like her happy. But Ryker…"

"What about him?"

Brodie grimaced, averting his eyes. "He's not your friend, sir. I don't have to tell you that."

Cass's smile was mirthless. He dropped his cigarette butt. It plummeted like a tiny meteor, sizzling in the slush before winking out. Just to make sure, he ground the stub into the water with his boot toe—imagining it was Ryker's face.

"Did you salt those steaks the way I told you to?"

"Yessir," Brodie said.

The boy pushed a package, wrapped in butcher paper, through the branches. Cass hid it under his duster.

"And the blueprint?"

"I made a sketch. Goddard's office is in the west wing, on the second floor. The library's on the south side, at the top of the grand staircase. You really think you'll find the Heart of Fire at Greyfell Manor?"

"It takes a thief to catch a thief."

"'Cause they think alike?"

"Now you're catching on, son."

Brodie looked pleased.

Cass winked, pocketing the sketch and saying his farewells. Tugging his Stetson low against the wind, he headed for the hitching post, where he found his buckskin huddled for warmth between two long-legged fillies. Ol' Pancake wasn't the fuddy-duddy Collie liked to think he was.

Cass's smile faded as he swung into the saddle and turned toward Colfax Avenue. The moon would be dark tonight, which he considered an advantage. Wyntir's birthday party would soon be in full swing. Too bad Don Dom had been forced to give his regrets. But Lucifire was looking forward to his rendezvous with a climbing rope and a mansard roof.

CHAPTER 18

———◆———

Sadie was struggling to strap her derringer beneath ten pounds of underwear when a knock rattled the penthouse door.

Assuming the caller was Collie, she blew a curl off her forehead. She hadn't seen the boy or his masked moocher all day.

"Just a minute," she muttered. "I'm coming!"

"Ciao, amore mia bella!" came the muffled response from the hall.

Sadie's hands stilled on her thigh holster. Now *that* voice hadn't been bred in Kentucky.

Dropping her skirts, she approached the door with caution. This morning, she might have appreciated the arrival of an Italian knight in shining armor, whose warm, rich baritone claimed her as his beautiful love—especially while Cass had been running amuck, smashing things.

But at 6:40 p.m., with her nerves as taut as fiddle strings, thanks to her worries about Maestro's mindless minions, she was tempted to shoot first, and ask questions later.

Struggling against the impulse, she stooped to squint through the keyhole. She spied a dashing sash of crimson silk, a trio of glittery medals, and a red rosebud clutched in a white-gloved fist.

What woman wouldn't open the door for that?

Hiding her pistol behind her back, she dared to turn the knob. To her surprise, a man in black swallowtails—with Mace's green eyes—clicked his heels and doubled over in a smart bow. She raised her eyebrows. Her fastidious boss had donned a coal-black wig, waxed a mustache into curly-cues, and fastened mutton chop whiskers to his jaw. He'd also given himself a paunch. She didn't know whether to be amused or annoyed.

"Baciami!" he cried, throwing his arms wide and puckering his lips.

Okay, that settles it. I'm annoyed.

"I am *not* going to kiss you," she hissed, pasting on a smile for the elevator operator, who stood gawking at them at the end of the hall.

Grabbing Mace's coat sleeve, she dragged him over the threshold and slammed the door. "You have a lot of nerve, showing up here. What do you want? Cass? I haven't seen him since this morning."

"I believe you."

"Well, *that* would be a first."

"Just doing my job."

"Yeah? And what's that supposed to mean?"

Amusement softened the impertinent gaze that drifted to her well-boosted bodice. "I heard you needed a bodyguard."

"No, Wilma *ordered* me to have a bodyguard. I'm perfectly capable of kicking some scumbag's ass at a birthday party."

"In that dress?" He whistled long and low, ogling her curve-hugging, spruce-green velvet. "All the more reason for me to tag along. To watch," he added drolly.

Hating that her cheeks warmed, Sadie glared with extra disdain at his gift. "I suppose that rose has thorns."

"You wouldn't like it if it wasn't thorny."

Hilarious.

Secretly impressed by Wilma's cunning choice of bodyguards—after all, as long as Mace was attending

Wyntir's party, he couldn't arrest Cass—Sadie decided to cooperate. But she didn't have to like it.

"Take your pick of vases," she said tartly, pointing at her empty tequila bottle and the brimming water pitcher beside it. "And just for the record, you're early. I'm not finished dressing."

"No problem, doll." He winked. "Just holler if you need my help."

That'll never happen.

Stalking behind the dressing screen, she finished fastening her pistol to her thigh then crossed to the vanity, where she retrieved the pearl earbobs Wilma had loaned her for the evening.

As Sadie clipped on the dangles, her eyes strayed to Mace's brawny reflection in the mirror. He was checking his weapons. He unbuttoned his coat to adjust his shoulder holster; he tested the wrist trigger that dropped a .38 into his fist; he straightened his hem over his ankle sheath. As he was inspecting his cuff links, which were standard-issue smoke bombs for male agents, he caught her watching him in the mirror.

He had the poor grace to smirk.

She scowled and reached for her powder puff.

With nothing better to do, Mace shoved his hands in his trouser pockets and strolled around the room, acting nosy, like a detective. "How come this wallpaper smells like honeysuckle?"

"Don't ask."

"There's a nice big stain here. Have an accident?"

She dusted her nose in the ever-futile attempt to hide her freckles. "That's right. An accident."

He paced off the steps to her fragrance tray. "You threw that perfume bottle at point-blank range and missed? Please tell me Cassidy had already ducked out the door."

She twisted on her stool to glare at the nuisance. "Do you just *like* pissing me off?"

"Come to think of it, I can't remember a time when you weren't pissed at me."

"Shouldn't that tell you something?"

"Yeah." He flashed boyish dimples. "I'm hard to resist."

Her eyes narrowed. *Why are my cheeks heating?*

Since her mind was annoyingly blank, with no pithy comeback, she swiveled to face the mirror and dipped a well-lacquered forefinger into her pot of lip paint. *Copper Shimmer.* Not her favorite shade. But her hair was darker now, and the season was autumn, so she'd made the concession.

Applying the paint, she watched Mace's reflection as it squatted. The tails of his coat had been hiding tight, round buttocks. Reluctantly, she admired the corded calves connected to his even more impressive thighs. Clearly, this was a man who didn't spend his days and nights in a saddle...

Damn! Her heart skipped a beat. Mace was picking a black splinter from the carpet. How had she possibly missed it? She'd crawled over that wool pile three times, hunting for pieces of the music box that Cass had smashed!

"What's this?" Mace's curiosity quickly dissolved to suspicion. Crossing to a lamp, he inspected his find. "It looks like wood. Painted with black enamel."

"Mystery solved," she retorted with practiced nonchalance.

He tossed her a sharp glance. She made sure she looked busy, blotting the excess paint from her lips.

"You kids must have had some cat fight."

"Am I allowed *any* privacy in my own bedroom?"

She didn't like the way he was assessing her reflection with that hooded stare. She sensed he was making up his mind about something.

"Nothing you borrowed from the agency vault appears to be missing. What got busted?"

"Why don't you figure it out, detective?"

She probably shouldn't have said that. He flipped open a hollow button on his vest and carefully fitted the splinter inside.

"I was joking, Mace."

"Never joke about evidence, doll."

"Are you always this creepy when you go courting?"

"Are we courting?"

Ugh!

"Let's get our story straight," she said briskly in an attempt to change the subject. "I am Fiore Torchia, the *Contessa di Montaldeo*. I live in an obscenely large *palazzo* in Naples. I'm a widow touring the Americas, because I'm rich and bored and have nothing better to do since Luigi's death. Who are you?"

He inclined his head. "I am Don Niccolaio Brianza Assante, *Barone di Monte Somma*. The lover you were entertaining behind Luigi's back."

"Try again."

Unperturbed by her snub, he fitted a monocle to his right eye. "Very well. You can call me Nico. I'm your cousin."

"On my mother's side."

"If you insist."

"Must you wear the monocle?"

His lips twitched. "Rather Continental, don't you think?"

"You don't want to know what I think." With the magnified eyeball, he looked like a tree frog. "Why are you in Denver, Nico?"

"Duty calls. It's time to escort my favorite cousin home."

"No dice. I told Goddard my next stop after Denver was Frisco. Therefore, you want to grow grapes in sunny California. You hope to purchase a vineyard in Napa County."

"To expand the family business." Mace nodded. "Works for me."

Sadie sighed. If only their charade could be that simple. "How much Italian do you really speak? Apparently, Goddard travelled to Italy, and he's familiar with the language."

"I can get by," Mace said gruffly. "My Pa was a bricklayer in Blue Island, about a day's ride from Chicago. My neighbors were mostly Italian and German. Does Goddard suspect you're a fraud?"

She averted her eyes, recalling the music box.

"It's possible," she admitted reluctantly.

A moment passed as this dire news hovered like an executioner's ax between them.

Was Dante Goddard really Maestro? Sadie hated to admit it, but the suspicion was reasonable. He was a psychiatrist, with access to mind-altering drugs. Wyntir had said he disdained hypnosis, but he wouldn't need hypnosis to manipulate minds. He was an expert on human behavior.

And if he *wasn't* Maestro, Sadie thought grimly, then she'd hit a dead end. She was no closer to catching the bastard.

This realization was almost as troubling as the notion that she'd been so incredibly stupid. So thoroughly duped. She'd never once imagined Goddard as a criminal mastermind. Not even after he'd made lights flash in her head with his "therapeutic" neck massage.

Come to think of it, maybe I fainted because he drugged my champagne!

She shivered at the notion.

Now she was terrified to imagine what he'd *really* whispered in her ear at the auction, when her mind had been dazed and she'd been too weak to defend herself. Would the music box have triggered his command to steal for him? Kill for him?

Her skin grew clammy at the thought.

Mace crossed to her chair. She gripped the seat, bracing herself. She expected him to go bulldog on her, to start barking about her befuddled female instincts where handsome, pleasant-smelling psychopaths were concerned.

Instead, he dropped to one knee.

"Tonight, you will not leave my sight. Agreed?"

His voice had been quiet but firm. When his great, warm hand engulfed hers, she nodded, a tad mystified to recognize the concern in his fiercely green stare.

"But I'm not worried about me," she blurted, tugging her hand free and jumping to her feet. She was uncomfortable with the slow, slippery slide into trust that their newfound pact signified. Ten hours ago, hadn't Mace threatened her with house arrest? "I'm worried about Wyntir. She's in love with Goddard. Or maybe she's being *manipulated* to believe she's in love with him. In any event, she depends on him for everything—"

"I read your reports," Mace said grimly. "Wilma filled me in on the rest. Miss Greyfell's mind is fragile. She has been blacking out, and Goddard has been preying on her innocence."

"We have to save Wyntir before it's too late!"

Mace's jaw hardened. "If I know anything about a woman in love—" his smile was mirthless "—she won't listen to reason. In fact, she'll take the first opportunity to warn him of his danger. We have to tread lightly. Do nothing, say nothing about your suspicions. Goddard won't harm Wyntir until they're married, and he has full control of her inheritance. Tonight, we have one purpose, and one purpose only."

Sadie drew a shuddering breath. "Find proof."

"That's right."

The clock on the mantel was chiming seven o'clock when Mace retrieved her cape from the bed. Reluctantly, she let him wrap the sable around her shoulders. Reaching for her matching muff and beaded reticule, she left a light burning by the window. She hoped Cass would see it and come back. She'd been an idiot. She'd let her hurt and pride blind her to the real Dante, to the monster who lurked beneath the suave manners and impeccable tailoring.

But Cass, common coyote that he was, had sniffed out the truth beneath the sophisticate's lies. He'd been right all along. If all went well tonight, she would walk out of Greyfell Manor with the proof to hang Maestro and exonerate Daredevil. Maybe then, Cass would forgive her.

Stepping into the hall, she heard the elevator arrive. The operator rolled open the door, as if to cue her charade. She forced herself to take Mace's arm, to laugh up into his darkly fringed gaze like a woman who was fond of her long-lost cousin and his banal observations about American weather.

God have mercy. Tonight's going to be torture.

Some twenty feet above Wyntir's front yard, Cass crouched in a snow-dusted Ponderosa pine. He was puffing a cigarette and waiting for the last family on the guest list to arrive. The sound of wheels, crunching on the drive, would make the dogs start to bark and give him his opportunity to sneak inside the house without suspicion. His other plan— to drug the Dobermans—would have caused problems if he acted too soon. The last thing he needed was for some servant to find the unresponsive pups, before he could complete his mission.

"I figure it like this," Cass told his furry nemeses, who'd flopped belly-down in the snow to growl at his tree. "You and I are on the same side. You're here to protect Wyntir, and I'm here to save her."

Maximus's black lips curled away from gleaming, two-inch fangs. And he was the friendly one.

"Can't say I blame you," Cass commiserated, tapping ash into the wind. "I reckon I'd be annoyed, too, if I got banished out here to freeze my tail off. I bet Dante was responsible."

The dogs' ears swiveled. Their growls crescendoed.

"See that? *You* know who I'm talking about. Looks like we have lots in common. I hate Dante; you hate Dante. Why can't we all get along?"

In response, Brutus licked his chops. To the Alpha, Cass figured he looked like a big, black squirrel-steak with a Stetson.

"Now I understand why you wear the blood-colored collar, pal."

At last, the distant clopping of hooves, accompanied by jingling bells, pierced the crisp, Colorado night. Cass squinted past the steam of his breaths to spy bobbing lanterns. The driver was turning the coach into Wyntir's drive.

At last his chance had come.

Cass tugged his black neckerchief over his nose and slid the coil of hemp off a nearby branch. For a showboater who'd roped fleeing steers from the back of a galloping horse, lassoing a chimney wasn't much of a challenge—even if the moon was dark, his limbs were stiff, and two gaping maws of death waited to gobble him up below.

Amused by this melodramatic notion, he spun the rope in his black-gloved fist. Howling like hell hounds, Brutus and Maximus bounded to their paws.

"Whoa," the driver called to his team.

A coach door with gilded arms swung wide, loosing heat and perfume into the air. Maximus and Brutus were going berserk. They didn't know which was the bigger threat: the silver-haired granny, who stepped down to the drive, or the rope that whooshed through the air, snaring the brick smoke stack. Cass tugged hard to tighten the knot.

"Good God, what a racket," groused a man by the carriage.

The gent's back was turned, so Cass took a running leap and swung. Wind whistled through his ears. Brutus charged after him, leaping for the seat of his pants. The Alpha's teeth snapped air. Cass might have laughed if he hadn't been concentrating so hard on keeping his feet between his chest and the wall. He didn't want to crack a rib when he slammed into the second story.

His *oomph* sounded like an explosion to his ears. So did the scraping of his rowels on brick. But no one in the drive looked up to investigate the cracking icicles or the grinding metal as the rope bent the flashing. All his noise was masked by hellacious barking.

Half grinning, half panting, Cass began hauling himself hand over hand up the rope.

The dogs went apoplectic.

"I was *invited* here, you mangy menace!" the little, stooped granny scolded, wagging a finger at Maximus. "Tahoma, go bite him."

"We'll have none of your ghost talk, Mother."

"Are you *sure* you sprang from my womb?" Lilybelle grumbled, stumping up the cobblestones with her cane. "Because sometimes, I think the real Wortham was switched at birth with a fuddy-duddy."

Cass smothered a snicker as Lilybelle passed beneath him. He was pulling himself onto the roof's eight-inch ledge when he heard her cane rap the door. The butler took half a second to respond, but she snapped at him anyway:

"It's about time! I nearly froze to death! You want a blue-haired corpse on your porch? Move aside, Humphrey, you're sucking up my heat…"

The door slammed behind the long-suffering Wortham, whose arms were laden with presents.

Cass flattened his spine beside a dormer window and saluted his furry nemeses. "See that? There are worse things than being cold. You could be haunted by a dead fox."

The dogs continued to bark curses at him, so he unbuttoned his duster. A swift tug of his belt loosened the bundle of butcher paper, strapped to his waist. Brutus reared up, scratching eagerly at the bricks. Maximus followed suit.

"Aw, fess up. You knew I had these all along."

Cass hurled the steaks as far as he could. The Dobermans chased the package around the side of the house. A few moments later, the barking ended, and the feasting began.

Sweet dreams, boys.

Cass snapped open a glass cutter. No respectable burglar traveled without one. With its help, he got past the lock on the dormer window faster than Lilybelle could make a scene. And that was saying something.

Dust and lavender assaulted his nose. Smothering a sneeze, he struck a match. Judging from the clutter of cradles, rocking horses, and trunks, he guessed he'd crawled into a storage chamber. A string quartet's arrangement of *Roses from the South* floated through the floorboards. The music disguised his cursing each time his match burned out. Finally, he stumbled to the attic door.

Cracking it open, he let his eyes adjust to the low flame in the hall's single sconce, before he was on the prowl again, hunting for a stairwell.

Based on the diagram Brodie had drawn, the dining room, parlor, and conservatory were all on the first floor. Greyfell Manor had no ballroom, so Cass figured the hosts, guests, and servants would all be congregating on the lower level. If he was lucky, they'd stay there for hours, letting him scout the second story in peace.

With the stealth of his coyote namesake, he crept down the claustrophobic hall that served as the servants' staircase. *So far so good,* he thought, furtively poking his head past the door. He spied what he guessed to be Wyntir's bedroom, since tufts of white fur clung to the jamb, where her Persian must have rubbed against it.

In fact, the more he looked, the more cat hair he saw, sprinkled along the rug or jutting from the claw-foot legs of accent tables and chairs. Oddly enough, all these tufts seemed to be waving in the same direction, as if riffled by a gentle breeze.

Cass squatted, tugging off a glove. Sure enough, a cold stream of air tickled his fingers, about an inch above the floor. It seemed to be coming from a pair of open mahogany doors, which his diagram labeled, "The Library."

Casting a wary glance behind him, Cass hurried across the hall, slipped into the dimly lit chamber, and closed the doors. The aroma of burned pine emanated from the hearth. Although the library was warm at knee-level, cold air persisted near the carpet. It led him to a bookcase embedded in a wall. Frowning, he checked Brodie's painstaking diagram again. A dumbwaiter was supposed to be here. The shaft had been sealed—and poorly, judging by the draft.

Strange. Brodie had sourced city records to create his diagram. Any blueprint filed with the planning commission should have indicated a renovation to the house.

I'll be damned if Goddard gets charged with nothing more than city tax evasion.

Doggedly, Cass lit a lamp and held it higher. A male's *sanctum sanctorum* leaped into relief, including stuffed leather chairs, polished brass spittoons, a mounted elk trophy, and a cabinet full of liquor. Cass also spied a music stand and a highly polished violin, which rested with its bow on a stool, as if waiting for its owner to return.

But Cass was less interested in the fiddle than the leather-bound volumes that stretched to the edge of the oak rafters. He scanned for disturbed dust. Scratches. Fingerprints. Worn bindings. Anything that might indicate one of the books had recently been removed from its shelf.

A smart thief, who didn't have a suitable buyer, would distribute his cache in several hiding places. A cocky thief, who'd purged the household of witnesses, would continue to use hiding places that had been convenient in the past. Cass figured Goddard fell into both categories.

Finally, he spied what he'd been looking for: a spine bound in nondescript brown with slightly worn gilt lettering. The volume jutted about a straw's breadth past its neighbors. Titled, *Frygt og Bæven,* which to Cass's mind was gibberish, the work was authored by some foreigner named Johannes de Silentio. More to the point, the book was situated on the fifth shelf, which was too high for Wyntir but within stretching distance for a man of Goddard's height.

I've got you now, you bastard.

Eagerly, Cass reached for the book. When it rattled in his fist, his anticipation sharpened. Which stolen treasure had he found? The Heart of Fire? Mephistopheles's Jewels? The Namdaran Emeralds?

Before he could find out, footsteps echoed in the hall. They were coming closer fast. Muttering an oath, he shoved the book back into place and blew out the lamp. He barely had time to jump for a rafter and pull himself up among the spider webs before Wyntir burst into the room.

CHAPTER 19

◆————◆————◆

"Look, Tahoma! It's Lady Coyote!"

Sadie groaned, her smile growing strained, when she spied Lilybelle. The impish dowager plowed through a field of jewel-colored ball gowns to corner her and Mace in the conservatory.

"Howdy, stranger!" she greeted, shamelessly ogling Mace below the belt. "I'm Lilybelle. My friends call me Lil. I own most of the banks in this town. Who are you?"

To his credit, Mace managed to keep a straight face. *"Signora."* He did the whole heel-clicking, waist-bending bit, and somehow, the monocle never popped from his eye. "I am Don Niccolaio Brianza Assante, *Barone di Monte Somma.* At your service."

"I sure do like that last part—about being at my service." Lilybelle wiggled suggestive eyebrows over her rose-tinted spectacles.

Sadie coughed into her fist.

"So tell me, Baron Montezuma—"

"Monte *Somma,"* he corrected her politely.

"Whatever. You gonna marry this gal?"

Sadie was sure her cheeks turned fire-engine red.

But Mace remained as suave as ever. "Alas, *signora.* Lady Fiore insists I behave like a proper cousin."

"No kissing?"

"Not even a peck."

Lilybelle shot Sadie a reproachful look. "Haven't you learned *anything* from me?"

Sadie wondered if she could plead insanity and throttle the pest. "Perhaps I shall have better luck this evening," she conceded dryly.

"That's the spirit." Lilybelle nodded, stroking her fox's snout. "Tahoma thinks you're all right—for a coyote. You just say the word, and we'll fix you up with a nice Navajo. Or maybe that raccoon exterminator. I reckon he's around here somewhere."

Sadie cleared her throat, glad Mace wasn't privy to *that* nickname for Cass. *"Signora,* have you seen Wyntir since the engagement toast? The darling seems a bit...distracted this evening."

"Head-over-heels is more like it. I expect I'd be that way, too, if a fella put a rock that size on my finger. Last I heard, she went looking for chamomile. Butterflies in the stomach, poor child."

"Che peccato," Sadie murmured, her eyes narrowing speculatively.

Wyntir's behavior had been peculiar all evening. Absent-minded, agitated, and a shade too pale under her rouge, the young heiress had complained privately of a headache. When Goddard insisted that she drink a willow-bark tisane, she'd snapped:

"Quit telling me what to do! I'm not a child anymore!"

Sadie had wanted to applaud Wyntir's new-found backbone, but she'd restrained herself. If Goddard somehow intuited that he was a suspect, he might get spooked and flee. Or worse, harm Wyntir.

Lilybelle, meanwhile, was making a hideous face and shooing away a waiter with a champagne tray. "You ever try that stuff?" she asked Mace. "Tastes like burnt wood. And the bubbles go straight up your nose."

"Perhaps a fruitier vintage would be more to your liking, *signora.*"

"I'm fruity enough. Or haven't you heard?"

Mace blinked. Sadie imprinted the moment on her memory. For the first time in their acquaintance, she witnessed her wiseacre boss at a loss for words.

He bowed again.

Lilybelle elbowed Sadie in the ribs. "Does your cousin tip over that way a lot?" she whispered.

"All the time," Sadie whispered back.

Lilybelle flashed her mischievous grin. "Seems like I should go stand behind him then. To see the show."

Blowing kisses, Lilybelle wandered off to find a better vantage from which to watch Mace's butt.

"You're blushing, *carino,*" Sadie purred.

His lips twitched. "American women. They are—how you say—spirited."

"I find her charming."

"Gloating does not become you, *mia cugina.*"

She chuckled.

"Ah. Our foreign dignitaries," a lazy Boston accent greeted behind her shoulder.

Sadie stiffened.

Mace's eyes glittered.

In that moment, another historical first occurred: Sadie was glad to have Mace by her side. She might not like him, but she could admire his cool head in a game of cat and mouse.

"Are you enjoying yourselves in my home?" Goddard had the audacity to ask.

'It's Wyntir's home, you parasite!' Sadie wanted to shout.

However, the stakes were too high to give her temper free rein. She forced cordiality into her tone.

"Si, dottore. It has been a lovely party. But where is your fiancé? Surely you have not lost her so soon."

"The kitchen, I believe. Something about finding another candle for her cake." He turned his keen, assessing stare on Mace. "You honor us by attending our little celebration, Lord Assante. Lady Fiore did not mention she had a cousin coming to town."

"Ah, business. She is a stern mistress, *no?* A few, stolen moments of leisure are all she permits. But what of you, *signore?* Will you and your charming bride travel abroad for your wedding tour?"

The key to a convincing undercover performance, Sadie reflected, was to ask questions while volunteering as little as possible about your invented background. Usually, this feat wasn't difficult. What civilian didn't love to blather about himself?

Goddard, however, was an expert on human behavior. Even if he didn't suspect she was a Pinkerton—yet—he would recognize Mace's attempt to deflect questions and conclude something was amiss. As a master of disguise, Mace was canny enough to understand his risk.

Sadie's scalp prickled as the secret enemies fenced, every word dripping with politeness, every nuance crackling with danger.

"I suspect we'll postpone our travels until next winter," Goddard said. "Denver can be so bleak that time of year. What is your take on *Punta del Nasone* as a destination?"

"Your bride, she is fond of rigorous hikes? During blizzards?"

Goddard's eyes hooded. Sadie's heart tripped. She'd never even heard of *Punta del Nasone.* Thank God Mace had, because Goddard was clearly testing him.

"Breathtaking country, I hear. But perhaps better traversed in the summer," Goddard agreed silkily. "I understand you hail from Campania. Rather rugged terrain for vineyards."

"Ah, but it is a multi-faceted region—like a jewel! You have heard of Avellino?"

"Where the renowned reds of Taursis cluster on the vine."

"*Taurasis,*" Mace countered enthusiastically, deftly navigating another landmine by correcting Goddard's pronunciation. "You and *Signorina* Wyntir must travel there, *dottore.* Then you will witness for yourselves the finest black Aglianico in all of southern Italy!"

Sadie was secretly impressed. Mace had diffused a third bomb, one which would have blown her cover sky-high. She'd had no idea that red wine came from black grapes.

"I daresay a vintner must know his competition," Goddard recovered smoothly.

"The vintners of Taurasis put our humble family cellars to shame," Mace said. "Fiore has agreed to help me tour possible new holdings in California, where—it is said—the land yields great wealth. But I tell you what you already know, eh? You traveled west to seek your own fortune, and you found *Signorina* Wyntir."

Goddard's eyes narrowed at this double entendre.

"Cousin Nico is an expert on all manner of sparkling things—wine, women, and jewels," Sadie interceded lightly. "You are men of similar passions, *dottore*. I was greatly impressed by your choice of diamonds. Such fire! Such brilliance! Much like the love you bear dear Wyntir."

Goddard inclined his head, but his smoldering gaze moved far too leisurely up her bodice, like an unwelcome caress, before it reached her eyes. "It takes a woman of passion to recognize the fire of the spirit," he said. "Come. Let us drink to love, friendship, and good fortune."

Sadie tensed as he snapped his fingers. A waiter in swallowtails materialized almost immediately, bearing an uncorked bottle of Chateau Lafite-Rothschild and three empty glasses.

As if the toast was pre-planned.

Uneasiness coiled in her belly as Goddard prepared the first glass of vintage Bordeaux. Etiquette dictated he pour a sample for his guests—in particular, Mace.

But Mace wasn't privy to the warning Fowler had blurted that afternoon: *"Eat nothing. Drink nothing, unless it is poured by your own hand."*

Sadie intercepted the crystal, scooping it from Goddard's fingers. *Better safe than sorry.*

"Mmm," she purred, gazing seductively into her host's eyes. She didn't know whether to be terrified or triumphant when she watched the dark fires kindle there.

Like a European sophisticate, she went through the sanctified ritual of the taste. She swirled the burgundy liquid. She inhaled with deep appreciation. The smell of normal tannins was all she could detect. But then, poison didn't always have a scent.

Her lips curved in a luscious, crotch-swelling smile. She hoped Goddard limped in pain for the rest of the night. "But you tease us, *dottore,*" she accused playfully. "Nico, isn't he the most darling of pranksters?"

Trusting her lead, Mace played along. He chuckled, tapping a finger on the side of his nose. "Ah, you test us, *mio amico.*" Inhaling deeply, he waved the bouquet from Sadie's glass toward his face. "Flowers, black truffles, red fruit…" He *tsked.* "But where is the cedar, you devil?" Like a good-natured sport, who realized he'd been played, Mace gestured expansively and "accidentally" swept the bottle off the tray. It toppled to the tiles with a resounding crash.

Sadie took her cue. She jumped back, contributing to the chaos by tossing her Bordeaux across the waiter's knees. *"Oh mio dio!"* she cried, acting mortified.

Mace did her one better. He spewed a stream of rapid-fire Italian, waving his arms and slapping his forehead with his hand. She had no idea what he was saying about their messy *faux pas,* but it sure sounded authentic.

Surrounded by gawking guests, all breathless with waspish anticipation, Goddard had no choice but to swallow his dish of crow. Graciously, he declined Mace's effusive offers to pay for the Bordeaux, the crystal, the carpet, the waiter's uniform—"Anything that *Signorina* Wyntir should require to repair her spoiled evening."

"No harm done," Goddard assured Mace with a wintry smile. "The splatter was contained. Humphrey will tidy up the glass."

In fact, the butler did materialize at Goddard's side in that moment. He was carrying a broom and dust pail, but the clean-up seemed the least of his concerns. He murmured urgently in his master's ear.

"The dogs, you say?" Goddard's brow darkened. "Very well." He nodded brusquely to Mace and Sadie. "Enjoy the festivities. We'll be cutting the cake shortly."

Sadie watched in speculation as Goddard headed for the foyer, where he conferred with a snow-dusted groomsman. The servant looked nervous. He kept twisting his cap in his hands.

"What do you suppose that's about, *mia cugina?*" Mace whispered, careful to keep up appearances. There was an old saying in the detective business: *the walls have ears.*

Sadie shrugged, watching a frowning Goddard dismiss the groomsman and stalk for the kitchen.

Suddenly, Mace jerked his head toward the central staircase. Sadie followed his gaze. She glimpsed Wyntir's sky-blue skirts disappearing through a door on the second level.

"Go," Mace whispered urgently. "I'll sound an alarm when he returns."

Sadie nodded.

Hiking her gown, she hurried after her young quarry. By the time she reached the top of the stairs, she heard the muffled sounds of thumping and clanking.

"Carina?"

Knocking once, she pushed through the library's doors. She spied Wyntir kneeling in a puddle of china-blue satin near the raised lid of the window seat. The younger woman started, shoving something under her skirts. When she turned, the guilt on her face was unmistakable.

"F-Fiore! Why aren't you downstairs?"

"Because you are not downstairs, *carina.*"

The chamber was cavernous, filled with hulking shadows, none of which Wyntir's tiny pool of lamplight could dispel. Sadie suspected the younger woman was trying to conceal her presence; why else would she keep the wick so low?

Wyntir raised her chin a notch. "I have a headache. I told you."

"Ah. But I fear you will find no willow bark tisane in a window seat."

Some of the color returned to Wyntir's cheeks. She averted her gaze. "I needed some time to feel better, is all."

"Come now, *carina,*" Sadie cajoled. "We are friends. You do not need to pretend with me. Something is troubling you. How might I help?"

Wyntir's bottom lip trembled. "I really could use a friend," she whispered, dashing away a tear.

Sadie's heart turned over. "Then we shall sit, *si?* And we shall talk. Come. Join me by the fire, where it is warm."

Sadie tried to keep her smile reassuring when Wyntir pushed down the window seat and hurried, like an anxious child, across the cavernous room. Clutched in Wyntir's white-knuckled fist was a blue-gingham book, its size only slightly bigger than her hand. Leaf fragments trickled from the pale green pages. The scent was unmistakable: mint.

The journal!

But something else was wrong. As Sadie waited for Wyntir to carry the book—and the lamp—closer, she was plagued by a fresh rash of goosebumps. She couldn't quite put her finger on the reason…

Then she sucked in her breath. Faintly, ever so faintly, she detected the aroma of cinnamon mixed with cloves, sandalwood mingled with leather.

Cass!

"Wh-what's the matter?" Wyntir whispered, halting like a nervous filly by her side.

"Nothing," Sadie lied.

Her lover was close. So close. She could sense him like an earthquake in her soul. A dozen questions screamed through her brain at once. How did he get in? Where was he hiding? What had he found? Did Goddard suspect?

But she forced herself to rein in her galloping emotions. She didn't have the luxury to worry about her renegade lover. If anyone could fend for himself, it was Cass. Wyntir was the one who needed her help.

"However, I am worried about you!" Sadie crooned with sisterly affection. "You are missing your party!"

"Oh, Fiore." Wyntir sank forlornly beside her on the settee. "I wish it was yesterday."

"Did you quarrel with Dante?"

"No." Her brow furrowed. "At least, not that I remember," she added uneasily. She clutched her journal closer, seeming to draw strength from it. "But there are so many things I don't remember. And now I'm getting…scared."

"You mean confused," Sadie counseled, hoping to nip panic in the bud.

"Y-yes." Wyntir drew a shaky breath. "Confused."

A great, crocodile tear rolled down her cheek. Her face looked like porcelain, and when Sadie gripped her hand, Wyntir's bones felt just as fragile. Sadie tugged a handkerchief from her reticule.

"Thank you." Wyntir sniffled, dabbing at her eyes. "Today started like a dream. The best kind of dream. I was excited about my party. I wanted Dante to propose. He was so secretive about the ring. Honestly, I didn't think he would ever give me one.

"I wanted to buy a few things—stockings and such—so I rode into town. I was scheduled for an early appointment with my seamstress, but I ran into someone, literally, at the Windsor. Boxes flew everywhere. He was such a gentleman; he offered to pay for the damage. He called himself Don Dominar, *Marqués de Oro Gran Polla*. A Spanish caballero with the most magnificent eyes. Like polished sapphires. They twinkled when he laughed…"

A muscle ticked in Sadie's haw. Lord Dominant, of the Grand Golden Cock, eh?

Cass, you louse!

"When I confessed it was my birthday, he took me on a sleigh ride. I've always wanted to go sleighing with a beau, but Dante…" She shrugged helplessly. "He doesn't do anything that isn't planned for days. Or practical."

Sadie filed that tip in her memory.

"Anyway, Don Dom and I sipped the most refreshing coffee. He called it a toddy. I felt wonderful. I practically floated home. But after a few hours, the headache started. And...I started to remember things."

Now Sadie was starting to see the bigger picture. Cass had set out to get Wyntir drunk so he could break Goddard's spell!

"What kind of things, *carina?*"

"Dreams. *Horrible* dreams. Only now, I'm not so sure they were dreams, because I remember writing them in my journal."

She tapped a shaking finger on the inscription, in mint-green embroidery: *"You're the Sister I Always Wanted. Love, Minta."*

Sadie struggled with her composure. "So...you have been reading your journal."

Wyntir blanched at the idea. "No! Not yet. I only just discovered it when you walked through the door. I'd lost it, you see. For months. Isn't that strange? Forgetting something so special?" Wyntir's brows knitted. "I must have blocked it out of my mind, for some reason. But during tonight's champagne toast, I had a flash of memory, as clear as a picture. I was sitting on that window bench, writing. And crying. So I figured I should look under the cushion."

"But why were you crying, *carina?*"

Wyntir squirmed in her seat. "For the longest time, I couldn't remember anything about the day Papa died. But tonight, I recalled how he argued with Reverend Fowler because the preacher told Papa to send Dante packing.

"But Papa would never do that, of course. Dante was like family, and besides, Papa swore by Dante's music. Whenever Dante played the violin, the neck pain from Papa's mining injury went away. Dante couldn't play the fiddle all day, so he gave Papa a music box. *By and By.* That was the hymn. Papa listened to that song over and over again. And when he did, he felt as good as new."

Sadie thought she might be sick.

"On the day Papa died, I heard him shouting at Reverend Fowler. He said that spirit messages were hogwash. I was appalled! I mean, Papa was the one who'd first suggested that we use a medium to contact Mama!

"But for weeks, he'd been acting so strangely. So alien to his nature. Before Reverend Fowler left the house, he warned me that Papa was in danger. That same afternoon, Papa shot himself," she whispered hoarsely. "It was horrible—*horrible!* But no one tried to hurt Papa. Even the police said so."

Sadie swallowed hard. In light of what she knew about Dante Goddard, she wasn't sure she agreed with the police. However, to send him to the gallows, she needed a reliable witness. Right now, Wyntir's recollections were confused by grief, guilt, and whatever insidious "therapies" she'd suffered at Goddard's hands.

"Tell me, *carina,*" she murmured, steering the conversation back to the journal, "who is this Minta who embroiders so beautifully?"

Wyntir hugged the book to her heart. "Minta was my best school friend. My goodness, I haven't seen her for years!" The glimmer of happiness faded from Wyntir's eyes. "And yet, I remember sitting on that window bench, writing about the eulogy she gave at Papa's funeral. That can't be right, can it?" Wyntir's voice broke. "You see, Fiore? I'm confusing my dreams with my waking life!"

"But your journal. You think it will help you recognize the difference?"

"Maybe." Wyntir bit her lip. "I hope so." She raised impossibly big, tear-filled eyes to Sadie's. "But I'm afraid! What if the dreams *are* real?"

"Then Nico and I will help you. We are your friends. And *we* have many friends. You are not alone, *carina*. Ever."

A tense little laugh bubbled past Wyntir's lips. She pressed shaking fingers to her mouth. "Oh, Fiore. I'm so afraid I'm going mad…"

"You are *not* mad, child. I assure you. You are strong. Resilient. We shall get to the bottom of your blackouts and your dreams."

Wyntir sighed. A great weight seemed to lift from her shoulders. "I suppose some dreams are easier to recognize than others."

"Like what?"

Her laugh was thin. Self-conscious. "Well, there was this one awful night, when I heard screams. From the basement. A woman was yelling my name. The voice sounded an awful lot like Minta's. I tried to find her. I walked forever down a claustrophobic staircase in a cold, dank crawlspace. Then I came to a cluttered place with broken furniture and empty barrels—like a basement. Across the room, a door was ajar. So I peeked inside and saw a sort of laboratory with cages and surgical tables! Isn't that bizarre?

"But the worst part was, Minta was locked inside one of those cages! I tried to get her out, but I couldn't find a key. Then we heard footsteps, so she told me to run. To go to the Pinkertons. But why would I go to the Pinkertons? Why wouldn't I go to the police?" Wyntir shook her head. "None of it makes sense—not that it should. It was a dream." She laughed with a little more conviction this time. "Something so sinister couldn't happen in real life."

Sadie wished she could share Wyntir's optimism.

"Since we are friends," Sadie said, striving for a warm, parental tone, "I shall take this journal from you. I shall keep it safe until you are ready to read the entries.

"But tonight, you will read nothing," Sadie continued, slipping the volume into her reticule. "You will speak to no one—*no one*—of these blackouts or dreams, *capisci?* Tonight is a celebration of *you,* of the beautiful, radiant woman you have become. Your house is full of loving friends and neighbors, who wish to celebrate your 21st birthday with cake, gifts, and champagne. And I shall be the first among them to toast all the wonderful possibilities of your future!"

Wyntir's giggle sounded like the ghost of her old self. Impulsively, she threw her arms around Sadie's neck, knocking her off balance. "I am so grateful you're my friend. Thank you. Thank you for *everything*. I love you, Fiore," she added shyly.

Then she bounded to her feet, her cheeks pink with anticipation, rather than gray with dread.

As Sadie gazed up into Wyntir's sweet, hopeful face, her eyes were drawn to a metallic glint in the rafters. Something long and shadowy was hiding there, with silver spurs.

Cass's eyes locked with hers.

She swallowed hard. *Dear God, is he working alone? Where's Collie?*

"Come on, Fiore." Wyntir grabbed her hand and pulled her off the settee. "Everyone's probably wondering where we are."

Reluctantly, Sadie let herself be dragged toward the door. *"Watch your back,"* she mouthed to Cass.

He nodded and winked.

The door swung closed behind them.

As Cass let his eyes adjust to the dim light in the hearth once more, he had to admit: he'd been impressed. Sadie had diffused an emotional bomb and bought him time to search Greyfell Manor. He couldn't help but admire the flawless way she'd acted her role, gaining Wyntir's trust, coaxing her to spill her guts, then walking out the door with the Pinkertons' first solid evidence in the case. Sadie deserved extra points for accomplishing these feats in under 10 minutes, without alarming Wyntir or spooking Goddard.

Yep, Sadie was a smooth operator, all right. He had to give credit where credit was due. He might not like the idea of his woman working as a Pinkerton, but at least he could sleep easier, knowing she was good at her job.

Now it was time to do his.

Grimacing, he flexed his cramped muscles. He knew better than to plunge through nine feet of darkness without first pumping some blood through his limbs.

But before he could swing from his perch, the dumbwaiter shaft began to glow. Light radiated from the cracks between the books. Cass heard a faint scraping. The next thing he knew, the bookcase swung away from the wall, and Goddard ducked into the library with a lamp.

Cass drew a restraining breath. As the bookcase swung back into place, his fingers twitched, yearning to trigger the .38 up his sleeve. He wanted nothing better than to blow off Goddard's devious head. But his conscience wouldn't let him gun down an unarmed man.

Too bad I don't have a search warrant. I could have cuffed the bastard in front of all his pretentious, pinky-crooking friends.

Gritting his teeth, Cass watched Goddard cross the room. Something was troubling the thief. Otherwise, he wouldn't be speeding like an arrow for his loot.

Someone must have found the dogs!

Even as Cass drew this conclusion, Goddard's light struck the fifth shelf and its treasure box. The thief muttered an oath. Cass wanted to do the same. In his haste to hide from Wyntir, he'd shelved the book upside down. Even from this distance, he could see the gilt letters gleaming on the wrong side of the spine.

Goddard snatched the book from the shelf. But when he peeked inside, his panic quickly dissolved to relief. He began stuffing his clinking cache into his trouser pockets.

Over the next few minutes, he raided the shelves, grabbing five more volumes—situated in different bookcases—and shoving their contents into his pockets. Cass glimpsed a crimson flash, like flickering flames, which he suspected was the Heart of Fire. He also spied the serpentine slither of rainbows, which he recognized as Dolce's necklace.

At last, Goddard turned away from the shelves. He was frowning. Crossing to the liquor cabinet, he flipped open a humidor. The aroma of cognac-laced tobacco wafted to the rafters. Striking a match, he puffed his Cleopatra Federal cigar. Then he propped his rump on the padded arm of a leather chair. Cass could almost hear the fiend's mind at work as he tapped ash and blew smoke rings:

Someone—most likely Daredevil—broke into my house. Daredevil located the Heart of Fire, but he didn't steal it. Why? Was he spooked in the act? Is he waiting for the guests to leave and the servants to retire?

Maybe Daredevil isn't a thief. Maybe he's an undercover dick. Too bad. Police can be bribed. But a Pinkerton? Not likely.

So who is this elusive prick of a Pinkerton? Is he downstairs mingling with the guests? Is he hiding in the woodwork like a cockroach?

And how do I get the most pleasure out of killing him?

A few minutes passed before Goddard roused himself from his reverie. He glanced at the clock on the mantel. It read 9:40. Rubbing out his stogie, he straightened.

But as Goddard set off for the hall, something on the floor attracted his attention. He grew still. *Stalking-wolf still.* Cass didn't dare to breathe.

Goddard chuckled. Low and ominous, the sound vibrated with triumph as he squatted before the settee. Cass didn't know exactly what the murderer plucked from the carpet— some small, white gleaming thing—but every hair on the nape of Cass's neck stood straight. He didn't consider the omen a good sign. Sadie had been sitting on that couch!

With a dastardly smile, Goddard tucked his find into a vest pocket. Then he blew out his lamp and exited into the hall.

Son of a—!

Cass was cursing like a muleskinner when he swung down from the rafters. He'd run out of time. Because of that book, Goddard was looking for him. Soon the bastard would have all his servants looking, too.

But he probably won't have them looking in the dumbwaiter shaft.

Reason punctured Cass's sense of failure. He drew a fortifying breath. Steeling himself against impatience, he studied the bookcase by the scarlet glow of the hearth.

Now if I was a low-down, double-crossing thief—who thought I was too clever for a U.S. Marshal—where would I hide the lever that opens the door to my lair?

Acting on a hunch, Cass ran his hands over the unlit sconce near the bookcase. He found what felt like hidden hinges. When he tugged on the fixture, it bent forward, like a lever.

How original, he thought snidely, watching the door swung open.

Now he faced an especially narrow, spiral stairwell—just like Wyntir had described. The space could barely accommodate the shoulders of a six-foot man. Cass wasn't too surprised; the shaft had originally been built for a dumbwaiter, after all. What did surprise him was the eerie silence of the door as it swung closed. And the cushiony quiet of the steps each time he stepped on one. He suspected they were covered with some sort of rubber.

That would explain the stink, he thought, wrinkling his nose.

With his spurs echoing faintly in the shaft—and setting his nerves on edge—he descended past the kitchen, recognizable by yeasty smells. He knew he'd drawn close to the basement when he detected the pungent odor of mildew. He felt like he'd been descending for hours through the claustrophobic darkness, with its seeping walls and scurrying spiders.

Finally, he reached a locked door.

Untethering his Colts, he dragged a widdy from his hatband.

Cracking the lock took mere seconds. On the other side of the door, he found an old loom with a half-woven tapestry. Pushing past it, he stepped into the basement that Wyntir had described.

His heart quickened.

Upon first glance, the chamber looked like any other cellar in a house where the inhabitants had more space than they required. His lantern illuminated arched, brick buttresses and cobwebs. The hulking shadows to the left proved to be a furniture cemetery, featuring a ripped settee, a broken roll-top desk, and other relics too cumbersome to haul up the narrow stairs to the attic. To the right were barrels of corn, sacks of flour, pickled beets, and other preserved vegetables. A thick layer of dust coated everything—except the pristine tiles of limestone on the floor.

Cass's smile was mirthless. *Sweeping away your footprints, Goddard?*

He approached the farthest wall. It was remarkable for two reasons: first, its location. Why would a house, the length and breadth of Greyfell Manor, have a basement that was only 80 feet wide?

Secondly, Cass questioned its masonry. The clay of the bricks was similar in color—but not the exact shade—of the deep, dark red that characterized the other walls. The clay was also less stained by mildew. Clearly, someone had built this wall after the rest of the house had been constructed.

The odd wall was lined with open-shelved cabinets, loaded with bushels of onions, potatoes, and beans. A rack overhead stored kegs of ale. Cass figured the door that Wyntir had described must be behind one of the cabinets. He hunted for a lever and soon found it in the form of an empty beer keg's tap.

You're not as clever as you think you are, Goddard.

Visions of a terrified young woman, incarcerated in this hellhole, fueled Cass's fury. With a Colt gripped in each fist, he kicked the door wide, ready for anything.

But the scene his lantern illuminated was truly disturbing. At the center of the chamber were a hospital table and a throne-sized chair, equipped with thick leather straps for restraining heads, torsos, and limbs.

The chamber's left wall was lined with animal cages. Some contained live specimens—mostly rats and scorpions—but the human-sized cage, which hung from the ceiling, was empty, thank God. Suspended above it were an enormous lamp and three church bells, which were just incongruous enough to give Cass the creeps.

Shuddering, he turned his attention to the right side of the chamber. Above a long panel of mechanical levers, he saw a wall clock with a swinging pendulum. Below the panel was a table laden with musical novelties, ranging from pocket watches and humidors to a phonograph and organette. A neighboring cabinet with glass doors was filled with medicine bottles and instruments, such as scalpels, syringes, and some spooky-looking tongs with teeth.

Suddenly, his gaze alighted on a leather-bound journal. It rested in plain sight, atop a three-legged stool, which abutted the panel.

Had Goddard kept a record of his experiments?

Cass's neck prickled like his coyote namesake's. Using the warning to sharpen his awareness, he scanned for threats one final time before venturing into the chamber.

Ignoring the squeals of the rats, which were agitated by the lantern light, Cass flipped hastily through the open journal. The precise, neatly-penned entries contained names he recognized: Sheridan Welbourn, Mendel Baines, Malcom Renfield. By the time he reached the pages pertaining to Araminta Merripen, his skin was crawling.

> *Oct. 16:*
>
> *Subject is a Pinkerton female. Clever, strong-willed. Resists verbal commands. Detects hallucinogens in food. Syringe required. Flashing light protocol initiated. First test: subject lost consciousness at 1 hour 21 minutes. When revived, refused to smash glass with fist...*

Oct. 18:

Subject vulgar and violent. Music protocol initiated. Bells induced screams at 28 minutes. Subject lost consciousness at 36 minutes. Upon revival, demonstrated strong hesitation to obey smashing command. Still feels scorpion sting...

Oct. 20:

Subject no longer fears scorpion threat. Takes beatings in silence with some flinching. Succumbs to trance state fastest through music set to 3/4 time. Making progress...

Oct. 23:

Subject obeys blindly. Feels no fear or pain. Carries out kill command to Farewell My Darling. *Upon revival from trance, remembers nothing. Ready for field test...*

Cass was shaking so hard when he reached the last line of that entry, he wanted to puke.

So help me God, no attorney is going to talk a jury out of hanging this unholy bastard. If I have to, I'll kill him myself.

Setting his jaw, Cass slammed the journal closed and lifted it off the stool. Only when he turned to leave did he notice the tether attached to the book's spine. By that time, it was too late. He'd already yanked the wire, springing Goddard's trap. A sickly-sweet puff of air blew in his face.

Cass staggered. His vision blurred, and his muscles went slack. A metal door came crashing down, sealing off his escape. Overhead, the bells were pealing at a thunderous pitch. He sank to his knees, trying to cover his ears, but he couldn't make his arms stretch high enough.

Then the ceiling lamp began flashing with the brightness of the sun...

CHAPTER 20

Five Hours Later

A shadow had fallen across Sadie's heart. And it kept growing darker.

She'd first noticed her nagging sense of doom during the party. At the time, Wyntir had been dragging her through the library doors. When they'd reached the foot of the staircase, they'd found Mace waiting.

The senior agent's boisterous "Nico" soon brought the bloom to Wyntir's too-pale cheeks. She must have laughed with him for ten minutes. Sadie was glad to see Wyntir's good spirits restored, but soon that lunkhead of a butler reappeared. Standing behind his mistress like some tuxedoed Grim Reaper, Humphrey kept clearing his throat like a foghorn, until the conversation lulled long enough for him to speak.

"I regret to inform you, miss, that your animals are ailing."

Wyntir gave a little cry of dismay. "Tallie?"

"No, miss. The dogs. The groom moved Maxi and Brutus to the stables, where he can keep an eye on them. They're warm and comfortable."

"Does Dante know?"

"Yes, miss. He went to examine the dogs himself. He

couldn't rouse them, but he said you shouldn't be alarmed. They're only sleeping."

Sadie struggled not to show her own dismay. She would have bet her Pinkerton pension that Cass had drugged those Dobermans. Now Goddard knew an intruder was prowling the premises!

Needless to say, Wyntir ignored her fiancé's advice. Grabbing a cape, she wrapped a scarf around her head and dashed for the stables, heedless of the fact that her cake still needed cutting and most of her guests were milling around the dining room, waiting for the big event.

"You wouldn't happen to know why the Dobermans are ailing, would you?" Mace asked dryly, keeping up his Nico pretense.

"I know as much as you do, *carino.*"

He didn't look convinced, but apparently, he had more important matters on his mind.

"Wyntir's eyes were red. Why was she crying?"

Sadie shrugged, trying to look like she was discussing some triviality with her bombastic cousin. "She's remembering things."

"Useful things?"

"Sì."

Several well-coifed guests promenaded past. Mace bowed and murmured greetings. Too canny to demand details in such a public setting, he let the subject drop. "So…what's that bulge in your reticule?"

Sadie was secretly impressed. Mace's sharp, pine-needle green eyes missed nothing. "A young woman's private reminiscences," she said lightly.

Like the fuse of a firecracker, anticipation flared between them.

"Brava," he murmured.

"Grazie."

"By the way, you lost a dangle."

Damn! Sadie's hands flew to her earlobes. Wilma was going to kill her! "How long has it been missing?"

Mace looked amused. "The last time I saw it, you were pitching a glass of 20-year-old Bordeaux at the waiter." His voice grew husky-warm with approval.

Her cheeks heated. Uncomfortable with their chummy new familiarity, she averted her gaze. That's when she spied Goddard, strolling out of the library. As if by magnetic force, their stares locked. She'd been in the process of removing her orphaned earring.

A mocking little smile curved his lips. He inclined his head.

She did the same.

Finally, he released her from the dark fires in that burning gaze. Air whooshed from her lungs. She hadn't even realized she'd been holding her breath.

"What's wrong?" Mace raised his eyes in time to see Goddard turn toward his office. Mace's face darkened. "How'd he get past me?"

"You must have been distracted."

"Like hell. I've had a clear view of the upper landing since you climbed the stairs. Is there another entrance to the library?"

"Not that I saw."

"There has to be."

Sadie battled a frisson of panic. Did that mean Goddard had eavesdropped on her and Wyntir? That he'd found Cass hiding in the rafters?

Mass didn't miss a single nuance of emotion, flickering across her face. "All right, we're leaving."

"But we'll look suspicions if—"

"It's too late for that," Mace said grimly. "He knows."

The memory of Mace's words pounded like a death knell in Sadie's head.

He knows.

Was it any wonder she couldn't fall asleep?

Cass, where are you?!

Anxiously, she checked the time. The mantel clock read 3:12 a.m. Except for its monotonous ticking—and an occasional, creaking timber—the hotel was quiet. *Too* quiet for a woman who'd spent half her life in a brothel. At this hour in Dodge's Long Branch Saloon, she would have expected to hear banging headboards, whooping cowboys, smashing bottles, and the occasional gun fight.

Sighing, she glanced at her bedside lamp. The flame had been burning for hours. Now it was running low on oil. She'd been hoping Cass would brave the snow and climb through her window. But she couldn't blame him if he didn't. The wind was howling like a hellhound.

Unfortunately, that wasn't the worst part.

The worst part was Mace. Her annoying bulldog of a boss had insisted on watching over her for the rest of the night. When she'd protested, he'd offered her a choice: he could spread his gear in the hall, or he could camp on her chaise lounge. So in essence, he'd given her no choice at all.

But Cass didn't know that. Nor did Cass know that Mace, in his overbearing but well-meaning way, was trying to protect her rather than ambush him.

Feeling restless, Sadie punched her mound of pillows and repositioned her spine against the headboard. Wyntir's open journal beckoned on the quilt beside her lap. So far— by reading between the lines—Sadie had learned how Goddard had ingratiated himself with Edmund Greyfell; how he'd moved into the manor to take advantage of an old man's pain; how he'd started stealing sterling and jewelry; and how he'd pinned the thefts on the butler and two maids.

Throughout these early entries, Wyntir was often impatient with Goddard, whom she'd described as "handsome enough" but "priggish." Then one morning, she woke up—literally—with a whole new regard for the man who'd been "such an angel of mercy to my poor, bereaved papa." On that particular date, the fervent mantra, "I love him; I can't live without him," first appeared in the journal. To see the declaration scrawled in black and white gave Sadie the creeps. She couldn't prove it—she would probably *never* be able to prove it—but she felt as certain as a hanging judge that Goddard had planted that mantra in Wyntir's sleeping mind.

To his credit, Edmund Greyfell was also suspicious of his daughter's abrupt change of affections. At least, that's what Sadie intuited when Wyntir wrote about her father's quarrel with Goddard. Greyfell threatened to cut off Goddard's retainer and kick him out of the house for "inappropriate overtures" toward Wyntir. About 12 hours later, Greyfell committed "suicide." The implication was all too clear.

Sadie tasted bile.

Turning grimly to Wyntir's journal, she braced herself for the worst.

> *Sunday, Sept. 23:*
>
> *On the most awful day of my life, a ray of sunshine pierced the gloom. My sweet, childhood friend, Minta Merripen, arrived for Papa's funeral. Her visit was the most welcome of surprises! We hugged and cried for hours. She was the one who gave me this beautiful new journal, lovingly constructed by her own hand and smelling like mint—just like the one from graduation! Strange, isn't it? I still can't find that most beloved of journals. It vanished so thoroughly, I had to start writing in this one...*
>
> *Monday, Sept. 24:*
>
> *Dante doesn't want Minta staying in the house. He was perfectly beastly about it. He said he found her nosy and impertinent—an unholy influence on me! The gall of that man!*
>
> *Minta was gracious and offered to stay at a hotel, but I wouldn't hear of it. I told Dante if he didn't like it, he could sleep with Wind Chaser in the stables...*

Tuesday, Oct. 2:

For my sake, Minta finally made peace with Dante. Yesterday evening, she wouldn't stop praising his musical virtuosity. At breakfast, she hung on his every word when he commented on some boring old medical article about conditioned response—whatever that means. Is it any wonder he seems to have a new regard for her? She's killing my darling with kindness!

This afternoon, unfortunately, I suffered one of my wretched headaches. I couldn't attend the new botanical exhibit with Minta. Since Dante didn't have any patients scheduled, he agreed to escort her in my place, which was très galant of him, considering how little interest he has in flowers...

Thursday, Oct. 4:

While Minta and I were shopping for new, Halloween chapeaux, we ran into Prof. Baines. He was so understanding about all my cancelled appointments since Papa's funeral. I finally confessed how Dante forbade me to have any more hypnosis sessions because they were dangerous.

"Poppycock," the professor said. (I always want to laugh when Prof. Baines says, Poppycock!) "Hypnosis is nothing more than deep sleep. It has no risks whatsoever—unlike the sedatives your so-called guardian prescribes for your night terrors."

Minta was intrigued by what Prof. Baines had to say. Especially when he urged her not to let Dante drive away all my friends. (Such a peculiar thing to say!) Minta volunteered for one of the professor's experiments...

Friday, Oct. 5:

This afternoon, I caught Minta in Papa's study, rummaging through his desk drawers. I can't imagine how she opened them, since only Humphrey has the key. She said she was hunting for a stylus, because she wanted to write a letter to Geoffrey...

Monday, Oct. 8:

One of Dante's patients cancelled. I already had an appointment for a dress-fitting. Poor Minta was bored out of her mind. She invited Dante to go riding. They returned in high spirits, even though Minta took a fall. Her hair was mussed, her riding jacket was grass-stained, and her bodice was missing a button.

At dinner, Minta announced she couldn't possibly impose on my hospitality any longer. Despite my heartfelt pleas to change her mind, she insisted on staying at the Grand Central Hotel...

Friday, Oct. 12:

Today, I caught Minta in the most outlandish lie! We were having tea in the parlor, when a gullible young man (a violinist from the opera,) called for her. He asked for a Claudia Dunlap.

Humphrey tried to turn him away, but the caller was lovesick and duly persistent. I approached the door. My intention was to prove I was not Claudia. However, the gentleman spied Minta, peeking through the parlor doors. He identified her as the one and only Claudia, a reporter who'd interviewed him for the Leadville Democrat.

Minta turned white at this pronouncement. Truthfully, I thought she was going to faint. She called him a half-baked loon and stormed into the foyer to slam the door in his face. I was stunned by her behavior. A lady of breeding would never *treat a suitor that way! What is happening to my poor, dear Minta?*

Dante overheard the entire exchange from the landing. I swear, he's always lurking behind a potted plant or a bookcase or something. Anyway, he confided to me later, in his professional opinion, that Minta is suffering delusions. He blamed Prof. Baines's hypnotism experiment. But Dante assured me he would take care of her...

Saturday, Oct. 13:

Minta is acting stranger than ever. After dinner, while Dante was playing his violin, I accidentally bumped her elbow. She'd been pawing through her reticule, and a tiny gun dropped to the floor! I was stunned. I think Dante was too.

Minta laughed it off. She said the derringer was a gift from Geoffrey. Since he couldn't accompany her to Denver, he'd wanted her to have protection.

I still don't understand why she would bring a derringer to my house...

Monday, Oct. 15

I just woke from the most disturbing dream. At least, I think it was a dream. Things are sort of fuzzy in my mind; but then, they always are after I faint!

Dante was with me when I woke. He said I fell and struck my temple. That would account for the bruise, I suppose. I asked him where Minta was, and he reminded me she'd become a guest of the hotel. He said she hadn't called at the house all day—which was a huge relief, considering my dream!

It started with me and Minta in the library. She asked if Dante had left the house. I said, "Yes, he's not expected back until dinner." Then she shooed away the servants, claiming they couldn't be trusted. She called them spies for Dante's "great evil."

That comment was a bit off-putting, even from Minta!

But I swallowed my annoyance. I tried to be supportive. When I asked what was troubling her, she burst into tears. She confessed Dante has been coming to her hotel room every night for the last week—and she let him stay! She begged my forgiveness for being a horrible friend and a fool.

As if that wasn't shocking enough, she said I wasn't safe in my own house. She insisted that I must leave Dante immediately. She called him the worst kind of predator, and she said she had proof. She quoted something Prof. Baines supposedly said about Harvard. How Dante conducted unethical experiments, using real human subjects. How he got wind of an inquiry, so he framed Baines.

I couldn't help but wonder if Minta was having another "episode"—which is what Dante calls delusions. I mean, if she was really his lover, she would have every reason to make me want to leave him. How can she expect me to believe such preposterous tales about my danger?

I don't remember much else about the dream. I heard footsteps behind me. Then I heard a lovely lullaby. It sounded like Brahms.

Tomorrow, I think I'll invite Minta to lunch. Then we can have a good laugh about my dream...

Tuesday, Oct. 16:
I felt compelled to leave the house today. Since Minta never responded to my lunch invitation, I guess I was lonely. I spent the morning and afternoon at the orphanage, reading to the

children. Then I dined with the Moffets in their home. I was glad for the diversion. It was lovely to join a large family, carving jack-o-lanterns and making candy apples till well after eight bells.

I forgot to mention: I did stop by the hotel before dinner, just to check on Minta. The clerk didn't remember seeing her all day, but I suppose that's to be expected. The poor fellow sees so many faces pass through his lobby. He did promise to give Minta my updated lunch invitation.

As I write this entry, I can hear the clock chiming 10 bells. I haven't seen Dante since the same hour last night. That's when he examined me. He was so concerned about my vision after I fell. To test my eyesight, he made me count backwards, ticking off the number of times his pocket watch spun on its chain. But that was 24 hours ago! Where could he possibly be?

I wonder if he really is having an affair with Minta...

Wednesday, Oct. 17:

Something horrible is happening! I can't find Dante, and I don't know what to do. Am I going mad? I keep hearing screams—a woman's screams—coming from the old dumbwaiter shaft. It sounds like Minta, calling my name!

None of the servants can hear the screams, or the spooky footsteps on the other side of the wall. It's as if my whole household went deaf! Cook said the noise must be rats. Humphrey said it could be the wind. When I ordered him to search the basement, he said sternly, "We must never go to the basement, miss."

And I said, "Why?"

And he said, "It is forbidden."

So I said, "By whom?"

And he looked me straight in the eye and said, "God."

The creepiest part was, he wasn't joking.

So tonight, after everyone falls asleep, I'm going to search the basement for myself.

I hope Humphrey's right. About the wind...

Sadie thought she might be sick. The journal abruptly ended with that entry.

My God, my God, what did he do to you, Minx?

Shuddering violently, Sadie reached for her gun and made sure every chamber in the cylinder was loaded. She decided to keep the holster by her pillow, rather than on the nightstand.

Now the clock read 3:30 a.m. There was no way she was going to fall asleep after reading Wyntir's last few entries. She considered waking Mace and telling him what she'd learned, but he'd already given her crystal-clear instructions:

"If you want an arrest warrant for that unholy bastard, consider carefully. No judge wants to be dragged from his children—or his Maker—on a Sunday morning. That journal needs to say something that will hold up in court.

"So if you don't want to make an enemy of a hanging judge, make double-damned sure you're not wasting his time."

Fighting tears, Sadie gazed at the cheerful, green message stitched upon the journal's cover: *"You're the Sister I Always Wanted. Love, Minta."*

Could the ramblings of a wide-eyed school girl convince a judge to sign a search warrant for Greyfell Manor? Sadie honestly couldn't say. She didn't know the nuances of the law—or the personalities of the local judges—the way Mace did.

Her biggest fear was that some fork-tongued lawyer would convince an all-male jury that Wyntir was a delusional young woman, who suffered nightmares and recorded fiction for posterity.

If Goddard got acquitted, he'd disappear. He'd change his name, alter his appearance, and start a new reign of terror on some other, unsuspecting heiress!

Rubbing bleary eyes, Sadie reached for the bottle of tequila she'd ordered Brodie to smuggle into her room.

Somehow, Goddard had to hang. Maybe Cass had the evidence she was looking for…

Cass was dreaming of Lucifire.

And Hell.

Only Lucifire's Hell wasn't the fiery abyss of legend. It was a dank, cold place. A clanging, glaring place. The air stank of rats and urine, chemicals and burnt flesh.

Although this Hell held no fire or brimstone, it held pain. The shrieks went on and on, like some demonic fury was teetering on the brink of madness. The only way to end the torment was to obey the Fiend in the white lab coat.

"Kill," the Fiend said.

So Lucifire aimed and fired. He pulled the trigger again and again, until his palms blistered, his fingers bled, and his eyes were seeing double. The revolvers were never loaded. They couldn't strike down the Fiend. And that, perhaps, was the greatest torment of all.

In this hellish dream, the Fiend determined the targets. They were porcelain dolls with fancy clothes. Each of the dolls possessed names. Some of those names were known to Lucifire. But his hatred ran deep. He imagined another doll, wearing charcoal pinstripes. He dubbed this target, "The Fiend."

But soon even that secret rebellion was denied him. Struggle was futile; screaming brought no relief. The only release was to surrender to the darkness of oblivion…

Cass woke with a start. Something wet, smelling of horse, nuzzled his cheek. He groaned, pushing a slobbery muzzle away from his face. Pancake snorted. The sound was loud enough to wake a hibernating bear—in the next county.

No wonder my ears are ringing.

Cass curled into a ball and tried to go back to sleep. His head hurt. His arms hurt. His stomach wanted to heave. He was pretty sure he was half dead.

No sense waking up for that.

Pancake nudged his shoulder.

"Don't have apples," Cass mumbled. He was trying to reach the fuzzy, dark place. The haven deep in his brain where time and torment didn't exist. In the Dark Place, the sky was black; the black was quiet; and no creepy-crawlies were winding up their tails to strike.

I hate scorpions.

Cass wasn't sure why. He just did.

But Pancake was persistent. He stomped. He jingled his bridle. He swatted Cass's backside with his tail. When all else failed, the gelding reached his great yellow teeth for Cass's hat brim.

And Cass let him.

Wait a minute.

Black, wispy tendrils were inviting him to dive into the Dark Place, to surrender his will and deaden all sensation in the fog. But something was wrong. Pancake was chomping his Stetson. His prized Stetson!

I should be madder than a teased rattlesnake right now.

"Bad pony," he rasped.

Pancake nickered affectionately.

"You wanna become wolf bait?" With a Herculean effort, Cass opened his eyes. And instantly regretted it.

"Ow."

Privately, he conceded just how useful that Dark Place had been. Now pinpricks of light jabbed his brain. The sun was glaring him straight in the eye. But at least it wasn't flashing.

Funny. A flashing sun...

Chuckling weakly, he winced again. His throat was as raw as carrion. A sea of fresh straw surrounded him. In his arms, he clutched an empty bottle of Talisker whisky. His clothes stank of urine and sweat. He had no idea where he was; no idea how he'd gotten there. And why the hell had he been drinking a prissy man's Scotch?

He pushed it aside.

"Must've been some bender, eh, Fiddle Foot?" he told his horse.

Pancake stomped and jingled some more.

"Ow," Cass whispered again.

Sound hurt. Light hurt. Breathing hurt. He was surprised when his arm actually obeyed his command to retrieve the Stetson. He'd been worried he had some smashed bones.

How'd my wrists get so bruised? And my ankles?

"I'd hate to see the other fella," he rallied, testing his legs. "The one who lost the brawl."

Grabbing hold of Pancake's stirrup, he pulled himself to his knees. Gripping the saddle's girth strap, he dragged a foot under him. By the time he'd hauled himself high enough to reach the horn, he was panting hard.

Retching felt good. So he did it again.

At last, he was able to stand—or more accurately, lean. He pressed his cheek against Pancake's neck. It felt warm and soft—comforting, like home.

"Ponies don't go to hell, right?" he murmured into that golden-brown fur. "So if you're here, I must be somewhere north of Hades."

Pancake stood like a mountain. Strong and silent. Still.

"You must've pulled me out of some jam, pal." Cass patted the gelding's neck. "Always working that apple angle, huh?"

Pancake's tail whacked his calves.

"Again: *Ow.*"

He caught the pony's bridle and led him out of the stall. Some fine-looking horse flesh stared back at him across the aisle. They were all thoroughbreds, judging by their deep chests, high withers, and long legs. Not a single groom was in sight. Cass could have rustled his pick.

But Pancake had saved his life. As far as Cass was concerned, his rustling days were through. He wouldn't trade his buckskin quarter-horse for a king's ransom in gold.

"I'm gonna make you a Ranger's horse, Pancake."

The gelding's ears swiveled skeptically.

"Believe it, son. You and me, we're a team. Like eggs and bacon. Biscuits and gravy. Chili and beans."

Cass's stomach heaved, threatening to turn inside out.

"All right. No more food talk," he said weakly. "But you get the idea. When I get us back to Texas, we'll both be heroes."

There was just one little thing he had to do first. Some nagging thing, he couldn't remember. The memories scattered like smoke on the wind. He frowned, blaming the Talisker.

Damned prissy man's liquor.

In the crackling chill beyond the stable's doors, his breaths formed puffs of steam. He halted to get his bearings. Frozen ruts stretched under a canopy of icicle-laden conifers. He recognized carriage tracks, winding off through the woods. Around a bend in the drive, he glimpsed a chimney and a mansard roof.

Nice neighborhood.

He'd been expecting Holladay Street.

Screwing up his face, he squinted at a white mass of brightness, behind a lowering, gray cloud. The sun appeared in the three o'clock position. He still had time.

Time for what?

He rubbed his forehead, but the massage didn't help. He couldn't remember.

"If today was my birthday," he told Pancake, "and I couldn't remember where the party was, that would be a bad thing."

A birthday party?

His humor ebbed. A spark of memory flared. Just as quickly, it got snuffed out by the tentacles of fog, stretching out from the Dark Place. He had the oddest sense he wasn't supposed to remember. And that pissed him off.

"I don't suppose *you* can tell me, Batter Head."

Pancake's great, liquid-brown eyes blinked. Somewhere in that bottomless gaze hid all of Cass's secrets. Or at least, all his secrets since he'd rustled the big, amicable buckskin from a hitching post in Pancake, Texas.

"Maybe a bath would help. Don't worry, I meant for me, not you. Find me hot water, pard."

He heaved himself into the saddle. The earth pitched. The sky spun. He choked the saddle horn for dear life.

"But find it real slow," he wheezed, fighting off another dry puke.

Pancake obliged. Slow was his favorite gait.

Somehow, as they made their way down the avenue, Cass didn't topple into the bushes. He paid no attention to the magnificent houses behind the brick walls and wrought-iron fences. He was too busy trying to remember things: like where he'd gotten the whisky. And who owned the thoroughbreds. And why he had welts, like giant bee stings, on his neck. He was deathly allergic to bees. Shouldn't he be buzzard bait by now?

The clopping of hooves distracted him from these uneasy musings. An unmarked carriage rattled around the bend. The well-bundled whip clutched a flask in one hand and the reins in the other. Cass guessed the hack was a rental.

As the team of Morgans drew abreast of Pancake, the whip raised a toast. Cass pinched his hat brim. As far as he was concerned, they were two chilly strangers, passing in a ditch. That's why he didn't waste a second thought on the bespectacled youth, gawking at him through the isinglass windows.

A moment later, he heard a disgruntled *whoa*. Cass glanced over his shoulder in time to see a coach door swing wide. A beardless beanpole, dressed in red livery with epaulets, jumped into the slush.

"Ranger Cassidy!"

Cass winced. Loudness wasn't his friend. He waved a greeting and urged Pancake to continue onward.

"It's Brodie, sir!"

Brodie. The memory hit Cass straight between the eyes. *Brodie, the Pinkerton.*

Something cold and cunning whispered from the Dark Place: *Kill...*

Cass shook his head. Mostly to clear it.

Turning Pancake, he rode back toward the coach. Brodie waited, fresh-faced and eager.

"I *reckon* you didn't recognize me in my valet disguise," the boy said proudly. He looked like a lobster with golden scrub brushes on his shoulders.

Cass hiked an eyebrow. It was one of the few things on his body that moved without throbbing. "So that's why you're all ragged-out?"

The boy nodded, pushing his spectacles up his nose. He was finally able to take a closer look at Cass's welts and bruises. Or maybe he smelled the urine. In any event, his forehead puckered.

"You've been missing for hours, sir! Where've you been?"

"Around."

"You look like you tangled with a grizzly bear!"

"So?"

Brodie flinched at his brusque tone. "Um...I reckon that bear wasn't anything you couldn't handle, sir."

"That's right. And that bear will stay our secret. *Comprende?*"

Brodie nodded vigorously, wide-eyed and breathless.

Cass relaxed his wrist, preventing his .38 from sliding into his fist. Apparently, he still had a loyal mole in Ryker's organization. "What's the word on the street?"

"Ryker came up empty-handed," Brodie reported disdainfully. His dislike of Ryker was the main reason why Cass had been able to recruit him. "Sadie's the one who saved the day. She snatched Miss Wyntir's journal. The trouble is, today's Sunday. Ryker's trying to get a search warrant, but Judge Hadley is on holiday in New York. Ol' Judge Mad Dog—er, I mean, Maddox—has a grudge against Ryker. Sterne might have to step in. Unfortunately,

Sterne's got a strike against him, too, 'cause Maddox can't abide Rangers. He thinks they're all murderers, sanctioned by Texas to wear a badge."

Cass cocked his head. Little of this report made sense. "So...I'm in the clear?"

"Oh. Um, that." Brodie fidgeted. "Not exactly, sir. Ryker and Sterne have been distracted by the warrant, that's all. But if you found some evidence to help them, something to earn their trust, that would sure go a long way toward clearing your name."

Cass grunted.

"Did you?" Brodie prompted.

Cass blinked blankly at the boy.

"Last night at the house."

Cass still didn't have a clue what the kid was talking about. And that worried him. But pride compelled him to keep his mouth shut. To play along and not ask questions.

"Maybe. I reckon it'll take someone wiser than me to know for sure."

"So it wasn't the Namdaran Emeralds?" Brodie looked disappointed. "Or the Heart of Fire?"

That insidious, sibilant voice was whispering again from the Dark Place.

Cass frowned. He rubbed his forehead.

"Ranger Cassidy, sir? You all right?"

Cass winced as the boy raised his voice. "I'm not deaf, kid."

"Oh. Um...sorry."

"Take a message to Sadie. And *only* to Sadie. Got that?"

"Yessir."

"Tell her to meet me at dusk at the corner of 20th Street and Welton. In the churchyard. Tell her to come alone."

"But Ryker—"

"Do it." Cass drilled the kid with his gunfighter stare.

Brodie gulped. "Y-yes, sir. Do you still want me to deliver Don Dom's purse to Miss Greyfell?"

Cass had forgotten about Don Dom. He'd forgotten about a lot of things, apparently. "Change of plans. I'll do it later. You fetch Sadie. Leave Ryker to me."

The boy nodded uneasily. He handed the purse to Cass.

Satisfied his orders would be obeyed, Cass turned Pancake in the direction of his original destination, Holladay Street. There were things he needed to do before nightfall: Feed his horse. Take a bath. Bind his wounds. Clean his guns.

There was one other thing too. Something that had to happen in a churchyard with a bell. He didn't know what it was, exactly.

But something told him he'd remember when he saw Sadie.

CHAPTER 21

S adie jolted awake in her chair, her Smith & Wesson aimed at the penthouse door. Someone was pounding on it. The whole wall shook. Even the crystal teardrops, dangling from the sconces, were swaying.

She scrubbed a hand over her face. She figured the caller couldn't be Goddard or a minion from his secret army. Any of Goddard's puppets would have tried to lie their way into the penthouse, not break down her door.

Dragging her fingers through her hair, she made a cursory attempt to look presentable, pinching her cheeks and hiding her .32 beneath the sleeve of her bolero jacket.

"*Coming!* Coming," she muttered, appalled when she glanced at the mantel. The clock read 3:35—*in the afternoon!*

Somehow, she'd lost three hours off her day. She'd only intended to rest her eyes after Pryce had escorted her back from the Grand Central Hotel. She'd ridden there for a powwow with Wilma, Rex, and Mace about Wyntir's journal. Mace seemed to think they had grounds for a search warrant. Arranging for that warrant had been Rex's job.

Not trusting Mace to be sensitive to Wyntir's innocence—or her grief—Sadie had asked Wilma to accompany Mace and Rex to Greyfell Manor. In the meantime, Sadie was keeping up her *contessa* charade, in case the search proved fruitless.

Eager to know if her colleagues had unearthed the "secret laboratory" that Wyntir had described, Sadie cracked open the penthouse door.

She'd been expecting Mace. Instead, she found Collie.

"Shh!" she hissed, grabbing the boy's deerskin sleeve and dragging him over the threshold. "I'm being watched!"

Vandy wriggled his way through the maze of skirts and trouser legs, just barely clearing the threshold before the door swung closed.

"Hey! Watch the tail!" Collie snapped.

"Sorry."

Vandy didn't seem to mind her negligence. Full of forgiveness, he flopped on her shoes, kicked up her skirts, and generally made a nuisance of himself. She had to tug her petticoats from the playful coon's teeth.

"Did you find Cass?" she asked hopefully.

Cass had been missing for hours, and he hadn't found a way to communicate with her. Thanks to Dolce's accusations, every law enforcement agency in town was looking for him.

Collie wanted to find Cass too. The difference was, Collie didn't want Cass arrested. She'd had the devil of a time convincing the boy that she was on his side, mainly because Mace had ordered his most loyal men to watch her around the clock. In fact, he'd replaced the elevator operator with a Pinkerton.

Now Collie's flinty, streetwise glare darted beneath her bed, the chaise lounge, the draperies—anywhere a grown man might hide. Sadie wasn't sure whether he was hunting for Cass or Pinkertons.

Finally, a shadow passed over the boy's sun-gilded brow.

"I was hoping Cass sneaked in here," he admitted.

Damn!

Sadie struggled to ignore her frisson of dread. "Well, he knows he's being hunted. He knows they're watching me and you. He's a coyote. He knows where to hole up. Besides, he hasn't even been missing for 24 hours. I wouldn't worry about him, if I were you. I'm not."

"How the hell are you a Pinkerton? You can't lie worth crap."

She sighed. So much for playing Big Sister and trying to ease the boy's mind.

"Did you try Mattie's? The Bust-a-Gut? The Bonanza—"

Collie was nodding impatiently. "I tried every brothel on Holladay Street and every saloon in the Highlands. I even went to Porfi's. Nobody knows where he is."

"He probably convinced some bawd to cover for him."

"You mean he told her to humbug a kid with a coon?" Collie shook his head. "No way. He would have told her to let me in."

"But if he was worried you'd been *followed*—"

"I know how to ditch the law," he snapped. "I do it better than he does."

"In the wild? Maybe. In an unfamiliar city? Not so much."

They locked stares. Collie didn't like to be told he was wrong.

"Look," she said, struggling with her own notoriously short temper. "All I'm saying is, he's canny. That's why no jail can hold him. Besides, Rex would have sent word if Cass was arrested."

"Arrest ain't what I'm worried about," Collie said darkly.

Sadie quailed to see her worst fears mirrored in that troubled, pewter stare.

Suddenly, a polite rap shook the door.

Collie's Colt was in his fist faster than she could blink, which secretly impressed her. His quickdraw had come a long way since Cass had started training him last year. The boy jerked his head to the side, ordering her out of the line of fire. Vandy growled softly.

"*Donna?*" a muffled young tenor queried in Italian. "*Sono io, il valletto di Don Nico.*"

Sadie hiked an eyebrow. Mace had sent an agent to play his valet? The boy's accent wasn't half bad.

She waved Collie out of sight, tossing him a warning look for good measure. He'd eased his thumb off the gun hammer, but he'd refused to holster the Colt.

Cass has been training him, all right.

"Buon pomeriggio," she greeted, adopting a regal mien as she opened the door.

Brodie inclined his head. *"Si, donna."*

Sadie hid her amusement. So much for the junior agent's Italian. Apparently, Brodie had memorized just enough vocabulary to get him in the penthouse, and '*good afternoon*' hadn't been on the list.

"I came as fast as I could," he confided as she closed the door behind him.

Collie's narrowed gaze swept over Brodie's red coat, brass buttons, and white gloves. "Bellhops are supposed to wear blue around here."

Brodie straightened his spectacles. "You are Collier MacAffee," he said in some surprise. "Ranger Cassidy's friend."

"I know who I am. Who the hell are you?"

A flush rolled up Brodie's neck. "That's not important. What's important is Ranger Cassidy sent me." He turned his shoulder on the boy and locked stares with Sadie. "He wants you to meet him alone. St. John's Cathedral. At dusk in the churchyard."

Collie's thumb strayed back to his gun hammer. "Prove it."

Brodie's Adam's apple bobbed a couple of times. He looked to Sadie for help.

"Put away the gun, Collie." She felt like the weight of the world had lifted off her shoulders now that she knew Cass was alive. "I trust this messenger."

"Yeah? Well, I don't trust anyone associated with Ryker."

The boy had a point. But she wasn't going to let Brodie know she felt the same way.

"Then you mustn't trust me," she said impatiently.

"You're female. That's different." Collie's flinty gaze drilled into Brodie. "And dressin' like a girl don't count."

Brodie huffed, straightening his spine. "I'll have you know, Ranger Cassidy asked me to impersonate a valet to corroborate his Don Dominar alias!"

"Don Dom?" Collie cocked his head. A grudging acceptance vied with the suspicion on his face. "You dressed as a bootlicker for Cass?"

"Well, *you* wouldn't," Brodie said indignantly.

"Damned straight. You look like a crawfish. After a boil."

Sadie cleared her throat to hide her amusement. "If you boys are done cuss-fighting, I'll need a little help sneaking past Pryce."

"He ain't your only problem," Collie said grimly, holstering his Colt. "The fella in the elevator's got shoes that stink like rubber too."

So Collie noticed Pinkertons wear soft soles to tail suspects? That boy's going to make one canny tin-star someday.

"I have an idea," Brodie volunteered.

Sadie and Collie exchanged dubious looks.

"Mr. MacAffee will need to loan you his hat, coat, and cartridge belt, of course," Brodie said eagerly. "Oh. And his coon."

Collie blinked. "My coon?"

"Well, Miss Sadie can't very well impersonate you without Vandy."

A comical look of horror spread across Collie's face. Sadie coughed into her fist.

"What are *you* laughing at?" the boy growled.

She winked at Brodie. "Well, there is an alternative solution," she said in lilting tones. "I could loan Collie my bustle, corset, and lip paint—"

Collie was already stripping off his coat and scowling like a gargoyle. "When you find Snake Bait in that churchyard, tell him I'm gonna whup his ass. Oh, and make sure Vandy bites him."

By the time Sadie had finished dressing like a boy, the clock read 3:50. She spent another 10 minutes learning how to mimic a certain corn-cracker's gangly stroll, much to Collie's humiliation. By the time the boys had loaded Vandie into a knapsack and strapped the coon to her back, the clock read 4:05.

"Good God," she huffed, hefting her furry stowaway higher on her shoulders. "How many pecan trees have you eaten, Tubby?"

"For your information," Collie retorted, "Vandy doesn't *have* to volunteer for this mission. He could leave you to rot under your tiara, princess."

"That's *contessa,* smartass. And all I'm saying is, I don't think you should be giving him that biscuit—"

"You want him wiggling like a fish and popping out on your head?"

Sadie shot Brodie a withering look. The junior agent was snickering.

"I didn't think so," Collie said loftily.

Vandy reached eager forepaws for the treat. Sadie winced at the amplified sound of coon teeth, crunching in her ear.

"Now don't forget to let him pee before you ride back. And cinch that belt real tight so he doesn't tip out. And remember to—"

"*Yes,* Mother," she interrupted, tossing the boy an exasperated look.

She cracked open the door and peeked into the hall. She could see Pryce sitting on a stool by the stairwell. He was reading a newspaper. The masthead of the *Rocky* was illuminated by slanting shafts of afternoon.

She squared her shoulders.

Brodie nodded in encouragement. Collie folded his arms across his chest. When the door swung closed, he looked worried. She had no illusions about whom.

The good news is, sneaking past Pryce will be the most harrowing part of this journey, she consoled herself.

Even so, her heart wouldn't stop hammering her ribs. She thought for certain the agent would hear it.

She gulped a bolstering breath.

All right, Moocher, it's show time. Do me proud.

With Vandy's hot little breaths blowing in her ear, Sadie sauntered toward her Pinkerton bodyguard. She wasn't able to stop Collie's spurs from jingling—like he'd shown her—but she steeled her expression against a show of frustration. She kept Brodie's advice firmly in mind:

"Pryce has no reason to suspect the switch, so don't give him one. Just walk. Keep your head down. If you have to, grunt like you hate the world."

"Hey!" Collie had protested.

Somehow, she managed not to smirk at the memory.

Now she was five feet from the agent. She kept her chin tucked in Collie's bandanna and the boy's chocolate-brown Stetson pulled low over her tell-tale eyes.

Fortunately, the sun was dipping in the sky, and the stairwell was full of shadows. When Pryce glanced up, she angled her face away from the window and toyed with Vandy's paw. She could almost feel the agent's probing stare as it roamed from her muley boots, to her fringed deerskin jacket, to her furry sidekick, who was leaving a trail of crumbs in her wake—not to mention dropping them down her collar.

"Hold."

She nearly strangled on her breath.

"You got a smoke?" Pryce demanded.

Fighting down panic, she shook her head.

The agent looked annoyed. "This stairwell's colder than a witch's tit. What's the time?"

She shrugged and grunted, trying to look surly and sound insolent—just like Collie would.

Pryce scowled. Her scalp prickled. She thought he'd taken offense.

"Becker's late, I'll warrant. Probably losing his shirt at craps," he grumbled, shaking open his paper again. Pryce waved her forward and buried his nose in the boxing pages.

The ruse worked!

She fled. By the time she reached the hitching post and heaved her 50-pound knapsack onto Collie's horse, the clock on the Windsor's tower read 4:18. She needed to hurry if she wanted to reach the cathedral before sunset.

The snow had stopped, but the wind was brisk. Rhubarb's canter made it even brisker, causing air gusts to sting her cheeks. She was grateful for Vandy's warmth, pressed against her spine. He didn't mind the chill. In fact, he seemed to enjoy the way the wind riffled his fur and caused little puffs of steam to rise from his snout. He even swatted at his breaths, playful to the core. She smiled to hear him snuffling at scents she could only imagine.

Eventually, he hooked both paws around her neck and rested his chin on her shoulder, the way a toddler might. His childlike trust made her heart sigh. She hadn't anticipated this sneak-attack of female yearning. Her brain promptly turned to mush, envisioning a dimpled, tow-headed urchin with Cass's mischievous blue eyes on her back.

Somehow, she managed to drag her attention to the road once more. St. John's Cathedral loomed around the bend. Its spire rose like a silver flame against the western backdrop of sun-drenched mountains. The peaks were ablaze with orange fire. She wouldn't have minded taking a few moments to enjoy the view, but Rhubarb distracted her, tossing his head. He whinnied.

A distant, but friendly neigh answered the roan.

Pancake!

An overwhelming surge of relief made her eyes burn. She didn't know whether to laugh or cry. Cass was here. All the hours of worry had been for naught. He was safe, and he was on time. She suspected if she turned into the wind, she'd catch a whiff of cinnamon and cloves, and the aroma of his tobacco would lead her to him.

Planning to do just that, she dismounted, gathering Rhubarb's reins. But the minute she stepped beneath a stand of pine trees, Vandy started squirming like that fish Collie had warned her about.

"What on earth—"

Now Vandy was growling. Coon fangs were daunting at any distance, but when they were bared two inches from your throat, that was cause for serious alarm.

"All right, all right, I'll let you down!"

She lowered the knapsack to the snow. Wriggling out of his leather prison, Vandy barreled through the drifts like a chubby torpedo.

She blew out her breath. Either Cass had loaded his pockets with coon treats, or a female was busily spraying a tree. In either case, Sadie didn't know how the devil she was going to get Vandy stuffed inside that knapsack again.

I'll deal with that catastrophe later.

She tethered Rhubarb and wandered through the trees. The sun was sinking fast, and midnight-blue shadows were lengthening across the snow. The grounds were larger than she'd anticipated; she wasn't sure where to look for Cass. He wasn't smoking; at least, not that she could smell. The church was dark, and the yard appeared vacant. To her left loomed the Episcopal rectory, to the right sprawled a graveyard. She couldn't spot fresh hoof prints. But then, Cass was dodging the law. He wouldn't have left an obvious trail.

The sudden clanging of church bells startled her. They pealed at a thunderous pitch—not once, as they should have done to mark half past the hour. They rang five times. Eight times. Twelve times.

A curse and a whimper were distinct between claps.

"Cass!" she called again.

Lord. Enough of the bells already. She couldn't believe they were still tolling. The timing mechanism must have been faulty in the clock tower.

She spied movement. A dark-haired man in a black duster was stumbling into the graveyard with his hands over his ears. He fell to his knees.

Cass?

Shouting was futile. She hurried after him, leaving her tree cover behind. He struggled to his feet. She lost sight of him as he ducked behind a monument.

Suddenly, the clamor stopped. The utter silence of the boneyard was eerie. Every bird—and even the wind—seemed to be reeling in the aftershock. Her own ears throbbed as she crossed beneath the vaulted, wrought-iron gateway that marked the cemetery's entrance.

"Cass!"

Her voice pinged off the headstones, the cathedral, the trees. He didn't answer. He didn't show himself.

Halting, she tugged Collie's coat collar higher. She was getting chills. She supposed that was normal. Dusk was leeching what feeble warmth the sun had pumped into the yard. Maybe Cass didn't recognize her. She shoved back her hat, letting her hair tumble past her shoulders.

"It's me! Sadie!"

Yew trees soughed; elms creaked and moaned. Above the mournful sounds, she could just barely discern the tinny strains of mechanical music. The tune was an old soldier's lament. Her memory supplied the lyrics:

> *"Bury me alone at sundown,*
> *When the sky's last lingering rays,*
> *Flee before the coming darkness,*
> *Thus to end my wicked days."*

A suspicion—a terrible, horrifying suspicion—sneaked inside her brain.

Twigs snapped.

She spun around.

It was too late to trigger her .32. All she could do was quail before her worst nightmare:

Cass had emerged from a hedgerow. His expression was blank. His eyes were cold. And his gun was pointed at her heart.

CHAPTER 22

◆◆◆

"C-Cass?"

Sadie's shock was giving way to real fear. He stood like stone in the long, lingering rays of the sun. His .45 glinted like a lethal shard of lightning in his black-gloved fist.

"Don't you recognize me?"

A flesh-prickling chuckle answered from the shadows. It was followed by the flare of a match. She could see Goddard now, about 10 yards to her right, dressed in his own disguise, the patched overalls and drooping slouch hat of a common miner. His impoverished look, complete with a day's growth of beard, was belied by his fancy, Cleopatra Federal cigar. She could smell the tell-tale aroma of cognac as he puffed the tobacco to life. The music was coming from the open humidor he'd balanced on a tombstone.

"You're in a trance, Cass! Wake up! You have to fight it!"

"Oh, he's quite beyond your influence, my dear—Sadie, I believe you called yourself."

Tears stung her eyes. Never had she hated anyone more in that moment than Goddard. For whatever he'd done to Cass, she wanted to draw her stiletto and stab it a thousand times into Goddard's black heart. *No, better.* She wanted to draw her .32 and blast the bastard's balls to smithereens.

But she didn't dare to move. She barely dared to breathe. Whoever was staring out of Cass's glacier-cold, unblinking eyes was a stranger. And that stranger wouldn't hesitate to kill.

"What did you do to him?" she whispered hoarsely, the horror of Wyntir's last journal entry creeping into her mind.

"Trade secret." Goddard strolled closer, smug. Arrogant. Utterly confident in his control over his puppet. "But I must say, Mr. Cassidy was a refreshing challenge. An outlaw with a murder record, who'd convinced some fool to hand him a marshal's badge? Now that must have taken real charm. Or cunning." Goddard chuckled, halting about 10 feet from her side. "I know something about cunning, you see."

'How dare you compare yourself to Cass!' she wanted to shout. *'You're not fit to lick a horse turd off his boots!'*

But Sadie steeled herself against the fury churning in her breast. She knew something about cunning too.

"However did those fools at Harvard fail to recognize your genius?" she deadpanned.

He looked amused. *"Brava.* As hoydens go, you're rather clever. And far more resourceful than that other piece of fluff the Pinkertons sent to investigate my thefts.

"But sending a girl to do a man's job? *Tsk,"* Goddard continued in that same grating tone of conceit. "The Pinkertons should be ashamed. I'm sure you'll agree, in light of your own dismal failure, that your superiors should be punished for luring foolish young women away from the scullery. Or in your case, the brothel.

"But do not fret, my dear. As accomplished at gunplay as Mr. Cassidy—or should I say, *Daredevil*—is, I'm sure he'll have no difficulty carrying out his task to execute your pretend cousin. In fact, I think Mr. Cassidy is rather looking forward to ventilating Agent Sledgehammer. Isn't that right, Mr. Cassidy?"

Cass's nod was mechanical. Devoid of all emotion.

Sadie drew a shuddering breath. "You know about Sledgehammer?"

"Your silly little colleague told me all about him. Or rather, her reports did. Miss Merripen even predicted another agent from the Sisterhood would come to her rescue. She was most helpful in that regard—a real peach. She handed over all her files before jumping into the Platte."

A muscle ticked in Sadie's jaw. "And here I thought you'd pushed her."

Goddard hiked a mocking eyebrow. "Murder? How untidy. No, Miss Merripen killed herself. As did Renfield. And Baines. And the clerk at the Windsor Hotel. I daresay Judge Maddox will do the same. Once I decide he's no longer useful."

Sadie's heart trembled at this revelation.

"But your methods aren't infallible," she countered. "Sheridan got caught. And she's still alive."

"Of course she did. I wanted her to suffer the ultimate agony: her fall from grace." Goddard was gloating. "Now she'll be refused at every soiree, every afternoon tea. Whispers of contempt will haunt her footsteps for the rest of her days." He smiled pleasantly. "Socialites are far more brutal than juries when doling out punishment. Rather like piranhas at feeding time."

"So you wanted revenge? Because Sheridan hired Baines?"

A glimmer of spite flickered in those dark, burning eyes. "An act of sheer madness. Sheridan should be locked in an asylum with her crackpot of a mother-in-law."

"You've been played, doctor." Sadie pounced on the first sign of weakness that he'd shown. "Lilybelle's no crackpot. Her eccentricities are nothing more than affectations to annoy her relatives."

He blew a long, spiraling stream of smoke. "So now you're the expert?"

"She hid her jewelry from you."

His amusement returned. "In point of fact, she hid her jewelry from Sheridan."

"Not according to my sources. Lilybelle was warned about you. So was Edmund Greyfell. That's why Wyntir overheard you quarreling with her father. What happened, Dante? Did your hold on Edmund slip? Did a cleverer, more charismatic charlatan persuade him to sign over his fortune?"

Goddard's brow darkened. Her barb had struck home.

"So you found Wyntir's diary. Commendable. Where did the scatterbrain leave it?"

"Trade secret."

"My, aren't you brassy."

"Brass and balls. The top two requisites for a Pinkerton." She carved out a pleasant smile.

She was stalling for time. She knew that humidor couldn't play *Bury me at Sundown* forever. She was hoping the mechanism would wind down, that Cass would come back to his senses.

"So let me guess," she said boldly. "It's what we Pinkertons do best. Edmund was in pain. He was trying to avoid a morphine addiction. He hired you to play the violin, because it soothed him. You drugged him, hypnotized him—whatever—and began your reign of terror. You implanted suggestions in his brain, so he would invite you to live in his home; so he would construct your secret basement; so he would blame his servants for your thefts; and eventually, so he would appoint you Wyntir's guardian. But somehow, Edmund broke your spell. How do you think he did that, Dante?"

Goddard's smile was snide. "Now let *me* guess. You hope Mr. Cassidy is listening to our conversation. That my answer will give him the clue he needs to recover his senses. You think your ruse will restore your lover to you. After all, I only had 12 hours to break him in my lab."

Goddard's casual use of "break" and "lab" made Sadie sick to her stomach. In the fading light, she could see the ugly sores and welts on Cass's neck, the dark circles beneath the midnight-blue of his eyes. He'd been through hell.

"A valiant effort, my dear. But 12 hours of—shall we say, *duress*—are sufficient to divide any human mind into its most basic personalities. In effect, Mr. Cassidy has become two men: one with a conscience, and one without. As a matter of fact," Goddard taunted, "I was astounded to see just how readily he took to my conditioning.

"But then, Mr. Cassidy's lawless side has always lurked just beneath the surface. All it needed was a little push to rise up against the tyranny of its oppression. Now his primal self can happily do what it has yearned to do for years: Kill without remorse."

Sadie trembled, struggling to remain calm, to draw faith from her love. She refused to believe Cass's killing instinct was stronger than the good man who lived inside him. A killer would have ventilated those three, unarmed bushwhackers in Mattie's alley. He would have plugged the zombie-like Baines, when the professor was shooting up Porfi's bakery. And he doubtless would have blown off Collie's head for unrepentant sassing. Hell. In that context alone, Cass was a saint!

"You're wrong about Cass," she said fiercely. "I knew him before puberty. And in all these years, he has *never* wavered from his determination to protect the weak and defend the innocent. To make the world a safer place for little kiddies to play!"

"Your little kiddies, my dear?" Goddard's chuckle raised every hair on her scalp. Flicking ash, he turned to Cass. "Tell me, Mr. Cassidy. Why did you come to the churchyard this evening?"

"To kill the Pinkerton whore."

She quailed. Cass hadn't blinked. He hadn't hesitated. He'd spoken with a chilling finality that made the blood drain to her toes.

"And after you kill the Pinkerton whore, what is your next mission?"

"Kill Ryker."

"And Ryker would be?"

"Sledgehammer."

"Very good, Mr. Cassidy. But what if a marshal comes to investigate? What if he tries to question you?"

"I kill the marshal."

"Yes, but marshals have posses. What if you cannot escape?"

"I kill myself."

Sadie trembled.

"Excellent, Mr. Cassidy." A cruel little smile teased Goddard's lips. "Shall we begin?"

She struggled to keep a grip on her reason, to dam the mortifying tears of fear.

Maisy, if you really are my Guardian Angel, now's the time to pull out all the stops!

"My God, Dante, what happened to you? You wanted to be a doctor, once. Doctors heal people not…not *torture* them!"

"I am a man of *science,*" he retorted loftily. "When my test subjects are clever—and they execute their missions successfully—they wake, remembering nothing of their adventures. My research has no permanent ill effects."

"I'd say *death* is a permanent ill effect!"

"A matter of perspective, my dear. If I exposed you to one of the Nightshades, you'd be begging for death."

"T-the Nightshades?"

"A family of plants. One yellow-and-white flower in my possession is particularly nasty. If I were to blow its pollen in your face, you would do whatever I desired. Screw yourself with a whisky bottle, if I commanded it." He smiled pleasantly.

She swallowed hard. Was she imagining it? Or had a tremor just moved down Cass's gun arm?

Hope clutched her heart. *He's fighting. Good Cass is alive inside and fighting!*

"Is that what you did to Minx?" Sadie demanded, desperately trying to give Good Cass the time he needed to win. "Screwed her with a whiskey bottle?"

"I didn't think of it at the time," Goddard admitted wryly, "but it would certainly have kept her from spawning."

"So you sent Minx over the bridge with your *baby* in her womb?!"

"Genius such as mine can only be bred from a pure lineage."

My God, my God, Cass kill him!!

"And Wyntir? Is *her* lineage pure enough for you?"

Goddard laughed. The sound was freakishly sane. "That harebrained twit? You add to your sins by insulting my intelligence.

"But no matter. Despite the best efforts of your entire Pinkerton Agency, my stay in Denver has made me a wealthy man. The Heart of Fire, the Namdaran Emeralds, and Mephistopheles's Jewels are but a few of the treasures I've tucked away for safekeeping. After the heat dies, I'll return to Denver to retrieve them.

"In the meantime—" he dropped the stub of his cigar, letting it smoke and sputter in the snow "—I must bid you *adieu.* The Union Pacific waits for no man. With your curiosity satisfied, I trust you can die fulfilled—or at least, as fulfilled as an abominable failure can be.

"Mr. Cassidy."

The air iced in her lungs.

"Kill the Pinkerton whore."

Cass's thumb cocked the hammer.

Sadie's eyes brimmed. *This is it, then? Good Cass lost the battle?*

As stiff and pale as alabaster, the hauntingly beautiful face of her lover swam in the kaleidoscope of her tears. Despite her tremors, she raised her head and stood her ground. She told herself she wasn't afraid to die. Maisy, Mama, and Papa were waiting on the Other Side. Cass would shoot straight and true. She would feel no pain.

She just had one last piece of unfinished business. "I forgive you, Cass."

His gun barrel quivered.

"I love you. I've always loved you," she whispered, the tears sliding free.

"Mr. Cassidy," Goddard barked. "You have your order. *Kill the Pinkerton whore.*"

She braced herself.

Time slowed.

The air became sharper, fresher. Her heart hammered harder to sustain her ending life. The rush of her blood was dizzying. Her entire existence telescoped to that moment. To Cass, her childhood friend, her adolescent sweetheart, her Beloved. The man whose fiery spirit burned like the twin flame of her soul.

And then in the deep, dark winter of those colder-than-cold eyes, she saw a spark.

The spark became a flame.

A hellish rage blazed to life.

Lucifire was reborn!

Slowly, methodically, he depressed the gun hammer. The .45 slid from his glove and plunged, muzzle-first, into the snow.

No! My God, Cass, what are you doing?!

She wanted to trigger the .32 up her sleeve, but she couldn't move. She couldn't breathe. It was as if angelic forces had immobilized her body with invisible wings.

Goddard's mask of civility melted away. His once handsome face twisted with noxious malice. She was sure he was shouting something vicious and blood-curdling, but she couldn't hear the words. Her pulse was roaring like a speeding locomotive in her ears.

She saw Goddard shove a hand inside his hip pocket.

She saw the ghost of a smile touch Lucifire's lips.

When Goddard's fist reappeared, it was cocking a pistol. The demon in Cass unleashed. Striking like black lightning, he triggered the .38 up his sleeve. The first bullet drilled through Goddard's maniacal brain. The second ripped through his fiendish heart.

Bullets three and four shattered the humidor, scattering cigars, metal gears, and splinters of wood across the snow.

But Lucifire wasn't satisfied. He dropped his spent .38 and yanked the .45 from the snow. Sadie ducked, covering her head, as bullets zinged off the bell tower. The clock face shattered. The minute hand spun circles around the numbers. Chunks of sandstone tumbled off the masonry.

Now the .45 was spent. Lucifire's vengeful, burning eyes sought a new weapon. They alighted on Goddard's fallen pistol.

"Cass, stop!" Her limbs shaking like jelly, Sadie forced herself to step between him and the spreading blood stain in the snow. "It's over! You've won!"

Lucifire's lethal stare pinned her like a fly on a wall. Tears spilled down her cheeks.

"Cass, hear me," she pleaded, forcing the words past her constricting throat. "He can't hurt you anymore. He can't hurt anyone. Not even me."

Confusion muddied that fearsome gaze. He blinked. He scrubbed a hand over his face. When he staggered, she wrapped him in her arms. He buried his face in her hair.

"My God, Sadie." His muffled voice cracked with shame. "All I wanted to do was protect you."

"You did, Cass."

"I'm so sorry…"

"No one will ever know what he did to you," she vowed fiercely. "No one will ever find out."

He dragged her into a crushing embrace. When he folded her body against the wild cadence of his heart, his shoulders quaked.

That's when she realized he wept.

CHAPTER 23

———— ◆ ————

Over the next few days, the *Rocky* pieced together sensational stories of Maestro's crimes. The shocking headlines spared few reputations:

Maestro Unmasked:
Evil Mastermind Disguised as Wyntir's Guardian

Dolce Eats Crow:
Daredevil Revealed as Undercover Cop

Lilybelle Donates $100K:
New Asylum Named 'Sheridan's Shelter'

But the *Rocky* also published a glowing testament to Denver's newest celebrity:

Raccoon Hero Saves the Day:
Maestro's Stolen Jewels Recovered

Sadie couldn't help but smile as she clipped an adorable etching of Vandy for her Pinkerton report. The coon was romping in the snow, his furry neck adorned with rubies, emeralds, and diamonds—or rather, glass replicas.

Minutes after the shootout in the cemetery, Cass had spied the chubby prankster tangled in the real jewels and somersaulting into a tombstone. Apparently, Goddard had tucked the Heart of Fire, the Namdaran Emeralds,

Mephistopheles's Jewels and some lesser-known treasures inside a former taffy tin and stashed his cache inside an abandoned critter den. Needless to say, Vandy's matchless nose had sniffed out the candy.

But the biggest surprise of the hour, at least to Sadie's mind, had been Mace's commendation. Before closing Minx's case, the senior agent had made a special effort to apologize for doubting Sadie's instincts, especially about Goddard's *modus operandi.* In his report, Mace had praised her for the quick thinking that had saved them both from Maestro's tainted bottle of wine.

Even so, Sadie wasn't looking forward to traveling with her boss to headquarters in Chicago for a debriefing tomorrow. Too many long, arduous hours of staring out a train window were dangerous temptations. She might inadvertently blurt out something about Cass's ordeal. To a mind as keen as Mace's, even an innocent, off-hand comment might help him connect the dots. Since he carried a grudge against Cass, she didn't want him to have the barest inkling that Goddard had tried to turn Cass into a mindless killer.

The muffled ding of the elevator distracted Sadie from her thoughts. She glanced at the mantel clock.

Good grief! It's 5:40 already! I haven't finished dressing for Wyntir's Thanksgiving party!

Sadie barely had time to clip citrine dangles to her ears before a fist pounded on her door. Her heart skipped, anticipating a reunion with Cass. Hastily, she checked her reflection. Her cheeks were flushed beneath her powder. Her eyes were luminous above her kohl. She looked like she felt: nervous. Excited. Dangerously in love. Cass had promised her a surprise this evening.

Hiking her amber-colored skirt, she hurried to the door.

But when she threw it wide, her elation deflated a notch. Collie stood on the threshold, scowling more than usual.

"What's wrong?"

"News maggots," he grumbled, letting Vandy streak past her ankles. "They keep pestering me with questions. How'd

I train a coon? Is he smarter than a hound? Will I be taking that offer to sell him to the circus?" Collie snorted at the sheer stupidity of this latter question. "Cass said a deputy's supposed to keep the peace, so I threatened to fill their britches full of buckshot. The reporters thought I was joking."

Sadie's eyes widened. "You mean—?"

"Yeah," Collie grumbled. "Cass confiscated my shotgun. He told me to fetch you while he holds them off in the lobby."

Sadie loosed an exasperated breath. She wasn't sure what to think of the boy's story. Reporters *had* been dogging Collie's heels. His surly façade hid a painfully shy streak, so she could understand why Cass might wade into the fray, distracting the reporters to let the boy escape unwelcome attention.

On the other hand, Cass and Collie were thicker than thieves. She wouldn't have been surprised if the boy was only telling half the story, since Cass had been avoiding alone-time with her since the cemetery shootout. She'd been hoping Thanksgiving would be different...

Suddenly, she realized Collie's hair was slicked back. He smelled of lemongrass soap, and he was wearing a black string tie. Since the kid didn't own a stitch of frou-frou, she suspected Rex's influence.

She hiked an eyebrow. "You're looking mighty fine this evening."

"Don't start." His neck had turned beet red. "You ready?"

"Uh...I just need some lip paint."

Muttering about skirts and "war paint," he stalked across the threshold and made a beeline for her tequila bottle. "You'd better hurry. You're gonna be sorry if you're late."

"Oh?" She tried to hide her curiosity. Without a doubt, Collie was aware of Cass's surprise. "Why's that?"

He tossed her a withering look. "'Cause Wyntir's dogs will eat the turkey."

Liar. She smirked. "Why do I get the feeling you're still sore that Vandy's escaped from the knapsack?"

His jaw jutted.

"Honestly, Collie." She shook her head and reached for her paint pot. "Your coon made out like a bandit."

"What's Vandy gonna do with a $10,000 reward? Even he can't eat that many crawly-fish."

"Maybe Vandy will make you a loan," she said dryly.

"What am *I* gonna do with $10,000? I already got a horse and guns. Ammo only costs 50 cents a box, and Wilma promised me five cases of Wild Turkey if I mend her roof."

"That should last you till Christmas."

"That's being optimistic," Collie deadpanned. Then he grew thoughtful. "Maybe I should buy a still. And brew my own mash."

"Or here's a thought. Why don't you hire a tutor to help you with your ABC's?"

"Book-learning?" Collie looked horrified. "Are you trying to kill me, woman?"

Sadie sighed. Collie didn't understand how much he was missing by being semi-literate. She hated to say it, but his ignorance had actually worked in her favor. His contempt for books had let her keep her promise to Cass—namely, that no one would ever learn what had happened in the cemetery.

After the shootout, she'd searched Goddard's corpse and found his lab journal. Finding the entries about Cass, she'd nearly retched on the spot. The Pinkerton in her had demanded that the book be surrendered as evidence. The woman in her had feared for her lover's badge. Conflicted about her course of action, she'd slipped the journal into her pocket and hurried off to help catch Vandy.

Hours later, when Collie had retreated behind her dressing screen to don his clothes, she'd panicked, remembering where she'd left the journal. But she needn't have worried: Collie had no use for books.

"Here," he'd said, tossing her the grisly record. "You left this in my coat."

Sadie drew a shuddering breath and tried to push aside the memory of how she'd broken the law, burning every last page in that little book of horrors. She prayed that all of Goddard's victims would live out their lives with no ill effects, as the psychiatrist had claimed.

"I'm ready to leave now," she announced to Collie.

The boy muttered something that sounded like, *"Hallelujah,"* then lunged for Vandy, who was trying to wash one of Sadie's earbobs in her tequila glass. She hid her amusement as the furry thief fled into the hall.

When the elevator doors opened in the lobby, Sadie realized that Collie hadn't been exaggerating about the reporters. Three men with pencils and notepads circled Cass, who was entertaining them with gun-spinning tricks.

"So far so Good," Collie muttered, scooping Vandy into his arms. "The maggots didn't hear the elevator ding. Keep hidden till I make my getaway."

"But where are you going?"

"Telegraph office. I'll catch up with you later."

Sadie's lips quirked as the boy hauled his chubby, bright-eyed load across the lobby and bolted out the 18th Street entrance.

Then her eyes strayed to Cass. He'd drawn quite a crowd. He was cracking jokes and accepting dares. Cass lived to showboat.

Gladdened to see the return of the winsome Coyote, Sadie perched unobtrusively on the arm of a settee and watched her lover perform. He juggled; he spun; he tossed guns over his shoulders and caught them behind his back. Clearly, he was feeling better. The rings around his eyes weren't as pronounced as they'd been that harrowing night in the graveyard. The fading welts on his throat were now hidden beneath a high, starched collar and cravat. Cass looked like the happy-go-lucky Coyote of old except, of course, he was wearing holiday swallowtails.

But beneath the fancy broadcloth, Sadie worried that the man she loved had changed—and mostly, toward her. For three days, he'd holed up in a darkened hotel room with tequila. He'd refused the meals she'd ordered for him. He'd barked at well-meaning chamber maids to go away. The only visitors he'd allowed through the door were Collie and Vandy, as long as they'd smuggled his favorite physician, "Dr. Cuervo," past the elevator operator.

Sadie had understood that Cass was trying to cope with the horror he'd lived through. She'd tried to be patient.

Then, yesterday morning, she'd learned that Allan Pinkerton wanted her in Chicago. With the clock ticking on the precious hours she had left with Cass, she'd practically begged him to let her inside his room.

Yesterday had been the first time they'd been utterly alone since the cemetery. Her throat constricted as she remembered how he'd tossed an uneasy glance at his gun belt before edging away from the bed post, where he'd hung it.

An aching silence had descended like an invisible barrier between them. She'd imagined she could hear the soap foaming in his shaving bowl.

She'd tried to find something light-hearted to say.

"Vandy made the headlines again."

"Is that a fact?" Turning his back to her, he concentrated on his shave.

"Boone started a petition. He wants to get Vandy elected mayor. Some lunatics, from a group called The Brotherhood of Rascals, actually signed it."

"Boone'll do anything to sell papers. I'll bet he drafted his poker pals."

"Boone has 287 poker pals?"

Cass hiked an eyebrow. "How many signatures does Vandy need?"

"Three hundred. Collie's pitching a fit."

Cass laughed. The sound was a deep, warm rumble of mirth. Her heart swelled to hear it. Since his ordeal, Cass hadn't laughed much.

She watched him expectantly, hoping for some wisecrack. Some banter to keep the conversation going.

She was disappointed.

"Wyntir's planning a spectacular Thanksgiving feast," she reported, trying to find another topic to ease the tension. "Lilybelle promised to come. So did Rex and Wilma. Fowler and Rebekah will be making an appearance, too.

"As a matter of fact, Wyntir helped Fowler pay his tax penalty so he could spend the holidays, celebrating with his ward, rather than rotting in jail. He and Rebekah are going to move in with Wyntir—at least, until the snow clears and the spook show travels south. In the spring, Wyntir wants to move to Texas."

Cass grunted, scraping off the left side of his beard. "So Wilma recruited her, huh?"

"Actually, Wyntir figured out why Minx carried a pistol and posed as a newspaper reporter."

Cass frowned. "You really think Wyntir has the gumption to be a Pinkie?"

Sadie sighed, toying with the slender gold chain that Cass had given her, by way of Vandy. Now that she wasn't a *contessa* anymore, she could finally wear Daddy's Confederate, brass button in plain sight.

"Wyntir does have a romantic streak. But she's strong-willed. And resilient, too. Most young women would have taken to their beds with laudanum after the trauma she lived through. But Wyntir got busy. She set up a scholarship in Minx's name. She got herself a language tutor and a firearms instructor. She even started remodeling the basement."

A shadow passed over Cass's face. Sadie could have kicked herself for mentioning Goddard's lair.

"I reckon some folks are just cut out to be a Pinkerton." Cass's eyes met hers briefly, uncomfortably, in the mirror. "You're one of those folks, Sadie. I was wrong about you. One hundred percent wrong. You're a helluva agent. I was impressed by how you convinced Denver's high-society you were a *contessa*. And how you fought off those ruffians in Mattie's alley. And how you figured out the music box clue.

"And then there's the way you handled yourself in the graveyard." His voice broke, and his chest heaved. "That had to be one of your finest hours."

Tears glazed her eyes.

"You were meant to be a Pinkerton," he continued gruffly. "Just like Roarke Michelson was before you. I think he would have been proud of you. I know I am."

"Thank you, Cass," she whispered. "That means a lot."

He nodded, dunking his razor to rinse off the soap. "And I won't ever doubt you again. Or stand in your way. You don't need some gunslinging hothead hanging around, risking your cover."

"Cass..." She didn't like where this conversation was heading. "We solved the Maestro case together. We made a good team."

Grimacing, he reached for his towel and began scrubbing his face. "You don't have to throw this ol' dog a charity bone, darlin'. You and I both know I got in your way."

"From the beginning, you saw Goddard as a fraud," she insisted staunchly. *"You* were the one whose instincts never failed."

He fidgeted.

"Cass." When he refused to face her, she crossed to his side and took the damp terrycloth from his fist.

He actually flinched at her touch.

"Please look at me," she pleaded quietly.

When he did, her heart broke into a thousand pieces. Tears glimmered in those haunted, sapphire eyes.

"We're going to get through this, Cass," she said firmly. "Just like we got through your Cousin Bobby's death. And the crazy misunderstanding about Rex. And the fire at the Satin Siren. And Poppy Westerfield's mad scheme to have your babies. We've beaten the odds before, Cass. Lots and lots of times. We're stronger for it." She reached for his hand. "We're stronger than *ever*."

Sadie's eyes stung at the memory. She blinked hard to stave off tears. She didn't want Cass to see her waiting for him on the settee and blotting her face with a handkerchief.

He was ending his show. A rousing round of applause paid him tribute. With a broad smile, he returned the unloaded revolvers to their owners and instructed a bellhop to store Collie's shotgun in the vault.

Still chuckling, Cass joined her by the sterling statue of Tabor.

"Bravo," she purred.

"Gracias," he quipped in his *caballero's* voice. He swept a courtly bow. Then he pressed a hand to his heart and raised incredulous eyebrows. *"Ay, caramba!* The most beautiful *contessa* in all the world has no escort for Thanksgiving dinner?"

Her heart swelled to see the spark of mischief in his eyes. It was kindling to an amorous flame.

"Why, if it isn't the legendary *Don Dominar,"* she drawled, offering her gloved hand so that he might kiss it. "But I must warn you, *carino.* You are not alone in your affections for me. *Signore* Vandy has been most persuasive in your absence. He showers me with gifts of fish bones and pumpkin seeds."

"The impudence!" Cass feigned indignation. "I shall lop off his whiskers!"

"A duel? Over me?" She flapped coquettish lashes. "How delicious. I've heard that Spaniards have fierce and fiery natures. Tell me, Don Dom. How do the men of your lineage live up to their intriguing family name?"

Cass's grin turned wolfish. "Save that thought, *querida,"* he whispered, tucking her hand beneath his elbow.

Their carriage ride steamed up the windows. Only this time, she wanted him. Needed him. Couldn't let him go.

"Love me, Cass."

"Always, Sadie."

She sat in his lap, facing him, cradling his princely shaft like a treasure deep inside her velvet heat. He moved so tenderly, so sweetly, she felt every nuance of her rising pleasure. In the luminous blue beneath his dusky lashes, she saw all the mingled shades of heaven. She was falling into him, sighing into him, sinking to a perfect rhapsody of bodies, minds, and souls.

> *"Through all time, you and me*
> *Heart to heart..."*

She smiled against his lips. He was crooning the lyrics of *Destiny* when she felt the deep shudder of his bliss.

Forever. For the first time in her life, she dared to dream of it with him. She dared to hope that she could keep him, and love him, and cherish him for the rest of their days.

He smoothed the tumbled curls off her cheek. She traced the chiseled lines of his breathtaking face.

"The first time I saw you," she whispered, admiring the shimmer of starlight on his hair, "I thought you were an angel, disguised in scarecrow clothes."

His grin lit up the brazier-warmed darkness. "I remember that day. I was wearing a ratty, old straw hat. And I'd stuffed my pockets full of corn cobs."

"The ones you stole from Farmer Hinckley's field."

"His fat old hounds couldn't have caught a crippled coyote."

"Luckily for you," she teased.

"And I thought *you* were mighty fine," he drawled, "sitting in that window, munching strawberries. I didn't mind one bit when you smuggled me into Madam Snake Eye's liquor cellar."

She snickered. "You were so green back then."

"Naw. Just shy."

"Well, you sure got over *that* in a hurry."

His chuckle was supremely male. "I figured it was the gentlemanly thing to do. You took off your clothes, so I took off mine…"

She sighed wistfully, resting her cheek against his chest. "I wish you'd been my first."

"Me too," he whispered, kissing her hair. "But at least you were mine."

"I remember…" She smiled dreamily, letting her eyelids flutter closed.

"I never wanted anyone else."

She stilled, half afraid to breathe.

"It was always you, Sadie," he continued fervently. "Every redhead I've ever known. I wanted to learn. I wanted to please you…"

Her throat constricted to hear the Rebel Rutter's confession. "You never told me."

"That's because I was too pig-headed to realize it—until now. I'm sorry I hurt you. I'm sorry about that damned Judas Kiss. I just can't think straight when I'm worried about the people I love…"

The coach was slowing. The world was intruding. Lamplight, clopping hooves, and jingling bridles hammered at her senses. She pouted. She didn't want to leave the circle of her lover's arms. She didn't want to disrupt their newfound intimacy.

"Let's skip dinner." She snuggled closer. "Tell the whip to keep driving."

Cass's rumble of mirth vibrated beneath her ear. "But it's Thanksgiving."

"Don't like turkey."

"What about your surprise?"

"Don't like surprises," she mumbled.

"Liar."

His fingers strayed to her ticklish midsection. She gasped, sitting bolt upright.

"Cass! You—"

Her good-natured threat died on her lips. The coach hadn't stopped on Colfax Avenue. She could see Tabor's stately opera house, gleaming like a bright, blurry jewel through the condensation on the windows.

Her brow furrowed. "Have I been kidnapped?"

He smirked, twirling a pretend mustache. "How easily you fell into my trap, Detective Know-It-All."

"What?!" Childlike glee replaced her confusion. "This is my surprise? You brought me to the opera? *You?"* She

laughed and grabbed his lapels, smacking a kiss on his lips. Hastily, she began repairing her mussed hair and clothes.

"Wait a minute." Suspicion sneaked inside her Pinkerton brain. "*Faust* closed on Sunday. What's on the program?"

He tossed her a sidelong glance. "Let's go inside and find out."

Sadie's mind was spinning as he bustled her under the twinkling lights, past a solemn-looking usher, and into the red-and-crystal opulence of Tabor's Grand Opera House. To her amazement, every person in the audience rose as she entered the auditorium. Enthusiastic applause, mingled with rousing whistles, bounced off the elegant dome. She recognized Rex and Wilma, Wyntir and Lilybelle, Brodie and Porfi, and the Greek's three kittenish mistresses. Enoch Fowler and the entire cast of his Spook Show took up at least 20 chairs. Boone and Dimples sat companionably with Silas Tate and his brood. Sadie estimated that close to forty people had congregated in the orchestra section, below a massive, grand piano that gleamed like onyx under the lights.

Something rustled in the shadows near the stage steps. Like a sultry, scarlet flame, a dark-haired beauty in a stunning, low-cut gown sauntered up the aisle.

"*Ciao, mia bella!*" Dolce greeted, grasping Sadie's hands and kissing her cheeks. "I am delighted to meet you at last, *Signorina* Michelson. I feared this dashing devil had spirited you away in his coach!" Dolce tossed Cass a sly wink. "But then, it is a diva's prerogative to arrive fashionably late, *si?* Come. Your audience awaits."

"M-my what?"

"But surely you don't think this fanfare is for me? *Signore* Cassidy, he has gathered all your friends. They wish to hear you sing."

"But I haven't rehearsed!"

Dolce patted her cheek. "They love you. Do you think they care?"

The whistles crescendoed.

Sadie laughed through her tears. Giddy and flushed, elated and terrified, she turned to her lover. "You did this for me?" She threw her arms around his neck. "Oh, thank you, Cass! Thank you so much!"

Cass tightened his arms around his woman, clasping her to his heart for one precious second longer.

"Knock 'em dead, Tiger," he whispered huskily.

Her eyes were shining like twin stars when she kissed him. Then Dolce grabbed Sadie's hand, dragging her down the aisle and up the stage steps.

Cass dug his fists inside his trouser pockets. He pasted on a smile in case somebody happened to look his way. He might feel like he was dying inside, but he refused to let that spoil Sadie's evening. He wanted her to be happy. He wanted her to remember this night because she was finally living her childhood dream—not because her lover was a walking time bomb.

You mean more to me than life, Sadie.

For weeks, he'd been secretly planning an event to celebrate her music. He'd conceived the idea when Porfi had suggested he steal Mephistopheles's Jewels. Wilma had brought copies of Sadie's sheet music from Lampasas. Rex had hired a pianist to accompany her during the recital. Wyntir had painstakingly penned the invitations. Brodie had hand-delivered them to the guest list.

But Cass's greatest coup had been Dolce. Mortified to learn how wrong she'd been to lambaste him in the *Rocky,* the diva had shown up on his doorstep Monday afternoon with a key to the opera house. She'd arranged for lighting and stage props, ushers and waiters, champagne and caviar—in short, Dolce had improved on his idea of a common recital by turning it into a full-scale production.

"I am forgiven now, *si?* " she'd demanded sheepishly.

Yes, Dolce. You're forgiven.

The real question is, will I ever be?

Alone in the darkness, he stood beside a cherry-wood pillar that disguised the auditorium's emergency exit. As the woman he loved took the spotlight, he'd never seen her look more radiant. In her amber velvet, with her chestnut hair spilling in soft, silken waves across her bodice, she reminded him of some voluptuous, autumn goddess. Her voice was a honeyed balm, pouring over his frayed nerves and secret wounds—wounds that no ointment or bandage would ever heal.

He closed his eyes. His mind was transported to yesterday, when she'd stood so vulnerably before him, stripped of all pretense, the mirrors of her eyes reflecting the pain of his soul.

"We'll get through this, Cass."

She was fighting for them. She was fighting for *him.* Guilt twisted like a burning knife in his gut.

"As much as I want that, Sadie—as much as I want *us*—when I look in the mirror, I…I don't know who's staring back at me. Lucifire or the Ranger."

"In time, you *will* know," she said staunchly. "Until that time comes, I'll be the only mirror you need."

He ran rough fingers through his hair. "My God, Sadie, how can you believe in me? How can you possibly trust that I won't—?" His throat constricted, sealing off the horror of the words. "When I think of what I almost did in that graveyard—"

"But you *didn't*, Cass. That's the point. Something inside you was too strong. It couldn't be broken. In that graveyard, you fought your greatest enemy: the man in the mirror. And you won. That means your light is stronger than your darkness. You're a *good man*."

Am I? He swallowed hard. *Am I really?*

He'd packed his bags. He'd hidden them under the straw in Pancake's straw. He didn't know where he was heading, just that he had to get away from everyone he loved. Everyone he might hurt. Sadie, Collie, Wilma, Lynx, Sera—none of them would be safe if the demon got a hold of his guns. Hell, even Rexford Sterne couldn't beat Lucifire's draw, and Rex was the fastest gun the Marshals had!

Sadie's voice soared like angel wings, vibrant with love. She was singing *Destiny*. She was singing it to him.

> *"Suns may rise, stars may fail.*
> *Worlds collide; love prevails.*
> *Through all time, you and me,*
> *Heart to heart, destiny.*

His throat worked. Four weeks ago, he'd thought she'd written those lyrics for Sterne. *Funny.* That Devil's Eve concert in Lampasas, Texas, seemed like it had happened a lifetime ago...

> *"Never doubt, you're my man,*
> *Through God's vast, Master Plan.*
> *Always yours, I shall be.*
> *Born for you, destiny."*
> *I've always loved you, Sadie. I always will.*

The song was ending. The crowd was cheering. Cass did too. She grinned and curtsied, blowing kisses. Cass pasted on a smile. He drew a bolstering breath.

The time had come.

His heart was breaking. He gasped like a drowning man. Staggering, he pressed a hand to his chest.

That's when the strangest thing happened.

All the pain and horror that had been haunting him got blasted apart from within. The Dark Place exploded in a cataclysm of light, proving once and for all, that goodness was the universal power.

'*You must not leave her,*' Lucifire said sternly.

'*Staying is the right thing to do,*' the Ranger insisted.

Faced with the most important decision of his life, the demon and the lawman had finally agreed. They'd forged an alliance to love and protect Sadie. Half laughing, half sobbing, Cass realized the division of conscience was over.

He was free.

Joy fizzed through his blood like cherry sarsaparilla. A

cool blast of air riffled his hair as the door behind him swung open, but he promptly forgot the new arrival. He was too busy grinning like a halfwit, watching his woman, *his* Sadie, prance around that lofty opera stage, belting a bawdy ditty that she'd once popularized in a saloon.

The crowd loved it. They stomped. They clapped in time. At least half the folks knew the refrain, and they roared it out as she sang:

"Purty Pansy Primrose, now that she's full grown,
Will jump a randy Ranger like a dog jumps on a bone!"

Cass popped two fingers in his mouth and whistled like a hooligan. *Ranger star, be damned. I'm gonna marry that woman!*

He laughed at the notion, picturing the mother of his freckled, red-headed tots singing *Pansy Primrose* in the nursery.

That's when he noticed the somber figure approaching him from the lobby. As silent as shadow, Collie halted at his side.

Vandy was nowhere to be seen.

Cass's scalp prickled. The boy's lips were pinched. His eyes glistened like winter rain.

Dear God, if something happened to that coon…

"What's wrong?" Cass demanded in an urgent undertone. He didn't want to disrupt Sadie's performance.

A muscle ticked in Collie's jaw.

"Found your saddle bags, packed and buried in the stall."

Cass blew out his breath. *Oh. That.*

"Look, kid. I had a really bad bender, that's all. It's over now."

"You weren't going to tell me you were leaving? Or Sadie either?"

Cass winced to hear the hurt in Collie's voice. "I've always believed a bandage should be ripped off fast," he admitted gruffly. "But, hey. That was yesterday. Today, I decided to ask Sadie to come to Texas with me. Why don't you flag down a waiter? Drinks are free."

Collie's face was stony. He was staring at the stage, but he didn't seem to see it. "I'm glad you changed your mind."

Cass frowned. The kid didn't sound glad.

"What's really eating you, son?"

For a long moment, Collie said nothing. Tension rolled off him in waves. Cass was beginning to wonder if the kid had heard the question.

"I know you went through hell," Collie admitted finally. "I saw your welts and rope burns. I heard you mutter about scorpions in your sleep. After the *Rocky* listed the kinds of vermin that Goddard locked in cages, it wasn't hard to figure out why you went missing all those hours.

"I was going to talk some sense into you—man to man," the boy continued gruffly. "After Sadie's singing, I was going to give you the train fare, so you could visit Doc Jones back home." Collie's voice broke over the word, *home.* "So I telegraphed Sera…"

Dread seeped into Cass's soul.

"Is Sera all right? Did something happen to the baby—"

"Not Sera." Collie drew a long, shuddering breath. "Lynx. He was shot."

The air fled from Cass's lungs.

"Dead?" he somehow wheezed.

"No. But Sera says it's bad. He might not have long. Meanwhile, a killer's on the loose, and Blue Thunder doesn't have a sheriff. She asked us to come. Tonight."

Cass's world was imploding. Lynx was the brother he'd never had. The one man he could count on to ride into hell with him. The Cherokee half-breed had saved Cass's life more times than he could count from stampeding steers, blood-thirsty bounty hunters, rampaging honey bees…

Dammit, Lynx, you can't die! Life was just getting good—for both of us!

Cass's eyes burned. He thought of Sera and her unborn child; Doc Jones and his wife, Eden; wily old Aunt Claudia and little Cousin Becky. His closest friends, his last surviving kin—they all lived in Blue Thunder. They were all at risk!

Collie produced two train tickets. The departure time was clearly stamped: 6:30 p.m.

Cass cursed a blue streak inside his head. *Half-past six is just 12 minutes away!*

"It's a good thing you packed," Collie said darkly. "Another train won't leave for Kentucky for three days."

Cass felt sick. He turned his eyes toward the stage. Sadie was still performing. Oblivious to the tragedy, she was trilling in abject bliss by the piano with Dolce. The diva had suggested the *Carmen* medley. Singing a duet with an international opera star wasn't just the highlight of Sadie's program, it was the highlight of her musical career. He couldn't barge onto the stage and ruin her big number!

"She'll understand," Collie said impatiently. He thrust a pencil at Cass, along with the tickets' envelope. "Write her a note. Tomorrow, she's heading for Chicago, anyway."

That's true.

His mind in an uproar, Cass dashed off a few lines. He didn't have time to compose a sugar-coated love note; he just blurted out the news. Waving for an usher, he instructed the man to give the envelope to Sadie as soon as the performance was over.

Then, as quietly as he could, Cass slipped out the emergency exit with Collie. It was a rotten trick. He hated leaving Sadie on the sly. But fate had been cruel. In his upset, he couldn't think of a better plan. She knew that Lynx was his blood brother. Collie was right. She'd understand.

So why do I feel like Satan just tapped me on the shoulder?

The door swung closed.

In the shadows huddled against the auditorium's wall, the crimson lining of an opera cape stirred. A hawk-nosed figure stepped out of hiding and flashed a Pinkerton badge.

The usher hastily surrendered the envelope.

"Not a word of this," Mace growled, "or you'll never work in this town again."

"Y-yes, sir."

The usher fled.

Mace waited for the next round of applause. It disguised his retreat into the alley.

Lightning hissed. The air crackled with the promise of a bitter storm. He turned his back on the keening wind to light a cigar.

At long last, he turned his attention to Cassidy's envelope. Beneath the cold, winking eye of the moon, Mace scanned the outlaw's scrawl:

"Forgive me, Sadie. Lynx was shot. Left for Blue Thunder. Don't know when I'll return. Tell Sterne I'll wire him when I can."

Mace grunted and puffed his stogie.

Once the embers were good and hot, he lit the envelope's corner. Patiently, he shielded the sputtering flame, helping it gain momentum. After the wind scattered the ashes, he rubbed out his smoke and tucked it inside his pocket.

Confident that he'd left no trace in the snow, Mace returned to the theater to enjoy the performance.

You're Invited!

Thank you for reading *Dance to the Devil's Tune*. Now I hope you'll come "behind the scenes" with me! Enjoy all the fun and excitement of birthing a new book. From brainstorming new character names to plotting key scenes, you'll get a bird's-eye view of the writing process. Ask questions; share opinions; and win some fun prizes.

If you'd like to join my special family of Romance readers, visit this link: http://wildtexasnights.com/join-my-romance-club/. I look forward to hearing from you!

In the meantime, page ahead for a sneak peek from *Devil Plays with Fire* , Book 3 in my *Lady Law and The Gunslinger* series.

Best wishes,
Adrienne deWolfe

Austin, Texas, USA

LADY LAW & THE GUNSLINGER SERIES

Shady Lady
Included in the Western Romance Anthology,
Pistols & Petticoats

Devil in Texas
Dance to the Devil's Tune
Devil Plays With Fire

*Turn the page for an
excerpt from*

DEVIL PLAYS
WITH FIRE

Lady Law and The Gunslinger
Series

Book Three

❖

Adrienne deWolfe

Spring, 1884

Wearing little more than longjohns and a week's growth of beard, Cass stood up to his calves in Kentucky wildflowers. Behind him, his morning campfire smoked, adding the pungent aroma of chicory coffee and buttermilk flapjacks to the breeze. Before him stretched an alpine pasture, wet with dew and silvery with the night mist the rising sun had yet to burn off.

"Listen up now, Pancake." Cass fixed his playful pony with a stern stare. "We practiced this drill yesterday. One stomp means animal approaching. Two stomps mean human bushwhacker.

"Okay. A noisy squirrel chases you through the hickory trees. What do you do?"

Pancake bolted like a lunatic, running circles around the pasture.

"I said a *squirrel,* you big lunkhead, not a wolf!"

Whinnying at his jest, Pancake pranced all the way back to Cass's side and reached mischievously for the bottle in his right fist.

"Hell no." Cass swatted the gelding with the vegetable in his other hand. "That didn't deserve a sip of whiskey. That didn't even deserve a *carrot!"*

Pancake returned the favor by swatting Cass's backside with his tail.

"How'd you like a punch in the nose?"

Pancake snorted. Dropping to his haunches, he began rolling in the daisies.

"Are you sure you're not a big, mutant coonhound in disguise?" Cass groused good-naturedly above all the equine grunts of pleasure.

Pancake heaved himself to his hooves and stomped twice.

"That's great, pal." Cass shook his head. "You're a day late, and a dollar—"

A twig snapped. Cass choked back an oath. Dropping the carrot, he spun to face the threat, a .45 cocked in his fist.

To his bemusement, he saw a stocky hiker with balding, auburn hair and a long bushy beard emerging from the trees. Dressed in a plaid cap and matching knickers, the Scot stumped through the wildflowers with a canvas knapsack on his back and a hand-carved walking staff in his right fist.

Pancake bared his teeth and flattened his ears.

Cass hiked an eyebrow. *I reckon ol' Batter Head really did learn something from me yesterday.*

"That's far enough," Cass barked at the intruder. "How'd you find me?"

"I am *the* Pinkerton," the Scot deadpanned.

Cass's smile was mirthless. Oh, he recognized his nemesis, all right. About six weeks ago in Chicago, after a colossal argument with Sadie, Cass had sneaked inside the headquarters of the famous detective agency—mostly to prove he could outsmart its security measures—and had come damned close to smashing Allan Pinkerton's face. Settling for a less satisfying revenge, Cass had told the detective chief (rather loudly) what he thought of Pinkerton's contemptible plan to let young women bait psychopaths and get murdered so the Scot could pay the rent.

"Get your plaid ass back to Chicago," Cass growled. "You're not welcome here."

"Still sore about the Palmer House, eh?"

Cass ground his teeth at this reference to Sadie's hotel, where she'd accused him of "ditching her in Denver." Their argument had escalated to volcanic proportions after Cass had realized just how cozy she'd become with Ryker during the three months that he'd been combing the Kentucky backwoods, hunting for Lynx's would-be assassin.

What's worse, Cass mused bitterly, *is that the whole damned fracas erupted on the day I intended to propose marriage!*

His throat constricted. He hadn't seen Sadie since Chicago, mainly because he had no idea where she was. Pinkerton had sent her deep undercover. Even Brodie hadn't been able to ferret out her location.

Cass shoved his .45 back in its holster. "Heard about that little incident, did you?" he countered gruffly.

"Lad, everyone within five blocks heard. Your row inspired Chicago's first noise ordinance. The mayor dubbed it, *The Cassadie,* in your and her name."

"You see me laughing, smartass?"

The Scot winked. "I always have my most passionate rows with my woman. That's how she knows my love is true. Besides, the make-up sex is like riding a hungry tigress."

"If you're trying to cheer me up, you're doing a lousy job."

"Aw, buck up, laddie. Ryker didn't get her to the altar yet."

Cass scowled. "Whose side are you on?"

"Sadie's." Pinkerton struck a match and squinted, puffing his stogie to life. "That reminds me." He blew out the flame. "Are your guns still for hire?"

Cass folded his arms across his chest. "You sure got some nerve, Flatfoot."

"Yep."

"Maybe I didn't make it clear what I think of you and your army of scum-sucking weasels."

Pinkerton blew a leisurely ring of smoke. "Things change."

"As far as I know, hell didn't freeze over."

The Scot shrugged. For a long moment, he appeared to be studying the proliferation of ivory blossoms in the dogwood trees, the colorful carpet of periwinkles and sun drops beneath Pancake's hooves; the majestic circle of conifer-laden mountains, towering over Cass's head.

"Blue Thunder Valley sure is pretty country," Pinkerton drawled. "Peaceful. Quiet. I can see why a man might come here to mend his heart."

"My heart's just fine," Cass snapped.

"Course, there's not much in the way of excitement," Pinkerton continued in that same grating tone of conciliation. "No Injuns on the war path. No outlaws jumping stage coaches. No mobsters running opium dens."

"I got plenty to do around here, Pinkerton."

"Is that a fact?"

"I'm training my horse to fend off road agents."

As if on cue, Pancake hiked his tail and let one rip.

"I can see that," the Scot said dryly.

Cass's cheeks flamed. "Good. Then you can see I'm busy. So scram." He grabbed Pancake's halter to lead him away.

"Too busy to earn a $10,000 reward?" Pinkerton challenged.

Cass scowled. "I told you," he snapped over his shoulder, "I—"

The protest died on his lips. In Pinkerton's hands was a crumpled murder warrant. *"WANTED,"* the parchment screamed. Beneath the usual list of aliases was a sketch of a big-breasted outlaw with a saucy smile. Below the murder suspect's chin was printed, *"$10,000 Reward. Deliver prisoner to the nearest Consulate of Mexico for extradition."*

The breath whistled past Cass's teeth.

That international felon, in all her buxom glory, was Sadie!

———◆———

DEVIL PLAYS WITH FIRE

available in print and ebook

Adrienne deWolfe is a national bestselling author and the recipient of 48 writing awards, including the Best Historical Romance of the Year. She consistently delights readers with sexy, action-packed Romances, including her *Wild Texas Nights* series and her *Velvet Lies* series. In addition, she is the author of the bestselling non-fiction ebook series, *The Secrets to Getting Your Romance Novel Published*.

A fiction-writing instructor who has taught at the college level, Adrienne continues to mentor aspiring authors. She offers fiction coaching and story critiques through her website, http://WritingNovelsThatSell.com.

To read news and excerpts featuring Cass and Sadie, the star-crossed lovers from the Lady Law & The Gunslinger series, visit www.LadyLawandtheGunslinger.com.

www.ingramcontent.com/pod-product-compliance
Lightning Source LLC
Chambersburg PA
CBHW030920260626
47169CB00002B/340